Beyond Two Realms

MAZRINE L. AMARIS

This book was edited by Kat Betts of Element Editing Services.

Cover design by Beck of Whimsy Book Graphics.

-

EPUB ISBN: 978-0-6457092-3-0

Paperback ISBN: 978-0-6457092-5-4

Hardback ISBN: 978-0-6457092-4-7

ALSO BY MAZRINE L. AMARIS

Two Realms Series

Between Two Realms

Note to Reader

I want you to feel safe and seen. The following book contains themes that may be triggering to you. They include but are not limited to; death of a parent, forced separation of a child from parent/s, memory manipulation, alcohol/drug use, child abuse, graphic sacrifice, mass murder, death of children, coarse language, sexual content, sexual scenes, graphic sex scenes, graphic fight scenes, torture scenes, and suicidal thoughts.

If there is a possibility that any of these themes trigger you, I urge you to reconsider reading this book.

Contents

Beyond Two Realms

Official Playlist

"Circle" – Allen Stone

"Chokehold" – Sleep Token

"Until I Found You" – Stephen Sanchez, Em Beihold

"Rain" – Sleep Token

"Alone" – Allen Stone

"I'm Kissing You" – Des'ree

"Song of Storms" from *The Legend of Zelda: Ocarina of Time* – Gentle Game Lullabies, Andrea Vanzo

"Through the Years and Far Away" – Eminence Symphony Orchestra

To those whose hearts once bled for someone unworthy . . .
I hope you find the starlight to your storm.

PART I THE RISE

Hurt comes in many shapes and sizes. Sometimes it is a flame that burns brightly, warding off those who ache to near it. Sometimes it is a shield, hard and steely, a tough defence to get past. Most of the time though, it is a wall, built to keep out the most devastating of storms.

See, a flame can burn out, wither to nothing but ash with a touch of water. A shield can become battered and broken, discarded upon a battlefield. But a wall? Sometimes they're built so high that no one would even think to climb it. Not even the person who made it to begin with.

1

KAINE

Love was a powerful thing. It was a feeling, an entity, a *thing* Kaine could never grasp yet longed for all the same. It was a *thing*, a name in which kings and queens started bloody wars. Soldiers died killing man, shouting its name upon their cracked lips. It was a fire that burned, strong and deadly, and by the full might of Faery did Kaine want, no, *need* to burn in its flames.

Kaine had felt it once. Love. Grazed along its edges, just by the tips of his fingers. Fleeting, yet he'd never tasted anything sweeter, anything so full of life. He'd had it. With Sophie. His purple-haired, bright-eyed human. His soulmate. Now? Her flames had dimmed. Stolen from his arms, and he would kill to feel its warm caress again.

"I've no one else to turn to." Kaine hung his head low, defeated. A dull ache pooled at his knee, sending twitches up his thigh. He'd been kneeling on Castle Terrin's cool throne room floor for far too long. But he needed this. He *needed* Queen Calliea. He needed the queen of Faery and her dark, ever-growing power. And once he took a hold of her power, mother of Faery, his potential would be limitless. His opportunities endless. But none of that mattered if he didn't have his Sophie.

With this newfound power, he would *destroy* the Tienthan. The guardian angels of the Godlands. *Angels.* The flying vermin that dared infiltrate the lands of Faery and steal his soulmate. Kaine's mouth soured at the words. He knew well that he couldn't defeat the Tienthan on his own. There was no doubt his mana was strong, but combined with the power of Queen Calliea? He would be unstoppable. A host unto himself. By the time their power melded and thrummed through his fingertips, nothing would stop him from stealing back his Sophie.

It had been weeks since Sophie was taken from his grasp by the Tienthan. Weeks since he vowed to start a war in her name. A love so brief, yet his soul ached for it like a phantom limb. Her. No one ever loved him like her. Who knew what the angels were doing with her? Soiling her, surely.

"Then take my blood-oath," Queen Calliea breathed from her throne. Her pointed chin moved higher in the air, as she looked down upon him, a smug smile on her alabaster face curtained by blood-red waves of hair.

Kaine would do anything for his Sophie. Even if it meant siding with the enemy and relinquishing his rightful claim to the Faery throne. For if he took this blood-oath, the most coveted bond second to the soulmate bond, he would be doing just that. He would be sworn to protect Queen Calliea for all his life. A price Kaine was more than willing to pay to get his Sophie back.

Blood-oath.

Blood.

The word shot through his mind, triggering a dark thirst within him that only craved the sweetness of revenge. A dark blindness that addled him since the days of his torture in this very castle. Violent images of his mother dying in his arms, of Sophie writhing underneath Cam, of Sophie being *stolen* from him, flashed through his mind. Kaine tried to shake the cold, spindly grip of them. The memories. The hallucinations? No matter what they were, they came often.

Kaine looked up to Queen Calliea, his face cool and calm despite the spike in anger the flashes had caused.

He nodded. Determined. Sure.

A deft swipe of a taloned nail against her porcelain skin had crimson blood sliding down her forearm shaping into the roots of an age-old tree. The queen extended her wrist in silent command.

A beat passed.

"Drink." Her cold voice echoed through the empty room.

Kaine stood quickly; the ache in his knee instantly ebbed. He took the steps of the dais in two strides and fell back down to his knees again.

There was no turning back now.

Her blood was sour at first. Bitter second. But by the time his lips warmed her skin, her blood tasted sweet. Kaine drank in full dregs of Queen Calliea's blood, intertwining her magic with his. From this moment on, she was his queen. In all meanings of the word. He would obey every command and will, his blood was hers to control. But despite this obedience, there was something he was hiding from Queen Calliea. The lie sat just behind his teeth, the teeth that grazed her skin in a life-bonding promise. There was something else, beyond her power and alliance, that Kaine had sought to gain. Something of higher value than any being in *this* realm possessed. Something he wouldn't reveal until the time was right. Not until it was just within arm's reach. Queen Calliea couldn't know. Not yet.

And so Kaine drank. He drank her blood until his head spun, and his veins thickened with the weight of the blood-oath.

Everything in his life had been ripped away from him, and the raw pain it brought on was more than he could bear. At first, it was his mother, mauled to death by hellhounds, the Tienthan nowhere to be seen when he cried for their help. And now, his Sophie. Everything in his life had been ripped away, sure, but the true tragedy was not of his own. It would be the tragedy his enemies faced when they sundered under the full brunt of his wrath.

After all, the sands of time were irrelevant to an immortal Fae . . . so what else was there to fight for, except *love*?

2

SOPHIE

S ophie stirred.

Soft humming and hushed thuds of movement flitted around the room, dipping in and out of her ears. Firm hands tucked her further into the soft bed she lay in. She had no idea who it was, but her body lightened and eased in their wake. It was the type of ease that consumed one's entire being, knowing that after a long journey, home was just a moment away.

But despite the softness she lay upon, the leaden organ in her chest was heavier than she could lift. Sophie's heart ached deeply as she lay there. *Cam.* The name felt like a thousand daggers in her chest and with every beat of her stupid heart, their sharp edges would stab her, over and over again. Deservedly.

The low humming moved closer again. Gentle hands placed a cool towel across her brow. The soft material was heaven across her heavy, swollen eyelids – the consequences of never-ending tears. The sound of water being filled into a jug gurgled through the room. Sophie parted her lips, hoping her voice would find life again but it did not. She had no strength in her. She wanted to thank whoever it was that cared for her, but the aching of her throat denied her this simple gratitude. A small fire crackled and popped while her caretaker propped themselves down on a leather seat by her bed. The creaks and movements settled as they sat down.

Slowly, Sophie tried to open her eyes. Sorrowful tears began to form, as if in warning. *Are you sure you want to see the world again?* They seemed to say. She wasn't ready to see the world again, if at all. Not after what happened in the temple. Her eyes, burned with the outlines of Cam's lifeless form, were heavy stones, but she followed that deep male voice that hummed just beside her. It was her only lifeline.

Through her blurred vision, she could make out the silhouette of large, feathered wings peeking over a chair. In her caretaker's lap was a book. He was reading. "Come back from the deep," he said. "Your capable heart is strong, I know it, but even the strongest warriors need to be taken care of. Let me be that for you . . ." His low voice called to her like a lighthouse in the Fallen Seas. And like the daring Fae who never returned from its treacherous waters, Sophie couldn't quite find this lighthouse. She tried to speak but only a soft murmur escaped her lips.

He paused his reading.

And that silence? When the rhythmic beat of his voice no longer graced the stifling air around her? It was deafening. Suddenly, home was no longer a moment away. It was miles, aeons, if not realms out of arm's reach.

Tears fell freely down Sophie's cheeks as she let the pain in her chest resign to all the rusty daggers that were aimed at it. All at once, she let them go with a ruthless *snap.*

ONE WEEK LATER

TWO WEEKS LATER

THREE WEEKS LATER

3

SOPHIE

Clouds. Sophie was in a bed of clouds, she was sure of it. Her muscles, sore, melted into the bed she lay on. Something firm and warm pressed up against her legs, easing her muscles even further. In the distance, birds chirped freely and happily. The sound of moving water trickled through the crisp, clear air and into . . . this room. Her room? No. Surely not.

Sophie's eyes fluttered open to find a ceiling made of pure white marble.

Oh gods, am I still in the temple?

Panic raced through her as quickly as a flame took to a match. Sophie shot up, taking in her surroundings, her stiff neck working against her. Her bearings were nowhere to be found. She had no idea where she was.

Shit.

The bed lay flush against the wall in an open-air room. There were no windows, just white marble columns with pristine white curtains, billowing against the soft wind, blocking out the sun. Where in Faery was she? Summeira perhaps? The air felt fresh and clear as if it were so.

Sophie blinked her eyes to clear her vision again, her focus falling upon the moving mound of dark fur against her leg. That heated mass that nestled against her legs earlier? Yep. It was a fully grown *hellhound*.

Sophie let out a silent shriek. Yes, silent, because she knew better than to poke a grizzly bear, albeit a snoozing grizzly bear, but one with razor-sharp teeth all the same. The jolt of fear of seeing Terr's – king of the Shadow Realm – very own minion dog *napping* against her had yet to settle. Was she in the Shadow Realm? She had to be. It was where hellhounds were born and bred – vicious, bloodthirsty creatures who wreaked havoc wherever they went. They would maul everyone and anyone who stood in their master's way. The Elite, Faery's strongest warriors, had lost their parents in vicious, unprovoked hellhound attacks.

Great. Sophie had landed herself in the Shadow Realm itself. Not only had Kaine managed to slaughter Cam, but he'd most likely succeeded in killing her too. It was the only explanation for the hellhound that lay right next to her.

As slow as possible, Sophie slid herself out of the lush white bed, careful not to disturb the creature. It's flaming tail burned brighter, acknowledging the movement.

Holy shit. She'd have to make a run for it. Sophie shot her eyes to the small courtyard, just beyond her bed. It was cordoned off by hedges. Not an option.

There. The door.

Mustering all the energy she could, she bolted for it, her legs like two pieces of uncooperative jelly. She needed to put distance between herself and this monster.

The hound's ears perked up, but it didn't move. In fact, it just watched her flail toward the door. Her body was still weak from all the power she used in Wrenntian temple . . . and the grief that held her heart hostage.

Sophie wrenched the door open, slamming it shut behind her. She leaned against it, catching her breath. That was a close call. Holding her ear against the cold door, she listened for movement. There was none. The hound must've gone back to sleep.

"He's not going to eat you," a dark sensuous voice rumbled from behind her.

Her heart involuntarily skipped a beat, making her swift heel-turn, turn into a stumble of sorts.

She faced the voice's owner now.

She knew that long dark hair.

She knew those turquoise eyes.

Kaine.

Sophie had never felt such poisonous rage before. The type that boiled your insides, but despite the pain, pushed you to feel unspeakably deep, pushed you until your world was painted in red. Pushed you to the point where you knew no world but the one doused in the angry colour of blood.

She started toward him, teeth bared, fists clenched, eyes promising a torturous death. Caution, sense and control fell to the wayside. How dare he show his face to her after what he'd done to Cam? After what he did to her? Sophie flung out her arm, willing all the mana she could to blast him, but nothing came through.

"Woah, is that how you normally treat people who save you?" He shot his hands up in the air, dodging her advances.

Was that surprise that laced each word? He'd just murdered one of his best friends. *Her* friend.

"How *dare* you show your face to me after what you did? How could you?" Sophie's voice was dark and murderous. A mask for the trembling, ice-cold rage that simmered beneath her skin. Tears blurred her vision entirely. Her heart tore over and over again as a glimpse of Cam's laughing face flashed before her. A glimpse of her own bruised wrists and arms that she hid from Ellie threatened to pull her down into a darkness she was afraid to live in. And that was enough to break the dam that held together her punishing fury.

She moved. Her heart obliterated itself as she pummelled and raged against the person who made her very nightmares come to life. Her knuckles cracked and her nails sliced against her own palms. She held nothing back as she beat into his chest.

Yet he just stood there, taking it all. Taking all her rage, absorbing it all until the fiery rage calmed to a tranquil stream.

He did not lay a hand on her.

"Why can't you say something?!" Sophie cried, defeated.

She leaned her head against his strong chest, feeling entirely small and helpless.

He smelled different.

Silence.

A pause.

Then he spoke with a tenderness, as if his own heart had been broken. "I have no words for a male who would hurt a female, let alone a female he supposedly loves. And love hurts, I know, but never in that way. Never." His voice was different, clear, more confident and deeper.

Sophie looked up to find a face, while similar to Kaine's, was in its own way, different. Where Kaine's face was sharp and determined, this stranger's face was kind, strong and . . . softer. His lips were fuller, lines dipping and curves peaking in a way that called upon Sophie's intrigue. A large scar slashed across his left eye, running down to touch his cheek in the shape of a lightning bolt. The movement in his turquoise eyes reminded her of billowing smoke . . . like a time-lapse of a cloud-filled, mountainous valley being kissed by the sunrise in a perfectly turquoise sky.

Sophie's foot almost slipped from under her as she attempted a feeble step back.

This was not Kaine.

The realisation seized her throat in a catastrophe of confusion.

Sophie tried another step back, flinging a hand to her throat in surprise.

The being before her was taller, his shoulders broader and his muscles thicker. Tattoos covered both arms and shoulders, and while his hair was the same length as Kaine's, this stranger had an undercut that accentuated a strong jawline. An underlayer of pure white hair peeked from under layers of his inky hair as if he'd been struck by lightning. His fingernails were painted black. White wings peaked high above his head and fluttered under her gaze. He had *wings*. White feathered wings that were neatly tucked behind him.

How could she have missed those?

"Who . . . are you?" Sophie managed to whisper.

The stranger's eyes softened with . . . what? Pity? Sadness? Sophie couldn't place it, but she didn't miss the way his full lips turned down just the slightest before he found her eyes again.

"My name is Acheron, though you can call me Ash." He smiled handsomely; his soft, now hope-filled eyes watched her carefully. He extended a hand and despite the festered, infected heart she carried in her chest, she beheld those eyes and the face that reminded her so much of Kaine. The one who betrayed her heart when it already lay beaten, encrusted with dirt and debris from the ground of her past.

Different, she had to remind herself. This person was a different person. Sophie gingerly placed her hand in his, swallowing a knot of embarrassment. Before she could stop him, Acheron bent low, placing a soft kiss on the back of her hand. His angel wings extended behind him, in a show of beautiful feathers. The tenderness of it all sent shivers up her arm. And she *hated* it. The tenderness. It was not something she deserved.

Sophie cleared her throat. "Sophie. Sophie Taliesin." It was pathetic. She wanted nothing more than to drown in her embarrassment and confusion in the confines of the bed she was just in.

"Welcome to the Godlands, Sophie," Acheron bowed, his hand still holding hers. Not once did his eyes leave hers.

The Godlands . . . holy mother of Faery. Sophie's knees almost buckled.

She was in the Godlands – Heaven.

4

SOPHIE

There were two things Sophie learnt in her short time in Heaven. One, hellhounds weren't as vicious as they had been chalked up to be. Two, angels of the Tienthan, Aerial Legion of the Godlands, weren't that bad either.

For now, at least, Sophie thought as she sat on the stone steps of her courtyard. Her arms wrapped around her knees as she watched the starry night sky above. The hellhound – Calypso, Sophie learnt – snoozed away softly by her side. His snoot lay gently on top of her feet to keep them warm.

After her embarrassing outburst and case of mistaken identity, Acheron had insisted that she rest in her room. He was sent to help her. It was by the will of the Fates, he explained. He had heard her cry for help and he answered. He was her *guardian angel*. It all sounded suspicious. Make-believe. Nonsensical. Guardian angels didn't exist, they failed to save Kaine's mother. They ... Sophie scrunched her eyes shut, stopping her thoughts from the deadly spiral they craved to turn down. She didn't want to be thinking about him. Them.

Like a Band-Aid to a bullet wound, her scrunched eyes failed to staunch the bleeding that came flooding in the form of uncontrollable tears. The thought of the friends she'd left behind in Faery. Of her mother who would be worried sick. She couldn't shake the sadness that manifested in her chest each time she met Acheron's gaze. He was a different person, sure. But the small similarities he shared with Kaine were enough to make her heart wrench in pain. It was an irrational feeling; she knew that much.

Acheron must have felt it. Must have caught on to the small wince that she failed to mask each time their eyes met. He quickly left her to her own devices to rest and recover. "Nothing will harm you here," he had said before he left. "Cal will protect you always."

Cal, short for Calypso. The name of the hellhound she woke up to, cuddling up against her. While technically he was a hellhound, he wasn't raised in the Shadow Realm. Acheron had found him in Faery while he was on a mission many years ago. They'd bonded and Acheron had said he had no other choice but to bring him back to the Godlands. He had made a promise to an old friend to raise the pup to be a strong and kind warrior.

Strong, kind and warrior were words she would not use to describe Cal – that much was certain. He was like a puppy despite being almost nine years old. Each time Sophie would move or make a noise, Cal would be at her feet, tongue out, waiting for pats or with a ball in his mouth waiting for her to throw it. When sobs of pain racked her entire body, Cal would nuzzle his way through her arms to lick her tears away. Despite his hellhoundish features – short black fur and flaming tail – he was very sweet. Especially with his pointed ears, with one that constantly flopped.

Sophie looked up to the night sky again. There, the moon spun graciously among the dancing stars. Perhaps, Sophie thought, there was one more thing she had learnt in her short time here.

Sophie gulped.

There wasn't a place where she truly belonged.

In Sotera, she'd always yearned for more. In Faery, she got what she asked for and paid the ultimate price. Here in the Godlands, among gods and angels she was but a mess. The clarity of it made her chest sink into deep, dark waters and tonight, she was drowning.

Her throat restricted.

She couldn't see.

She couldn't breathe.

But she knew exactly where she was.

The soft lining of a rotting coffin closed in on her. The coffin that was meant for her. And the worst part? No one knew she was inside.

You did this to him, *a multilayered voice echoed accusingly in her ears.*

"I didn't mean it I swear, I didn't mean it!" Sophie sobbed.

The air in her lungs burned.

She slammed her hands against the coffin, hoping a nail would come loose.

The wood barely croaked out of place. It was pointless, until . . .

Sophie barrelled out of the coffin door that had vanished, landing on a mound of something soft and sticky.

She knew what it was. Who it was.

She'd had this dream a thousand times over.

Before her lay Camrine with his short red hair, but his beautiful green eyes did not shine. They were milky white, fresh from the clutches of death.

"I'm so sorry. Please, please forgive me," Sophie sobbed as an invisible force took control of her wrists and slammed the short spear repeatedly into Cam's lifeless chest.

This was the worst part.

His body jerked with every movement. The crunching sound of the blade against his bones would haunt her for an eternity. But still, she could not stop it.

No matter how hard she tried, she never could.

5

ELOWAN

"That's your third cup this morning, Ellie," Regin said lowly into Elowan's ear, eyeing the cup she held firmly in her hands.

They sat at the family dinner table together with Alfre and Alston – Regin's mother and father. A sense of sadness hung in the air as they waited patiently for Zala to return from Fyllera's town centre.

The room that had always emanated warmth felt cold as of late.

Ellie was tired.

All of them were.

It had been weeks since Cam had passed. His body burned upon the funeral pyre they had built in the field by Regin's family home. Weeks had slipped through her fingers. Weeks where the pain and hollowness in Ellie's heart had not abated. The only semblance of solace she could find was in the bottom of a bottle or cup of hard liquor. It was only in a state of numbness she could function without wanting to the tear the world apart.

"And?" Ellie didn't care. So what if it was her third or fourth cup of the day and it hadn't hit noon yet?

Ellie could feel the heat of Cam's short spear burning against her hip. A reminder for her to carry. A reminder that you couldn't trust anyone. A reminder that you could never let your guard down, because if you did, someone dear to you would twist a knife into your back as if the dirt they walked upon was more valuable.

Ellie could feel the pressure of Alfre and Alston's eyes on her now, like two hot blades pressed precariously upon her neck. She didn't mind the bite.

"Nothing. I just want to let you know I—" Regin was cut off.

Zala the wraith, hurriedly opened and closed the door behind her, pulling her dark black hood off her head. Silently, she looked to everyone in the room, her head dipped in sorrow.

Alfre was the first to get up. Her chair screeched as she did. "It's true then…"

Everyone paused.

"It's true," the wraith confirmed.

Everyone except Ellie shot to their feet, chairs screeching.

Ellie sat still, staring into the cup that had just a sip of rum left.

"So Queen Calliea has secured Faery's strongest warrior by her side?" Regin wrung his hands through his long blond hair.

"We've still got hope," Zala said firmly.

"We do." Alfre stood tall, with a hand on Alston's shoulder. Regin's father nodded in support of his wife, his purple eyes determined.

"The Lord of Fyllera will stand with us. Summeira has not yet stated their allegiance, but I imagine they are partial to Kaine with him being Summeiran. Soxis is our next best shot," the wraith said plainly.

After Cam's untimely death, Kaine disappeared. Convenient.

Word had quickly spread across the courts of Faery. The blood-red queen had given life to her namesake and confessed to the mass murder of the promised children. A bartering tool, she had so regrettably explained. A "necessary sacrifice for the greater good" she said without so much a bat of an eyelash. She didn't even bother allowing the parents of the children lost a moment to mourn. Queen Calliea's confirmed union with Terr was the heavy axe upon all of Faery's neck. "To save Faery from the blight that has crept into the edges of Fyllera and Summeira," she announced. The blight. *She* was blight.

The power-hungry rich flew to swear allegiance to Queen Calliea like a moth to a flame. The parents who had lost their children over years and decades however, mourned. And from the ashes of their anger rose a rebellion. One not led by anyone but by the common goal of peace and righting what had been wronged.

"The Lady of Wrenntia and her people have sought refuge in Soxis too. It would increase our chances of doubling our allies," Alfre added.

Alston signed to his son and Ellie, his hands moving swiftly.

"I think that's the best way, Father. Zala, Elowan and I will make for Soxis, secure our allies there while you and Mother make your way to our potential allies in Windspire Cay. We'll cover as much ground as possible," Regin nodded confidently, before looking to Zala who responded with a curt nod – agreeing to the plan they'd just hatched.

Dark times were brewing. The air was thick with the threat of war, like the moments before a catastrophic storm. This was the start of a war to end the twenty-year blood reign and now, it was just a matter of moving their chess pieces. The queen had just secured her strongest knight while the rebellion made way with the pawns they had available to them. It wasn't a strong start for the rebellion, no, but they would not let a tyrant reign supreme. They would not let Queen Calliea's chokehold on Faery remain any longer. They'd break free of the chains and the conqueror who crossed the line.

Alston, Alfre and Zala now looked to Ellie who had finally lifted her sorrowful gaze from her only vice. "I'll go pack," Elowan rose quickly from her seat without another word. The alcohol had settled itself in her legs and she wobbled slightly.

Righting herself, she walked out the back door of the Fylleran cottage that once felt so full. She could feel the pitiful gaze of Regin, her soulmate, and the worried glances her friends and family no doubt shared among each other.

Elowan was sick of playing politics but if this was their shot against Queen Calliea and Kaine, she'd take it. What else was there to lose?

6

SOPHIE

Sophie never could. She could never run from the petrifying nightmares that paralysed her almost every night since that mournful day. She was the one to blame for Cam's death. If it weren't for her, well, he'd be alive.

Sophie shot up from her bed. Her sheets equally soaked and suffocating, burning her skin, no, melting her skin. At least it felt that way most nights. Her chest heaved with breaths she could barely grasp as she threw her bedsheets aside. The cool evening air bit into her skin as she paced and paced.

"What am I even doing here?" Sophie whispered harshly. Her jaw taut, her fists clenched and her muscles overflowed with tension. The pit of her stomach filled with dread and her heart pulsed with urgency as her feet stepped to the dire beat of a war drum.

She ran her balmy hands across her face.

Why was she here? In the Godlands when one of her best friends had just been murdered by a man that supposedly loved her? She needed to go. She needed to run. Back to Faery. She needed to right her wrongs, even if it hurt her to.

Cal started to whine, his head tilting as she paced and paced. The sound of his concern left fissures in her crumpled heart. "I'm sorry, buddy. I . . . I need to go."

He whined again.

"I'll be back soon." She wasn't.

Sophie dived deep into the pit of mana that pooled in her stomach. It was barely there, a blip compared to the tidal wave it once was. But she tried, oh how she tried. She stumbled through the words that Zala had taught her. Point A. Point B. Traverse the Between. Find the path and lock all the points in. Promising sparks of purple mana and matter set the room alight in quick flashes.

Come on.

She tried again.

I need to get back.

She pushed harder. Clawing at the mana that she felt was not entirely her own. Her hands flexed and tensed as she tried again and again. Her breaths grew louder, between the growing grunts of frustration.

I need to go. Please, she begged her mana. She thought of Cam, his bright smile as he embraced her in Fyllera. She thought of her mother and her flowing silver hair. She thought of the Faery, the one in her childhood, it's rolling hills and the vivid laughter of the boy who—

The purple glittering portal blew open, just enough for her to run through. Cal barked furiously.

Sophie didn't look back as she fell through the fabric between worlds. Violent wind rushed past her ears as she tumbled through time and space.

Take me home.

It didn't. The portal chewed her up and spat her out. She knew she was in the Godlands still. That faint smell of sea that clung in the air. That cool breeze that she had woken up to when nightmares cleaved her soul, greeted her again.

"FUCK!" She scrambled to her feet, not caring that gritty gravel clung onto her scraped skin. To her left, an unfamiliar house stood, it's curtains completely drawn. To her right stood a wall, twice her height covered in thick and thriving vines. She didn't think. She just ran to it. Her hands numb and her knees aching, she scaled the wall with panic. With her fingers barely gripping and her feet constantly slipping, she fell to the ground for what was the third time.

On the third fall, Sophie didn't get up. She—

"Care to explain why you've not only trespassed into my home but are now destroying my garden wall? What has it ever done to you?" His voice was low, thick with sleep.

Acheron.

She sat up straight and turned to him.

He rubbed his eyes of sleep and stifled a yawn.

Sophie gulped. Dirt clung to her skin and crumpled leaves she had accidentally taken with her on each fall, splayed guiltily around her upon the garden floor.

Acheron stood over her. His arms now crossed and his brows furrowed, though his lips gave way to a slight smirk.

She stared at him. His overbearing presence and those wings. She'd never get used to those wings, made of the starkest white and the softest of feathers. And she'd never get the chance to anyway.

Sophie's voice was shaky and urgent. "Acheron, please. T-take me home." She moved to her knees. She'd never thought she'd do this. Ever. But still, she clasped her hands together. Her eyes wide with desperation, brimming with fear-filled tears and her breaths, quick. "*Please*. I need you to—"

Acheron rushed to her. His knees hit the ground before his strong hands wrapped around her wrists to pull her hands apart.

"Sophie." He squeezed her hands. His voice was as tender as the soft moonlight that washed across his tattooed skin.

The tears were instant then, falling down her face in helpless streams. The softness at which he uttered her name was undeserved. She'd brought on the death of a good friend. She deserved no kindness. Her chest heaved as panic rolled through in unrelenting waves. Her head was barely above the water. "I need to get— I need to get back to Faery. Acheron, please. *Please* take me back."

She couldn't breathe. Why couldn't she breathe?

Acheron didn't let her go. His hands held on tightly, squeezing hers, fronting the storm that brewed inside her. "Breathe with me, Sophie." His eyes washed with concern as he breathed in slowly. Then out, just as calmly. Sophie's panic stilled for just a moment as he did it again. She followed this time.

In. Out.

Acheron nodded in encouragement as he practised slow breaths with her.

Deep breath in.

Calm breath out.

And as her breath steadied, the soft hum of cicadas returned. Her vision sharpened. The cool evening air breezed along her skin.

"I hear you, Sophie. I hear you. If it's going back to Faery you want then I will take you there. You are not being held captive here and I need you to remember that. I—" He dropped her hands between them, as if he never intended to touch her at all. The absence made her sway, or was it the mana she'd attempted to use?

Acheron steadied her with strong hands upon each of her shoulders. "You're depleted."

Sophie tried to blink away the weariness. "I'm fine. I just need to get back." She sniffled, her eyes scrunching in pain as she fought away the unsteadiness of the world around her.

He searched her eyes. She didn't really mean to, but she looked right back. She wished she hadn't. Those turquoise, moving eyes. They haunted her in more ways than one, blended into a deadly concoction of memories, nightmares and dreams.

"Sophie. You are swaying. You can barely stand. I know you want to go back to Faery, and I'll take you there, but not like this. Not given how I . . ." His voice trailed off, soft with sadness around the edges. He didn't have to say it. She already knew. He wouldn't take her back in the state she was currently in, depleted and broken, knowing full well the bloodbath that she would be returning to. The bloodbath that he'd found her in.

It was like her body had a mind of its own. Gone was the strength that controlled her muscles, and it wasn't too long before she found herself subconsciously mirroring Acheron. The way he sat. The way his body leaned. Like reflections, they sat under the moonlight.

"Not given how you found me," she finished for him. "You're right." She didn't want him to be. She wanted to get back and . . . and do what? She had no strength in her. What would she achieve, going back to Faery? How would she confront Kaine? "You're completely right. I don't know what I was thinking. I wouldn't be able to achieve anything in this state." Sophie sniffed, wiping the snot from her nose.

"You'll get there, Sophie. With all your power back. I know it. And like I said, if you really want to go back to Faery, I'll take you, *but* it might be in your best interest to rest at least for tonight. I can take you down to Faery at first light."

He meant it. Sophie could tell by the way his voice steadied, the way his lips and eyes turned into a reassuring smile.

Sophie looked away. To the ground. To the wall she so desperately tried to climb. Her voice was even more meagre now. Her hands twisted awkwardly upon her lap as her next words tumbled out with all her emotions. "I'm sorry. About this." She scoffed through tears, her arms gesturing to the ransacked leaves around them. She dared to look at her guardian angel then. "About how I treated you when I first woke up here in the Godlands. You didn't deserve any of that. Rage had clouded my thoughts and clearly my vision. Though it's not an excuse. I really am sorry." Her throat ached all over again. She hadn't meant to lay hands on him. She really hadn't. She was just so blind with rage that her body took on a life of its own. But that was no excuse.

Acheron leaned a fraction forward, but as quickly as he did, he moved back even farther than he was before, as if he was stopping himself from saying something. Doing something. He moved so subtly, Sophie thought she'd imagined it.

"Consider it a non-event. You don't ever have to apologise to me, Sophie. I understand." A small chuckle left his lips, and his hand lifted nervously to knead the back of his neck. "Though come to think of it . . ." Acheron's face winced overdramatically. ". . . my chest does hurt a little. I think it's a little bruised." He hissed as he rubbed his chest. The innocent movement showed the way his muscles peaked and the valleys of his tan torso.

Did he just make a joke?

Sophie paused. Then she stared. One, because Acheron, a guardian angel that looked like he'd enjoy killing demons, was making a joke despite the situation. Second, well, she didn't want to dwell too much on the second reason.

"Okay, too soon with the jokes. The girl's crying for fuck's sake, Ash," he mumbled underneath his breath. Acheron grunted as he stood, brushing off the dirt and gravel that clung to him.

Sophie watched every single movement with a small, bemused smile. Emphasis on the small.

He held out a hand for her. "Just sleep on it, okay? I'll take you at first light."

Perhaps it was the tiniest of smiles that had somehow found its way upon her face when it felt like all she knew was hollowing sadness. Maybe it was the fact that her hands were balmy for all the wrong reasons or that when she thought of home . . . the portal had led her here.

"I think . . ." She placed her hand in his. A steady thrum of electricity and pure power moved through her at their contact. Her stomach twisted and turned. Time itself paused for just a millisecond.

Acheron's brow raised in question.

"I think I'll stay," Sophie said at last.

At least just for a little longer.

7

SOPHIE

There were days where Sophie couldn't get up from her bed. The claws of pain and sadness pulled her back down whenever she tried to get up. She often found herself in an inescapable circle. A place where there were no corners to hide from the pain. A place where every line that she followed somehow led her back inside.

Snacks, hot meals and fruits continued to appear by her bedside table despite her non-existent appetite. She'd have to thank the servants when she saw them next.

Sophie shifted in her bed. Cal stretched out over her legs. She reached down to scratch his head. Last night was the first night in a while where she did not dream. She felt lighter than she'd ever felt since arriving here.

The birds in the courtyard chirped cheerfully and the trickles of water in the distance called to her. She longed to feel the sun on her skin and breathe fresh, cool air.

Today felt . . . different.

Trying her best not to wake Cal from his peaceful slumber, she slipped out from the bed and made her way to the bathroom to freshen up. She brushed her now mid-length, purple-silver hair, pulling it into a neat braid. She walked over to the wardrobe, wondering if anything had been left for her.

She scoffed.

In the wardrobe were various garments from loose blouses and loose shirts to sundresses all in black, trimmed with tiny regal jewels. She pulled on one of the sundresses, over her ribs that showed and her arms that no longer felt strong. She stepped into golden slippers and for the first time, she made her way to the door where Cal was patiently waiting. The hellhound had a silly grin plastered across his face and his feet tip-tapped in utter excitement.

"I thought you were asleep, cheeky boy!" Sophie said as if she were talking to a baby. "How about we go out on an adventure today?" she asked, scratching just underneath his chin.

Cal wagged his tail furiously and let out a puff of smoke from his nostrils in agreeance. Sophie laughed at the show he put on.

Before she reached for her bedroom door, she took a deep breath. Was she ready to face the outside world? To finally get up and do something about the way she felt?

Through her nightmare-filled sleep and hours of reflection, she knew she needed to find her way back to her mother and somehow find a way back to Elowan and Zala too. She needed to get down to the bottom of who she was. She still needed to help Faery, but right now . . . all she wanted to do was put herself first. She wanted to explore the Godlands while she had the chance, and when she was ready, she would return to Faery and finish what she started. One step at a time. She'd take this one step at a time and nothing more.

Sophie pulled the bedroom door back to let Calypso bolt out. The poor pup had been cooped up with her, keeping her company for days. He ran all around in the living room area, barking, howling and spinning in excitement. Various white velvet chaises were strewn across the centre of the room and to the right was a kitchen of sorts. Like her room, there were no windows, just open air. Beyond the living room was an extension of her courtyard with a small circular pool.

While shutting the bedroom door behind her, ensnared by the Grecian architecture and decadent furnishings, Sophie's foot nudged something small and soft. A little crocheted sun with a smiling face, the size of a small mandarin, had been left in front of her bedroom door. There was a small note attached to it. It read, *For when the sun does not shine*. If the mission was to make her smile, the servants were successful.

A small warm feeling started in her chest as she held the tiny sun in her hands. Cal tippy-tapped eagerly in front her, eyes hyperfocused on the small crocheted sun.

"Not a toy, silly. A gift," Sophie smiled as she pocketed it.

Cal whimpered in protest, his flaming tail burning brighter.

She padded over to the main entrance of her accommodation. By the white, gold-trimmed door, a folded letter with her name scrawled across it lay neatly on a silver platter. She unfolded it.

If you've made it this far, I trust that you are ready to explore. As the humans say, what's mine is yours. You are free to roam the Isle of Deos, the city where the gods live and Tienthan train. I'll most likely be on a mission and will come back as soon as I can to see how you are faring.

In the meantime, Cal will be your guide. You'll find that he has a strange way of understanding what you're saying. I sometimes think he can speak though he has not revealed anything to me yet . . . I am rambling. Apologies.

If you want to see or buy anything, feel free to let the people of the Isle know that you are under my guard. They will see to it that you have everything you want and need, at no cost to you.

PS, I would highly recommend not punching people you've just met – commonplace for you as it may be.

Acheron.

The first part of the note made her laugh. She couldn't imagine a giant guardian angel sitting down to write this for her. The thought was absurd. She'd seen draekins, Dakin spiders and magic, but this was downright absurd. The second part of the note made her want to reach into the past and throttle his thick angel neck until the cows came home.

Sophie placed the letter back on the platter that she grabbed it from and looked to Cal who stared patiently up at her with his big loving eyes. "How can a sweet furbaby like you have such a cruel, annoying master?" She sighed. "You ready?"

Cal huffed with a puff of smoke and rapidly wagged his tail. Of course he was ready.

Together they stepped out the front door, ready to take on the Godlands. One step at a time.

8

KAINE

"**W**hat I struggle to comprehend is how you remain unaware of what has transpired in your very own court . . . it was not long ago that you left Summeira to live in Castle Terrin. Forgotten your roots, have you?" Lord Gulliver raised a sleek eyebrow, his voice thick with mischief.

Is twenty years ago considered not long ago?

The Lord of Summeira, a tan-skinned, middle-aged male sat stone faced in his war room in Daybreak Keep. His golden silks and sandals matched his pristine blond hair but despite his bright façade, he looked less than impressed with Kaine who had sauntered into the Summer Court's keep, requesting its allegiance to Queen Calliea.

The rebellion was rising. And they needed all the courts to swear their allegiance to the throne. In blood.

The Summeiran lord stood from his chair and wandered over to Kaine, who stood just a few metres away. Silken curtains billowed carelessly in the war room. The sounds of summer – water lapping, birds chirping and insects buzzing – were the only sounds that stifled the heated, hungry gaze Lord Gulliver raked over Kaine. The Summer Court's lord was known for his greed. He had a harem of males and females and more servants than anyone ever needed. Gluttony aside, he was a renowned war general and a powerful one at that. At his beck and call was a garrison full of trained soldiers that would prove useful, should

Queen Calliea need. Because that was who Kaine was here to appease. At least for now.

While decades stood between Kaine and the male before him, Kaine knew he was more powerful. He also knew that Lord Gulliver would do anything in his power to fortify his court and riches, both of which Queen Calliea and Kaine were willing to offer should the lord swear his allegiance to them.

Kaine stood squarely, hands behind his back. Relaxed. Nonthreatening. A guise. "I have been . . . preoccupied"—Kaine chose his next words carefully—"her majesty Queen Calliea and I swear on blood and bone that we will serve and protect Summeira like our own, so long as it willingly stands with us." He fixed his eyes upon the lord. An offer.

"Ah yes, if I have heard correctly, you are blood-oathed to her . . ." Lord Gulliver said sweetly, raking a tanned finger along Kaine's broad shoulders. "What are you getting out of this? I'm curious . . ."—the lord paused just behind Kaine, leaning in closely to his ear—"is it something I can offer?"

Kaine stiffened. He could feel the Summeiran lord's sensuous breath brushing the shell of his ear. Kaine's fist clenched, straining to refrain from breaking the lord's neck. He bit out, "Revenge."

"Sweet, sweet revenge," Lord Gulliver sung, sauntering past Kaine, toward the marble chair he had occupied earlier. He sat upon his throne with the arrogance of a thousand kings and paused, smiling sweetly at Kaine. "I swear allegiance to Queen Calliea and the abomination that is Terr in return for protection and service, whatever form that may come in, but . . ."

That was baiting if Kaine didn't know any better. The insolence. A low, warning growl began to rumble in the back of Kaine's throat. "Say it."

"Before you go back to your blood-oathed with the news of our allegiance, you must do something for me . . ." The blond male before Kaine spread his legs wide suggestively, his hands resting on the arms of his chair.

A tick started in Kaine's jaw. He had to secure Summeira as an ally. Queen Calliea had ordered, under the blood-oath, that he do everything in his power to have them swear allegiance, even if it meant doing things he didn't really want to. She needed to prove to Terr that her following was strong. Kaine had no choice in the matter, but this? This was crossing the line and the smug lord before Kaine knew exactly how to take advantage of it.

Kaine sent out a fraction of his mana. That was all he needed.

Lord Gulliver's head swung back with a vengeance. His face crumpled in pain as Kaine's mana dealt an invisible blow that would surely rearrange the lord's nose.

Kaine's mana sprung into the air in a rush of glittering magic, turning into giant clasps that wrapped around the lord's neck with ferocity.

Feeble breaths managed to escape the lord, but Kaine did not relent. He pushed harder.

With hands clawing at his neck, the lord managed to let out a measly, "I . . . yield."

At the words, Kaine released his mana.

The lord sagged with relief, a violent gasp for air.

"Try me again and you will regret it," Kaine sneered.

Lord Gulliver rested his hands on his thighs, panting. He scoffed, "It turns out the loyal dog is not all bark . . ." Rolling his neck and shoulders, he wiped his brow and all but spat out, "Fine. I swear allegiance to the blood throne. I will stand with Queen Calliea and Terr."

Lord Gulliver stood from his chair, attempting to tower over Kaine and said, "Just promise me that you'll get rid of the hellhounds that are terrorising the outskirts of Pleasure Alley." The mention of the Summer Court's sin-filled district almost made Kaine laugh. They were on the verge of an uprising and that was all the lord wanted to protect. His reputation preceded him. He was a man of greed and gluttony indeed.

"Consider it done." Kaine waved the request off.

The Lord of Summeira pulled a small silver blade from his waistband and made a quick incision to the inner part of his arm.

On bated breath, they both watched as three drops of blood fell ceremoniously to the ground, sealing the alliance between the blood crown and the Summer Court.

Without a word, Lord Gulliver, with his now ruffled blond hair, walked to one of his windows and gazed out into the distance – a dismissal.

"Lord Gulliver, your allegiance to the blood crown is valued and celebrated." Kaine bowed swiftly before turning on his feet.

He tried his best not to smirk at the small win. As he walked out of the war room swiftly, he swore he heard the lord scoff.

Pleasure Alley. Dirty. Dingy. Dark and seductive. Narrow alleyways lit by red glass lamps teemed with travellers seeking their moment of ecstasy. Seductresses of all shapes and sizes draped across doorways and beckoned those who dared step close.

With his hood fastened over his head, his dark black cloak billowing behind him, Kaine stormed through Summeira's red light district. His short spear glinted in the moonlight and Fae of all kinds shrank in fear as he charged through the alley's chaos.

Dark. Menacing. Unwanted. That's all he was.

He finally reached the alley's end – the only exit.

He took cover behind a dark building wall, out of sight. Without a shred of remorse in his immortal heart, Kaine reached into his pocket and pulled out a vial the size of his palm. In it was a thick dark red substance that sent his mana curling away in disgust.

Oh how things had changed.

Now he needed it. Depended on it even. For the substance brought him closer to what he wanted. Power, revenge and justice. The vial filled with the blood of the promised children felt heavy in his palm. He pulled the cork off the top, dipped his finger in it and crouched low, his cloak completely concealing him in darkness.

Like he'd done many times before in this very alley way, he drew an ancient-Fae symbol of various swirls and curves. Queen Calliea had taught it to him after he took the blood-oath. Kaine swiftly moved to the other side of the alley and repeated the same thing. Dipping his bloodied finger into the vial, he drew the symbol that represented how far he'd come in possessing a power that transcended realms. As he drew the last curve, both symbols burned to life in a show of red anger. They pulsed several times before guttering out.

Then, it began.

A sonic boom sounded, then a crack in the air. The smell of sulphur and decay began to rise and slowly, a deep red portal began to rip apart the fabric between Faery, opening a temporary gate to the Shadow Realm.

From his crouched position, Kaine watched it all unfold with unbridled pride rumbling through his chest. For his attitude and advance, Lord Gulliver would pay – just one more time.

Kaine drew his hand toward his mouth, curled his tongue and blew a sharp whistle. The sound of paws padding the soft earth grew to a crescendo. Black dust rose from the ground, spilling over onto Summeiran soil.

From the portal came a pack of hellhounds. Twenty of them. They barked, yipped and growled, waving their flaming tails and baring their razor-sharp teeth.

Kaine used to fear them. Hated them even. Perhaps he still did but what he hated more was the Tienthan. The good-for-nothing angels took away his Sophie, and if this was Kaine's only way to secure the alliances he needed to win this war, he'd do it. He'd do it in this lifetime and every other lifetime the Fates allowed him.

For fear was leverage. Kaine's allies needed to understand that he was their saviour. Many were convinced the hellhounds had slipped through as the fabric between realms weakened. But no, Kaine was also the male responsible for setting the rabid dogs upon them – but they didn't need to know that.

Kaine stood from where he crouched and leaned against the edge of the alley way. He watched, arms crossed over his broad chest as chaos ensued.

The hellhounds did not hold back tonight. As the hounds mauled and terrorised Pleasure Alley's patrons and the sorrowful sound of agonising screams overtook the sounds of pleasure, Kaine turned on his heel and smiled.

"Well done, my pet," Queen Calliea said proudly upon her throne.

Kaine remained on his knees, his head bowed in respect. Silent and ever obedient.

"With Wrenntia unoccupied and Summeira now sworn to us, we have secured the northern courts," the queen continued.

"That's correct, my oathed." Kaine hated the way that word curdled on his tongue. Oathed. It was rough and unruly. Something he didn't want yet needed all the same because his soulmate was waiting for him. He knew it.

"Very well." The red queen stood up from the blood-red throne. "Now see to it that Seaspun Bay swears their allegiance by whatever means necessary. I *command* this."

Kaine didn't miss the venomous uptick of her mouth.

The invisible collar that tethered him to the queen tightened ever so slightly. He hated the feeling, but he only had to endure it a little longer. He had to persevere because there was one being that surpassed her in greatness. Terr. Ruler of a realm filled with demons, hellhounds and creatures no one dared to even imagine. Commander of undead army with a posting strength of hundreds, if not thousands worth of tortured souls. There was an opportunity there. Kaine could smell it. All he had to do was lie in wait.

"Yes, my oathed. Your will is mine."

Seaspun Bay. The undersea court was one of opulence and extravagance, but historically had remained neutral in all Faery conflicts. Ruled by Lord Zavis, a mer-male of centuries old, the court was known for being cut-throat, demanding and insufferable. Prideful would also be a good word to describe them. Kaine had better things to do than tread in waters where he was most likely unwelcome, but he had no choice. The blood-oath that chained him yet provided him with so much power, commanded that he do this much.

Kaine bowed his head lower.

And that was the thing about soulmates. They never gave up on each other and by the Fates, for Sophie, he would do it all.

9

SOPHIE

The Isle of Deos – the city where the gods lived and the Tienthan trained. Surrounded by giant, tree-covered mountains, the small town felt like it was deposited onto the set of *Jurassic Park*. The island was covered in lush tropical jungle, various birds flocked and flowed as if they were dancing to a secret song. Island folk dressed in various colours of floating linen, laughed and waved. Together with Cal, Sophie walked through the town centre, a sheen of sweat coating her skin, and her eyes wide in appreciation.

In the distance, nestled between the mountains was a breathtaking waterfall, larger than any Sophie had ever seen before, whose waters ran upward instead of down. It was an island paradise. One that distracted her from the deep pain she couldn't seem to shake.

Everywhere she went, she was met with smiles from people of all ages. Some were Fae, some looked human, and some were outright glowing – beings surely from other realms she did not know. Children ran up to pet Cal, who revelled in all the attention. The Isle of Deos was really something else. What else would you expect from the proverbial Heaven itself?

But the smiles, the sunshine, the joy, all combined to highlight what she had not felt in a long time. The sneaking claws of anxiety began to crawl and creep up her chest.

She swiftly pushed it down.

Its talons however, remained embedded in her skin.

"How about we find somewhere with more adventure of the natural kind? Maybe with fewer people?" Sophie asked Cal, wanting a bigger distraction from the darkness she'd lived in for the past few weeks or months – she never counted.

The hellhound huffed, spun in place and pointed a paw toward the giant waterfall that centred the Isle.

"Ah, to the waterfall it is then." It was hard not to grin.

Acheron, despite his annoying letter, was right about Calypso. The hound had an extraordinary way of understanding and communicating.

Sophie and Cal walked silently side by side until they reached the edge of the waterfall where a pool of glistening clear water lapped up against her ankles. To the left of the large pool of water surrounded by rocks and the mountain walls, were stables. Sophie could hear the distant neighs and clopping of horses from within. To the right of the pool was what looked like a training ground. Ropes and obstacles were strewn across the sand and dirt, while racks of weapons neatly lined the edges of a training ring.

"The Isle of Deos, the city where the gods live and the Tienthan train. I'm assuming that's where they train?" Sophie turned to Cal who lay next to her in the water blowing bubbles with his nostrils.

Sophie scratched behind his ears at the endearing sight. Cal perked up at her touch and huffed once, which Sophie understood was a yes. "How about we check out the stables then head to the training ring?" It'd been a long while since Sophie trained her body. The least she could do was have a go at the obstacle course while no one was around to watch her fall on her face.

Cal huffed once more and shook the water out of his coat. His flaming tail sizzled as water brushed against it. Together they walked over to the stables where the horses seemed to have calmed. Unlocking the latch before her, Sophie stepped inside. The smell of hay shot up her nostrils with a vengeance, but it did not prepare her for what lay before her eyes.

Before her was not a small, forgettable stable. Before her was a marble-made, open-air stable that led out to endless, rolling grassy hills. It was like a pocket into a different realm. It was an optical illusion.

Along the grassy field, horses – no, arions – roamed freely. She'd read about the illustrious, Heaven-made, winged horses before. The most famous one being Pegasus. Fifty or so arions of different colours – black, brown and white – roamed and galloped about. In the distance, a team of arions flew in formation. It was like they were practicing for war Beds of clouds lined the walls of the stable itself. Some arions grazed lazily at hay and fruits that had been laid out on the floor while others napped on the beds of clouds. It was some sort of illusion that Sophie's mind had not yet processed.

When she was outside by the waterfall, the meagre stable was most definitely surrounded by rocks and mountains, yet in here . . . it was somewhere else entirely.

She stood in the stable with her jaw wide open.

Holy mother of Faery. This is . . . wondrous. Sophie spun in place, taking in all the sights and sounds of this pocket of heaven within Heaven.

Carefully, Sophie moved forward, closer to the arions that grazed peacefully. Their wings, so intricately made and majestic, fluttered and twitched with the breeze that crept through the place. Their eyes twitched. Noticing her presence, they moved toward her. Some neighed and some nickered. A graceful white mare approached her first. It bowed its head closer to her outreached hand. Slowly, but surely, Sophie greeted the mare with a light brush of her muzzle.

"Hi there, beautiful." Sophie's voice was all soft and airy. The white arion pushed against her hand wanting more attention. "What's your name?" The arion nickered again and its wings shook with excitement.

"Her name is Aika," a masculine yet chirpy voice said.

Sophie jumped and shrieked, startling all the arions that surrounded her. Her voice echoed onto the grassy hills where all the arions in the illusion-stable whipped their heads toward her. Her shriek echoed for a few moments more before dying out.

Well, that was embarrassing.

Sophie winced and dared to turn on her heels to face the stranger that surely thought she was crazy. Before her stood a tall pale-skinned, handsome male with strawberry-blond curls that almost covered his eyebrows. His strong, muscled shoulders bore pure white wings that stretched out behind him. His light-silver armour accented a cinched waist and strapped to his back between his wings was a silver bow and arrow. His face, however, was scrunched with something that looked a lot like pain . . . or mortification.

"I think I spooked the horses?" Sophie shrugged and tried not to drown herself in her own embarrassment.

"That you did." The blond angel sighed. He looked down toward Sophie's feet. "Cal, my boy! What are you doing here?" The angel crouched down to give Cal a good scratch on the head.

Cal sat patiently before the angel, savouring as many pets as he could.

That little attention-loving demon, Sophie groaned.

"Oh, you're showing this screaming lady around? What a good boy! Does the scream-y lady have a name?" The angel cooed and looked up at Sophie expectantly.

Sophie figuratively facepalmed herself but somehow pushed through the public humiliation. "The name is Sophie. Nice to meet you . . . ?"

"Eros. The name is Eros." The angel beamed and stretched his hand out for Sophie to shake.

Sophie gulped. "As in Eros, God of Love and Attraction?"

"Tis I!" he smirked and bowed dramatically.

Sophie almost rolled her eyes. Almost. She would've done it outright if the gods didn't have a reputation of being a little bit chaotic, easily offended and bloodthirsty.

"Oh, oh shit. Do I need to bow or something?" Sophie scrambled to her knees and looked at Cal for help. The hellpup just looked at her and tilted his head.

"Oh no, no, no. No need to grovel. Gone are the days . . . as unfortunate that may be." Eros laughed deeply and helped Sophie off the ground. "Since Calypso here is taking care of you, I'm assuming I have Acheron to thank for several spooked arions?"

Sophie nodded. "Yes, that would be the case. Acheron said I could roam the Isle of Deos as I pleased. I realise I'm probably not meant to be here . . ."

"Nonsense! The Isle of Deos is an open city. Come with me. You've arrived just in time to watch me kick some angel ass." Eros snickered.

He offered his elbow to Sophie.

Angel ass. Now that *would be a welcome distraction.*

Eros's cheerfulness reminded her so much of Camrine. Her friend. She tried not to think about it; the pain that permanently lived inside her chest. *Come on, Sophie. You're in the Godlands! And the ACTUAL god, Eros, is about to show you around town. Eighteen-year-old, Greek-mythology-obsessed Sophie would be dying! Enjoy it while you can.* Sophie tried to convince herself, but still, her heart ached tremendously.

Sophie placed her hand in the crook of the elbow Eros offered. "Lead the way." She smiled, though it did not quite reach her eyes.

Eros had led her to other side of the waterfall, where a small amphitheatre surrounded a dirt-covered training ring.

"Lady and Pain in the Ass, please meet Sophie Taliesin, Acheron's special guest here on the Isle of Deos." Eros waved his hands about Sophie like she were part of his magic show as she stood in front of two other angels.

"So lovely to finally meet you! You're looking nice and alive." The female angel with long chestnut-coloured hair hugged Sophie as if she were an age-old friend. The angel's chestnut-coloured wings wrapped around Sophie. She was dressed in similar fighting gear as Eros and her eyes glowed white. Sophie couldn't help but marvel at their otherworldliness. "Oh, you'll get used to these." The angel pointed at her eyes. "They're a little bright at first." The female pulled back from the embrace. "My name is Nemysis, but you may call me Nemy, and this . . ." She motioned to the tall broad-shouldered male angel with short, silver hair. His grey wings were the colour of ash. His eyes were wholly black with bright yellow irises. He looked terrifying, as if he enjoyed bathing in the blood of his enemies. "This is the second biggest pain in the ass you'll ever meet – Deymos."

The silver-haired angel Deymos, who looked a lot like death incarnate with an eight-pack, rolled his eyes and casually saluted Sophie. "Lovely to meet you, Sophie. Welcome to the Isle."

Sophie nodded back in greeting. "Deymos, as in the god of dread and terror?" It explained the way he looked.

"Correct," Deymos said, giving Sophie a cheeky wink.

"Wait, if you're the second biggest pain in the ass . . ." Sophie pointed at Deymos and scrunched her brows. "Then does that mean Eros is the biggest pain in the ass?" Sophie glanced over to Eros, who looked as if she had just shot an arrow through his heart.

Silence.

Nemy and Deymos both burst out into laughter.

Eros stood there with his arms crossed and his eyes narrowed at his two friends. "Remind me to never introduce new people to you two again."

His reaction only caused more hysteria.

"She's been here for five minutes and she's already got jokes!" Nemy moved closer to Sophie and wrapped an arm around her petite shoulders. Nemy was beautiful. Godly even. She stood about six foot and her skin was perfectly tanned – as if she spent hours in the sun. She looked to Sophie who felt infantile next to all the gods. "You'll fit right in."

I sure hope so.

Eros and Deymos moved to the rack of weapons that were placed around the training ring. They pushed each other jokingly. Eros lifted himself off the ground to scruff Deymos's hair. Deymos swatted him away, disgruntled.

Sophie turned to Nemy who led her to the amphitheatre steps where Sophie could watch them train. She had already mentioned she wasn't feeling too well physically but would love to see them in action. "Nemy . . . Nemysis, as in the goddess of retribution?"

Nemy's eyes grew a touch brighter. "Ah, you're a clever girl too. Yes, the goddess of retribution. If anyone has wronged you, come to me and I will handle it for you."

Sophie laughed nervously but considered the goddess's offer for just a second. Okay, maybe it was more than a second.

"Refreshments are down there if you need." Nemy pointed to a table beside the ring where fruits and water had been laid out. "Otherwise, enjoy the beating that these two are going to get." She smiled sweetly and gave a knowing nod to Sophie before traipsing to the training ring.

Sophie didn't smile back. The friendship that these gods shared reminded her of Cam, Elowan and Zala. It made Sophie's heart break again into a million irreparable pieces, and she had no idea how to put it back together. She wasn't even sure if she wanted to.

Cal leaned his head on Sophie's lap and looked up at her with his puppy eyes.

He whined.

"I know, boy. Sometimes I'm okay and then sometimes, out of nowhere, it hits me." Sophie softly brushed her hands through the scruff of his neck. "If only I could keep you forever. You read me so well."

Watching gods and a goddess battling it out in a training ring was something else. Sparks flew, loud crashes of thunder roared and echoed against the mountain walls. Eros and Deymos created a violent storm of throws, grapples and strikes while Nemy critiqued their every move.

Sophie mentally practised their graceful movements. Perhaps she could train with them one day. One day when she had the energy and heart to do it, but today wasn't the day.

Nemy roared out, "You're slower than you were yesterday, Eros! What happened?" She hovered just around them, her chestnut wings flapping elegantly.

"He stayed up watching *Emily in Paris*!" a familiar, deep male voice sounded from the entrance of the training ring.

All heads, including Sophie's whipped around to the owner of that voice. Sophie's heart clenched. Their truce last night and her decision to stay didn't soften the blow of who he reminded her of. It made her uneasy. Awkward even.

Eros stopped his sparring to stare at Acheron who stood with his arms crossed over his bare chest. "I told you to keep it a secret!"

Acheron chuckled and his broad chest rumbled with the movement as he casually swung a war hammer emblazoned with flames along its sides. Sophie couldn't help but stare. A mixture of hate, sadness and gratitude filled her chest. He had saved her, and yet . . . he looked so much like Kaine. When she thought of Kaine, she thought of Cam and how he should be alive. Next to her. Laughing and enjoying life just as the angels were. The feeling burrowed deeper in the emptiness in her chest.

Nemy and Deymos joined in on the laughter.

"I can't help it. I love love, okay?" Eros threw his hands in the air and floated down to the ground to greet Acheron with a brotherly hug. "Good to see you back, baby brother."

Before anyone could notice, Sophie walked down from the amphitheatre steps with Cal in tow. "C'mon boy. Let's go home." The hellhound whined and pointed to his master with a furry paw. Sophie stopped her hurried steps. "You're welcome to stay, pup. I'll see you at home." She gave the pup a reassuring scratch behind the ears and hurried her steps out of the training ring – back toward the town centre.

As she walked, hot tears flowed down the peaks of her cheeks. Sophie didn't dare look back. She knew she was being unfair but every time she looked at Acheron, he reminded her too much of Kaine. On paper they were different, but their features were similar enough for Sophie's heart to wrench in all the wrong ways.

As she neared the small villa she'd been occupying, her throat eased and the tears stopped. Sophie moved quickly up the few steps to the front door but slowed when she noticed a small gift left for her. Bending over, she picked it up.

A tiny, crocheted Cal – flaming tail and all – stared back at her. That negligible warmth in her chest pulsed again. The small note attached to the crocheted dog said, *A best friend to keep.* The small gestures chipped away the darkness that ate her heart away each day.

Entering her bedroom, she fished out the crocheted sun the servants had left for her earlier that day and placed it on her bed stand next to the tiny, crocheted Cal.

And there it was. Small and imperceptible. But it was there.

A smile.

10

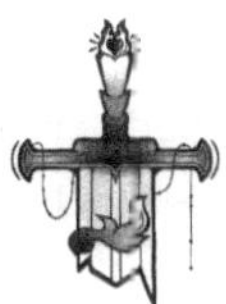

ELOWAN

Heartsprung Hills.

The rolling, grassy hills that surrounded the Spring Court's hold had always been a warm welcome for Ellie – except today. How could the insects revel and the birds rejoice when death and decay had consumed other parts of Faery? Elowan wanted to rip out the grass and stomp on all the flowers. How could the world around her be so happy when inside she felt dread and despair that would last her a thousand years?

It was unfair, Ellie thought.

"You're sulking," Zala stated flatly, her two rapiers gleaming in the Faery sun.

Elowan huffed and ploughed forward, ahead of the wraith and Regin who trailed quietly behind her. "What do you want me to do Z, have a fucking party?" Elowan threw her hands in the air and stomped on a flower as they crested another hill, moving closer to Asteria Hold – where the lady of Soxis ruled.

"You can start by getting your shit together." The wraith stormed ahead, now silent.

Elowan shook her head in annoyance, muttering her grievances to herself.

Tension had managed to wedge itself between Ellie and Zala since Camrine's death.

"Please, you two. We have got to remain focused." It was Regin who spoke. The voice of reason that Ellie listened to . . . every now and then.

He was right. Zala was right. Ellie had to get her shit together, but she feared that if she did not wallow in her self-pity and anger, and feel her emotions fully, it would feel like Camrine no longer mattered. It would feel like Sophie was never here. And she didn't want her friend's death to be in vain.

Ahead, sitting peacefully in the Faery sun, was Asteria Hold. With its high-reaching, flower-and-vine-covered white stone walls, the place where Lady Ollette had long ruled, had now become a refuge for the displaced people of Wrenntia too. She was always charitable. A fierce female who would welcome everyone.

Before them, Fae milled about, carrying loads of washing and supplies. The supply stalls, from what Elowan could see, were dwindling. Shelves were left bare. No doubt the court that now housed two courts worth of Fae was struggling to keep up. The town centre's fountain however, gurgled with happiness. Butterflies fluttered about without a care in sight.

The people of Soxis nodded with warmth and acknowledgment as they made their way through the town centre. Lady Ollette would be waiting for them. They had sent word via raven not too long ago. As they neared the receiving room, a young female ward dressed in a flowing green dress smiled brightly at them. "Welcome. Lady Ollette is eager to see you," the young female said. She ushered them forward, toward a green wooden door. Its golden handles were carved in the shape of fern leaves and there were flecks of gold scattered throughout the green paint.

On a silent wind, the door before them opened.

Asteria Hold's receiving room was . . . Elowan took a moment to soak it all in. Florals panelled the high walls and domed ceiling. Underneath their feet was a completely grassed floor and above them a circular skylight that encapsulated a perfect sliver of the Faery sky. A small stream circled the room, trickling with delight, constantly turning around the space on the whim of some mana. The smell of freshly cut grass and sweet jasmine was just the proverbial bow. Exquisite. That's what the room was.

In the centre of it all, sat upon a lilac picnic blanket, was Lady Ollette. And next to her, sipping a cup of what looked to be warm tea, sat Lady Firtha – the head of Wrenntia.

Elowan, Zala and Regin bowed their heads in greeting.

It was Lady Ollette who stood first, opening her arms wide in welcome. She trotted over to the three of them with a warm smile and hugged them all. "How are you, my dear friends?" Her voice was small and sweet, but she was not someone to be reckoned with. Her brown hair flowed effortlessly down to her waist and her orange dress swished melodiously along the grass. She wasn't wearing any shoes.

"We've seen better days, Lady Ollette, as I'm sure you are aware," Elowan said with a touch of sadness.

Lady Ollette hummed in agreement and motioned for them to sit down with her upon the grass. "Speaking of someone who's seen better days, I'm sure you've all crossed paths before. This is Lady Firtha"—the Spring Court's lady gestured to the raven-haired female who sat graciously on the blanket—"Lady Firtha, this is Elowan, Zala and Regin," she paused, "our allies."

Lady Firtha, with her dark raven hair and olive skin, smiled brightly. "A pleasure to see you again, Elowan, Zala. And it's so lovely to meet you, Regin." She nodded politely to the three of them.

Elowan had crossed paths with the Winter Court's lady on several of her missions. She was an exceptionally kind and warm soul despite heading Faery's coldest court. She loved her people fiercely and sought to protect them at all costs.

"I'll skip the niceties. We,"—Lady Ollette motioned between herself and the lady of Wrenntia—"understand that an uprising is nipping at our heels. War, even. Our courts and our people remain our respective focuses."

It was Lady Firtha who moved first. She reached into the basket beside her, pulling out a carafe filled with a black glittery concoction.

Elowan gulped. She felt Zala and Regin tense beside her too.

"Blood promises can be manipulated if the right words are uttered," Wrenntia's lady stated as she poured the carafe of black glittery liquid into three small glasses. "You can declare your alliances until dawn breaks, swear upon the lives of your loved ones, but these are all fleeting promises; oaths and declarations that change with the wind. *But*, if you know your enemy's darkest secret? They'll keenly fall upon your blade, just so their one darkest truth never sees the light of day. That is the power of truth." Lady Firtha handed the shot glasses to Elowan, Zala and Regin.

They all looked at each other with natural hesitation.

This was Veritas. A truth serum.

But not just any run-of-the-mill truth serum made by local witches. No. This was one crafted in the Godlands. One that was used only when necessary. In most important moments. Moments like this, where taking sides could cost the livelihood of your people.

The two ladies of Faery's courts lifted their teacups from where they had left them.

"To the revolution," Lady Ollette said proudly.

Elowan eyed the concoction, her hands shaking ever so slightly. It's not that she had anything to hide, right? The hesitation was because Veritas was a burning sword of truth that when ingested felt like the gods had sought to rip apart every molecule that you were made of. The endless hours of nausea were the least of their worries. It was the ease at which their deepest, darkest truths would divulge that worried Elowan the most.

Elowan swallowed thickly as she cast an eye to Zala and Regin. They nodded as they caught her gaze. Together, they held up their glasses. "To the revolution," they said in unison.

They gulped down the serum.

One.

Two.

And then she felt it. Like a demon born from the depths of the Shadow Realm, Veritas clawed down Elowan's throat, leaving red-hot burns in its wake. She could hear Regin sputtering. Zala somehow remained silent, but Elowan could tell she was struggling as the wraith white-knuckled the grass beneath her.

A sweat broke down Elowan's face. She wanted to scream but her numb throat denied her the privilege.

Lady Ollette propped up onto her knees before the three of them. Lady Firtha sat beside her with a reassuring hand placed on her companion's shoulder. With a stern voice, the lady of Soxis stated, "I'll keep it quick." She cleared her throat before continuing. "By the power of Veritas and the gods that be, the words before me shall only be spoken truthfully."

The air around them all stilled at the words.

Ellie could not move as the tips of invisible knives hovered by her throat. The more you resisted Veritas, the closer the invisible knives drew to your throat. The thousands of needles that you felt like you ingested would seek their way out through the walls of your skin. It was truly harrowing. But for Faery and for Camrine, Elowan would have to push through.

Lady Ollette crossed her arms. "Where do your loyalties lie?" Her meadow green eyes pinned Elowan's.

Elowan blurted out first, "To Faery, the land and its people."

Regin coughed before adding, "We want to see the wrongs of the queen righted."

"And you all promise to serve and protect its people in ending the blood reign?" Lady Ollette pressed.

"Yes," they all said in unison.

Lady Ollette paused for a moment, taking in the struggling faces of Elowan, Zala and Regin. She dipped her head and rolled her lips in what Elowan could only interpret as regret. ". . . and what is the one truth that you would much rather die for, than face?"

She stared the three of them down.

Lady Firtha tightened her hold on Ollette's shoulder, nodding encouragingly.

Lady Ollette stood from where she knelt and moved to Regin first. His long blond hair now clung to his face. Sweat rolled freely down his reddened cheeks as he clutched the grass beneath him. His eyes darted back and forth between Elowan and the lady of Soxis.

Elowan watched helplessly as Lady Ollette knelt in front of her soulmate and leaned in, a hand cupped to her ear – for privacy.

As pale as ever, Regin leaned in, his entire body shaking with pain.

Elowan could not hear the words that her soulmate had whispered into the lady's ear.

Lady Ollette nodded and murmured a thank you before moving to Zala. She moved her dress eloquently out of the way before kneeling and repeating what she had done for Regin. The dread that had already snuck its way into Elowan's stomach grew into an unruly beast. Veritas' needles began to prick her innards. Sharp. Deadly.

Zala leaned into Lady Ollette's awaiting ear. Moments passed as Zala divulged her one truth. While they were close, Elowan could not hear over the blistering pain the Veritas served. Lady Ollette cleared her throat, and like before, murmured a thank you before moving to Elowan.

Elowan's breath turned heavy, her shoulders lifting with increased cadence. She was not ready to face her truth.

As Lady Ollette knelt before her, Elowan began to sob. She didn't mean to but still they came rushing out. Painful, heart-wrenching sobs. The invisible daggers that danced around Elowan's throat closed in with painstaking slowness. The needles from the pit of her stomach began to make their way through her skin. She could almost hear the popping sound they made when they did.

She didn't want to say it. Her truth. Because if she said it, it would all come true.

And Regin would hate her.

Zala would hate her.

The world would hate her.

And she would die alone.

Lady Ollette, paused, wiping a tear from Elowan's face with the pad of her thumb. Without a word, she cupped the shell of her ear and leaned in. An invitation.

Like a string puppet, Elowan met the lady of Soxis halfway. "I . . . was,"—Elowan dry-heaved from the pain—"too naïve." It was all she could manage as the invisible daggers pierced her throat all over again.

Lady Ollette nodded patiently. "You must stop fighting it, Elowan," Lady Ollette said sorrowfully.

"I can't face it!" Elowan screamed. Her vision blurred as she sobbed. She wished the invisible daggers would pierce her throat fully, rendering her unable to speak. But that's the thing about the daggers of Veritas, they were only invisible.

"You swear allegiance to the true Faery, to the revolution, do you not?" Lady Ollette asked.

"Yes."

"Then you must tell me your one truth. What is the one truth that you cannot bear to face?" Lady Ollette now had her hands on Elowan's shoulders. Her touch burned like a hot blade, fresh from a blacksmith's fire.

"Let it go, Ellie!" Regin's warm voice pierced through the calamity.

So Elowan did.

She screamed.

She sobbed.

And all too loud, she admitted, "If I hadn't been so *painfully* naïve, my best friend would not be DEAD. His blood lays on my hands and my hands alone. I willingly, knowingly, led Sophie to the slaughter while I clung onto a shred of false hope and for what? I alone set into motion the demise of Faery and it's a weight I no longer wish to bear . . ." Elowan sniffed back tears. "I thought about it time a plenty. My inconsequential life is one that is not worth living anymore."

Elowan let out a gasping breath as she fell forward onto her hands. The invisible daggers and needles of the Veritas relented. The words that had hung above her head since Cam's death had rolled off her tongue all too easily. Her vision began to steady.

Before her with watery doe eyes, Lady Ollette stood. She murmured, "Thank you."

In place of the invisible daggers now sat the pain of embarrassment, shame and fear. Elowan much preferred the pain of the blades against her skin.

Lady Firtha moved swiftly to the picnic basket, fetching three vials of clear liquid. She moved to place a vial in Regin's hand. Then Zala's. Then Elowan's.

"I know your deepest fears – the truth that you believe does not deserve to see the light of day." Lady Ollette scanned the three Fae who had slumped to the floor before her. "Will you remember this?"

"Yes," they responded.

"Then drink. The truth has set you free."

Feverishly, they all moved to open their vials of antidote, the liquid that would abate the piercing pain of Veritas.

"Today, you gain not just one ally, you have gained two. Soxis and Wrenntia will stand with you," Lady Ollette declared. She pulled a small knife from the pockets of her skirts and Lady Firtha did the same. At the same time, they made a small cut on the inner part of their arms.

All in the room watched on with bated breath as three drops of blood for Soxis, and three drops of blood for Wrenntia, hit the floor.

The deal was done.

The rebellion had gained two strong allies.

Elowan had to admit it, the lady of spring was smart. She didn't just unwittingly side with anyone. She would extract their truths – painfully – and use it against them if they dared step out of line. It was a masterful assurance. One that Elowan had deeply regretted walking into.

11

ELOWAN

"UGH, I cannot shake the nausea," Elowan dry-retched with an arm braced against a building wall in Soxis's town centre. The thick night air of Faery's Spring Court was almost a physical wall against Ellie's senses. The jeers and shouts of joyful citizens flooded the town centre, doing the nausea that hung high in her belly no favours whatsoever. The smell of spices and cooked meats wafting through the humid air urged her to projectile vomit. Again.

It had been two hours since they all took a shot of Veritas. An hour and forty-five minutes since they took the antidote for it. They only endured fifteen minutes of interrogation. Fifteen measly minutes. It was no wonder people passed out or died from Veritas ingestion.

Zala, who stood a metre behind her was now back to her normal steely self – quieter in fact, if that was even possible. Regin was still flushed, pink warmed his cheeks, but he held it together with a firm hand on Ellie's back. Soothing her between her bouts of groans and dry heaving.

"Let's get a fucking drink," Zala sighed.

"Finally, something we can agree on." Elowan groaned again, straightening herself.

Zala brushed past Elowan without another word, storming ahead.

Elowan took that moment to reach for Regin's hand. "Are we okay?" Elowan asked, peering into his light-purple eyes. The loose tendrils of his blond hair framed his face perfectly.

Regin reached out to cup Elowan's face with his broad hand. His hands were calloused from working tirelessly in his workshop, but Elowan didn't care. They were hers to hold. "Always." Regin smiled, the corner of his mouth twitching just the slightest. It was his tell.

"But?" She could always read him.

"But I need you to know that I will love you no matter what. When you are at your darkest, I will be the light, Elowan. You can turn me away or tell me I am not worthy of you, and I will still shine just for you. I am yours to keep. You can tell me anything. Everything."

His voice, deep and soft, ached with a pain she never intended to inflict. He was hurt that she didn't, or rather couldn't, tell him how she had been feeling since Cam's death. An ache started in the back of Elowan's throat. She tried to swallow it away. "It's hard. You know me . . ." It was Ellie's turn to start tearing up now. "It's always been hard to tell you how I feel. I'm scared. I'm scared that you'll leave me if I say the wrong things."

Elowan leaned into his hand farther. Her lips wobbled.

"I won't leave you. It's not written in my destiny. You're it for me. You're the gravity that holds me together." Regin's voice quivered. He took in a breath before pulling Elowan into his embrace.

She leaned into his warm chest. His sweet smell nestled itself into her nostrils. His long blond hair shielded her eyes. And that's when she crumbled.

"What can I do to make you realise that I will never leave you?" Regin said into Elowan's hair.

"I don't know." Instinctively, Ellie tensed. Regin had never given her a reason to believe that he would leave. Never. But with her mother gone, her father unknown, her lower brain couldn't help but equate their leaving to her existence. It was an illogical thought and an equally impossible one to rewire.

"It's okay if you don't know. We can work it out together." He pulled back enough to wipe the tears from Elowan's tanned face. "Now let's go get a drink before Zala drinks the entire town under the table," he said, laughing lightly.

Elowan took Regin's outstretched hand and followed the wraith's trail.

The Sleeping Rabbit. Soxis's local watering hole. You could hear it from a mile away and as you inched closer, you could practically smell its sticky floors. It was mouldy eighty per cent of the time and packed to the rafters one hundred per cent of the time. Which only meant one thing. The drinks were good.

Thank fuck.

As Elowan stepped inside behind Regin, the crowd teaming inside the tavern cheered – a custom for the Sleeping Rabbit. For anyone who walked in, you had to cheer them on in welcome. It was sweet.

Playing cards, fanned among the grubby fingers of patrons, scattered and flew across tables. Coins clanged against tabletops as they met the eager hands of hopeful winners. The heavy thump of cups reverberated against wooden bar tops and tucked away from the chaos, was Zala, sitting in the shadows of a corner booth with two tankards before her. Like a predator lying in wait for the next kill, she was surveying. Watching. Looking for details.

Regin waved to the wraith, who nodded back in acknowledgement, and then turned to the barman before him.

"What can I do ya for?" the bartender asked, his burly hands braced firmly on the bar top, a towel draped over his shoulder. He winked at Elowan.

She growled in response, of course.

The bartender cleared his throat and swiftly turned to Regin, who beamed with pride. "Two house ales, sir."

"Coming right up." The bartender moved with seasoned grace, pouring two tankards full of ale to perfection.

He handed them each a cup. Regin tossed him a silver coin in return.

"Thanks, chief. Next!" the bartender shouted over the jeering crowd.

Avoiding the sweaty armpits and musky-smelling patrons that danced around the room, Elowan and Regin made their way to Zala. Regin slid into the booth. Elowan slid in after him without a word. She was mortified that Regin had to hear her truth, let alone Zala. Zala who sat there with her arms crossed. Her piercing blue eyes narrowed on Elowan.

In true Zala fashion, the female of little words, she had managed to say everything yet nothing at all as she silently pushed one of her cups in front of Elowan. A peace offering.

Elowan nodded in understanding. It felt like Zala had finally understood where Elowan's mind had been for the past several weeks. Elowan sputtering out her truth in front of her friends wasn't ideal, but that was the way it unravelled. There was nothing to be done about it. And from that, Zala understood. Which was all that mattered, right?

Elowan felt like she finally had the chance to break the surface of water she'd been held under for so long. It was refreshing.

Elowan took the cup that Zala offered and raised it into the air. She looked to Zala, then to Regin and cawed, "Cheers!"

They clanked their cups together ceremoniously and downed the house ale.

It was crisp.

Tart.

Perfect.

Elowan flung her arm around Regin's shoulder and kissed his cheek. Zala made a noise of disgust. "Get used to it Z, we're in for the long haul," Ellie laughed.

Zala just shook her head.

A barmaid, short with red curly hair waltzed toward their table with three more cups of ale. She plonked them down on the table, the liquid spilling on the sides.

"Oh these aren't—" Elowan started.

"They're on the house," the barmaid said lowly, winking as she waltzed her way back to the bar. Tavern revellers called to her from all sorts of directions asking for more alcohol. To her credit, she nodded, acknowledging them all and moved to pour their orders.

Ellie looked to Zala who had begun sniffing all their cups. Checking for poison no doubt.

"Nothing," the wraith stated plainly.

The buzz of the alcohol had finally started to settle and Elowan started to feel warm – it was one of her favourite feelings. "Well, cheers again then." Ellie pulled her cup in the air. "To an eye-opening night."

"To an eye-opening night!" Zala and Regin laughed.

As they downed the whole tankard, a flash of white underneath Zala's cup caught Elowan's eye. A piece of parchment. She waited until the wraith finished her drink before swiftly switching their cups.

Zala followed the movement.

"Might be worth getting us another round Z."

The wraith nodded, gracefully slid out the booth and glided to the bar. Elowan picked up the cup, peeling the parchment from the bottom and clasped it in her hand. It was small and folded. Clearly it was meant to be a secret, but who was the messenger?

Elowan turned to Regin and whispered, "Just play along." He squeezed her thigh underneath the table in response. The crowd in the tavern burst out in a cheer as more citizens piled in. Elowan took the moment to embrace Regin around his neck and pulled him in close so she could use him for cover. Regin wrapped his arms around her waist dutifully. She unfolded the small parchment behind his neck. From this angle, no one could see what she was doing. All they would see was a tipsy female getting handsy with a male.

The secret parchment read: *Some freely fly above neutral waters. -O*

Elowan immediately crumpled the parchment into her palm, drew back and kissed Regin passionately. He leaned in, breathing in her scent. She loved it when he did that.

As they shared this intimate moment, Elowan burned the parchment with a tiny wisp of her mana. Elowan pulled away for a moment to whisper, "Let's dance." To which Regin let out a small growl of excitement, pushing her out of the booth with two firm hands on her waist.

As if on cue, the concoction of stringed instruments and tambourines that played lowly in the background of the tavern grew into a joyous crescendo. Patrons stood up from their card games, their chairs screeching against the floor. They all took their cups and downed their alcohol. Burly males grabbed the shy females that had spent the night coyly admiring them from a distance, old friends grabbed new ones they had just met, and together, bright eyed and a little drunk, they all danced to the merry music.

Elowan took Regin's hand and pulled him into the eye of the storm, giggling and jumping to the rhythm of the music. Regin bent back in laughter as Elowan pulled the silliest dance move she could muster. She loved the sound so much. How did she ever think life wasn't worth living?

"Move!" Zala's voice was a knife to the throat – all business, no charm. She pushed her way through the cheerful crowd with three tankards of ale in her hands. The crowd thankfully made way for the wraith. Made way? More like *scattered*.

"Finally!" Elowan shouted over the raucous. She took the two cups from the wraith's hands and handed one to Regin who was still moving to the music. Elowan pulled an arm around Zala and hugged her lifelong friend as hard as she could. She leaned in and whispered into the wraith's ear, "Some freely fly above neutral waters."

Zala responded with a squeeze of Elowan's shoulder.

She knew that Zala understood.

"Cheers!" Regin came in with his cup, he took them both in his arms and pulled them close. It made Elowan overflow with joy.

They danced and they cheered. Letting loose on the one night that seemed appropriate for them to. Even Zala let her hair down a little. She swayed lightly to the music taking sips from her tankard. It was the most fun the wraith showed in a while.

Elowan and Regin on the other hand, danced like two drunk idiots. For a moment it felt like nothing had changed. For a moment it felt like they were back to the good old days when it was bearable to hear Kaine's name and when Cam was . . .

A ringing, soft at first, grew to a stifling climax.

Elowan stilled.

Then Zala stilled.

The strings of the band fell flat as the room too, grew silent.

The revelry grinded to a deafening halt.

Everyone turned to the front door of the tavern.

To listen.

One second.

Two.

The wooden door catapulted from its hinges, spraying shards of wood in all sorts of directions.

Then the screaming started.

The Fae closest to the door fell to the ground, supporting whatever body part had been pierced by free-flying shrapnel. Growling and yipping sounded near the door.

"Everyone, get back!" shouted Elowan. The patrons yelped, eyes wide as they moved swiftly away from the door. Some even scurried. Others helped those who were injured. Whatever had just blitzed the door into tiny shreds smelled of another world. Another realm.

Elowan pulled out her short spear from her belt, fastening it in her left hand. She pulled out Camrine's short spear and fastened it into her right hand.

Slowly, she advanced.

She'd done this a million times. Walked straight into danger, that is, but it didn't prepare her for what she saw growling, dark blood dripping from their maws.

Three hellhounds.

They pounced.

Chaos ensued as Elowan dropped to the floor with what had to be seventy to eighty kilos of solid muscle. The air in her lungs left her with a painful thump. Razor-sharp teeth shaped into a nasty growl, mere centimetres from her face, threatening to shred it into tiny unrecognisable piece. Terror filled every vein in Elowan's body as the hellhound pinned her down. All Elowan could think of in this moment was . . . that this was the last thing her mother saw as she was mauled to death.

The hellhounds were like shadows. Their obsidian fur contrasted the bright red flames of their tails. Only their jagged demon teeth stood out from their fur – yellowy and plaque covered. As terrified as Elowan was in this moment, she knew could she not let them run free.

Patrons of the Sleeping Rabbit screamed as the other two hellhounds terrorised them. Nipping and mauling those who were closest. A push of dark shadow matter sent the hellhound above Elowan flying to the side. It whimpered as it hit the ground. Zala.

"You okay?" the wraith breathed. She gruffly picked up Elowan by her shoulders.

Elowan's vision refocused with a shake of her head. "I'm fine."

The bartender that served them earlier shouted over the pandemonium. "Everybody get downstairs! Now!" The crowd moved, trying their best to avoid the hellhounds.

From the corner of her eye, Elowan could see Regin helping the patrons who were most intoxicated and confused. They all headed downstairs to safety, Elowan hoped.

Elowan stood up swiftly, standing back-to-back with Zala whose two rapiers were now out and ready for action. "Hey, fido, come get some!" Elowan called out.

The three menacing hellhounds began to circle Elowan and Zala. They barked and growled, their hackles fully erect.

"A part of me thinks they're cute." Zala chuckled.

Elowan scoffed. "Of course you would."

Elowan pulled back her two short spears, ready to strike, when the hellhounds snapped out of their trained aggression. In sync, the hounds turned their heads toward the front door as if they all heard the same thing.

"What the . . ." Elowan didn't even finish her sentence when the hounds bolted out the front door, leaving a trail of blood in their wake.

Elowan ran after them.

Zala did too.

As soon as Elowan breached the threshold of the Sleeping Rabbit's front door, she gagged. The smell of blood shot its way through her nostrils like nothing else, grinding her sprint to a halt. Elowan watched in terror as another twenty hellhounds ran past them from the town centre and out toward Heartsprung Hills.

She had no words to describe the carnage that the hellhounds left. Bloodied paw prints scattered themselves across the town's pavement as if a war had been waged. Elowan traced the paw prints all the way back to the now silent town centre. In the distance, lifeless bodies slumped together. Limbs and innards were strewn haphazardly across the ground.

She whipped her head back to see where the hellhounds were headed. Just above a hill, Elowan spotted a deep-red, glittering portal. A portal headed straight for the Shadow Realm.

Without thinking, Elowan sprinted for it. The pack of hellhounds had started to stream into the portal. Elowan was so close. If she sprinted harder, she would be able to catch one or two of the last ones.

She pumped her arms and legs as hard as she could. She was just fifty metres away from the back of the pack now. The pavement of the town centre turned into brittle grass. The smell of ash and blood melded together as she ran. The portal began to shrink. *No. Not yet.* Elowan ran harder, trying her best to catch them.

"Ellie, stop!" It was Regin.

Harder. I've got to go harder. I can catch them. Elowan gritted her teeth and pushed herself. But she was too late. The last hellhound bounded into the portal and as the tip of its flaming tail crossed the border, the portal closed with a *woosh*.

Elowan fell to her knees, skidding to a halt. Panting. She was only two metres away. She could've stopped them.

And do what? a little voice inside her asked. She had absolutely no idea.

"Ellie, are you alright?" Regin shouted, worried. He fell to the ground before her and held her tight.

"I'm fine. I'm fine," Elowan repeated.

"Don't ever fucking do that again," Zala said flatly. The wraith appeared into Elowan's line of sight with an annoyed look upon her face. Zala crossed her arms then turned swiftly, quickly examining the grassed area where the portal had appeared, looking for anything notable.

Regin helped Elowan off the ground.

"I'm sorry, I just . . ." Elowan trailed off. She didn't know how she felt right now nor the root cause for her failed act of valour. She was angry with the hellhounds, she hated them for what they did to her mother. She wanted them to pay for what they did to the citizens of Soxis. She wanted to know why they were doing it and who was tasking them to do what seemed like pointless slaughter.

Elowan's gaze fell to the ground. The flowers that bloomed as they walked to Asteria Hold just earlier that day had wilted and greyed. She crouched down to inspect them further. Elowan brushed her hands through the grass. The grass itself had greyed and stiffened, withering away into meaningless particles with a slight touch.

Elowan looked out to the rolling hills ahead and what she saw lodged a sadness deep in her throat. The once beating heart of the Spring Court, the luscious Heartsprung Hills, was now dead. All life that had blessed the earth here had disintegrated into greyness.

The blight had finally reached Soxis.

12

SOPHIE

Sophie woke to a soft hum of mana that brushed against hers. The ends of her hairs stood up. Someone was at the front door of her villa. She could feel it.

With Fae grace, she slipped out of her bed and snuck over to the small fireplace across from her bed to wield the fire poker. Bits of ash fell delicately across the marble floor as she paced across the room. As she made it through her bedroom door, Sophie wound the fire poker back in the air, ready to strike the intruder that dared hover just outside.

On silent feet, she advanced to her front door and swung it open with lightning speed.

In front of her stood Acheron and in his giant hands was a crochet draekin – its pink-and-purple body lay in his left hand while its tail lay in his right. He stood there with his jaw open like a koi fish. Sophie craned her neck as she surveyed him, and she would do it all again just to see his silly stunned face.

Sophie pulled her fire poker higher, pointing it at him. "What are you doing?" She looked to the crochet draekin that lay in his hands then back to his face.

Acheron straightened himself and cleared his throat. "I . . . you . . ." His majestic angel wings fluttered behind him nervously.

Sophie pulled down her threatening fire poker and twirled it nonchalantly in her hands. She watched as Acheron's bare chest tensed, holding his breath. He was wearing the same uniform loin cloth she saw the other angels wear.

Sophie tried not to smile. The large handsome angel was undeniably nervous. "Do you normally go around destroying people's gifts?" Sophie nodded pointedly at the crochet draekin that had its tail ripped apart. She crossed her arms and leaned against her front door.

"Here." He shoved the crochet draekin into Sophie's hands and quickly turned around. "I found it that way." Acheron's wings flared out with a whoosh, creating a wall between them. He cleared his throat. "You have a visitor in the courtyard. I suggest you get dressed for this one." His voice was all commanding again though Sophie heard a hint of a smug smile. Just a small one.

Without another word, Acheron shot up into the air with a thunderous thrust of his wings.

"Wait, who's the visitor?!" she screamed after him. She let out a groan of annoyance just as the smallest of breezes caressed her skin—

She looked down at herself.

Are you fucking kidding me?!

Sophie had been far too preoccupied to realise that was she was basically naked. With all but a see-through polka dot bra and matching thong. The angel wasn't undeniably nervous, he was undeniably *uncomfortable*. And given the way she was toying with the fire poker like she had a point to prove, she was a complete numpty! Sophie could have died right then and there from sheer embarrassment, but clearly the gods had other plans for her.

Quickly slamming the front door behind her, Sophie sprinted to her room, threw the fire poker and crochet draekin across the room and flopped onto her bed face first. She let out a groan that stirred her long-dead ancestors. Rolling onto her back with exasperation, Sophie mocked in a high-pitched annoying voice, "I suggest you get dressed for this one." It sounded *nothing* like Acheron.

But as seconds rolled by, her annoyance gave way to a toiling unease that unsettled all her insides. She had a visitor . . . who could it be?

Clothes, check. I'm off to a good start.

After triple checking that she'd dressed herself appropriately, Sophie made her way to her separated courtyard where Acheron had mentioned her visitor was waiting for her.

On a stone bench sat a woman with long silver hair. Her skin glowed a faint gold and a small breeze picked up through the courtyard that filled Sophie's nose with the scent of fresh strawberries. Sophie's throat choked and her feet lost their ability to move. Tears prickled her eyes.

It couldn't be. Here? In the Godlands?

With her piercing golden eyes, the woman turned to face Sophie. It was Danna, her mother.

The sight of those familiar, warm golden eyes sent the waterworks on full blast. Sophie ran across the courtyard with all her Fae speed and grace to embrace her mother. This hug. Right here. She'd wanted this hug for so long.

Danna laughed through her own tears and hugged Sophie right back. They stayed like that for a few moments before Sophie pulled back. "I can't tell if I want to throttle you or if I should keep hugging you." Sophie sniffed and pulled her mother into another embrace. "I've missed you so much."

"I've missed you too, Sophie. More than you can imagine." Danna wiped her tears away with the pads of her fingers. She cleared her throat and pulled Sophie down to sit with her on the stone bench. "I am so sorry, Sophie. More than you can imagine. There's so much to tell you, I don't even know where to begin."

"Let's start with promising to never hold back secrets, no matter how difficult they are to navigate. We're family. We've only got each other." Sophie held her mother's hand between hers.

"Agreed." Danna softly smiled and cleared her throat again.

"I can't believe you're here in the Godlands." Sophie laughed, though it fell flat when Danna's face dropped imperceptibly.

"Well . . ."

There was something about that downward tone that had all remnants of Sophie's smile fading. "Well?"

"Have you heard of the goddess of all lands?" Danna pressed her lips together.

Did Sophie know the goddess of all lands? What sort of question was that? Of course she did. Sophie had spent nights pouring over every page of the thick leather-bound mythology books her mother gifted her. She spent days out in the sun, nose deep in their vivid stories, until the pages creased and the pictures faded from the oils of her curious fingers. "Of course, she blesses lands with flowers, fruits, harvests across all the realms . . ." Each word Sophie spoke grew more soft, suspicious.

"Yes, that's right! I'm happy to see those mythology books I gave you were put to good use." Danna's laugh was all nervous as she explained something that left Sophie's worldview askew.

Those books, her mother told her, failed to mention that the goddess of all lands had fallen in love with a Fae. They failed to mention that despite her family's wishes and ridicule from other gods, the goddess chose herself. "In the eyes of the gods, Fae were lesser beings, made by the gods themselves, though it never mattered to the goddess. She never saw a difference." At this point her voice softened, a thread of warmth filling the spaces between words. "Together they had a daughter."

Sophie's heart began to thunder.

"And like all children of gods and goddesses upon the age of five, half or full-blooded, her daughter was presented to the Fates. They bestowed upon her a gift. She would be the demigoddess of Faery. 'Blessed', she was, to save a dying kingdom. 'Destined' she was, to wield an unruly amount of power." Danna looked up at Sophie, golden eyes brimming with tears. "But what is a blessing in the eyes of the Fates is oft times a curse – a heavy burden." Gone was all the warmth. What filled the breaths between Danna's words was a quiet warning that stirred Sophie's unease.

A pregnant pause filled the courtyard.

The words turned over and over in her head.

Insects hushed and stilled.

The air itself stiffened and crackled with suspense.

"I should have told you. Whether you understood or not, I should have told you . . ." Danna's hands were startling cold compared to the blood and adrenalin that coursed through Sophie. ". . . I'm the goddess of all lands."

Sophie let those words sink in.

She then laughed nervously, the sound caught between a scoff and a strangled cry.

Silence.

A rug had been pulled out from underneath her.

I'm the goddess of all lands.

Sophie's world did a backflip and all the theories she'd ruminated over in her head fell to the wayside. She had theories that her mother was Fae which explained away Sophie's heritage, but this?

Her hands began to shake despite Danna's firm hold.

"This was the very villa I used to live in." Danna's eyes were searching Sophie's, prying for some sort of validation or a response that Sophie couldn't give. So she pushed on. "When you disappeared from the face of the earth for several days, I knew I needed help that was far beyond my capabilities, Sophie. So I came back. A friend of mine helped me track you down and ever to my surprise . . . here you were."

Sophie stared at her mother. She tried to speak but her words were slippery. She couldn't grab a hold. "So– but– wait . . . but *I'm* your daughter."

"Which makes you a demigoddess." Danna grimaced.

The air around them stilled.

Sophie's face dropped into a deadpan. "Okay, it was nice seeing you too, Mum." She got up from where she sat. "Full of jokes as always! Ha."

Danna quickly grabbed Sophie's hand before she could move any farther. She shook her head. "Honey, I know. I should have told you the truth from the start. That's on me."

Sophie looked to the warm hands that held her and soothed her throughout her childhood. The warm hands now encased in a golden glittery film. She followed that glow all the way to her mother's golden eyes. Her silver hair. Features, so painfully otherworldly.

Danna's eyes shone, etched with a plea.

"It's true then. You're the goddess of all lands?" Sophie watched her mother's face closely.

Danna nodded.

Oh. My. God.

Sophie's eyes were impossibly wide as all blood drained from her face. A small dying squeak escaped her lips as the reality of her being came into full view. That's when the pacing started. "So . . . So I'm a demigoddess destined to save a dying kingdom?!" Sophie surveyed her arms, legs and body. She didn't feel like a demigoddess.

"The Fates blessed you with the destiny to save Faery . . ."

"Faery?! What does that even *mean*! That can't be right!" She wasn't a *demigoddess*. No way in the several realms of the universe! She'd JUST found out that she was Fae and now she was something else entirely?!

Danna rocked back on her feet. "Your real father—"

"Is Fae!" Sophie threw her hands in the air. Step. Step. Turn.

"How did you—"

Sophie pointed to her delicately pointed ears. "Well these were a dead give-away." Sophie paused. "And I bumped into Uncle Alston and Aunt Alfre on the way here too." Step. Step. Turn.

Danna let out a whimper and placed her hands on her chest. "Are they well?" Her face washed over with a hopeful sadness.

That whimper made Sophie stop. She nodded. "They're alive and well. At least I hope they are . . . I kind of sent the entire Faery realm into a tizzy." Sending the entire Faery realm into a tizzy was the biggest understatement of the year. Sophie had unleashed the wrath of Queen Calliea and damned the entire realm to hell since denying her and Kaine's fate. Sophie's stomach dropped and dread rooted itself deep within her soul at the thought. She found it hard to form the words. To tell her mother what had happened, but maybe she could . . . "A lot of things happened to me in Faery, Mum. A lot. You're welcome to see my memories. If you want to, that is." Sophie had nothing to hide. Ever since she landed in Faery all she wanted to do was show her mother. She wanted to tell her mother all that had happened, everything including Kaine, as much as she knew it would hurt her reliving the past.

Sophie moved closer to her mother and lifted her hand to her own forehead.

"Are you sure?" Danna asked tenderly.

"Certain." Sophie closed her eyes. A faint golden glow washed through her eyelids and then she felt it. Instead of a shadowy presence, like she did with Zala, Sophie felt a golden glow roaming through her head. The memories of her time in Faery unfolded before her. Travelling through the tunnels with Ellie, Zala and Cam. Fighting the Dakin spiders. Being trapped in the dungeons with Kaine. Learning how to use mana. Turning Fae. Kaine's rescue and Kaine's deterioration. The golden presence flinched at the sight of Cam's lifeless body. Then it retreated, filled with sadness, from out of Sophie's mind.

Sophie opened her eyes. Tears already filled them.

Danna's eyes were scrunched with worry, tears spilled freely from them, and her throat bobbed with heavy emotion. The flowers and plants in the courtyard wilted as Danna brushed the tears away from her face. She grabbed Sophie's hands softly and glanced at the ghosts of bruises that used to lay there.

"I should have been there for you. I'm so sorry that I wasn't. And I know that sorry in this instance won't be good enough, but I'm hoping that you'll allow me to make it up to you, Sophie. No one deserves that kind of heartache." Danna pulled her daughter into a tight hug.

"I'm fine, Mum. Really. I'm fine." Sophie wasn't fine but at least she felt better than she had since she first arrived in the Godlands. It seemed like everyone in her life had the ability to lie. To omit the truth. Her trust had been razed on all fronts. The real question here was, could she find it in her heart to forgive? Could she find it in her heart to trust again? Sophie wasn't so sure, and that made her feel all sorts of uncomfortable. "So . . ." Sophie cleared her throat. "Care to explain how we ended up here?" She chuckled softly through tears.

Smooth.

Danna paused, squeezed her daughter's shoulders, and said, "Better yet, I'll show you."

13

SOPHIE

Sophie floated in the air over Castle Terrin, except it wasn't as all doom and gloom as she knew it to be. The grand castle was covered in lively vines and flowers of rich, vibrant colours that bloomed freely across its walls.

"When I was younger, I often visited all the realms, imbuing their lands with prosperity in the form of crops and flowers – whatever the land needed at the time. My favourite place to visit was Faery," Danna's voice echoed in Sophie's head.

"Holy shit, this is like a cinematic cut scene of a movie or—"

"Sophie, pay attention. I'm trying to tell you the story."

"Sorry, Mum, sorry. Go on."

Sophie watched as her mother's memories played out before her like they were on the big screen. Clouds rolled across the bright blue sky and the Faery sun rose and fell bringing with it buds of beautiful flowers. Pixies danced to a secret song, birds sung freely and children played chase across the castle grounds.

A young Danna sat on the ground with a group of young girls who were dressed in rags and covered in dirt. Next to them, a fountain that sparkled with the golden coins of those that dared to dream and wish, flowed happily.

"See, of all the realms, the people in Faery were happy. It was nothing like I'd ever seen before. It was something I wanted for myself," Danna continued.

Young Danna manifested crowns of flowers on each of the girls' heads. They cheered in excitement and hugged her. Suddenly, a tall, handsome silver-haired

Fae soldier bearing a short spear towered over them. He cast a menacing shadow over the group. The young girls shrunk in fear for a moment, before they realised who he was. They knew him. Danna's golden eyes met his of bright purple.

"And then I met Lou. Your real father. I finally had a reason to stay in Faery beyond my responsibility as the goddess of all lands."

The silver-haired, purple-eyed warrior knelt on one knee and murmured a few words that Sophie could not hear. Young Danna smiled and raised her hand for him to kiss. He slowly bent down to place a lingering kiss on the back of her hand. He did not look away from the golden eyes that had so clearly captivated him.

"Our love was a whirlwind. It was a storm that I never saw coming but one that I revelled in. A storm that I never wanted to go away."

Sophie saw her mother and her father running across the hills of Soxis, embracing one another. Then she saw them lying in a field of flowers like Sophie had seen in the photos that her Uncle Alston kept. Then a scene of them holding baby Sophie in their arms, tears of joy running rampant down their young faces. The scenes warmed Sophie's heart.

That's what love is meant to be like, Sophie thought.

"We were living out our fairytale until one day, the goddess of rebirth, Cerri, came to our doorstep, crying."

A small woman with long dark red hair sobbed in front of their cottage door. Lou brought the crying woman a cup of hot tea while Danna soothed the woman with the reassuring circles of her hand across the goddess's back.

"See, her child had been prophesised over, as infants of gods and goddesses do. By their fifth year, they receive a reading from the Fates that could take the form of a blessing or a curse."

Lou and the two goddesses huddled together before the fireplace. Cerri sobbed as she animatedly explained what the Fates had said.

"Her child, Lethe, born from her entanglement with Terr, was cursed."

The vision of a small boy with dark red hair appeared. He looked sad and alone.

"He was cursed to be the Breaker of Realms. It was a prophecy that struck fear in the gods and goddesses of the Godlands."

The world around the small boy crumbled with red-hot ash. His eyes turned red and bloody as his mouth fixed into a permanent roar.

"But what it did not change was that he was her son. Cerri loved him."

The world around him pieced back together. Bright light surrounded him as his mother, Cerri, embraced him with tears in her eyes.

"It so happened that Faery was facing its own demise. See, shortly after the arranged marriage of Queen Calliea and King Gydeon, Gydeon found his true soulmate."

Before Sophie flashed an image of the young Gydeon in his royal robes, arms shielding a small woman with dark hair and silver swirling eyes. Riviera. Before them stood the never-aging Queen Calliea who had a permanent snarl fixed across her porcelain face. She was ready to strike the small female.

"Calliea learnt that Riviera was pregnant. She wanted Faery's heir dead. She wanted every threat to her throne destroyed. So together with Riviera and King Gydeon, we struck a deal with Cerri."

The familiar warm-hearted woman with dark black hair and silver swirling eyes appeared before the fireplace of Danna and Lou's cottage. Behind her stood King Gydeon with his dark black hair and turquoise eyes. Across the small coffee table sat Lou and Danna. They were planning something. Tears teamed in all their eyes. Reassuring looks and nods were passed around the table.

"We tried to deceive Queen Calliea in hopes to save all our children from their fates, but some things did not go to plan."

The scene flashed again. Now Sophie was on the edge of the Red Oak Forest, watching as Cerri crouched down on her knees. Her cheeks were flushed, and her hands braced the shoulders of her red-haired, cursed son, Lethe. He was shaking his head, lips pouted and eyes red from angry tears.

Sophie could just make out the words Cerri mouthed to him. *It's going to be okay. I will love you forever.* With those words a shimmer of golden magic encased the boy. It glowed bright for a millisecond before rolling off the boy in a shimmering, billowing fog.

Sophie's stomach dropped.

Before Cerri stood the young, turquoise-eyed boy Sophie had always dreamt of. The boy she had memories of . . . except here, he had no scar running on the left side of his face nor did his eyes swirl and smoke.

"What Cerri and Riviera did for their sons took great courage . . . at least, more courage than I ever possessed."

Sophie watched as a sudden movement caught Cerri's attention. From the brush appeared Riviera with her son, a boy with dark black hair, turquoise swirling eyes and a scar across the left side of his face.

From a distance, the boys were identical.

The same inky hair. The same tanned skin. Even the same height.

Up close however, were the telling signs that these were not the same boys. Tiny little cracks upon a vast façade.

Where Acheron's eyes were moving and vivid, Lethe's were not. Where Acheron had a fresh scar upon his left eye, Lethe did not. Where Acheron's shoulders were sure and calm, Lethe's were not.

With reassuring nods from their mothers, the boys took a few steps forward and swapped places.

Next to Cerri now stood Acheron.

And next to Riviera, now stood Lethe.

"It was agreed that Acheron would be kept safe in the Godlands while Lethe and Riviera would escape to Sotera with us."

Sophie understood.

To escape the wrath of the gods, Cerri gave up her son.

To run from the queen who promised death to who she loved most, Riviera did the same.

While Sophie understood, it didn't stop her from feeling physically ill.

With a gentle wave and a knowing nod, Cerri and Acheron vanished into thin air. Riviera gave Lethe a reassuring squeeze of his hand. She leaned down to wipe his face free of his tears. Together they ran east, through the Summeiran forest to Wrenntia. To Northern Helm station.

Their pace quickened. Riviera constantly checked over her shoulder, pushing young Lethe to his limits. In the distance, small flames appeared between the staggered trees. The flames bounded, leapt and moved closer and closer to them. They weren't flames. They were hellhounds.

Riviera scooped young Lethe up from the ground and sprinted as fast as she could. He clutched onto her for dear life. His little fists were white-knuckled but still, Riviera ran with all her might. Try as she did, she wasn't fast enough for Terr's hellhounds.

A loose root caught a hold of Riviera's ankle, and she came crashing down to the ground. Lethe crawled to the woman to help her up, but her ankle was badly twisted. Riviera sobbed. She pulled the boy close to her and yanked off the chain she wore around her neck. The sleeping sun necklace shone bright as she placed the necklace firmly in his small hands. *Protect this at all costs*, she mouthed as tears and pain washed over her face.

The boy, wide-eyed, nodded then shook his head and he tried to help her up. But he couldn't.

The hellhounds circled Riviera who lay helpless on the floor. Her mouth screwed into a fierce *Go!*

The boy scrambled back but fear had rendered his legs useless. He watched as hellhounds circled, nipped, then pounced onto Riviera's helpless body. Her hand stretched and strained for the boy. Dirt piled underneath her fingernails. Then her strained hands fell limp.

The colour in her eyes dimmed to a milky white.

The boy had watched it all unfold.

With the sleeping sun necklace in his hand, the boy ran as fast as he could. He dared look back once, but the hellhounds did not give chase. They sniffed and continued feasting on the remains of the kind-hearted Riviera.

"The oracles showed me. Riviera did not make it."

Danna's voice shook with a quivering anger whose edges were softened with sadness.

The world shifted again, the edges glowing and fading, returning to show a young Danna. The bright moonlight made her skin glow and the darkness underneath her eyes even more devastating. She stood upon a grassed clearing, a young Sophie grabbing onto her thighs. They were waiting. *"When Riviera never showed, we knew. We knew that Queen Calliea had found out that we were hiding something from her. Your father . . . Lou, he loved you so much. He loved Acheron just the same and to buy us time he . . ."*

The scene cut to Sophie's father, confronting the queen at the gates of Castle Terrin. Sophie couldn't make out the words, but she knew he was stopping her from moving. His strong arms were outstretched as if to say *"you'll need to get through me first"*.

Queen Calliea had looked the same as she did back then. All the way down to her spindly red nails that she lodged in Lou's neck.

Sophie could read the words that spat angrily from their mouths.

Get out of my way, the queen sneered.

Lou's eyes narrowed on her from where he knelt on the ground. *Never,* he mouthed.

With otherworldly speed, Queen Calliea sliced his neck open and kicked his flailing body to the ground.

Sophie choked.

"Your father did not make it."

Sophie could feel tears streaming down her face. Her throat ached heavily.

"But we made it. Barely."

A young Sophie swaddled in blankets clung onto her mother's chest, fear wrapped heavily around them both. Danna sprinted from Northern Helm pier to the station that lay just across the grassy hill. Their hot breaths billowed out before them.

"I feared the gods would seek retribution for my helping Cerri. I masked my power and we escaped through Northern Helm."

Sophie and her mother had made it onto the Faery train. Danna soothed an extremely distraught young Sophie, who cried and cried on her mother's shoulder.

Together, they vanished through the portal.

"As soon as we made it through the portal, I blocked all your memories of Faery."

Golden, sparkling mana weaved in and around young Sophie's head.

"After a while in Sotera, I glamoured you with round ears and black hair so no one could pick on you at school."

Young Sophie stood in front of a dressing table as Danna twirled a wind of mana around her. Her silver and purple pig tails turned black and her delicately pointed ears rounded.

"But I couldn't get rid of your eyes. Taliesin eyes."

The vision that played out before her eyes faded into reality. Her mother sat in front of her once more. They were back in her Godlands courtyard.

Sophie stared at her mother. Speechless. She had spent months upon gruelling months wanting answers to her questions and here they were. The answers roiled in her stomach. Unease and anger wrung her chest dry. But her mind . . . there was a smidgen of clarity there.

Sophie was a demigoddess, destined to wield some sort of great power. That explained her affinity for all the elements of mana. It explained why she could use her mana against iron while others couldn't. She was part Fae and part goddess. One blessed by the very Fates to save Faery.

It explained her muddled memories and visions. Kaine was not the boy she always dreamt of or grew up with. It was Acheron. It explained why Kaine and Acheron shared similar faces yet were so different. Acheron had been raised in the Godlands while Kaine, or Lethe rather, remained in Faery under Queen Calliea's thumb. Which meant Kaine was prophesised to be *the Breaker of Realms.*

Bile rose in Sophie's throat.

A sinking feeling started in her chest. No, he couldn't be. If he was, then . . . it really did mean that Sophie had left the entire Faery realm in the lurch. She'd just given the Breaker of Realms a reason to break realms. A reason to start a war. He thought she was his *fated.* Kaine said himself that he would do anything for her . . . even start a war.

For a brief moment, Sophie was transported back to Faery. Back to the intimate moment Kaine and her shared before his fireplace.

"You don't remember at all?" Sophie asked softly.

With every memory of their childhood that she divulged, Kaine shook his head.

Each head shake was a death knell.

The answer was within arm's reach this whole time. Kaine didn't remember any of their childhood memories. Of course he didn't. Because *he* wasn't the one that shared a childhood of vivid laughter and warmth with Sophie.

It was *Acheron.*

All along.

Sophie vomited all over the bushes of the courtyard.

She wiped the remnants of bile from her face with the back of her hand and panted, "So all the fairytales you told me when I was younger are true?" Sophie turned to her mother.

"Yes."

"And these prophecies, about Faery's strongest and the Breaker of Realms – they're all true?"

"Yes."

"My visions?"

"They're your memories resurfacing."

Sophie cast her mind back to the time she'd gone back to Sotera. Sitting at the kitchen bench, covering up her small tattoos – Elowan's favour. There was a tiny reaction there, like a flinch. Small, but still, Danna had made a face as if in recognition of what Sophie's new tattoo meant.

"Have . . . have I been to Faery before this? After we fled?"

". . . Yes."

"And you took my memories then too?" Sophie was scared to know the answer. She already knew what it was though. Sure, her mother feared the gods would track her down but still, it didn't wipe away the icky trail of having her memories forcibly removed.

"Yes. Honey. I'm sorry. You must understand that I had to."

She did. But it didn't mean she had to like it. "So you knew, this whole time? You had the opportunity to tell me, and you didn't?"

Danna started but couldn't seem to get the words right.

Sophie swallowed thickly. Danna didn't have to say to a word really. Her failure to articulate was answer enough. Disappointment. That's what Sophie felt right now. "Can I get my memories back at least?"

"You can, but I can't give them to you. You must go to the Stagnum De Memoria. The Pool of Memory. I can't undo the spells I've done." Danna scrunched her face apologetically.

Convenient. "I would be lying if I said I wasn't hurt by this. I'm not mad at you. Annoyed maybe, but not mad. I just– I just need a moment." She needed more than a moment.

Sophie stood up, walking back to the confines of her own room.

It was all too much. Her memories being stolen. The gods. The prophecies. It felt like sharp teeth were sinking into her and no matter how hard she tried, she could not shake them off.

"What am I going to do?" Sophie let out a heavy sigh. She was stretched out on the grass of her small courtyard with her hands resting behind her head. The moon, big and bright, spun leisurely in its place.

Calypso let out a whine. Sophie looked to him. He lay on his back with all four paws in the air, watching the moon with her.

"I mean, I could just leave Faery to rot and stay here in the Godlands forever, right? Avoid all my responsibilities?" Sophie said out loud.

Cal let out two huffs of smoke which Sophie learnt meant *no*. Cal gave her the side eye.

"Okay, okay, okay. I won't do that," Sophie let out another sigh. "I just want to wallow in my own self-pity a little longer, but saving the world can't wait, can it?"

Cal stood up from where he lay on his back to shower Sophie with licks and kisses. Sophie squealed, "I'm going to take this as your agreement."

Sophie laughed as she gave the hellhound the belly rubs that he loved so much. Despite the laughter, the aching unease in her chest did not quell. There was a newfound piece of knowledge that left her heart in a state of disarray. It was heavier than before, knowing that she'd left Faery to hands of the Kaine. Yet at the same time her heart was much lighter, knowing it was Acheron she had dreamt of all along.

This changed everything.

14

SOPHIE

Sophie was going to get up. At least that's what she told herself several times over this morning. Funny how her world view had shattered into tiny unrecognisable pieces, and yet the sun still filtered through her curtains. The slight breeze still swept across her skin. The distant sounds of the Isle's waterfall still trickled on. The world continued as it was, despite the storm that swept through her mind. She was everything she thought she wasn't and still, she felt like nothing at all. Especially in this godsforsaken bed she wanted to desperately disappear into.

Cal let out a loud yawn beside her, pawing at her arm.

Breakfast time. More like lunch time given the position of the sun in the clear blue sky.

"Alright, alright, I'm getting up."

At her words, Cal jumped off the bed and spun around on the spot for good measure before running to the kitchen Sophie begrudgingly shuffled after him.

Upon the white kitchen counter sat a platter filled with fruits, cold meats, bread, and chocolate-filled pastries. At least she was being fed well here, or at least been given the option to. She hadn't quite worked up her full appetite.

Sophie stretched and yawned, taking her time in moving around the counter to grab a bowl of Cal's food.

She should've moved faster. She should have been more alert. Because as soon as her back turned, the guilty sound of Cal's claws upon the kitchen counter sounded. Sophie whipped back around. But it was too late. From out the hellhounds mouth, hung several pieces of cold meat.

"Hey! I thought I could trust you! That's *my* breakfast!" Sophie lunged for him, but the hellhound was too agile. He gulped the remaining cold meats and even had the audacity to sneak a chocolate croissant into his mouth.

Chocolate.

Sophie's eyes widened. Her heart raced. She backed off, her hands in front of her, trying to calm him. "That has *chocolate* in it, buddy. Chocolate is bad for puppies. Very *very* bad."

She swore the hellhound was snickering. Tendrils of smoke left his nostrils as if to say *Ha! I recognise this folly. You cannot fool me.*

Chocolate was poisonous to dogs. Granted, Calypso was a hellhound from a different realm, but still, Sophie couldn't risk it.

They began to circle each other in the middle of the living room, a trail of croissant crumbs littering the floor.

"You're a good boy, aren't you Cal?"

Cal let out a single puff of smoke.

"And good boys don't like tummy aches, do they?"

Cal stopped, his head tilting as he looked at Sophie.

She closed in on him. "That's a good boy. Now give the poison croissant to me . . ." Cal inched in a few paces closer. "That's it, *good* boy."

Too much. Too soon.

Cal bolted from the living room, through her bedroom and into the court-yard. Sophie gave chase. "You little shit!" She jumped and dodged furniture, pain shooting along her sides. She wasn't as fit as she used to be, but at least she could still move.

Before she knew it, Cal had jumped the entire fence, a trail of pastry crumbs clung to the shrubbery around the courtyard.

"You're fucking kidding me!" Sophie was embarrassingly out of breath as she shot through the front door in nothing but a silk cami, shorts and no shoes. "CALYPSO! DROP THE DAMN CROISSANT!"

There's chocolate in it, godsdamnit.

Sophie hollered and howled after him. He was darting all over the street, dodging her. And when she thought she was close enough to grab him, he ran up the steps to the villa whose owner she didn't quite want to see just yet.

Of course.

The black door of the villa swung open. Acheron pulled back, brows ruffled in confusion. Not only was Cal bolting for him, Sophie was too.

"HE'S GOT A CHOCOLATE CROISSANT IN HIS FUCKING MOUTH!" Sophie shouted.

"By the Fates—" Acheron swung into action, chasing after the hellhound whose tail wagged furiously. This was a game to him. A freaking game!

Sophie jumped into Acheron's villa, invitation be damned. Together, Sophie and the angel worked to corner Calypso. There was barely any croissant left in his mouth and yet, his furry black bottom wagged in the air as if he had a point to prove. They were a calamity, running around the room in silly circles. Lamps and picture frames crashed to the ground. Furniture screeched across the floor. As Cal cornered himself onto a couch, Sophie made a lunge for him. But clearly, Acheron had thought to do the exact same thing.

Their heads collided with a painful *THUNK.*

"Ah!" Like all of Acheron's precious furnishings, Sophie crashed to the floor, bracing her forehead that pulsed with a heartbeat of its very own.

"Sophie, I'm so sorry!" Acheron winced, a tattooed hand covering his right eye as he reached for her.

"It's fine, it's fine! Get the croissant." Sophie could already feel the swelling of her head. She'd need to ice it.

When Sophie thought her day couldn't get any worse, the wet sounds of Cal choking on the dastardly croissant sounded through the room.

"Cal!" Acheron's hands flew to the hellhound's jaw, prying it open. "Sophie, I'll hold his mouth open. I need you grab the stupid pastry out!"

Swelling forehead be damned, Sophie moved to assist the angel. She stuck her entire hand down Calypso's throat, fishing out the giant wad of wet croissant. "I've got it! I've got it!"

Acheron let go of his furry friend. His furry friend who just sent them running around like fools. His furry friend who was, just a moment ago, choking on a poisonous croissant. His furry friend who now *trotted* over to the window, picking out the perfect sunspot to laze in, as if he hadn't just sent them both into a panic.

Sophie gasped, the damning wet croissant remnants still in her hand. She looked to Acheron who sat on the floor, his breath beginning to steady and his face, equally incredulous as hers.

"Are you open to adopting a hellhound?" Acheron's deep voice was still breathy, a laugh curling at the end of his question.

Sophie leaned back on one hand and lifted the croissant-filled one in the air. "Hell no! That's your dog!" She bent her head back in burst of laughter.

Acheron's wings fluttered for just a second before he joined in on the laughter with her. "I suppose he is."

They stayed on the floor for a little while longer, surrounded by tousled furniture, broken lamps and croissant crumbs.

"I thought you'd be above this," Sophie said, broom in hand, sweeping up crumbs from Acheron's living room floor.

"Above cleaning?" He stood a few strides back from Sophie, a steaming mop in hand.

"I mean you're a guardian angel in the freaking Godlands. You're part of Zeus's Aerial Legion. Doesn't that make you . . . some elite being?"

"No, I'm just a lieutenant in the Tienthan, but that doesn't mean I can't get my hands dirty. We made a mess, and now we're going to clean it."

"Don't you have servants that do this?" She gestured to the glass strewn across the floor. "Being holy entities and all that."

Acheron laughed. "I don't know if you've noticed, but we don't have servants here in the Godlands. Sure, there are people that cook by trade, but they aren't servants by any means. Everyone on the Isle pulls their own weight and we help each other out where possible – no matter what rank or holy being you claim to be. Plus, who needs servants when you can manifest things with a click of your finger? It's small acts like this, cleaning after you've made a mess, or after a cooking a big feast, that remind us that with every action or inaction, there are consequences, *being holy entities and all that.* How else are we supposed to stay grounded?"

Sophie hummed.

Interesting.

The room crackled with questions that longed to be asked.

While Sophie didn't face him, she could feel his presence behind her. It was like a sixth sense that told her his exact whereabouts. Her memories of him. Of Acheron. Their past. They started to eat away at her and perhaps getting it out of the way now, rather than later was for the best.

She turned to face him, leaning her chin against the top of the broom that she was using. It took her a few seconds, but she drummed up enough courage to ask, "We know each other, don't we? Before this, I mean."

At her words, Acheron stilled like a predator trying to conceal itself. He stopped sweeping the floor. He turned to face her, mirroring her posture. His chin rested upon the top of the broom, though given his height he had to bend down a significant way. They were now levelled – eye to eye. "That we do," Acheron said softly. He searched her eyes, as if waiting for her to say something else.

"Acheron Taranis. True son of King Gydeon and Riviera the Kind." Sophie tilted her head with a soft smile. It was almost a question, but not quite a statement. She noted the lines of his face, his smoky eyes that watched her intently. The telling scar that ran across his brow and cheek from . . . the fall he took as they played along the river as kids. With each day that passed in the Godlands, he looked less and less like Kaine. He looked like himself. He was Acheron. Ash.

"Sofreya Brighid Taliesin. Daughter of Lou Taliesin, Right Hand of the late king and Danna Taliesin, Goddess of All Lands." He tilted his head just like she did and smiled. "Took you long enough."

Sophie paled.

He knew exactly who she was. What she was.

Her heart stilled. *Why hasn't he said anything before this?*

Before she knew what she was doing she dropped her broom and closed the distance between them. Her lips wobbled as decades-buried emotions made their way to her chest and through the tears in her eyes.

Ash's words of recognition broke her and mended her at the same time. He remembered her. Her best friend. The boy with *moving* turquoise eyes that she loved so much. The boy she cried out for as she was ripped from her home. The boy who promised to find her. He remembered her.

Sophie embraced Ash across the middle and sobbed. For the first time in a long time, she felt seen. She never realised the amount of numb anguish she'd armed herself with since stumbling across realms and learning her truth – until now. Everything came rushing through the flood gates.

Fine. She didn't have all her memories, but she had enough to know that he was her best friend. He was the faceless and nameless soul she pined after for her entire existence without really knowing why or how. She knew now. Her memories had been wiped clean but the feeling and connection in her heart remained. It was his connection. *Their* connection that she searched far and wide for... one she would never find unless she crossed two realms to him. To Acheron.

Ash enveloped her entirely with his wings as she wept and whimpered. The gesture made her feel safe and secure. She'd finally found the other end of the never-ending tether and the relief she felt was beyond profound. It felt like she was levitating, walking on clouds even.

"It's a lot, I know," Ash repeated softly, rocking her side to side.

Moments passed but Ash continued to soothe her until her breathing evened and her eyes dried.

Sophie didn't let him go.

She looked up at him with her swollen eyes and pouted. Her voice shook with emotion, and she sniffled. "I don't have all my memories. The last thing I remember is calling out for you in the river of Faery." She cleared her throat, pausing. "I'm thinking . . . maybe we're better off with a clean slate anyway."

Some words were left unspoken. She would not be retrieving her memories from the Stagnum De Memoria. She didn't need to or want to. To be frank, it scared her.

Ash stilled.

Sophie felt his heart race.

He swallowed before saying against her ear, "Whatever you want to do Sofreya, we'll do." Ash continued to rock her back and forth, his arms around her upper back.

The use of her real name was a precious gift. It was a bittersweet feeling that she'd savour for a long time, along with the feeling of this moment. Safety.

15

ACHERON

There was very little that distracted Acheron Taranis – Lieutenant in the Tienthan. A guardian angel. All the accolades that made up who he was had one thing in common. Lives depended on him. Distraction, in and of itself, meant lives lost. He couldn't afford to be anything but focused. A razor-sharp blade oiled to perfection.

"Alright, boys, next point wins." He grinned, panting. The sun at midday was sharp, beating down on his skin. Acheron wiped the rivulets of sweat that ran down his face. In a crash of shirtless muscles, the angels of the Tienthan rushed against each other in a rugby scrum. The sound of it cracked and thrummed through the air. Ash loved that sound – the power that emanated from the deadliest legion across all the realms.

The leather ball rolled between their feet as the two teams charged against one another with all their might, fighting for the ball. Ash broke from the scrum, took hold of the ball and flew to the other side of the field to lead his rugby team to victory. His friends tried to tackle him, but he deflected them easily with a strong push of his hands. He dodged, spun, and sidestepped swifter than a lightning strike. That was until he saw Sophie sitting on the other end of the try line.

His step faltered, falling shorter than he intended. Sophie. Her purple, un-bound hair shone brightly in the sun. She wore a sheer black chiton covered in small sparkles. The sheerness of the dress pulled his focus, reminding him of how he found her at her front door yesterday morning, wielding a fire poker in her hands. It looked like she was about to murder him. And that thought alone made Ash's wings flutter involuntarily.

Shit.

The next thing he saw was dirt as Deymos spear tackled him right in the guts with a *CRUNCH.*

Ash groaned. By the time he recovered, his face was covered in dirt and his knees were torn up. He sat up, slicking the dirt off his face.

"You're getting sloppy, Ash," Deymos teased.

Ash gave the god of dread a flat stare as Deymos helped him up with a clasp of a strong hand.

Eros poked his head into Acheron's vision. "More like, he's getting *soppy.*" Eros grabbed Acheron's shoulders and straightened him, so that he faced Sophie, who was waving at them from the try line. Cal sat by her feet with his tail wagging.

Eros waggled his eyebrows at Acheron like an absolute deviant. If Acheron could, he would start an outright brawl with Eros and Deymos. Right here. On the field. In favour of not causing a scene, he opted to narrow his eyes at his brothers.

Eros shot his arms up in surrender and slowly backed away. Ash shot him another dirty look before righting himself. His immortal heart fluttered the slightest as he flew over to Sophie.

Be still.

The mighty push of his wings as he landed close to Sophie made her chiton billow. The strands of her hair, made from sparkling starlight itself framed her face, just like how the night sky was destined to frame the moon. There was a perfection in which the way her features aligned.

Ash bowed his head in greeting. "Come to perve on all the shirtless angels, have we, my lady?" He smirked, knowing he'd get a rise out of her.

Sophie crossed her arms and narrowed her eyes at him. The way her nose scrunched and how her brow furrowed when she looked at him that way. Adorable.

"If you weren't my guardian angel, I'd strangle you right now."

Ouch. It almost sounded like she meant it.

"Don't threaten me with a good time, Sophie," Ash teased, making his way to the refreshment table to grab himself a drink. He sipped the cold water, as he turned and leaned against the table to face Sophie. He felt rivulets of sweat trickle down the expanse of his torso.

Is it getting really hot out here?

Sophie sighed and pinched the bridge of her nose. "I've come to ask a favour actually."

"A favour?" Interesting.

Sophie moved closer to the table, eyeing his wings as if she wanted to touch them, "The Tienthan train almost every day. Eros told me that as the Godlands Aerial Legion, you are the most powerful legion across all the realms." She lightly caressed one of his feathers, examining the delicate barbs with her slender fingers and curious eyes.

Ash tried to focus on anything but that touch that sent shivers down his spine. What was she talking about? Right. True. The Tienthan, made of twelve gods and goddesses blessed with the gift of angel wings, was the legion called upon to settle cross-realm battles the gods and goddesses from all pantheons dared to raise.

Focus. "Where are you going with this?" The question came out softer than he intended. Ash held his breath and tried his hardest not to move as she took a closer look at his wings.

"I've got some things to take care of in Faery." Sophie brushed her fingers along the edge of his wings and they ruffled in response to her heated touch.

A flash of the scene in Faery that Ash had found Sophie in left a pang of feral sickness and rage in his stomach. He'd heard Sophie's echoed wails from the Godlands. Her voice called to him – loud and clear above the chaos. A voice that needed a guardian angel. When Ash raced across to the Faery realm, he was surprised to see the male that looked so much like him. Ash knew who the male was the moment he saw him. Lethe. Cerri's son. Ash didn't have the full picture of what transpired between Sophie and Lethe, but he could easily draw conclusions.

Sophie continued. "Some things that require me to be a bit more physically ready. What better way to prepare than with the best legion known to the gods?

I want to train with you." She paused. "And the Tienthan, of course," she added too quickly.

"But you're not an angel of the Godlands," Ash noted. Not that there would be an issue with her training with them as she was, but Ash wanted to test something.

"Just because I don't have wings doesn't mean I can't participate in the training aspect. C'mon, I promise I won't slow you down!" Sophie pleaded with puppy dog eyes.

Ah there it is. There was fight in her still. "And what do I get out of this?" Ash spread his wings just a little closer to Sophie so she could examine them more easily.

Sophie turned swiftly to perch herself on the table, to face his side. "Surely watching me fail at weapons or falling flat on my face trying to wield my own mana would fetch a decent price?"

"Hmm, that does seem like a decent trade-off but I'm not entirely sure . . ." Ash stroked his chin dramatically.

"How about an IOU? A favour that is." Sophie beamed from where she sat, her purple eyes dancing in the sun.

Oh, Ash *loved* favours, especially ones that were owed to him. Ash pushed himself off the table to stand before her small figure. He raised his tattooed hand between them. "Deal."

Sophie jumped down from the table onto sure feet. She took his hand in her own. "Deal."

As their hands met, electricity thrummed through the air. Trees rustled. Flowers stretched awake.

"Training starts in an hour by the waterfall," Ash said smugly.

Sophie's smile was all trouble. "Game on." She wanted a challenge; he knew that much. And a challenge was what he was going to give to her.

Their hands fell away.

With a sharp whistle, Sophie called Cal to her. She nodded a thanks before making her way toward the town centre. Ash watched as Sophie disappeared into the distance with his furry best friend.

"You can come out from behind that tree now, Eros," Acheron sighed, folding his tattooed arms.

A groan of annoyance sounded from the tree line not too far from where Sophie and Ash had been speaking. Eros appeared before Ash. His strawberry-blond curls were now pushed back with a hair band. The god crossed his arms and eyed Ash suspiciously. A mischievous grin splayed across his face, and he teased, "You let her touch your wings."

It wasn't a question. It was a statement. "It was nothing." Oh, it was definitely something.

"You keep telling yourself that," Eros drawled. With that, Eros turned to peel away. "See you at training!" he called behind him.

Ash waited for Eros to disappear before flexing the hand he swore still tingled with electricity. The hand that touched Sophie's.

Did she know?

When Sophie awoke in the Godlands all those weeks ago, Acheron prayed to the Fates that she remembered. Years, they'd been apart. He searched her eyes for a glint of recognition, a morsel of memory, but all he heard was the heartrending whisper of "Who . . . are you?"

He never prayed to the Fates, but in that moment he did. And when that innocent question gutted him from navel to chest, he vowed to never pray again.

But there was something warm about her today. Soft. Like a flower bending to the sun, she seemed more grounded. Given who she met with yesterday . . . maybe she did know.

Like that darned day Sophie finally moved from her bed, Acheron dared to do something stupid.

He dared to hope.

16

SOPHIE

First day of training. Hopefully he takes it easy on me.

"Ladies and gentlemen, I trust you had a good break. Today is test day," Acheron called out from the centre of the training ring by the Isle's waterfall.

Test day? Fuck.

Across Acheron's forehead sat a delicate, gold diadem in the shape of two wings that glinted in the afternoon sun. Each wing for each temple. He stood tall and proud as all eyes in the training room were fixed on him.

"Today, we also have a special guest, Sophie." He gestured to where she stood beside Nemysis, dressed in black fighting leathers and boots. Sophie waved shyly at the group of twelve extremely fit angels. She felt so out of place. They smiled at her warmly, shouting various greetings and welcomes.

"She may not have wings, but that is no excuse to take it easy on her," Acheron continued. Sophie's stomach dropped along with her jaw as she stared at Acheron incredulously. Sophie hadn't trained in what felt like months and her muscles were atrophied from the amount of slumber needed to quell her sadness. She was hoping to take it easy during her first few weeks of retraining, but it seemed the Fates had other plans.

Acheron grinned at her and raised his eyebrows. A challenge. Oh she would make him pay for this by beating his sorry angel ass into the Shadow Realm when she had the chance.

"Is he always this annoying?" Sophie muttered under her breath, leaning in so that Nemysis could hear. Sophie didn't let her eyes leave Acheron as he briefed in the rest of the group.

"Eh. I think he's got a sweet spot for you." Nemy shrugged casually. Sophie's cheeks flushed at the words, though she couldn't think of anything worse. They were just friends, right?

"Alright, two warmup laps then straight onto the obstacle course in pairs. The two slowest pairs will battle it out in an extra round. Losing pair repacks the obstacle course. Reminder: no wings. It's all about teamwork," Acheron called out from the front. With that, he beat his chest with his fist once. The Tienthan beat their chest twice in response before breaking away into pairs.

Nemy turned to Sophie, her chestnut eyes coloured with excitement, and started, "Do you want to part— Oh, it looks like you're spoken for." Nemy quickly shuffled away, clearing her throat as she did.

Acheron strode toward Sophie with the grace of a god. His muscled body glinted in the sun. He was a sight to behold.

Am I nervous?

"My lady," he bowed deeply as his wings stretched out behind him.

"Please don't call me that," Sophie huffed.

"What should I call you then? My queen?"

A muddy memory pulled at her mind. It was a low male voice that told her she was safe and that no one would hurt her. *You are safe now, my queen.* Her throat caught at the words and where they were uttered. She didn't want to be reminded of that moment. Not now. Not ever. Sophie shook her head to clear her mind. "How about the first Fae in history to beat your slow angel butt?" she smirked. *Fae and demigoddess, I guess.*

Acheron stepped closer to tower over her, but she did not cower. In fact, she stood taller to meet his stare. "I'd like to see you try," he said lowly. His dimples made an appearance as he looked down at her.

A quiver of excitement and thrill coursed through Sophie's veins – a feeling she hadn't felt in so long. The fire within her, the fire that kept her alive and focused, woke up, and a sinful smile filled with promise splayed across her face. Oh, she'd show Acheron what she was made of. She'd show him who the new demigoddess on the block was. And she'd beat his ass while doing it.

Sophie almost vomited at the sight of the obstacle course. She'd never been so eager to eat her own words until now. Before her stood an obstacle course that put the Witcher School course in Kaer Morhen to shame. It turned out that the small obstacle course she spied during her earlier days in the Isle of Deos were cut-outs used for warming up. Smaller versions of what they really trained on. Before her was the real deal that stretched several hundred metres in distance and what also seemed like height.

Like the illusion-stable she stumbled upon weeks before, this obstacle course was hidden in the mountain wall itself. Thick, heavy vines covered the entrance that could easily be mistaken as dense foliage but what really lay behind it all was a giant cave, with an obstacle course of axe-swinging pendulums, rope swings, rope climbs, free falls – basically anything that would send Sophie's stomach out her throat and into someone's unwitting face.

Sophie gulped.

She swung her head to Ash who stood next to her, rolling his shoulders, prepping his body for the physical onslaught that was about to ensue.

He noticed her panic. "Sorry, what did you say about beating my slow angel ass?"

Sophie blanched. She'd never regretted anything until now. Sophie grumbled profanities underneath her breath as she narrowed her eyes on the smug angel that stood beside her. She didn't let him get to her. Instead, she focused on the course that lay before her. They wouldn't be the slowest team if she could help it.

Come on, Sophie. You can do this, she repeated to herself. If she could survive this, in front of an entire group of gods and goddesses to boot, she could survive anything.

Sophie looked at the large clock in the distance which lit up green. It signalled their turn to run the obstacle. "It's go time." Sophie gave Acheron a saccharine smile, before jumping up and diving headfirst. The wind whipped against her ears as she aimed for the small pool of water that lay a several metres below. She felt like an assassin, nosediving off buildings into haystacks.

She heard Acheron softly swearing as he scrambled to dive in right behind her. He let out a whoop of joy as they plummeted toward the fast-approaching water. A stupid grin plastered itself across Sophie's face as the fresh air of the cave surrounded her. She was wholly in the moment.

Sophie was about to let out a scream as her stomach flipped and flopped around without gravity, but she didn't give in. She braced her body, tensing as much as she could, so she could break the surface of the water like a pin.

CRASH.

Her ears filled with water immediately. The coldness of the water hit her with such a force she almost inhaled it. With all her might, she kicked up and up to the surface, her boots, heavy stones upon her feet. Sophie broke free of the surface with a large gulp of air and swam as fast as she could to the edge of the pool. Acheron was already on the bank, shaking his wings free of water. He turned to reach out a hand for her to grab onto, but she declined by hauling herself onto the ledge.

Sophie tried to fight a smile as Acheron's mouth dropped and an incredulous scoff left his lips. He looked positively offended with his dark black hair clung to his neck and rivulets of water propelled down his tattooed arms and chest. He shook his head at her.

Sucker.

Sophie smirked and sprinted toward the next obstacle – a two-hundred-metre rocky wall climb with no rope to catch her fall. Her fighting leathers were sopping wet, and she could feel small rocks finding their way into her combat boots. Shaking the nervousness from her body, she began scaling the wall.

Naturally, Acheron had propelled himself up the wall within seconds, bounding left to right in a show of agility, strength and skill. Sophie looked up to see his head poke over the ledge. She was about halfway up the wall when her left boot squelched and slipped, sending rocks down range. A small yelp escaped her lips.

"Come on, Sophie. You've got this," Acheron called from above, "there's a rock jutting out to your left."

"I can't reach it," Sophie breathed heavily. Panic began to roil in her chest, but she willed her heart to calm. She had to leap and catch on to the rock before she could easily scale the rest of the wall. It didn't help that she was half the size of everybody on a course that was clearly made for beings of grander stature. Why did she put herself in this situation?

Sophie looked to the clock that hung up on the cave wall in the distance. They were still ahead of time. If only she could leap.

"You've got this, Sophie. What happened to that smart mouth of yours?" he chuckled.

The sound of his rumbling laughter made Sophie's blood simmer with a vengeance. "This smart mouth is going to give you one hell of a lashing once I get up there, you oversized bird!" she huffed.

"I could think of better things that mouth could do!"

Sophie gasped and let out an annoyed groan. She was going to flay the angel as soon as she got up on the ledge. With a push of her arms and legs, she swung herself upward to the rock that jutted out of the wall. With a grunt, she caught the edge with her fingertips; her forearms barked in pain as her shins slammed into the rocky wall.

That stupid angel, I'm going to kill him.

With a vengeance so fiery, Sophie scaled the wall like a possessed demon. She pushed and pulled to the rhythm of her adrenalin-filled heart and hauled herself up over the ledge ready to pummel the feathers off Acheron's wings. As soon as she stood, Acheron was there with the biggest, silliest grin she'd ever seen. Something like pride shone in his eyes.

"Get that stupid grin off your face." She narrowed her eyes.

"Apologies, my queen. I had to get you up here somehow, didn't I?" He shrugged his shoulders.

"Don't call me that." Sophie didn't mean to, but a little smile managed to escape. Acheron knew how to work her buttons. It made sense considering they spent their earliest years in each other's pockets.

Together, Sophie and Acheron turned to face the next obstacle. Giant logs suspended in the air swung back and forth at varying speeds. They needed to sprint across and land on the last log where they'd dodge large pendulum axes. Two hundred metres below lay thick, dark mud. While better than hard ground, it would be a painful fall.

Sophie's stomach turned as she realised that she was the only being without wings. The only being that would fall and splatter themselves on the ground.

As if reading her thoughts, Acheron assured her, "I won't let anything happen to you. I'll run first. Just follow my lead."

With the grace of a jungle leopard, Acheron bounced and leapt across the logs, pausing where he needed to time his jumps correctly. His wings were tucked neatly behind him.

With the adrenalin coursing through her veins, Sophie followed. She wasn't as graceful nor was her timing the best, but she made it through, landing on the last log where behemoth axes swung precariously close to them.

"Pay attention to my timing," Acheron stated before sprinting past the first axe. His feathers almost clipped against the sharp edges.

The axes creaked with heaviness and speed, lodging nervousness into Sophie's throat. She wasn't sure if she could get across the obstacle. She glanced to the clock. They were doing well compared to some other pairs. They needed to keep pushing. *She* needed to keep pushing.

With his godlike speed, Acheron dashed through several axes before barrel rolling past the last one.

"Are you serious? There's no way I can physically do what you just did!" Sophie shouted from across the log.

"Use your mana. You can sense the axes. Trust me."

Sophie completely forgot about her mana. The gut instinct that lived deep down in her stomach. The force that allowed her to sense danger. She dared not wake it up. She knew she burned it out and a part of her felt guilty. Guilty that while she had mana, she wasn't strong enough to stop her friend from dying. Tendrils of guilt and pain wrapped around Sophie's heart again. Though as annoying and insufferable as Acheron was, he was right.

In the distance she heard Eros and Nemy call out, "You've got this, Sophie!"

Sophie took in three deep breaths before reaching down to her mana. What she thought would be burned remnants, sat a small pool of mana that awakened at her call. She knocked on the glass box that it had been kept in for the past few months and let it do its . . . magic.

Sophie analysed the swing and fall of each axe, allowing her mana to add in an extra lens of clarity and logic.

Dash. Dash. Sprint and roll.

That's all she needed to do. Her mana told her so.

Throwing caution to the wind, Sophie broke free of her mental restraints and ran. She dashed. The axe fell swiftly behind her. Another dash. She felt the edge of the second axe nick the back of her boot, but she kept moving. Sprint. She sprinted by the three axes, lifting her knees up as fast as she could. Then roll. Her right shoulder crashed down on to the log with a crunch. She tucked her body close and barrel rolled all the way to the end of the log where strong hands pulled her up onto her feet.

"You did it!" Acheron looked like he was about to hug her senseless but thought better of it. Sophie was let back down on the ground so abruptly it almost made her laugh. Acheron cleared his throat as his wings ruffled. "We'll need to sprint across the totems and then we're there. We're doing okay for time too." He pointed to the clock.

Sophie nodded as she surveyed the totems. They were tall pillars that varied in height and distance. Some were farther apart while others were closer. What lay below were deadly metal spikes that promised a painful death.

"The only thing to watch out for is—"

"Last one there's a rotten egg!" Sophie cawed as she leapt onto each totem pole like a feline. Sophie could hear Acheron leaping after her and swearing under his breath.

"Sophie, wait!"

Sophie grunted with each leap and teased, "Your cheap tactics won't work with me!"

"Sophie!"

Sophie's stomach dropped as she fell through the totem pole in front of her. Through it. It was a mirage.

Mid fall, Sophie swivelled her head to the right where the true totem stood, just a few metres away. A scream worked its way up and out of Sophie's throat as she plummeted to the eagerly waiting metal spikes below.

Her hair whipped and danced around her vision.

Gravity wreaked havoc on her stomach as she fell. Weightless.

Acheron dived for her. His outstretched arms reached for hers. His face was screwed into a snarl as their fingertips grazed. He sped down, his wings tucked in behind his back. He gripped Sophie's hand.

His wings shot out behind him, stopping their descent in the nick of time.

Sophie's boot scraped precariously against the tip of the tallest spike as she dangled midair. Her only lifeline was Ash.

Sophie breathed heavily. Her heart was about to burst with gratefulness as she looked into his turquoise smoking eyes.

Ash pulled her up gently and nudged her legs, so they wrapped around his middle. She wrapped an arm around his neck and rested her head against him, panting. She felt the patter of his heart against her chest as she tried to calm herself with reassuring breaths.

As he flew them both back to safety, several metres up, he held her tightly across the back. Where his hand rested, her skin burned. And she became all too aware of how firm his grip was.

They'd reached the top of the final ledge in silence. With a sort of reverence, Ash set Sophie down on the grass covered ledge, high above the crowd of angels that chattered below.

Before he could say anything, Sophie burst out, "I'm so sorry. I should have listened to you."

"It's fine. Are you okay?" Ash brushed the hair out of Sophie's face.

"I'm fine. A little startled, but mostly fine," Sophie breathed.

Ash crossed his arms before her and gave a smile that was all *I told you so*. "Well, you know what happens when you play silly games, Sophie?"

Sophie furrowed her brows in confusion. "What?"

"You win silly prizes." Ash flicked her nose.

Sophie swatted his hand away with an unwarranted annoyance. If he hadn't just saved her life, for the second time, she would have argued. Instead, she settled on giving him a dirty look as he stalked off.

Ash chuckled one more time before walking down the stairs that led to the cave ground. "You better get your ass moving. You've cost us precious time and given I've just used my wings to save your sorry ass . . . it looks like we're the bottom pair."

Sophie whipped her head to the leader board that hung below the clock. He was right.

Damn it.

17

SOPHIE

Sophie woke the next day with a newfound brightness in her heart and mind. The darkness and sorrow still existed, lurking, though it lay dormant much like Cerberus guarding the entrance to Hades.

After test day, Ash walked her back to her place. They were leagues away from where they were mere weeks ago when Sophie punched him . . . on purpose.

Come on, it was a serious case of mistaken identity. Still, Sophie felt a little bad for it. Just a little.

On the way back home, Ash mentioned that he had a small library at his villa that she was more than welcome to peruse. Sophie wasn't so sure about their friendship before, but the moment the word "library" left his lips, she knew they were best friends for a reason. Better yet, he was only three doors down from her.

Sophie had spent the morning moving, stretching and of course making questionable, dying whale sounds. Her entire body was sore. Unbelievably so. She wasn't sure if she'd even make it to Ash's door, but after weeks of eating well and moving her body, her muscles were almost back to their fullest. Colour had finally reached her cheeks courtesy of the Isle sun, and the work she put in to moving and *doing* something had started to pay-off.

As she opened her villa front door, another crocheted gift was waiting for her. *We don't have servants*, echoed through her head. She picked it up. It was another draekin, this time it was black with its tail attached and large green eyes. Sophie smiled and popped it into her bag.

Closing the front door behind her, Sophie took a deep, relaxing breath. The setting Isle sun warmed her face. The birds chirped freely, and the crisp Isle air filled her lungs with joy. She could get used to this, living in the Godlands.

With quick, steady steps, Sophie walked three doors down to a villa shaped similarly to hers. The exterior white domes were a little bigger. Where her door was white, Ash's door was black. Catmints had been planted along the three-step staircase and unlit sconces donned each side of the door. It was perfectly kept and not at all what she'd imagine for Ash.

She knocked on the door. She knew no one would be home but thought it would be the polite thing to knock anyway.

She waited a moment. No one responded.

Turning the gold-brushed doorknob, she pushed the door open and stepped in. Finally, it was time for stimulation of the literary kind. She had gone so long without it.

The only way Sophie could describe Ash's home was Scandinavian, Norse Viking meets farmhouse living. Hung up against the dark-navy walls were wooden sculptures. Large, dark brown leather couches covered in thick furs surrounded a stone fireplace. It felt warm and lived in. Above the mantelpiece hung a polished wooden draekin head, baring its teeth. Ash had mentioned his library was downstairs. *Head to the draekin and pull the right horn*, he said.

Sophie was just tall enough to reach the draekin's horn. She pulled it down firmly, the smooth edges cool to the touch. The stone fireplace just below groaned to life, rotating to reveal a newfound entry way.

Hanging gracefully on the ceiling was a tiered rustic candelabra that cast beautiful shadows and shimmers. It hung above a spiralling black staircase just wide enough to fit one person. The warm light of the chandelier danced enticingly along each step, as if to welcome her. Sophie obliged.

Eagerly, she made her way down the spiral staircase. When she reached the bottom of the stairs . . . well, let's say she hadn't been this excited since the day she discovered what a Kindle was.

Sophie let out an audible and awfully dramatic gasp. Ash's personal library was the size of his entire villa. His *entire* villa. Floor-to-ceiling oak shelves with sliding ladders lined each wall. Books, embossed with gold-leaf bindings, packed the shelves. The floor was covered in lavish dark green rugs. Dark brown leather chaises were strewn around the room, perfect for lazy Sunday mornings spent reading. A giant candle chandelier took centre stage of the room, filling the library with a warm, inviting light, and the smell? By the gods, it smelled like the pages of books, new and old. Heaven.

Sophie walked along each shelf, surveying the titles, her head tilted sideways. The books ranged from the history of the Godlands, to war tactics and what Sophie saw next stopped her in her tracks. In fact, this discovery deserved one loud cackle.

"You've got to be kidding me!" Sophie shook her head. The coloured covers of red, green, pink, blue and grey of her favourite fantasy series lay in pristine condition on the shelf closest to the stairs. "You dirty, smut-loving angel! I'm totally giving you so much shit for this!" She laughed as she brushed her fingers against the spines. She read the next few titles . . . all her favourite books were easily ticked off. These were plainly mortal book titles and yet, they were here. Clearly, a lieutenant in the Tienthan had a lot of time on his hands. Sophie couldn't wait to embarrass the living daylights out of Ash the next time she saw him.

Quickly, she deposited a few of her favourites into her bag, hoping they'd bring her comfort over the next few days. Sophie kept moving along the shelves until she came across what looked like leather-bound sketchbooks with some dating as far back as eighteen years ago. They called to her. She was a moth to their flame. The spines were worn as if they were opened and closed every day, in various weather conditions. She had her finger pressed against the spine of the sketch book from nine years ago, when a soft knock sounded from upstairs.

Her Fae ears twitched at the noise. She stilled with a Fae-stillness she never thought she'd ever possess. The knock sounded again. It was the front door. Sophie sent out tendrils of her mana to sense her visitor. A warm, golden power thrummed back in greeting. She knew who it was.

Sophie pushed the spine of the sketchbook she fingered back into place and rushed up the stairs. As she crossed the threshold of the hidden entry way, the stone fireplace groaned back into place as if nothing had changed. As if nothing lay behind it or rather, underneath it.

A sense of unease clung itself onto Sophie's chest as she approached the front door. She hadn't fully forgiven her mother for lying to her or for keeping her from her truth. She understood why her mother had to do it, but now that she was in the Godlands and the gods clearly didn't care she was here, the cobweb of lies her mother spun seemed all for naught. Sophie opened the door slowly.

"Ash said you might be here. I bring apology donuts and ground coffee from Sotera." Danna stood at the door, dressed in a golden-spun sundress. Her silver hair billowed on a phantom wind and her tan skin was covered in a golden, shimmery glow. This was her true goddess form.

Sophie eyed the box of donuts and coffee grounds with reasonable suspicion. "This isn't me forgiving you by the way." She pried the goods out of her mother's hand before moving through the front door and closing it behind her. Sophie learnt on her trips into town that coffee did not exist in the Godlands. She couldn't think of anything more absurd or outrageous. The locals eyed her warily when she tried to source some to have with her breakfast. "Let's walk back to my place." Sophie tucked the bag of ground coffee into her mesh bag, slinging it over her shoulder.

They walked in silence to Sophie's villa.

It was Danna who broke first. "How've you been feeling?"

Sophie opened her front door swiftly. "Worse for wear." She took out the box of donuts and sat on one of the white velvet couches. "I guess that's what happens when you find out that your mother has lied to you your whole life and when you find out that the guy who you thought was your soulmate is in actual fact a psychopath culpable for killing one of your best friends." Sophie shrugged as she took a bite of her cinnamon donut. "Sprinkle in a bit of identity crisis, anxiety, fatigue, oh and coming to terms with knowing you've got a decent chunk of your memories missing . . . I think I'm doing okay," Sophie was as sarcastic as they came. She took another bite of her cinnamon donut and revelled in its sugary goodness.

Danna winced. "I'm sorry I asked."

"What's that line the kids these days are saying? A mental break down a day, keeps the doctor away?" Funny, because no one was saying that these days.

Danna remained quiet.

After a beat, Sophie tensed, sensing her mother's unease. "So . . . what brings you to my humble abode tonight, Mother?"

Danna leaned back on the chaise opposite Sophie's, with a delicate hand on her forehead. She closed her eyes and sighed. "The council is giving me a headache."

The council were a group of gods, goddesses and other holy beings that ruled over all realms including Sotera, Faery and the Godlands. And by the sounds of it, Sophie knew it was made up of a whole bunch of dinosaur-aged males who had no business running a realm let alone several. "What do they want?"

Danna breathed another heavy sigh before opening her eyes. "The wall between Sotera and Faery has been compromised."

Sophie stilled. Her heart stopped. She could only utter, ". . . and?"

"The council has it on good authority that an attack has been planned. Queen Calliea and Terr are making a move to rule over Faery by purging anyone who doesn't support their union. They're sending hellhounds out to slaughter." Danna swallowed and sat up straight, looking at Sophie. Worry creased her brow. It looked like she had more to add to that.

Fear shot through Sophie's heart. "Say it."

"Queen Calliea has a blood-oathed leading the charge. It's . . . Kaine."

Sophie almost vomited the donuts she'd just consumed across the white marble floor. She stood up from her chaise and paced across the room. Her hands clasped her mouth in a deadly concoction of fear and shock. "I need to go back. I need to stop him. It's all my fault." Sophie started burning a trail on the marble floor. Her chest was about to explode with anthills full of anxiety.

"Sophie, honey, this is not your fault at all." Danna stood.

Sophie shook her head. "It is!" If Sophie hadn't stumbled into Faery, if she hadn't given into basic desires, if she hadn't given Kaine any attention . . . this all wouldn't have happened. She would just be another human ticked off the list. Faery wouldn't be suffering. Cam wouldn't be dead. The thought struck through her like a serrated knife and that dark monster that lay dormant inside her came out to play once more. "I need to go back to Faery. I need to stop this before it's too late. Maybe I can talk some sense into him." Sophie made to rush to her room, but Danna caught her with a firm grip of her arm.

"And do what?" Danna breathed. "Sophie, my darling, please. This isn't your fault. It is Queen Calliea's. She's the mastermind. The driving force behind this all."

"It may have been her plan, but I set it all into motion." Sophie pulled her arm out of her mother's firm grip. "I was the one who started it all, and I'm the one who needs to end it. He'll listen to me. I know it. But I need to leave now."

"You can't. I won't allow it! You'll be up against Queen Calliea for Faery's sake. The limits of her power are unknown. You're up against Terr himself, the king of the Shadow Realm and that little demon-spawn of his, Kaine," Danna seethed, almost shouting now.

"What, and you don't think I can handle it? Like how you thought I couldn't handle the truth of who I am?" Sophie shouldn't have said it.

Danna took a step back, clearly hurt. She took a deep breath, eyeing Sophie with a sort of hesitation. It was like for the first time, her mother was seeing her. Actually seeing her. Who she was. What she was and how she was no longer a vulnerable six-year-old girl who needed her mother's protection.

Danna pulled Sophie into an embrace and said, "Go, if you must. All I ask is that you are physically and mentally prepared for it. Go with a plan, Sophie, please. Don't rush into what could be a battle to last the centuries." Danna pulled away from the embrace to search Sophie's face. Her mother's golden eyes watered. Oh how Sophie hated when her mother cried.

As much as she didn't want to admit it, her mother was right. How could she go up against a god, his spawn and an evil queen, when there were still days where she could barely get out of bed? How could she go up against such a force when barely a spark of mana left her fingers? It wasn't a viable option – as much as she wanted to rush into it. She needed a plan. She needed to find Elowan and Zala, and she needed to right her wrongs. She needed to master herself and her mana before she stepped foot back on Faery soil. She needed as much power as she could to stifle her enemies.

Sophie paused a moment longer and then nodded, wiping the tears from her eyes. "A plan it is then."

Danna pulled Sophie into another embrace.

After Danna left, Sophie crawled into bed without having dinner. She came up with a plan that started with lessons – demigoddess lessons – and she'd have to do more than train with the Tienthan to be prepared for whatever she was going to face in Faery.

Sophie tossed and turned in her bed. Her stomach grumbled violently but she wasn't bothered walking to the kitchen to satiate her hunger. She groaned out loud, frustrated.

A soft knock sounded at the front door. Sophie sent out tendrils of her mana. That familiar dark, powerful mana reached out in response.

"Come in!" she called, sitting up in her bed.

A moment later, her bedroom door busted open as Cal came bounding over. He jumped up with excitement and knocked her onto her back again.

"Cal! Down! Now!" Ash ordered with his deep, rumbling voice. Cal whimpered. His butt shook with excitement and his tail wagged furiously but he listened like the good boy he was. "Sorry, Sofreya. I told him not to do that, but he hadn't seen you all day . . ."

Sophie wiped the slobber from her face and grinned wide as she beheld Ash at her bedroom door. His tattoo-covered arms held a tray of what smelled like meats and roast vegetables.

"Is that for me?" Sophie beamed.

Without a word, Ash held it out for Sophie to take.

Sophie shot out of bed and grabbed the tray. "Oh, I could kiss you silly!"

"I heard the rumbling of your stomach from all the way in the Elysian Fields," Ash smirked as he leaned against the door.

Sophie gave him a flat stare. "Sorry, did I say kiss? I meant kill." Sophie pretended to lunge for him, but he dodged, laughing as he did. She moved to the fireplace with her tray of food, doing a little happy dance. She swore she felt Ash's eyes on her the whole time, but she didn't want to check.

Cal quickly found himself a spot at Sophie's feet, ready to catch any scraps.

Ash hovered at the door.

Sophie's eyes softened as that silly warm feeling filled her chest. "Thanks again, you didn't have to." She pointed at the tray of warm food.

"My pleasure. I was up anyway and thought you'd appreciate it." Ash turned to leave.

"Wait!" Sophie jumped up from her chair and ran to her bedroom door.

Ash turned in place, his majestic white wings tucked behind him. His smoky eyes shimmered with something like hope. He raised an eyebrow in question.

"I was in your library today."

"And?"

"Care to explain why a mighty warrior like you has a smut-filled, fantasy romance collection large enough to rival a bookstore?" Sophie grinned mischievously. She raised her eyebrows, daring him to give her any sort of excuse.

Ash turned white and she swore a bead of sweat rolled onto his forehead. In an instant, the strike of dread or embarrassment on his face disappeared. He turned without another word and stalked toward the front door. "Goodnight, Sofreya!" His expanse of muscles worked with every step he took.

Sophie gaped. "Hey, I asked you a question!" She called out behind him, a smile spreading across her face. She scoffed. There was no way in hell that Ash didn't think she would find his secret spicy-book collection. Her afternoon discovery was currency. Leverage she could use against him should he ever try to embarrass her, as he always did.

Sophie returned to her warm meal. She liked it here in the Godlands. Her being here felt right. Simply and truly right.

18

KAINE

S easpun Bay. The Sea Court of Faery located south of Fyllera, home to Southern Helm station, was a sight to behold. It was an island court with glass buildings and spires climbing from the sea floor to peak up and above the Altum Tides. The main hold where Lord Zavis held his court was located several hundred metres under the deep sea. Large glass domes interconnected like latticework were lit up by warm yellow lamps. Mer-Fae swam all about, rushing here and there through crystal clear waters. Sea animals and creatures of all sorts flitted about, dodging citizens who looked busy.

Historically, Seaspun Bay was neutral territory. In every old-time war or ruling, the Sea Court insisted on staying out of the conversation, operating in a world of their own – separate from the land courts of Faery. But all that was going to change today, Kaine thought. It had to. For the first time in Faery history, Seaspun Bay would have to choose. And it was Kaine's task of convincing its leader first – Lord Zavis.

With a breathing device he hired from the shores of Seaspun Bay, Kaine dived deep into the ocean, feeling the temperature drop and cool his skin the farther down he went. The breathing device was the size of a small harmonica with grooves to place your lips around. It was light and made of the same glass the buildings of Seaspun Bay were built from. Kaine would never truly understand the mana behind the device, but it worked. He breathed freely from his mouth.

The waters of the Altum Tides felt heavy and thick against his limbs, gliding through his fingers as he swam. The sounds of a bustling underwater city grew louder and more muffled as he dived closer to the sea floor.

It had been years since he visited the Sea Court, back when Lord Zavis had invited the few Elite to dine with his court. It was an opulent feast held in the grand hall. Kaine remembered it well because Camrine got so intoxicated he accidentally rearranged the seafloor with his mana and . . . memories of his betrayal spiked through Kaine's mind again. The sight of Sophie writhing under Cam. Visceral. Real. Raw. He hated it so much. The reality of the memories was impossible to ignore, no matter how hard he shook his head or scrunched his eyes.

Keep going, he reminded himself. Revenge had already been served.

Kaine kicked his legs, gliding into the airlock of the main entrance to the Sea Court. The entrance was wide enough to fit fifty beings. On the left, beside the main door was a switchboard with a bright red light on top and a green on the bottom. Swimming to it, Kaine pressed the green button. The glass door behind him groaned to life and began to close. Slowly, a warning tone blared through the antechamber. The water levels in the antechamber drained out, until at last, Kaine could stow away his breathing device and breathe with his lungs the way the gods had intended.

With a tendril of his mana, he dried himself up. His thin black fighting leathers creaked with every movement as he tidied himself. His short spear hung as a warning by his side and his long dark hair shielded most of his face. As soon as the door to the main entrance pushed open, loud chattering filled the antechamber.

Courtesans – scaled, skinned and shelled – peppered the grand hall with goblets of expensive wines in their hands. It was a sight to see. All these sea courtesans in one room, fancied and frivolous. It took effort to maintain their land forms, an hour at best before their skin ached for the touch of the sea. And a few more hours until their legs turned to fins and the like. But of course, like their lord, the courtesans of Seaspun Bay were greedy, using all they had to catch a glimpse of their court and all its happenings.

An obnoxious glass chandelier centred the room, stretching across all five levels of the grand hall. Thick golden tapestries, embroidered with stylistic interpretations of the Sea Court latticework hung from the very top level of the grand hall down to the floor, all meeting upon a golden and glass dais where Lord Zavis was no doubt sitting.

Kaine could not see the lord from where he stood, but he spotted the edges of a crowd upon the dais. Stringed music blared from the corner of the hall, bouncing across the walls in a cacophony of harmonic melodies. With one step across the antechamber threshold, Kaine entered the fray.

He walked tall, proud and straight to where he suspected Lord Zavis was seated. The crowd of seasoned courtesans stopped to watch him. Some leaned into each other to whisper, hiding behind their wine glasses. Others without shame, sneered at him. Kaine tsked. *Let them gossip*, he thought. He stalked along the golden carpet, underneath the glass chandelier, closer to the dais where, finally, he spotted Lord Zavis with his long white hair and sea-green velvet suit.

He was an old Fae, centuries old though his face remained quite young. He sat upon a glass throne. Beside him to his left, sat who Kaine assumed were his three daughters named after the three seas of Faery; Altumeda, Errida and Fallencia. Everyone knew they were Zavis's most cherished treasures, more often spoken about than seen. They were decades older than Kaine. Their skin glistened in the warm chandelier light – iridescent with a sheen of moisture. And before all of them were aristocrats and nobles spouting gossip and other nonsense they deemed important today.

Lord Zavis, to his credit, looked exceptionally interested in his courtly conversations until he spotted Kaine who parted the crowd as if he had the plague. They shared a look. Acknowledgment. As he reached the bottom of the dais, Kaine bowed at the waist. "Lord Zavis, it's a pleasure to see you again." He stood tall again after a moment, smiling and confident.

Lord Zavis, the white-haired mer-male, threw his hands up in welcome. With a commanding voice, the lord said above the crowd, "Captain Aaryn,"—the entire room quietened—"welcome back!"

Kaine strode swiftly up the dais and shook the hand of the infamous Sea Court lord. "How have you been faring?"

"Swell. Though I'm unsure what to say about what you've been up to . . ." Lord Zavis smirked, eyeing Kaine intensely.

Kaine knew what he meant. News of his blood-oath had spread wide across Faery. The Captain of the Elite had made a statement and had chosen a side. It made many Faery folk unsettled.

"I don't think you've met my daughters before," Lord Zavis gestured toward his daughter sitting directly to his left. "This is Altumeda, my eldest." With thick blue braids, sea-green eyes and a bored look upon her face, she nodded at Kaine. She was the most breathtaking of the three.

The lord then pointed to the mer-female next to her with light blue hair and the same sea-green eyes. She was much more palatable with a shy smile across her face. Kaine couldn't mistake her hungry gaze as she watched him; her throat bobbed as he met her eyes.

"This is Errida, my second eldest," Lord Zavis continued. Errida fluttered her eyelashes at Kaine and smiled sweetly. Kaine nodded in return.

"And my youngest, Fallencia," Lord Zavis said. His youngest daughter was the image of the first, though her hair was stark white, much like her father's.

Like sirens, all three daughters spoke at once, their voices melding together in a melody. "It's a pleasure," they said.

Kaine bowed his head to the three beautiful mer-females and returned to face Lord Zavis, the high lord of Seaspun Bay.

"Beautiful, aren't they?" Zavis winked.

"Certainly." Kaine did not pay the daughters any heed.

Zavis scoffed. "To what do I owe the pleasure?" The sea lord opened his arms, smiled brightly and leaned back in his glass throne. Insurmountable confidence and arrogance oozed from him which Kaine couldn't help but cringe at.

The crowd that littered the dais grew quiet, daring to listen. Their pearls, gowns and fascinators glinting in the light. Their dolled-up faces shied away, but their moisture-slicked iridescent ears shone with each micromovement, eager to catch each word.

"Perhaps we can discuss this somewhere more private."

A beat passed.

With a sharp inhale of his slitted nostrils, Lord Zavis sighed, "Very well." He stood abruptly from his throne. "Carry on," he declared to the grand hall. The lord clapped twice. The room erupted into a frenzy of music, chatter and dance. Those who had occupied the dais rushed to the dance floor, joining others who started a choreographed, erratic waltz. Kaine watched those in the grand hall, as if hypnotised, dance to the music.

"Follow me," Lord Zavis said low for Kaine to hear.

Kaine kept close to Zavis, who moved with water-like fluidity, as they exited to the right of the now empty dais. The lord waved to his daughters who remained seated. Altumeda, the eldest, rolled her eyes. Fallencia, the youngest, waved happily at her father. But Errida, she watched Kaine intently.

Kaine quickly averted his gaze back to Lord Zavis who guided them down an arched glass hallway. Between the thick glass walls was water, turning and twisting with every movement of the ocean they were surrounded by. Kaine could faintly hear the *wishing* and *washing*. Hung up upon the glass walls were shells of different sizes and shapes. As they walked down the hall, the music from the grand hall began to disappear and the smell of fresh citrus filled Kaine's nostrils.

They reached a gold-leaf infused glass door. Lord Zavis rested his hand upon the centre of it. As he did, the door glowed to life and disappeared into a swirling mist of water. The tall, white-haired mer-male graciously ushered Kaine in.

"After you," Lord Zavis said.

Kaine, with all his darkness, brushed past the lord, a contrast to Zavis's light skin, snow-white hair and green velvet clothes.

"Thank you," Kaine muttered. He walked into the room, the smell of citrus almost pelting him in the face.

As Lord Zavis stepped over the threshold, the gold-leafed door that had misted into nothingness appeared back in place with a warping sound as if Kaine had just dunked his head into water.

Kaine watched in appreciation. The reputation of Faery's Sea Court preceded itself. It was lavish, magnificent and the way that mana had been infused into the everyday was formidable.

In the centre of the room though, stood something Kaine never thought he would see in his entire immortal life. Like a glass icicle, it protruded from the floor. A rainbow, iridescent, lava-like fluid rushed about in its centre. Surrounding it were miniscule clouds with what looked like glitter particles suspended in the air.

It was alive.

It was a Wayfinder.

Kaine shot his eyes to Lord Zavis. The arrogant smirk he received in return was answer enough. This was the real deal then. An ancient bridge that connected Faery to the Godlands. The Wayfinder was cordoned off by a golden railing imprinted with the swirls of shells and sea creatures. An intense beam of white light that shone through several layers of large magnifying glasses fixed onto the ceiling, illuminating it as if it were a holy device.

"It is a shame the other two were destroyed," Lord Zavis said as he admired the ancient gateway.

When the gods and goddesses of the Godlands grew bored of Faery, not long after it was created, they destroyed the bridges that would transport them home – in fear that the Fae would follow them to their homelands seeking retribution for the females they took or the terrors they exacted upon unwitting Fae "for fun". The gods were ruthless, that much was true.

"A shame indeed. Does it work?" Kaine asked, leaning in closer to inspect the Wayfinder and its crystally surface.

"Can't say that I've tried." Lord Zavis sighed and began to circle the room at a leisurely pace.

The room was somewhere between an office and a library. Books lay open on display. Some suspended in the air on a wind of mana while others lay haphazardly on stools. The smell of citrus was strongest here. The room was cool and the sound of water gurgling through walls hummed peacefully.

Kaine turned his attention from the Wayfinder to Lord Zavis, who was watching Kaine intently. Kaine stood tall, hands braced behind his back, he puffed his chest. "I'm here upon request of Queen Calliea, to better understand where your loyalty lies."

Zavis scoffed. "Of course you are." He shook his head, circling the Wayfinder as Kaine stood still.

"Swear fealty to the queen and we will protect you, your family and the courtesans of Seaspun Bay like our own."

"I figured as much." Zavis stopped in his tracks and began leisurely sorting through the drawers that littered the office.

Kaine watched carefully.

"Seaspun Bay's neutrality has stood strong for centuries. For all of history perhaps"—the lord pulled open the top draw of a desk—"however . . . I understand that those days are coming to an end."

"Indeed, Lord Zavis. Faery is on death's doorstep."

"And let me guess, I have no choice but to choose now." Lord Zavis fished out a small dark green velvet box from the desk.

"Name your price."

The mer-male lord began to pace around the room again. A cheeky grin splayed across the lord's face which irked Kaine like nothing else.

He hated this game.

An impatient growl started in Kaine's throat.

"I've given you a critical piece of information." Lord Zavis gestured to the Wayfinder. "It's only fair that you give me something in return." Zavis tossed the small velvet box in his hand playfully. His sea-green eyes shone with delight.

"As I said, name your price," Kaine gritted.

"Fortify your protection and power with my family."

Kaine's immortal heart stopped for just a second.

"Marry one of my daughters."

"I can't—" Kaine cut off.

"You will." Lord Zavis's cheerful grin now turned serious, his white brows narrowed, and his broad shoulders squared. "You will because I've figured you out, Kaine Dormarth Aaryn." The lord drew out his name, leaving a beat between each name.

A growl left Kaine's throat. He bared his teeth but said nothing. He only gripped his short spear, wanting with every fibre of his being to throw it between the lord's eyes and have the conversation over and done with.

He couldn't marry one of Lord Zavis's daughters. He wanted to marry Sophie. But Sophie would understand, wouldn't she? Perhaps she could see that for Kaine, doing these deeds on behalf of the queen was a necessary evil. A way for him to get her back. Back with him, where she belonged.

"I'm no fool, Kaine. I know that you are Faery's strongest warrior. Queen Calliea has garnered immeasurable strength over decades, of which the source has finally revealed itself – Terr, the Shadow Realm King himself," Lord Zavis was basically spitting with anger now. "While the approach lacks tact, I admire the ambition. You've forced the hands of many – bow down or die. Bow down or face powers that go beyond the Faery realm."

He paused.

Kaine softened his knees, ready to attack. He could feel the energy pulsing off the Sea Court lord.

Lord Zavis took in a deep breath and straightened himself again. He softened his tone. "My family and my court are my greatest treasures. Nothing will stop me from protecting them. Nothing. I know you need the Sea Court's allegiance. Not just its resources but also the message it'll send to the rest of Faery. That a court, known for never deciding, has finally decided. And as a result, the blood reign shall reign on."

The lord hit the nail on the head.

"Correct."

Lord Zavis threw the velvet box into Kaine's hand. It was light. Soft.

"Then marry one of my daughters. I need a guarantee. That my court of all the courts that endeavour to align with you and the blood throne, remains your priority. *My* court above all else."

Kaine opened the velvet box. Inside sat a silver ring, emblazoned with the most breathtaking sapphire he'd ever seen. It seemed he had no choice in this matter. The blood-oath was a law that ran through his veins. By whatever means necessary, ordered Queen Calliea. He looked back up to Seaspun Bay's lord. "Very well. I promise to marry one of your daughters." Kaine didn't want to say it, but he had to. He slammed the box shut.

"This evening."

"This evening," Kaine repeated.

Without another word, Lord Zavis pulled out a small knife, pulled up the sleeve of his green velvet suit and made a small incision on his upper arm. The sound of his scaly-smooth iridescent skin against the sharpness of his knife sounded like leather being cut. Three drops of blood fell to the ground. The lord's eyes did not leave Kaine's the entire time.

"Lord Zavis, your allegiance to the blood crown is valued and celebrated." Kaine dipped his head in acknowledgement.

Lord Zavis scoffed. A devilish grin appeared on his face as if he had worked Kaine out like an open book. "So, tell me . . . who is she?"

19

KAINE

Evening came all too soon.

The private temple, tucked away upon the sands of Seaspun Bay wrought a sadness in Kaine's chest. It was not long ago that he himself was at a temple in Wrenntia, wanting to seal the soulmate bond he shared with Sophie. While this evening's ceremony wasn't one that melded the mana and life of two fated beings, it was a civil ceremony honoured in the eyes of Faery law. It would be upheld as such.

The one thing that the marriage would not overrule was the law of the Fates. The knowledge of that alone kept Kaine calm. He didn't feel cornered. His mind was clear, and his thoughts remained calculated. He would just have to get through the next hour.

The walls of Salsus Sanctum, Seaspun Bay's ceremonial temple was covered in crystal salts. The domed room Kaine found himself kneeling in smelled of the sea. The chilling evening wind blew in casually, whisking grains of salt and sand across the floor.

He'd been kneeling here for a good quarter of an hour. A priestess, dressed in a sheer sea-foam green chiton stood to his right, holding a candle, waiting for his bride to arrive.

Bride.

The word did not seem right. It repulsed him even. Because she wasn't Sophie. It was meant to be Sophie.

Lord Zavis hadn't detailed which daughter he'd chosen to marry Kaine. Nor did Kaine ask or care. He needed to get this over and done with so he could get back to Queen Calliea and work to gain Terr's favour. The end was so close, he could taste it on the tips of his teeth.

On a thrust of wind, the door behind Kaine burst open. In strode Lord Zavis, donning green scaled armour, a thick golden cloak draped across his shoulders. In his hand was his infamous golden trident – one that had struck down many foes. It echoed against the floor like a steady clock. *Tick. Tick. Tick.*

Behind Lord Zavis followed one of his daughters wrapped in a beautiful white gown. Seashells clasped onto her dress' trail, and an opaque veil obscured her hair and face.

They did not utter a word as they walked down the aisle. As they neared the end, Lord Zavis gracefully took his daughter's hand, kissed it and helped her kneel down in front of Kaine. The sea lord turned and took a place behind his daughter. To watch and to witness.

Kaine observed as the female in front of him fiddled with her gloves in nervousness. Her iridescent skin bobbed as she swallowed. With shaking hands, she pulled her veil from her face, revealing a slender face of sea-green eyes, cradled by light blue hair.

It was Errida. Lord Zavis's second eldest daughter.

Kaine didn't know how to feel. *This should be Sophie,* Kaine thought.

Tears began to well in Errida's eyes and to Kaine's surprise, it was joy and happiness that was written all over her face.

The priestess took her place in front of Kaine and Errida. She placed the candle she'd been holding onto the floor between the couple. The flames danced happily between the two, casting shadows across Errida's face.

"Tonight, under the eyes of the gods and the stars of Faery, we unite Kaine of Aaryn"—the priestess took Kaine's hand, extended it in front of him, palm up—"and Errida of Triton"—she then took Errida's hand, placing it on top of Kaine's, her palm touching his—"in love and light." The flame of the candle was close enough to warm the back of his hand.

Errida's skin felt smooth, dense, thicker than any land-Fae. As their palms touched, her skin shimmered with unearthly iridescence the way fish changed colours with each movement. Kaine watched her sea-green, hopeful eyes and he couldn't help but feel a sadness in his heart. What a waste of a perfectly beautiful female.

The priestess shifted in her chiton, lifting her delicate hand to her neck to unfasten her silver prayer beads. Everyone watched in silent reverence. She wrapped the beads around Kaine and Errida's upheld hands. "Kaine of Aaryn, do you swear to love and protect Errida of Triton so long as she lives?"

"By the gods, I do," Kaine said softly. His words echoed through the cold room. He didn't mean them though. There was only one person he wanted to utter the words to.

"Errida of Triton, do you swear to love and protect Kaine of Aaryn so long as he lives?"

"By the gods, I do," Errida's voice was soft, sweet and subservient.

"Then by the gods and your witnesses here today, you are now one, united under the eyes of the land on which you live. May the gods guide you to the ends of happiness," the priestess's voice was chirpy – genuinely happy to unite two people.

Together, Kaine and Errida blew out the candle, its smoke rising and encasing their hands. They were married now. By Faery law. Kaine leaned in over the billowing candle smoke. Errida met him halfway. With their hands still joined by the prayer beads, they kissed.

"I know that this isn't a conventional way for a husband and wife to meet but I'm willing to make it work . . ." Errida trailed off.

They sat side by side on the shores of Seaspun Bay. The sand beneath Kaine had found its way into creases of this body he never knew sand could even get to. He watched the waves of the shore lapping up and pulling away. The Faery moon rippled against the surface of the sea. His mind could not quiet. When he wasn't calculating what moves to do next, he wondered how Sophie fared in the Godlands. How brainwashed she must be. How he needed to get to her and save her. Then he remembered how Camrine had fucked his soulmate. It sickened him to the core, and it made him angry. The destructive thoughts continued to spiral the moment he kissed Errida. It all felt so *wrong*.

"You're a man of little words, I see . . ." Errida said softly.

Errida hadn't stopped talking since they were left alone as newlyweds. She was almost as tall as Kaine, with curves any sane male would die for, but Kaine didn't care.

"What could I possibly say in this instance? Your father forced me into this marriage. A marriage that I do not want but can understand is necessary. I'm surprised you haven't run away in terror," Kaine scoffed, gripping the sand beneath him in frustration.

"I've seen you before, Kaine. Traipsing around Faery with your Elite. Brooding. Handsome. Dangerous." Errida trailed a finger up and down his arm. Kaine moved away from the touch. "The moment I saw you years ago in the markets of Terrin, I knew we were destined to cross paths."

"By the Fates?"

"Precisely," Errida said into Kaine's ear as she moved closer to him.

Her voice sent a chill down his spine.

Kaine turned away, "I'm already spoken for." But it seemed his body didn't quite know that.

"My father told me as much. Sophie, was it?"

And there it was. The explosive anger that Kaine grappled with all day had suddenly spilled over the precipice. He didn't want to. He didn't mean to, but he did it anyway. With blinding Fae speed Kaine turned to Errida and death gripped her throat. He inched closer and closer to her face, breathing in her sea and sunshine scent. If he squeezed just a bit tighter, her life and light would cease to exist. He had the power to do it and his fingers were itching for blood.

Her eyes widened ever so slightly.

"I'll say this once. Leave her name out of your mouth," Kaine gritted, baring his teeth.

Errida, to her credit, did not struggle against his grip. Instead, she leaned back on her hands, pulling his weight with hers. She parted her lips sensually, staring straight into his eyes. His soul. The sight of her, full breasted and submitting, unravelled something in Kaine.

He loosened his grip.

Errida wrapped a hand around his wrist, keeping it firm against her neck. "Let me prove that I'm worthy of you."

Errida, with her light blue hair and sea-green eyes pushed Kaine back onto his haunches. She pulled his grip from her neck and trailed his palm to her chest, her heart beating thunderously under his touch. She slowly moved his hand over her breast and Kaine couldn't help it, he felt his cock pulse in reaction.

"What did she look like . . ." Errida's voice was thick with seduction. She pulled his hand away, placing it upon his thigh.

As if hypnotised, Kaine answered, "Her hair was purple, like starlight . . . her eyes were purple to match. Her face was sweet, a nose tipped to perfection and cheeks that filled with laughter . . ."

"You loved her?" Errida moved to place his other hand on his other thigh. Slowly, she pulled down her dress so that her breasts were exposed. Her skin shimmered in the moonlight.

"I love her still."

She moved to unbutton his pants, freeing him. Gods, he hadn't felt the touch of a female in so long. Since Sophie left, he hadn't been the same.

"Did she have any tattoos or markings?" Errida asked quietly. She moved to cup him with her bare hand.

Kaine grunted at the feeling, watching her has she seduced him with grace and confidence. "She had . . . tattoos along her left arm," Kaine managed to breathe as she tightened her grip around his shaft.

Fuck. Kaine stilled. He was too weak.

A shimmering layer of mana appeared over Errida's skin. And before he knew it, Errida's hair had turned purple with streaks of silver and grey. Her skin turned tan and markings formed up and along her left arm.

She was a shapeshifter.

Shit.

She looked up at him from where she was on all fours. Eyes of purple watching him. Without a word, she licked the tip of his cock.

The feeling was electric.

Irresistible.

"Please," Kaine begged.

For it was Sophie in front of him now.

It was Sophie who took his entire shaft into her mouth underneath the Faery moonlight.

And it was Sophie now, who worked him until he ran dry.

20

ELOWAN

Some fly freely above neutral waters. That was what the secret message Lady Ollette had slipped Elowan while they were in the Sleeping Rabbit. There were rebels and sympathisers in Seaspun Bay – the court of neutral waters. Thankfully, Elowan had a friend who owed her a favour.

Together in silence, Elowan, Zala and Regin looked up at one of the giant glass towers that housed hundreds if not thousands of Seaspun Bay citizens. Upon the bay was the central business district while underneath the sea, lay the Sea Court where elitist courtesans peered down their noses at lesser Fae. The towers, some shaped like spiralling seashells, was where all the fun happened.

The sand had clung to their boots and the fresh smell of sea spray clung to their noses. The late-night Faery sky sparkled brightly above and for the first time in a long time, Elowan felt at one with the land. Up there, in one of the towers, was a connection that could mean more allies for the rebellion.

"Should we split up?" Elowan asked as she looked up the seashell tower.

"Remember the last time we split up?" Zala mused.

"Which one Z . . . which one," Elowan trailed off as she stepped into the main entrance of the glass tower before them. Zala and Regin followed suit. They were all dressed in their plain fighting leathers. Dismissible. Inconspicuous.

"Do you remember where you're going?" Regin asked.

"Like the back of my hand."

Seventy-five sets of stairs later.

"Oh gods, when is this going to end?" Elowan groaned.

"Elowan love, you're the one leading us," Regin said, with a hand braced against Ellie's lower back.

"You'd think the sea-Fae would have an efficient method to navigate their towers," the wraith pointed out.

Elowan took in a deep breath before soldiering on. Just two more flights of stairs. Two more. "They do, however I'm not sure how we'd fare swimming up seventy-seven levels of water without breathing devices."

"Perhaps we should have prepared better. There were breathing devices being sold on the shore," Regin added.

"Not helpful, my love. Plus, we want to limit the contact we have here, just in case. We *could* purchase breathing devices like any sane land-Fae would but the stairs are notoriously empty."

Finally, they reached the seventy-seventh floor.

"Here we are." Elowan let out a heavy sigh as she turned the seashell doorknob. The heavy glass door slid open to a hallway. The echoes of laughter, the sounds of singing and dancing tumbled into the hallway of glass. Water filled between the walls masking most of it, but nevertheless, the joys the sea-Fae experienced spilled through.

Elowan moved quickly down the hall, hoping no one would catch them on the way to her friend's place. She turned the corner and almost crashed into a young sea-Fae with scaley skin and her crustacean-looking sea-Fae friend. "Apologies," Elowan said firmly, not making eye contact. She didn't need to turn around to see that the couple were watching them march down the hall.

Elowan slowed her pace until she could feel when the couple had turned the corner. She counted the doors.

One.

Two.

Three.

She stopped in front of the fourth, painted in a light teal with gold-flecked swirls. "I'd take a step back if I were you two." Elowan knocked on the door. A secret knock made just for her.

A second passed before light footsteps sounded on the other side. The door jangled as the knob turned. The door opened and like a tsunami, a team of children swarmed for her, cheering, jumping and hugging her across the middle. They had the combined might of a fully grown Fae male.

"You gremlins have grown so much!" Elowan shouted above the clamour and touched the foreheads of each child with the back of her hand – a way of greeting a friend among the common sea-Fae. She looked up to see the sea-female with long dark hair and dark-filled eyes that stood in the doorway with arms wide open. Beneath her arms were fin-like webs that shimmered with each movement, pulsing with happiness and delight. Sea-Fae wore their emotions on their skin.

"My Ellie!" the sea-female shouted with glee.

"Keeci! It's been an eternity." Elowan sighed, embracing a childhood friend she was long overdue to visit. The last time she saw Keeci, her children were only starting to crawl but now they bounced around the place like rabbits in the fields of Soxis. And they remembered her. That was the beauty of Fae memories. They were deeply tied to emotions, splendidly vivid and equally as sharp.

"I brought company. Hope you don't mind," Elowan pointed to Regin and Zala who peeked into the doorway.

"No of course, you are most welcome in." Keeci waved them in with a slender arm. She closed the door behind them. Keeci moved to embrace Elowan again, brushing a hand on her forehead as they parted. Elowan did the same. Smiling. Feeling the warmth and belonging in their greeting.

The apartment was exactly as she last remembered it. Family portraits framed and lined every inch of available glass wall. Toys were strewn haphazardly across the floor. Unlike houses in other courts of Faery, Seaspun Bay had only towers consisting of small circular apartments. Unless you had money pouring from your nostrils, the most you could get with your wage was a concentric circle-shaped apartment with four small coves. Each cove was a separate room of sorts, but in the middle, connecting all coves was the dining room. A place for family to meet and eat.

"This is Regin—"

"Your soulmate. I could smell the stench of love from down the hallway," Keeci smiled, moving to Regin. The sea-female brushed her hand on Regin's forehead and said, "Welcome to my home, Regin."

Regin bowed his head and with the politeness that Elowan was first met with, he said, "Ma'am."

Keeci moved to Zala. "It's a pleasure to see you again, Shadow Wraith."

Zala nodded.

Keeci then turned to Elowan. "Do I need to send my children to bed for this?"

"Better safe than sorry."

"Very well." Keeci knelt to the floor where her three children had clung themselves to Elowan's legs like barnacles. "Children. Mama needs you to go to bed, okay?"

All three, with the same dark hair and dark-filled eyes, simultaneously pouted. "Yes, Mama." They moved to give their mother a hug. Keeci rubbed the back of her hand across their foreheads.

Elowan watched as they glided to a cove tucked away on the other side of the apartment.

"They're good children, Keeci," Elowan's voice went soft with appreciation.

"I know. They're mine." Keeci laughed, beckoning her guests to sit at the dining table. Elowan, Zala and Regin obliged. The sound of glass gliding against glass made Elowan's ears twitch. They all took a seat at the round glass table.

"So, let's hear it, shall we?" Keeci nodded to the group. With a wave of her hand, a small stream of mana-willed water came dancing around the table. Along with it, several drinking glasses that graciously flowed through the stream, landed before each of them. With a wave of her other hand, she motioned toward the glass ceiling where several kegs were installed. Down on a flowing stream came alcoholic refreshments that filled everyone's cups. They all took a sip. Keeci, however, took a large gulp.

"Lady Ollette sent us," Elowan said quietly.

Keeci blinked at the name but said nothing else. Another wave of her hand brought down the sweet liquor sea-Fae loved to drink, filling her cup entirely. She downed the whole thing.

It was all Elowan needed to see. "Is there a way we could get a covert audience with your uncle?"

"Am I right in assuming you'd like to discuss his loyalties in the filthy war that wretched blood witch managed to conjure?" Keeci bared her sharp sea-Fae teeth.

"I understand that Seaspun Bay is neutral territory, but a side needs to be taken. We're on the brink of war. If we could just get an audien—"

"It's too late," Keeci said with finality.

Elowan didn't like that tone one bit. "What do you mean it's too late?" Elowan almost threw her chair back but Regin's warm hand upon her thigh eased the fire that burned in her chest.

"The barbaric heathen you call Kaine." Keeci poured herself another cup, filling everyone else's up, too.

Zala took a swig of her liquor and with a coolness, encouraged Keeci. "Tell us everything."

"He waltzed into the grand hall earlier today to see my uncle."

"Tell me Zavis denied him an audience and sent him on his way?"

Silence.

An anger so vile found its way to Elowan's throat. The only thing stopping it from catapulting out was the white-knuckled hand that currently gripped Camrine's short spear – a reminder to keep her wits about her.

"Seaspun Bay stands with the blood throne."

Elowan, Zala and Regin simultaneously expelled their favourite expletives.

"We need an audience with your uncle now, Keeci. Please do me this one favour," Elowan begged.

"Ellie, it's too late. He's already promised in *blood*, and he's offered marriage to one of his daughters as a security."

"But his daughters are his most prized possessions, are they not? Maybe we can stop the ceremony?" The panic in Elowan's voice was on full show.

"You are too late. They finished the ceremony about an hour ago. News has already reached all the seas." Keeci waved a hand, conjuring an image of a news bulletin, sharing an image of Zavis's daughter, embracing a sullen-faced Kaine before the Salsus Sanctum.

Shit.

Elowan raked her hands across her face, attempting to calm any shred of thought that was raging at the image of Kaine. The court known for its neutrality had finally chosen a side for the first time in centuries, and it was Kaine who beat them to it. Their former captain. Their former friend and brother. It felt like Elowan was living out a fever-dream and that everything she knew had been turned upside down or inside out.

Seaspun Bay was the rebellion's last bet. They were out of options.

The combined power of Soxis, Wrenntia and Fyllera and a few Elite – their mana, their soldiers, their weapons – measured just over three-quarters of what Queen Calliea already possessed in her arsenal. Now with the strength of Seaspun Bay and their resources, not to mention the message it would send the entire Faery realm, the deplorable queen tripled her power. This wasn't even taking into account the unknown power that Terr was feeding into the equation.

The rebel ship was already sinking, and the war hadn't even started yet.

"The news we received today, of Fyllera succumbing to the blight, has spooked him, Ellie. Summeira, who has publicly promised their allegiance to the blood throne remains free from the claws of what plagues the lands of Faery."

"A pure coincidence, surely?" Elowan argued.

"But not to a scared male, Ellie. Faery has never opened itself to the maws of the Shadow Realm in all the time it has existed. Until now. The game has changed, and the odds are not in our favour." Keeci looked to each and every one of them with sadness in her eyes. Her plump lips upturned, and the slits of her nose flared with anger.

Elowan looked to her childhood friend. "And where do you stand?"

"I'll wage my war until that witch kicks down my own front door. She has done nothing for us – the sea-Fae that barely have two clams to rub together. All she cares for are her riches. Her power. And by the mother of Faery, do not get me started on the promised children." Keeci snarled, her sharp, poison-coated fins flaring with every bitten word.

Elowan looked to Regin and then to Zala who was deep in thought. Her piercing blue eyes were glazed over, no doubt calculating their next best course of action.

"I never took you as someone who'd back down. Good to see things never change. Though with Seaspun Bay spoken for, it's probably best we return to Fyllera and help where we can."

Keeci eyes had glazed over too. Her scales on her skin, calming, and shining to an almost steady beat. She was thinking.

"What is it, Keeci?" Elowan asked.

"There's hope still." Her voice was just a whisper.

"Where?"

Keeci turned and flitted to her bedroom. The crinkling sounds of rustling paper echoed back to them. Within seconds, she was back.

She slammed a map, worn and dog-eared, upon the table. "In the Western Wastes." She circled a scaled finger around the empty, unmarked territory, west of Summeira. "A small beacon by comparison"—she gestured all around her, to Seaspun Bay—"but a strong one if it's still alive."

Keeci swiftly folded up the map and handed it to Elowan.

Thankful, Elowan pocketed it.

"We'll take the chance." Taking a chance was better than suffering the slow death of inaction. "Who do I contact once I get there?"

"They'll approach you. You'll need to pass through the Resting Ruins. That's how they'll know." Keeci looked apologetic.

Elowan's soul almost left her body at the words but before it flew up to the Godlands, she shot a proverbial arrow through it and dragged it back into place. "We can't just portal straight to them?"

Keeci shook her head. "It's a magic that goes beyond our means. Only the people that can withstand the Resting Ruins can pass."

Zala, with her impeccable timing, said rather frankly, "That's a suicide mission."

It was the perfect way to put it. For in the Resting Ruins lay the hundreds and thousands of Faery souls. Souls that had died and were deemed unworthy of ascending to the Elysian Fields but not wicked enough to descend into the depths of the Shadow Realm. No, these were the souls with unfinished business. Souls of the weary and the tortured who had no choice but to stay in Faery in a hellish state of limbo.

The thought sent a chill down Elowan's spine.

Keeci took Zala and Elowan's hand in each of hers. "You are two strong female warriors, blessed by the gods with the gift of bearing an element. If any being were destined, if not built, to withstand the trials of the Resting Ruins, it is you two. I feel it as I feel the water that courses through my veins."

Elowan's mana stirred, agreeing with Keeci.

Elowan looked to Regin who sat still. His brows furrowed in thought. "She's right," he said. "I'll return home to Fyllera. I'll be of more help there."

Elowan nodded. She squeezed her soulmate's thigh underneath the table. He understood. She could tell. Where they were headed, they needed to pack light and because he lacked any element-wielding mana, he would be a liability. His skills would be beneficial elsewhere; in this case, helping the people of Fyllera and establishing what connections he could there. Elowan turned back to her friend, her eyes now shining with a shimmer of hope.

"You can take my gliders. I've little to no use for them since having the children," Keeci insisted.

A glider. Elowan hadn't ridden one in an age. The last time she piloted the kite-like craft was with Cam. They were tumbling and turning in the sky along the edge of Mors Gorge on a mission for Queen Calliea. Cam vomited twice and Elowan swore she could still see and smell the splatters of spew across the glider's wings. A small smile pulled at the sides of Elowan's lips. She missed him.

"Are you sure?"

"Yes, just don't get caught." Keeci stood to embrace all three of them, brushing each with a kind hand upon their foreheads.

Friends.

Allies.

"Tell the children that I miss and love them," Elowan said quietly.

"Tell them yourself when you see them after this debacle." Keeci ushered them to the balcony that overlooked Seaspun Bay. "The gliders should be in fighting condition."

Elowan stepped out onto the balcony. The sea breeze caressed her skin with delight. Way above on the seventy-seventh floor, their problems in Faery, outstretched ahead of them, seemed so insignificant. Below, the lights – green, blue and purple – that illuminated up each tower of Seaspun Bay mingled in a carousel of colour. The train tracks that divided the two islands of the bay sat idle. Haunting even.

The train tracks that connected their world to Sotera. There were no humans spilling through the fabric between two realms now. Queen Calliea made sure of it by destroying the siphon train made decades ago. Perhaps the last symbol of symbiosis between realms if it ever even existed.

Elowan took a moment to soak it all in. One last moment of calm.

The sounds of Zala, pulling the buckles of a glider's harness, launched her back into reality. Elowan turned from where she stood admiring the sights and sounds of Seaspun Bay and faced Keeci, her childhood friend. With a sadness stuck in her throat, Elowan said, "Thank you. You've been a true friend and ally."

This favour needed no words. Elowan took a hold of her friend's wrist, pulled her mana from the depths of her stomach and broke off a tiny piece. She willed it into the essence of her friend's mana for safe keeping. A favour and a piece of her power.

"Thank you, my oldest friend. Stay strong." Keeci braced her hands on Elowan's arms.

"May the gods guide you," Elowan said with a bittersweet smile.

"To where we are all destined to be." Keeci's eyes were intense. Determined.

The slight change to Faery's old saying sparked hope in Elowan's heart. She was right. It was no longer an *I*, but a *we*. They needed to start thinking like a unit, a well-oiled machine with various moving parts if they wanted to win this war.

Zala threw Elowan a glider harness. She quickly strapped it on, pulling the buckles and levers to best suit her body's measurements. Gliders, hewn into the shape of a kite with the skin of a water craekin were imbued with mana – to not only glide through the wind of Seaspun Bay but through its waters. It was an efficient mode of travel and if Elowan pulled her mana right, they'd travel undetected.

Elowan moved up to Regin who was already fastened into his own glider. He turned and her heart squeezed when his light-purple eyes landed on hers. They always had that effect on her. She leaned in to kiss him deeply and whispered just for them to hear, "Stay safe, my love. I'll be seeing you soon."

She wasn't too worried. Whether it was alive in Faery or dead in the Elysian Fields, she would be seeing him soon. That was her only guarantee in life.

"I'll be seeing you soon. You have my heart. Remember that." Regin smiled as he squeezed her hand. With a nod, he took two steps back from the balcony's ledge, checked the glass frame of his glider and jumped into the air. The glider shot him into the sky on an arc and within a few milliseconds became invisible, headed straight to Fyllera.

Elowan turned to join Zala, who had clipped herself onto the glider already. She followed suit, clipping the two large straps to the wire frame that fixed the wings of the glider out straight.

"Ready Z?"

"As I'll ever be."

Side by side, they took two synchronised steps back from the balcony and ran to the ledge, pushing themselves off the floor, launching them both into the air with a *WOOSH*. Elowan took a second to turn back to Keeci.

Keeci held a hand to her heart as she watched the two glide into the air.

The sparkles of mana washed over the glider, then over Elowan and Zala. Together they would soar to the lip of Mor's Gorge where the Resting Ruins of the Western Wastes awaited them.

21

SOPHIE

This demigoddess shit is hard. What the fuck?

"You are destined to harness a great power that belongs to the infernal gods *and* elemental Fae. It's important to practise your powers, so that when the time comes . . . you're ready," Danna explained. Sophie met her mother in the Gardens of Incrementum situated before the Isle's waterfall before noon. Today marked day one of goddess lessons, as her mother coined them; "demigoddess lessons" didn't quite roll off the tongue.

Her goddess powers were different to her Fae elements. Bigger. Stronger. Where her Fae elements bent and shaped existing elements through the will of her mana, her goddess powers gave her the ability to create and destroy. Her strong suit, given her Fae heritage, was the creation of nature. Supposedly anyway.

The sun beat down on Sophie's shoulders and the humidity did no favours for her concentration. Her mother had her practise sprouting flowers in bushes, but her mana felt as if a stopper had been placed atop it. She could sense things and use her mana in small, inconspicuous ways but to create and form something? Sophie didn't stand a chance.

Strong suit, my ass.

Sophie threw her hands up in the air, after the hundredth attempt at sprouting a flower. If she tried any harder, she'd be getting a hernia. Several, most likely. Sophie sighed. "I just can't do it."

"You can, Sophie. I can feel your mana. It is strong and unruly. You could do wondrous things with it. I know you can." Danna was trying to be supportive.

Sophie scoffed. Her mana felt feeble. Insignificant. Useless. She couldn't even get a freaking flower to bloom. How was she going to save a fucking realm with this? Pathetic.

One more time. One more time, and then you can call it quits.

Sophie closed her eyes in concentration, dived deep into her mana and willed it to course through her veins . . . just like how Kaine had taught her. *Ick.* His name soured in the back of her throat and made her stomach sink into a burning pit of mouldy trash.

Nope. Nope. Nope. Sophie tried to shake it off and was about to give flower sprouting another crack before the sound of feet hitting pavement sounded in the distance.

Sophie's ears piqued at the noise. It was a large group of people running rhythmically. In time with each other. Sophie turned to face the oncoming crowd. It was the Tienthan – a team of muscled and winged bodies drenched in sweat. Leading them was an older male about her mother's age. His wings of pure white were rugged with a few dents and healed-over wounds. Tendrils of his golden hair whipped across his face which bore what looked to be a permanent scowl. He looked positively murderous as he barked orders that Sophie couldn't quite make out. The team of angels hit the deck to complete several push-ups. The older male barked out loud again and the team of angels shot up on their feet, resuming their thunderous run.

"Who is that?" Sophie uttered under her breath.

"That . . ." Danna let out an appreciative sigh. ". . . is Commander Ares."

Sophie gaped at her mother who stood with a dazed smile across her face. Even in her admiring another being she looked the picture of innocence. "Did you just sigh appreciatively at that man?"

"My heart still belongs to your father, but that doesn't mean I can't appreciate a godly piece of art."

Sophie made a small gagging noise. "Ugh, I don't want to hear it."

The two Taliesin women, or rather goddesses, watched in awe of the athletic angels that stormed the running path along the Gardens of Incrementum. The Tienthan and Commander Ares ran closer to them.

"Steady there!" Ares ordered his subordinates. The sweat-slicked angels skidded to a halt. "Three ranks!" They formed three rows facing Sophie and her mother. "Grandstand position, down!" The first row fell to their knees, the second row bent over by the waist and the final row stood tall, arms clasped behind their backs. They stood as still as statues. "Rest," Ares commanded, a little softer this time. His troops relaxed slightly, in place. "Grab a drink, whatever you need," he finished.

Commander Ares seemed just a touch older than Danna. His scarred tan skin glowed as if he spent days in the sun, wielding a sword and slaying enemies. It seemed fitting of the god of courage and war, Sophie thought. He stalked over to Sophie's mother, with a sense of purpose. Quickly, the god bowed his head in greeting.

Sophie could have sworn that her mother blushed. Great. Her goddess lesson turned into front row tickets to watch her mother flirt with Commander Ares. Sophie wanted to vomit.

"Dearest Danna," Ares smiled. Were those hearts in his eyes?

"Ares." Danna dipped her chin and fluttered her eyelashes. Her skin emanated that golden goddess glow and her hair floated around her. She was an enchantress. Danna quickly turned to Sophie. "This is my daughter, Sofreya." Her mother beamed with pride.

Ares shifted his focus to Sophie, ever the picture of calm and warm confidence. "A pleasure. Welcome to the Godlands."

"Thank you. It's an honour to meet you." Sophie dipped her chin, surprised that coherent words deigned to leave her mouth. To be fair, her response sounded like something a stiff courtesan would churn. She still felt out of place when it came to other gods and goddesses and was unsure how to carry herself.

"I'm glad I caught you two ladies . . ." Ares looked to Danna with an intensity Sophie wasn't ready for. Sophie noticed a bit of movement among the troops standing behind Ares. She felt a pull, like someone had told her to look in the direction.

Lo and behold, there knelt Ash. His hair neatly tied back into a braid and his muscled chest, glistening with sweat. He smiled brightly. Sophie's heart squeezed just a touch as she lifted her hand and waved. Eros clambered his way to Ash from the back of the troop to whisper something in Ash's ear. His expression immediately turned dark, and Sophie knew for certain that Eros had said something stupid.

Sophie let out a little laugh.

"Sophie?" Danna intruded Sophie's amusing distraction.

"Um yes, definitely!" Sophie blurted out, not sure what she was responding to. She quickly looked behind Ares to find Ash now with his arms crossed while kneeling. Eros, Deymos and Nemy stood laughing around Acheron. They were clearly making fun of him. Sophie wished she could hear what they were saying.

"Great, you're free to come by at eight." With that, Ares bowed slightly and turned swiftly back to his soldiers. He barked, "Alright you fuckers, attention!" The group of Tienthan straightened themselves immediately, their backs rim-rod straight, staring at the empty space before them. "Rest." They relaxed. "Jogging, change!" The pounding of pavement started again and Sophie watched as they left the gardens.

"I didn't peg you for a dinner-with-the-council kind of girl," Danna mused.

Sophie blanched. "Oh shit." In her absentmindedness she agreed to having dinner with the council. The last place and the last people she wanted to see or meet, let alone have dinner with. Sophie groaned and kneaded her temples. "I got distracted," Sophie admitted.

"Mhmm. I wonder who's got you so wound up that even the most revered Olympian couldn't hold your attention." Danna hummed in amusement.

Sophie narrowed her eyes at her mum. "Oh please. I saw you two undressing each other with your eyes."

Danna gasped.

Sophie snickered and turned to gather her belongings. She'd need to prepare for a dinner date with the council members. Sophie couldn't have thought of a worse way to spend her night. She'd rather shit in her hands and clap than sit in a room filled with aristocrats and politicians. But she couldn't back out now. She promised a damned god she'd be there and upsetting the god of war wasn't high on her priority list.

Sophie's head bobbed and her eyelids shut for longer increments each time she blinked. The council's dining hall was a flurry of activity. Chefs and their assistants roamed in and out, replenishing the table with succulent meats and vegetables. While the company was dull, Sophie thanked the gods that her food was undeniably scrumptious.

At the dining table sat Ares, her mother, Cerri, Diafonia, Dikastis, Vestes and several other council members Sophie didn't bother learning the names of. She knew the gods and goddesses that sat before her, sharing a meal. She'd read about them before.

Cerri was the goddess of rebirth and Sophie had recognised her from the visions her mother shared. Her eyes were worn, washed with hints of anger and resentment. Sophie remembered her worried tears as she let go of her son Lethe . . . Kaine. The goddess before her seemed like a ghost, dredges of the goddess she saw in her mother's visions.

Diafonia was the picture of her core power – discord. The bright colours she wore stood out painfully against the dull council dining hall. A permanent smirk filled with mischief and trickery etched her face. Sophie could tell she too was tired of the other councilmen who drawled on and on about trade routes with other realms. Sophie knew she'd get along well with the goddess of discord.

Dikastis, the god of justice and the goddess of discord's brother sat quietly, examining his food and politely nodding with the conversation. His bright blue hair was an interesting shade that Sophie had never seen before.

Last of the gods was Vestes. A shiver ran down Sophie's spine. She didn't know who he was or what his core power was. In fact, she'd never heard of him before, although the thrum of power that emanated from him and his air of arrogance could not be mistaken. The only thing Sophie knew about him was that he was head of the council, making him the right-hand man of Zeus – the god of all gods himself.

Vestes's pale skin was a contrast to the stubble that peppered his sharp jaw-line. His thin brows and wrinkled face clued Sophie in on how old he actually was – centuries or millennia, she wasn't sure. Though every time he opened his mouth to comment on something, Sophie fought to not roll her eyes.

"Sofreya, your mother tells me you've decided to embrace your powers," Diafonia mused. Her high-pitched voice broke the boredom spell that threatened to shut Sophie's eyes.

Sophie cleared her throat. "When destiny calls, you answer, I guess." She smiled politely.

Vestes scoffed. His pale skin, stretching with the movement.

Sophie looked around the room awkwardly. *Does this guy have something to say?*

Dikastis looked like he was going to facepalm himself.

Ares and Danna were too preoccupied with each other to even notice while Cerri sat there, wallowing in her own thoughts.

"Do you have something to share, Vestes?" Diafonia asked innocently, though the smirk on her face was contrary to her tone. She wanted mischief.

Vestes laughed aloud. "It's just that if I were a half-breed, I wouldn't even bother." His comment quietened the whole room.

Danna broke her focus from the charm of Ares. An anger Sophie had never seen before rose from her mother in the form of a nasty snarl. "You, of all beings, will not speak of my daughter that way," she warned from across the long table.

There was history there, Sophie could sense it.

Vestes took a sip of his wine, smiling into his cup. He leaned back into his chair and clasped his hands together. "Come on now, Dee, not everyone is *proud* of dallying with lesser beings."

Oh hell no.

Sophie stood swiftly, her chair screeching behind her. She stood tall, towering over Vestes from across the table. The god had the audacity to smirk, his sharp features turning with amusement. Sophie pointed at Vestes with the wrath of a seasoned goddess and said, "If one more unsavoury word comes out of your unpalatable face, I'll be sending you to the depths of the Shadow Realm where the only company you'll have is your own pathetic thoughts." The plates and chalices on the table shook with violence. It was all bark and no bite given the state of her powers, but no one else needed to know that. No one would speak ill of her or her mother. Not today. Not ever.

The remainder of the council room's eyes widened at each other and the vibrating table. Though Vestes did not falter, nor did he baulk at the rumble of mana Sophie had accidentally let out.

Vestes sat tall in his chair and gave Sophie a haughty look. He eyed Sophie up and down her entire body. Disgust climbed down Sophie's spine. The look Vestes gave her was slimy and something like hunger shone in his eyes. Sophie couldn't have wanted to vomit more than she did in this moment.

Lecherous bastard.

Vestes lifted his head higher, satisfied with his observations. He looked at her, maintaining intense eye contact and said, "I'd like to see you try."

The room violently shook again. Sophie was about to lunge across the dining table to strangle the creepy old god when a powerful, dark mana entered the room.

Everyone fell impossibly silent, including Vestes whose eyes darted to the being who had just entered, then quickly back down to his plate.

That was fear.

Diafonia leaned back in her chair, giggling. No doubt her core power of discord was revelling in its element in the council dining hall tonight.

Ares shot up from where he sat beside Danra, probably thankful for the timely interruption. "Acheron!" He stood up from his chair as Ash moved into the dining hall, his power electrifying the air.

The rest of the councilmen stood up from their chairs, murmuring their greetings as Ash strode by. They referred to him as the master of weapons. Sophie noted that. A weapons master at such a young age? That was a feat in and of itself. They were specialists in the field of weapons, often deployed in military units. Sophie didn't realise that the Tienthan employed them too.

Makes sense, I guess. Just look at him.

Ash's muscled form moved predatorily across the floor. He was a beast; Sophie would give him that. His white wings were by far the largest pair in the room. As he moved farther into the dining hall, Ash met her gaze. He gave her a curt nod. His only acknowledgment of her. His normally kind and playful face was now covered in a mask of stoicism. As he walked by Sophie to Ares, he lightly grazed her hand with the edges of his knuckles. It was subtle. No one else would have seen or known they touched hands except for them. She stilled.

What *was* that? Electricity shot up her arm from the contact as she pulled her hand back. He didn't look at her though, but she knew he'd meant for that to happen. Sophie averted her gaze elsewhere, hoping no one caught her movements. Her eyes unfortunately landed on Vestes who's head tilted in question. His mouth turned into a slow smirk.

Shit.

Before she knew what she was doing, Sophie turned on her heel and used the commotion of Ash's entrance to leave the council dining hall. She was fed up with being in the company of people she didn't care to know. At least that's what she told herself. It definitely had nothing to do with the spark of Ash's touch, stirring something inside her that she wasn't at all ready to decipher.

22

ACHERON

Even rigorous hill runs through the Isle's jungle couldn't stop Ash from thinking about last night's council meeting. Not even standing before the other Tienthan in the training ring lined with deadly weapons could stop him from thinking about how his knuckles felt against Sophie's. He knew he didn't have to, but he wanted to, in fact, something in him told him that he needed to. He wanted to let Sophie know that while his face was serious and stern, it was all for a reason. And he hoped – there was that word again – that she knew what he intended. The council was made of snakes, at least some of them were. Ares, Diafonia and Dikastis were harmless, but Ash wasn't sure where he could place the rest of the council, least of all Vestes. Ash had to play his cards right and he didn't want Vestes the vermin having any leverage over him.

Ever since Ash joined the Tienthan, Vestes had always voted against him. Doing everything in his power to put Ash at a disadvantage. The god had hated "half-breeds" as he coined them – children and beings born of a god and another being. Ash technically wasn't one. He didn't even know what he could classify himself as. His mother and father were Fae, but he had earned his wings in the Tienthan and by Zeus's own blessing that day on Mount Gehenna, he was gifted the powers of a god – several gods. That made him an anomaly. One that Vestes despised . . . and feared.

Ash stood in front of his troops, his favourite war hammer in his hand. "Today is weapons day." His favourite day of all days.

He surveyed his soldiers. A few of them were tired from the hill runs they'd just completed. To his surprise, Sofreya stood there looking worse for wear, but still, she stood there. Throughout the run she kept a steady pace at the back of the group, but never did she fall behind. She had grit and Ash admired that tremendously. "Those of you that have your master weapon, peel off and practise your drills. Those of you that don't, follow me."

All the angels of the Tienthan moved to the other end of the training ring where they unracked their preferred weapons, leaving his beloved childhood friend with her Fae ears and lack of wings standing alone. It reminded him of when he first joined the Tienthan – wingless and Fae but unknowingly powerful.

Angel wings in the Godlands were earned, not given. Anyone could try their hand at the Hrabrost Trials wingless, but only few would be able to get through and earn the illustrious angel wings. It was a test of courage, skill and grit. The last person to complete the trials and earn a pair of wings upon Mount Gehenna was him. And that was eleven years ago.

Sophie stood in front of him with her arms crossed, all her weight propped onto one hip. "If you wanted me alone, you could have just said so." She laughed.

"I'm not sure the rest of the team would appreciate me announcing how I'd like to see you . . . alone."

"Touché." Sophie nodded and stalked by, completely ignoring him as she walked past. Ash shook his head. For twenty years, he missed having his best friend beside him. It still felt like a dream.

It was now months ago that he'd heard a voice he hadn't heard in years echo down a bond that lay dormant in his heart. He heard her cries from all the way in the Godlands and he didn't hesitate. He flew faster than the speed of light to find her. To help her.

"So where do we start? Do I just pick one and start swinging?" Sophie peered over her shoulder back at him. Her purple and silver hair, now much longer than when she'd arrived in the Godlands, was tied into a battle braid.

Ash's wings fluttered as he watched her survey a smorgasbord of weapons from all realms strewn out across a table. "I mean that's a great way to start if you want a one-way ticket to the infirmary." Ash moved toward the table of weapons that had been laid out before them. Everything from shuriken to short blades, katanas and machetes lay on the table – oiled and ready for use. On the side of each table were racks lined with larger and longer weapons like wooden staffs and halberds. "Have you heard of the saying . . ." He set his war hammer down to pick up several throwing knives from the table. He turned to face Sophie and as she turned to him, he could have sworn his heart stopped for what was a millisecond. ". . . a jack of all trades is a master of none?"

Ash began idly throwing the knives in one hand.

". . . but often times is better than a master of one?" Sophie finished off for him.

"That's the one." He threw the knife toward the target that sat a few metres out from where they stood. *FWOOMP.* He knew it hit dead centre without even looking. "Well, the Tienthan, as Zeus's Aerial Legion, needs to be prepared for every case, every possible outcome in every realm." He threw another knife toward the target while he watched amusement dance across Sophie's face. She scoffed, knowing full well he was showing off for her. Well, he was. "We're the jack of all trades but . . ." He threw another knife. *FWOOMP.* Dead centre. "We are also the master of one."

Ash had one knife left in his hand. He toyed with it, tossing it over in one hand. "Today, we're going to find out what that one weapon is for you and we're going through the basics." Ash moved toward Sophie with a challenging smirk on his face. They almost stood toe to toe.

Sophie stepped in a touch closer, crossing her arms as she did. "Then show me . . . Master of Weapons."

Ash's immortal heart skipped a beat. *Clean slate. Clean slate. Clean slate.* He threw his last knife without looking. "I like how that title roles off your tongue."

"We'll see if you're singing the same tune once our weapons session is over." Sophie smirked. She stood up taller, challenging him.

If Ash leaned forward a fraction, they could— No, he couldn't finish that train of thought even though his body sang for her. He couldn't. She was his friend, and she insisted on a clean slate. He needed to respect her boundaries.

Ash shook his head to clear his thoughts and moved to the other side of the weapons table. "Come. I'll show you what's on offer." Using his peripherals, he spied the last throwing knife he threw. It was a hair's width off the centre mark.

"So, it's kind of like a sorting hat except it gives you your master weapon?" Sophie stared at the pair of leather-looking gloves that were made of the red threads of fate.

"Precisely." Ash stood on the edge of the weapons pit beside the racks of weapons.

"What if I don't like the weapon I get?" She gingerly put on the gloves as if she feared the power they held. They looked outright ridiculous on her small hands. Ash tried his hardest not to laugh.

He cleared his throat. "You will. Trust me. The Fates have already decided for you."

Sophie grumbled something about the stupid Fates, though Ash couldn't quite catch it. She shook her head and stood in front of the table and racks of weapons.

What the fate-threaded gloves did, was concentrate the wearer's mana and send a tendril of it through each weapon. A reactive pulse would return into the gloves, if and only if the wearer's destined master weapon was present. It was why the Tienthan always had an arsenal of weapons from all realms to work with.

Sophie stretched her arms out on front of her and breathed, channelling the mana that lived inside her.

Ash caught the wince of pain as she dived deep. It was something like resentment, anger and hurt that rang through the air. Ash had a sneaking suspicion as to the cause. He hadn't had the chance to speak to her about the scene he found her in, covered in blood and her skin almost blackened with the exertion of power. She had been on the brink of death, but that conversation would have to wait, and it would only happen on her terms.

Sophie furrowed her brows. "I don't feel anything."

"Be patient." Ash watched her as she begrudgingly pulled up another dreg of power. A white glow encased her hands and all the weapons splayed out began to levitate. Ash's lips parted, watching in awe as she moved all the weapons with little mana exertion.

"Got it." She smiled wide though her eyes were still closed. All the weapons she'd pulled to the air fell with a quick thump, except one. The rope dart. Possibly the most difficult weapon to master. Of course she was destined to master the most elusive, rare and complex weapon across all realms.

Ash scoffed and ordered. "Now pull it to you."

Sophie obeyed. The rope dart's red rope was spun from threads of fate. The darts on either end were forged in the underground volcanoes of Mount Gehenna. It was a choice weapon only few have mastered in centuries. The rope dart spun in place and flew to Sophie's expectant hand. She opened her eyes and confusion scrunched her beautiful features.

"I'm not going to lie. I'm a little disappointed. I have zero clue as to what this is." She held the rope dart gingerly in her hands, examining the unique sharp blades as if it were a dirty sock that would come to life and kill her.

Ash flew to her with one big beat of his wings. He loved how she did not cower or quake at the presence of him and his wings. His stature, standing six foot four, was intimidating for many. Add the height of his wings, it was a wonder he could fit anywhere.

"Let me demonstrate," he reached out his hand as she placed the weapon in his.

He released one end of the rope, swinging it casually as he walked into the centre of the weapons ring. Clashes of swords and spears echoed in the distance. With the grace of a leopard, the Godlands's master of weapons sprang into action. He sent the dart flying before him with a quick flip of his arm, his leg kicked up altering the dart's trajectory. He butterfly-kicked low, sending both darts flying out, piercing the necks of his invisible enemies. Quickly standing, he wrapped one side of the rope around his arm and the other side around his neck, building up momentum for his final killing blow. He swung his neck forward and kicked back at the same time – releasing the full length of the rope on either side of his body. If he were engaging armed combatants, they would have darts jutting out of their necks . . . several metres away. With swift rotations of his arms and a few spins around the body, he latched the rope dart by his side.

A slow clap sounded.

"So, um . . . can I pick another weapon? There's no way I can do that." Sophie grimaced from where she stood on the sidelines.

"If you want to argue with the threads of destiny by all means go ahead." Ash laughed. He knew no sane person would defy the Fates. But something in his heart told him Sophie would. She was crazy like that.

Sophie rolled her eyes. "I'm seriously considering having a word with these Fates. They've got a sick obsession with making everything hard." She groaned, stepping into the centre of the ring, stopping just before him. "Alright then, show me." She gestured to the rope dart that he held in his hands.

And so he did.

Sophie donned the rope dart. While she expressed her concerns about such a rare weapon, she took everything he showed her in stride. A growing smile panned across her face as she mirrored his simple dart strikes with ease. Flow. Strike. Flow. Strike.

She moved with ease, determination and skill. It took him hours to learn what she did in a few moments. There was a reason the Fates had chosen this weapon for her. She was a natural, and Ash was thoroughly impressed.

The next move would be the test. It took Ash weeks to perfect it.

Sophie moved to wrap the rope around her arm and tried to swing out both darts like he showed her, but she failed. "I can't get them to swing out like you did. They just fall . . ." Sophie screwed her face in frustration.

"You just need to twist more at your hips."

She tried but failed again.

Ash stood before her, analysing her stance. Her feet were too close. He kicked her front foot out a touch as she held onto the rope dart. He twisted her shoulders to face him. His hands tingled where their skin made contact and it felt like his head had been dunked into water. He wondered if she felt the same. Her purple iridescent eyes watched him carefully and he could hear her heart beat faster the closer he inched.

He softly pivoted her hips so that they were more in line with her feet. Electricity flitted through him at the contact. Ash noticed the bobbing of her throat. They watched each other carefully. It was like they had fallen victim to a spell that they both wanted but neither of them needed. At least that's what he tried to convince himself.

"Oi! Get a room!" A familiar male voice broke the dizzying spell they had both fallen victim to.

Eros.

Ash's entire troop turned to face where he and Sophie stood, unnervingly close to each other.

Thunder struck as Ash turned to face the god of love from across the training ground. He crossed his arms, made eye contact with Eros and shouted, "This entire training ground is my room!"

"Yeah, sure it is," Eros brushed him off, laughing as he walked away to get refreshments.

Ash felt his face turn red. He mustered enough courage to turn and face Sophie. "Apologies about Eros. He doesn't know what he's talking about." Ash kneaded the tension that had built up in his neck, waiting for his childhood friend to say something.

She didn't.

Instead, Sophie turned, placed her destined weapon on the table and stalked off to the refreshment table.

An emptiness started in Ash's heart. He wanted to say something, but he couldn't discount the tendrils of hurt and despair – guardedness even – that she left in her wake.

He knew she was hurting and deep down he wanted to be the one who would stop it.

23

SOPHIE

Without a word, Sophie walked to the table where fruits and refreshments were laid out.

It's okay to trust, Sophie. She continued to repeat this in her mind until the words jumbled and no longer made sense. Eros's teasing had struck a chord within her. If anything, she liked the teasing and that did not bode well with her at all. In fact, it fucking scared her.

Ash was too close. She let him get too close. And the last time she let anyone close to her, it ended with death. Destruction. How could she have so easily forgotten that? The thing with Ash was that with him, she felt like herself. She didn't think about anything else except the present when he was in her presence. She didn't focus on her time in Faery or the people she left behind. All she knew and all she felt, when she was with Ash, was herself. Not Sophie the demigoddess, or Sophie the fated of Faery's strongest warrior. She was just Sophie.

Sophie's lower brain was at war with her logical brain. Logically, reasonably, she knew Ash was a good person at his core. He gave her no reason to doubt his intentions. But her lower brain, her fucking subconscious, rejected the comforting arms of trust. To trust was to endanger. To trust was to suffer.

With her back toward the group of warriors, she heard Ash call out to all the troops – and that, unfortunately, included her.

"Alright, weapons down. It's mana time." He clapped his hands loudly, hastening the group of trained soldiers.

A thread of dread shot through Sophie's back.

"Want to partner up?" Nemysis's chirpy voice pierced through Sophie's train of self-deprecation.

Sophie downed the last dredges of water in her cup and nodded. "Yeah, sure." She painted a fake smile across her face. Using her mana was the last thing she wanted to do, but if she couldn't overcome it now, in a safe learning environment, then how could she face Kaine, Queen Calliea . . . least of all Terr?

Bile rose in her throat at the name.

Sophie and Nemysis squared up on the grassed area beside the weapons ring. Nemy's chestnut hair was tied up into a fierce ponytail and sweat clung against her porcelain skin. Her muscled arms bulged gracefully as she pulled herself into a fighting stance.

"Work on your combos!" Ash called out from the front of the group.

Everyone obeyed.

Nemy shot out two balls of fire and swept her leg out with ease. Sophie dodged – left, right, jump. The goddess beckoned Sophie to repeat the movement.

"Your turn, Sophie. One, two, sweep." Nemy shielded her face with both hands and bounced on her feet, ready to deflect Sophie's mana blows – but they did not come.

Sophie swallowed hard. She pulled at the mana pit that sat low in her stomach and chipped off a morsel. It was all she could stomach. Meagrely, she shot out two poor excuses for fireballs that Nemy dodged easily.

"Come on, you can do better than that," Nemy goaded.

"Unfortunately, mana doesn't come so easily for me."

"There's one thing that fuels me . . ."

"Let me guess. Retribution?" Sophie scoffed.

"Exactly." Nemy grunted as she let out two blades of bone-cutting air. Sophie dodged. "My offer still stands . . ." Nemy swept her leg out as Sophie jumped to clear it. ". . . I'll kill whoever wronged you."

Sophie knew who she was talking about. She should really take the goddess's offer and get it over and done with, but it didn't seem right. She wanted to be the one who righted her wrongs, not let someone else do the hard yards for her.

"It's fine," Sophie grunted as she mustered blades of air. They were barely strong enough to whisp Nemy's hair. Sophie kicked out with more fervour though.

"I can taste it. Your anger and your thirst to right whoever wronged you. I can do it for you." Nemy pulled from the earth and shot out two fist-sized rocks and kicked out again.

"I'm more than capable of doing it myself." Sophie managed to pull pebbles from the ground, flinging them toward the chestnut-haired goddess, a scowl now formed on her face.

Nemysis straightened herself from her fighting stance and crossed her arms. A smirk splayed itself across her face. "You can barely scratch the surface of your mana. What makes you think you could command the reins of such a glorious act as retribution?"

Something in Sophie snapped. She was capable. She knew she was, but she just couldn't pull the stopper from atop the glass bottle that encased her mana. As much as she tried, she couldn't. She pulled at her mana, wanting to prove the goddess before her wrong. Nothing manifested. If anything, her mana pulled back and dissipated. Hot anger brewed inside Sophie's chest – at herself, at Kaine, at the whole situation she found herself in. Sophie reeled back her fist ready to strike but Ash caught her wrist before she could.

"Nemysis. Leave Sofreya alone," the master of weapons commanded.

"She's got to get over it someday, Ash." The goddess crossed her arms, her brows furrowed.

"Well, she doesn't need you riling her up with your brand of retribution." Ash flicked his chin. A dismissal. Nemy rolled her eyes and gave Sophie an apologetic smile.

Sophie watched as Nemy left the grass they'd been sparring on. Ash wasn't a god of anything yet here he was, commanding centuries-old preternatural beings. And they listened.

Gingerly, Ash let go of her wrist and turned to her. "She's older than the earth we stand on and yet doesn't have an ounce of emotional intelligence," he scoffed under his breath.

"Hey, I heard that!" Nemysis shouted from across the field.

"You'll have to excuse her. She can be pushy when it comes to her core power."

"Understandable, I guess." The inch of rage Sophie felt dissipated like a raindrop in the sea the moment Ash touched her.

"Come on. I'll practise with you. If you don't want to use your mana, that's fine, just go through the movements." Ash braced himself and propped his hands up in defence. He towered over her so much it felt pointless. Sophie could barely reach him before he swatted her hands away.

They practised. Back and forth. Sophie would punch out – one, two – then sweep her foot out. They remained in silence, going through the movements.

But is was Ash who broke the silence first. "We're sending a few angels down to help patch up the wall between Sotera and Faery." He punched out and ducked quickly.

The words that came out of his mouth seized Sophie's throat. It was the last thing she had on her mind. How could she forget? How could she lose focus? Her worlds were colliding, and she needed to put an end to it. She didn't have time to be caught up in her own mind. "Are you going?"

"I'm not, but I can, if you want me to?"

"Why would I want that?"

"I know you have friends down there. I could check in on them . . ." Ash paused. ". . . on him."

Sophie turned white and muttered, "I don't know what you're talking about."

Ash's eyes washed with indecision. It looked like he was battling with himself to say something. Perhaps he thought that she loved Kaine still. Oh, how he was mistaken.

Ash lowered his voice, so she was the only one that could hear. "I don't know how to explain this to you without sounding like the biggest creep, but I can feel you and your emotions. It's like I have a direct link to your heart . . ." He slowed his strikes as if carefully calculating what to say next. ". . . and I can feel the shards and shadows that surround it as if it were my own."

Gone was the confident guardian angel that teased and annoyed her. In his place was someone who was cautious. Waiting.

Sophie swallowed. Tears began to prick her eyes. He read her so well. Was her pain shadowing her like a dark cloud? Was her pain that obvious? She fought the tears away, pushing more effort into the strikes she laid on Ash.

"Like I said, I don't know what you're talking about. I'm fine." She denied it, but she knew exactly what he was talking about – her hollowed-out chest that never seemed to stitch back together since she was saved from Faery.

She struck harder. Punch. Punch. Kick.

Ash's swift movements returned. He grunted. "You're not."

"You can't tell me what I am and what I am not." Sophie gritted her teeth. She struck harder than she should have but Ash took it all in stride. He didn't even flinch.

He accelerated his movements, pushing her off balance which stoked the rage that was rising in her chest. He was challenging her. She returned his advance with her own fire.

"Then tell me why is it that you purposefully dampen your mana?"

"I'm not purposefully doing anything."

"You are." Ash started using his mana. Two balls of fire flew their way to Sophie.

Without so much as a thought, she returned fire. "Am not."

They were like two kids, arguing.

Ash struck out with two swift blades of air. "Is he the reason why?"

Raging fire burned through Sophie's veins now. The strength of it was something she hadn't felt in a while . . . not since she was in Faery. "He's not the reason for anything," Sophie said flatly, slinging two giant air-blades at Ash's head.

She would deny it all. Deep down she knew Kaine was the reason. He was the one that taught her how to use her mana. Every time she dived deep to master it, it reminded her of him. And all the hard work she'd done in forgetting him, forgetting her idiocy and foolishness would come rising to the surface to suffocate her.

"It's your mana, Sofreya. You're in control of it." Ash flung two decent-sized rocks her way. She dodged them with finesse. "It's not someone else's to take."

Sophie's throat seized and tears rolled from her eyes. She furrowed her brows and said no more. She carved two dagger-like rocks from the ground with her mana and shot them straight at Ash's face that was so similar to Kaine's. She felt as if Kaine had a chokehold on her mana. And the last thing she wanted was to be reminded of him – the murderer, the betrayer . . . her abuser. He was the last thing she wanted to think about yet, each time she pulled at what was rightfully hers, his face was there. And it was fucking sickening.

"If you can't get a hold of your own mana, how can you expect to face him? Them?" Ash gritted through his teeth as he dodged and returned fire.

He didn't need to say their names for the words to hit home. He was right. About everything.

It drowned her vision in red. Sophie flung giant blades of fire at Ash. Then air. Then earth. Her onslaught on Ash was unwarranted, she knew that much, but so much rage and sorrow lived inside her that it all came pouring out. She couldn't hold it back any longer.

Suddenly, she felt the eyes of all the Tienthan watching her. She breathed heavily; her hands fisted against her sides. She saw it then. She'd pushed Ash back so hard that the dirt underneath him had kicked up from the force of it.

He stood there, panting heavily. His vambraces had even cracked from blocking her onslaught. Her power. She unlocked a level of mana she never knew she could reach again. She unfurled her fists. Her palms bled from the nails that had dug into them. That power. It came from her, but still . . . still it felt like she was in the dungeons of Castle Terrin. In that cell with Kaine as he taught her how to harness her true powers.

All of a sudden, she felt small.

All of a sudden, she felt detached from her true self.

She didn't want anything to do with her mana. It didn't feel like hers at all. It felt like it was Kaine's.

Sophie turned and ran. To where, she didn't know. All she knew was that she was running . . . from herself.

24

SOPHIE

Sophie found herself at the waterfall, behind several rocks tucked away from the prying eyes of the Tienthan who trained close by. Sophie sat there with her feet on the edge of the rocks. Water lapped up to calm her still rapidly beating heart. Her throat still ached, though her tears had abated. She felt numb. She felt like an intrinsic part of her was being held above her head, just out of reach and by someone who most definitely didn't deserve to have her.

She watched her reflection ripple with the flow of water. Her purple and silver hair reflected the sunrays like a star-filled galaxy, her pointed ears peeked through, and her glass-like skin shimmered – the only giveaway that she wasn't just Fae, she was half something else. A goddess. She looked like herself, mostly, but the bags underneath her eyes painted a different story. She was a husk. A woman with power and potential but a shadow of what she could be – who she wanted to be.

She heard the rustle of his wings before his reflection appeared next to hers in the water. Two halves of one whole. "If you're here to express your disappointment in me, I suggest you go away before I drown you in the water." Sophie scowled and turned away from Ash as he perched himself on the edge of the water beside her.

"Again, you've got to stop threatening me with a good time." His deep laugh rumbled through her. The harmonious reverberations pulled at Sophie's attention. She shot him a narrowed look.

He leaned back, bracing his hands on the ground as his white wings kept him perfectly balanced. His tanned skin, slick with a sheen of sweat glistened in the sun and for a moment Sophie regretted looking at him. His muscled form sat perfectly still, keenly aware of Sophie's burning gaze.

Their eyes locked.

"I shouldn't have pushed you," Ash breathed. He pulled his knees to him and leaned his head against them, watching Sophie.

Subconsciously, Sophie mirrored his movements, pulling her knees to her chest and resting her head atop them, watching Ash.

"Someone had to say it." She muttered. He only voiced what she already knew was true. That if she wasn't capable of overcoming the roadblock she burrowed herself in, then how could she expect to wage a war against three tyrants?

"I could've timed it better."

"Well, it's not your fault you were born with a big head and no foresight. Must be those damning wings getting in your way." She softly laughed and stretched out her hand toward him – a peace offering.

Slowly, hesitantly, he grabbed her tattooed hand with his, and it felt like they were their young selves running through the streets of Faery again. Except here, his hands were worn and much larger as they enveloped hers.

"Listen," Ash said, squeezing her hand, "I know you wanted a clean slate but …" Sophie's heart skipped a beat and her hand stilled. "… there's one memory that I think is worth reliving. One that I think can help you with your mana." He squeezed her hand again and quickly added, "Only if you want to."

The space between them fell silent.

Sophie did want a clean slate, but if what Ash offered would provide her refuge, a solution, *something* to get her sense of self back again, she'd take it – however high the risk would be.

"I do," Sophie wondered if she would regret uttering those words.

Like two souls born of the same elements, like reflections in a mirror, Sophie and Ash faced each other, crossing their legs, their knees just touching.

Sophie leaned into the space between them and closed her eyes, breathing in Ash's woodsy scent. His warm fingertips found their place on either side of her forehead. His mana felt like lightning as it thrummed through her veins and into her mind. And then there was darkness.

"It's like you're diving for treasure." The silver-haired Fae male animatedly swooped his hands high then low as if he were diving into water. "You want to jump down into the pool, pick out a piece and bring it up with you." He clawed his hand and picked at the air around him. "But be careful to not bring up too much or you'll burn out and that hurts." He winked. "Trust me."

Young Sofreya and young Acheron tilted their heads at Lou – the Right Hand of King Gydeon. And they burst out laughing.

"That's silly, Daddy." Sophie laughed. "My belly is too small. I can't dive into it."

"You're not actually diving into your own belly, my sweet Sophie." Lou guffawed. "You only have to imagine it." He pulled the two children off the grass where they sat atop a hill in Soxis, the dull roar of the Southern River not too distant. "Try it. Close your eyes. It helps."

And so the children did.

Together, they closed their eyes and tried to will their mana for the first time. Their task: to lift the small pebble from the ground and suspend it, midair.

Beside her, Sophie heard her best friend cheering. She opened her eyes to find his small pebble floating midair. He always found tasks like this easy which annoyed Sophie to no end.

Lou joined the boy in his cheers of glory. "Great job, Ash! Your father will be so proud of you." He walked over to the boy and scruffed his hair.

Sophie watched, a little jealous that her friend had beat her to the punch. It was always a competition between the two. Friendly competition. She furrowed her brows and shut her eyes harder, but she didn't understand what her father meant by taking up a morsel. When she dived deep into her belly, into her mana, there was just a big pit and all she wanted to do was take the whole thing and push it out. But all of it was too heavy.

She heard the sure footsteps of her father. Warm, caring hands braced her shoulders from behind.

"Relax your shoulders." A soft giggle left him. "And your face. You're going to get early onset wrinkles if you keep scrunching your face like that."

Sophie softened her face.

Her father placed a hand onto her diaphragm. "Now breathe in deep." She obeyed. "And breathe out." She let out a slow breath, her stomach expanding with the movement. "Now, dive into the pool but don't swim too deep. Just keep your head above the water." She felt her body relax. "Now let that feeling run through your veins." She felt it, a cooling sensation running down her legs, her arms and her spine. "And imagine that there's a string running from your hands to that pebble."

Sophie lifted her hand in front of her.

"Good girl." Her father let go of her shoulders and moved away. "This is your mana. Only you can control it. Now lift."

She obeyed. She imagined that the string she held was bound tightly to the pebble and she yanked it hard. Sophie opened her eyes and the pebble that was once on the ground in front of her, was now suspended midair.

A ribbon of excitement danced through her and she cheered, jumping up and down. Ash ran up to her, grabbed her tight and lifted her up, cheering.

"Well done, Sophie! You did it! I am so proud of you. I'm proud of you both," Lou shouted. With his long silver hair and purple eyes, he leaned down and stretched out his arms.

The two children ran into his waiting arms and cheered with happiness.

The darkness dissipated and Sophie was in the Godlands again. Her eyes fluttered open to meet Ash's. The scar across the left side of his brow, shining brightly in the sun. And just like the day in his living room, Sophie's lips wobbled. Her throat ached. Without a word she flung herself onto Ash's shirtless body and wrapped her arms around his thick neck. He did not falter, he caught her with ease and held her tightly with his arms as she sobbed. What he showed her was exactly what she needed to see. Her skin had been set alight for so long, she'd almost forgotten what it felt like to not be burning in hatred. Finally, *finally* she had met relief. She was grateful for it. Impossibly grateful. It was her father that had taught her how to wield her mana, but she was the one who took it by its reins and mastered it. No one else. It was hers and hers only. The chokehold that Kaine had on her essence and power relented because it was *hers*. It was Taliesin blood and Taliesin magic that ran through her veins and nothing in this world, nothing in this realm and all the realms, could change that.

She was power.

She was a demigoddess.

She was Sofreya Brighid Taliesin, and no one could stop her.

Sophie leaned back. Without even realising it, she had found herself in Ash's lap. His thick corded thighs the only thing supporting her, but she didn't care. "Thank you. Thank you for showing me that. I don't know how you do it." She wiped her tear-stained eyes with the back of her hand and laughed. She probably looked like a feral cat.

"Do what?" Ash beamed, his eyes shining in the sunlight.

Sophie's breath caught slightly. Striking was the only word she could describe Ash as. "You seem to know exactly what I need." She beamed right back.

"That's what friends are for, right?" He swallowed, eyes darting down to her lips then back up again.

"Best friends." Sophie nodded. The words didn't seem quite right given how they sat right now.

A momentary shadow of disappointment washed across his face but as soon as Sophie blinked, it was gone. In its place was the confident, powerful male she learnt to like, hell love – as a friend, Sophie told herself.

Ash looked at the sun. "Oh shoot."

Sophie stilled on top of his lap. "What is it?"

Ash reverently lifted Sophie from his lap and helped her to stand.

"I'm late." He brushed off the dirt that had clung to his legs and shook out his wings. He held out a hand for her to hold. "I think it's time we explore life outside the Isle of Deos." He smiled brightly. The two dimples that marked his tan skin were the embodiment of mischief and charm.

Sophie narrowed her eyes at him. "Where are we going?"

"To see my kids." Ash grinned.

"Your what?!" Sophie didn't mean to shout. Nor did she intend her voice to echo across the cavern. She just wasn't expecting him to utter those words let alone plaster a silly grin on his face as he said them. And it wasn't just one child, it was *kids* – plural.

It seemed like the gods, goddesses and angels on the Isle got busy when they had a moment to spare. She wondered who the female was. The female lucky enough to spend and create life with her best friend.

A pang of jealousy shot through Sophie – an unwelcome feeling that she didn't quite understand when it came to Ash.

25

ELOWAN

Rule number one when it comes to the Resting Ruins: Do not go through the Resting Ruins.

Rule number two: See rule one.

Like Zala had plainly stated in Keeci's apartment, it was a suicide mission for them. Despite this, it was key to adding potential allies to the rebellion, so it was a necessary risk they were willing to take.

Elowan and Zala aimed for the edge of a cliff along Mor's Gorge as dawn broke. Thick brush lined the entire cliff edge, painting the dust-covered rocks in a rich orange. There was no life here surrounding the Resting Ruins save for the hearty plants that could endure a thousand droughts.

They had officially landed in the Western Wastes – dry and dead land spanning to the horizon in every single direction. It was a place where many things came to die or waste away as punishment.

Elowan and Zala unbuckled themselves from their glider. Together, they collapsed the glider, neatly folding the glass frame. Tucking it behind a bush, Elowan's hands glowed faintly as she twisted them, camouflaging the glider with a quick masking spell. They'd leave the glider here, just in case.

If Elowan's map was correct, the Resting Ruins would be just a hundred metre's walk from where they stood. "Let's get this over and done with," Elowan sighed.

Zala nodded and made to move.

They strode in silence.

There it was.

The markings of where the Resting Ruins began.

Ahead, only a metre in front of them, black sand replaced the rich orange they'd landed on. Pillars of black stone stretched out in every direction as far as the Fae eye could see. It looked lifeless. Still.

There was no clear path through the Resting Ruins. It was a maze made long ago when Faery was in its infancy. The oracles, powerful beings of mana that could see deep into the past, present and future, had created this place for the troubled souls that endlessly roamed Faery. This was the place where stray souls got lost.

As if on cue, a soft whispering started, coating Elowan's skin in goosebumps. "You hear that too?" Elowan asked.

"Yep." Zala pulled her lips into a thin line of worry – a rarity for the wraith to even show an ounce of emotion.

"Then may the gods guide us."

"To where we're destined to be."

Using her short spear, Elowan sliced the bottom of her black shirt, creating two blindfolds. In unison, Elowan and Zala tied the makeshift blindfolds around their eyes and over their ears. A cautionary tale spun into an old nursery rhyme was their only saving grace today. It had been passed down through generations of families for centuries.

Resting Ruins oh souls with fear
How many years will we spend here?
Take our ears, take our sight
Perhaps that will give us might
To walk in limbo, past the screams of despair
None of them just or treated fair
Pray with light that our fates do not take flight
And lose their way through the maze in spite

The rhyme was vague at best and disconcerting at worst. The solution was simple enough, but it was no guarantee. They needed to cover their ears to mask the screams and pleas of the souls that were trying to claw their way out. They needed to cover their eyes so that the souls didn't trick them and guide them into a dead end. And they needed to pray like hell that the Fates didn't intend their final resting place to be the Resting Ruins.

Hand in hand – a physical grounding and link to one another – Elowan and Zala stepped foot onto the black sands of the Resting Ruins.

Immediately, the air grew still and stale.

The temperature plunged and along her skin Elowan could feel fog and mist wrapping itself around her. She squeezed Zala's hand and Zala squeezed back, calming her rapidly beating heart.

Silence. The whispers they heard along the border of the ruins had ceased.

And so, they walked.

Elowan would lead until her mana grew weary of navigating the unknown, then Zala would take over. Together, their manas would lead them to the end of the maze. How far away that would be, she had no idea.

They walked a few metres, feeling the sand crunch beneath their boots as they weaved through the black stone pillars. Elowan's mana guided them to a left turn but quickly coiled back from something. Elowan stopped moving instantly. It took every shred of willpower to not pull away her blindfold and look at what had caused her mana to recoil. She was smarter than that.

Zala squeezed her right hand.

Then a cold hand squeezed her left.

Elowan let out a scream, yanking her hand away from the soul that dared touch her.

"Z take over," Elowan urged.

"Roger."

Zala pulled Elowan closer to her and they weaved through the pillars with haste. The twists and turns Zala made started to make Elowan dizzy. That's when the begging started.

"Please take us with you!" a young female voice shouted from the left.

"GOTCHA!" a deep, croaky male voice laughed.

She could feel cold hands playing with the ends of her blindfold and hair. Elowan readjusted her blindfold so that it covered her ears better. Her heart worked itself up into a panic.

"We need to move faster. I'm not sure how much longer I can stand this," Zala shouted above the souls that had made it their goal to throw them off their path. So they picked up some speed, now weaving through the pillars at a steady jogging pace.

"Fuck. E, take over," Zala panted. Her mana must have coiled back from something.

It was unsettling how the ruins had a way of freezing and frightening their mana.

"On it," Elowan said, pulling Zala just behind her as they ran hand in hand. Elowan's mana had barely recovered, but it was enough.

"Take us with you!" shouted from the right.

"At least have the decency to look at us as you condemn us here!" shouted from the left.

Voices echoed and rolled into a cacophonous symphony of sound. Until thunder boomed right above them. The rain poured in tiny little pellets that pinched their skin as they whisked through the pillars.

Then the voices disappeared.

All but one.

"Where are you going?" a soft, female voice asked.

Elowan knew that voice. The first voice she ever heard. A voice that soothed her through all her aches and pains. A voice that stopped her dead in her tracks.

It was her mother's.

Hot tears started in the back of Elowan's eyes.

"Ellie, don't listen to it," Zala pleaded from behind.

Elowan remained quiet, her throat angry and her heart torn.

"Aren't you going to look at your mother?" the soul said.

"Ellie, don't," Zala warned.

Old Elowan would have torn the blindfold right off her face and embraced her mother in whatever celestial form she was in. But Elowan was born anew. The moment a drop of Veritas met her lips, she was faced with her truth. She could see clearly. The broken heart that she wore on her sleeve, had finally healed.

"You're not my mother. My mother is dead," Elowan said to the left where the soul spoke. Elowan felt a cool caress on the back of her neck.

This is not good.

Elowan ran.

Wherever her mana took her, she didn't care. They needed to get out of this blasted place, stat.

"Run, you little bitch," her mother's voice whispered into her ear.

Maniacal cackling followed Elowan like a shark in the water with its prey. It stung, but only for a moment. Elowan swatted the voice away as she ran. Blind. They needed out.

Zala's grip grew tighter, panicked. She was being pulled away. "Ellie! Don't let go!" Zala shouted.

Souls took a hold of Elowan's ankles, and they too began to pull. Elowan fell to the ground, panicking as her hand ripped free from Zala's. Elowan could hear Zala's grunts of pain and struggle.

She'd hit the ground too.

"Z! Z! Fuck!" The absence of Zala's warmth in this hellish nightmare was debilitating.

"Ellie!" Zala's voice disappeared into the fray.

"NO!" Elowan bellowed, engulfing her entire body with raging flames. Droplets of rain pelted from the storm brewing above her. Water sizzled and hissed before it even touched her skin. The souls shrunk back in fear. Elowan could hear their hushed whispers moving farther away from her.

It dawned on her that she had to run the rest of the ruins alone. It was what she and Zala agreed to on their flight from Seaspun Bay. If they were separated in the ruins, they would do everything in their power to get to the other side, even if it meant leaving the other person behind. This was a war they were waging, and sacrifices needed to be made. It would be better that one of them made it, than neither.

Elowan gripped Camrine's short spear and took in a deep breath. If running was the only way to escape the Resting Ruins, then she would leave a burning trail through it.

It felt like Elowan had been running for miles. She probably had. The only string of hope that managed to deafen the screams and pleas of the souls she ran past or collided into was the thought of seeing Zala on the other side.

The grit and grime of the black sand eased, growing finer and finer until the air came to life again. The rain ceased and alas the harsh sun of the Western Wastes blessed her skin. Elowan slowed down and fell to her knees.

Never in her life did she imagine crying at the feel of dead brush beneath her knees and the feeling of cool, fine sand between her fingers. Gone was the smell of death and its place was an earthy fragrance.

Elowan pulled off the blindfold with relief and braced herself for the brightness of the Faery sun. It was high in the sky. Midday. She had spent six hours running. Her knees were shot, and her shins felt like she'd smashed them against the edges of rocks. With numb hands, Elowan pulled the skin of water she had not dared drink from, from the waist of her belt and drank deeply. Water spilled everywhere and it felt like a divine blessing upon her face.

Putting the skin of water away, Elowan pushed herself up from the ground. Her body begged her not to, but her heart and her mind pulled her off the floor in search for Zala.

Elowan turned back to face the Resting Ruins. It sat still, undisturbed and unassuming. It turned out that Hell was a place on Faery, and it was here in the Resting Ruins.

Elowan waited, surveying the border of black sand for any disturbances.

Come on, Zala, come on.

Nothing.

The sound of shifting sand grew louder just ahead of her. Elowan ran toward it. It had to be Zala. It had to. At first it was just her hand, then her whole body came tumbling through the façade that encased the entire Resting Ruins.

Elowan opened her arms, ready to catch the wraith.

With a harrumph, Zala collapsed into Elowan's arms, her laboured breathing an absolute blessing to Elowan's ears.

Elowan quickly stripped her friend of her blindfold and unfastened Zala's skin of water. She helped the wraith drink.

"You made it. Z, it's Ellie. We made it," Elowan repeated.

Zala came to after a few more measured breaths and leaned back on an elbow. The wraith took the skin of water from Elowan's hands and drank deeply. "Let's never do that again," Zala breathed.

"Agreed, Z. Agreed," Elowan said, laughing. They sat there in silence for a little while longer, recouping whatever shred of energy was left. Above them flew a bird. No, a large raven, bigger than Elowan had ever seen before. It circled above them for a moment before spiralling down, landing a few paces away from their feet. "Shoo," Elowan waved the bird away.

At the words, the bird exploded into a plume of black smoke. In its billowing wake, a hooded and hunched figure appeared.

Elowan and Zala pounced from the ground, drawing their weapons.

"That won't be needed," a scratchy, old feminine voice drawled. The hooded figure lifted an obsidian-coloured hand to its hood. Long black nails like knives tipped each finger, dragging back the hood with the stillness of a being centuries old.

Elowan held her breath, a hand poised to release her short spear at any moment.

Underneath the hood was the wrinkled face of an oracle. A species deemed extinct only a few years ago. The oracle's piercing green-filled eyes smiled in delight as it registered the surprise undoubtedly written across both Elowan's and Zala's faces. The oracle stretched out a hand, pointing to the dead land behind them.

Elowan turned. Gone was the wide expanse of dead brush and nothingness. Peppered throughout the dry land were tents of all shapes and sizes. Beings and animals milled about. Smoke billowed. Vegetation grew all around. Life had suddenly sprouted in a dead valley right before their eyes.

"Welcome to the Untold Valley," the feminine voice croaked.

26

ELOWAN

*H*oly mother of Faery.

"But I thought your kind had been wiped out?" Elowan could barely form the words.

Supposedly. Oracles had slowly disappeared over years, but the final "cleanse", as Queen Calliea had called it, was carried out by Kaine. Elowan wasn't part of the Elite operation, but she felt responsible all the same.

"It takes more than brute force to kill an oracle, Elowan Nahvi," the oracle said with a smile.

"Wait, how do you know my name?"

"We know everything." The oracle paused. "Come." The obsidian being moved with a quickness that contrasted its overly hunched back. Sure, it hobbled, but it moved with intention and pace.

They stormed through the brush toward the village ahead. As they walked, the short brush turned into tall, lively grass reaching up to Elowan's knees. Several small tents made of animal skin and wood surrounded a larger tent that centred the village. Families covered head to toe in warm-coloured linen, matching the orange dirt of the Western Wastes, went about their day. The smell of spice and herbs from the cauldrons that boiled before tents wafted through the camp.

Elowan couldn't make out what the beings were. Some looked Fae and others didn't. But what was certain was that they were all watching Elowan and Zala. Some even told their children to go inside their tents. Something like shame sat in the back of Elowan's throat.

The oracle moved along without acknowledging the people around it. They reached the largest tent in the centre of the camp and pushed through the flaps. A wall of smoke greeted them and the smell of burning sage clung to Elowan's nostrils. She could barely see anything.

"Sit," the oracle ordered.

Elowan didn't really know where, so she felt around the ground only to find cushions. She knelt upon them. Zala had done the same just beside her. Elowan could hear the rustling and bending of the fabric.

"I see the Resting Ruins have shown you mercy," a different feminine voice pierced its way through the billowing smoke. The voice was a tad lower than the first oracle's, but it sounded younger.

"Hardly," Elowan responded into the smoke.

"You are alive, are you not?" the feminine voice said with a touch of annoyance.

In a blink, the smoke that encased the tent reeled back, disappearing into spindly, obsidian black hands, the room suddenly clear.

Before Elowan and Zala sat the oracle they'd met on the outskirts of the Resting Ruins. Next to it, a younger oracle. Its hair was long, black and stringy. Its eyes were the same piercing green and its black talons were long. They both wore the same dark cloak, darker than the shadows that Zala possessed. Cross-legged and arms relaxed by their side, it looked like they weren't even breathing.

Elowan had never seen an oracle before, let alone two in one day.

"Thank you for letting us into your village. It is pleasant." Were those the right words? Perhaps "peaceful" would have been a better choice.

The oracles did not react. They acted as if no one had said a word and continued staring into the space between them.

Elowan cleared her throat and quickly looked to Zala for some sort of support. But Zala did not look at her, she stared into the space between them all too.

This is getting weird.

Elowan cleared her throat again and loudly interrupted, "We need your—" The ground rumbled. The dirt once packed to the ground started to lift. Dirt particles suspended in the air, forming a vortex in the tent. Elowan's vision started to double. A force so strong struck her chest, winding her. Her neck craned to the sky by the pull of invisible hands. The pressure and sound of gale-force winds rattled her ears almost bursting them.

Then her vision turned black.

Silence.

She pushed open her heavy eyes. Sore, dirt-covered and teary. Wildfire burned the busy village ahead of her. Screams and shrieks of pain filled the air. It was all she could hear above the ringing in her ears. And the smell, oh the smell was horrible. Everything was on fire. Large Fae brutes ran through the village with their short spears, grunting and shouting. Some wielded weapons. They dragged people out from their tents.

No. No. What are they doing? Why are they harming these people? Elowan's throat was dry and aching from the tears that ceased to end. She scrambled to her knees, running to the closest Fae soldier. He wore purple breaches and golden armour just like . . . the Elite.

Elowan's stomach lurched. He picked up a little girl by the scruff of her neck. She had been hiding behind a wagon.

"Where are they hiding, little girl?" the male demanded.

The little girl cried as she shook her head.

"Fine." The male grunted. He shoved her down into the mud, her neck almost cracking from the force. Elowan ran for the soldier, trying to spear tackle him but she fell right through him.

What?

He stormed into the nearest tent and dragged out a young female who shared similar brunette hair as the young girl. The female came out kicking with a cloth tied around her wrist and a gag around her mouth. It was the young girl's mother. The little girl cried louder.

"Where are they hiding?!" the Fae male shouted.

To her credit, the little girl said nothing. She just cried harder. Her mother's eyes were wide, shaking her head, telling her daughter in any way that she could to keep her mouth shut. The little girl began to wail.

"Suit yourself," the soldier grunted. The male wound his arm back, lifting his short spear and aimed for the mother's heart.

Elowan quickly turned and ran. She already knew how that was going to end. The little girl's cry of despair chased her heels as she ran.

From a large tent ahead, a haunting hum beckoned Elowan. Closer and closer to the large tent she ran. It was like the one in the Untold Valley but it was older, different.

She tumbled in through the flaps to find the tent shrouded in dark smoke. Elowan couldn't see a thing. She fell to the ground in a panic, feeling for something, anything. A cold hand snatched her wrist from the ground and pushed her back onto her knees.

A click sounded in the room. The black smoke flew back into the centre of the tent to reveal three oracles sitting side by side. Their legs crossed and their eyes closed in meditation.

Elowan's heart pounded. Her breath heavy.

She waited.

And waited.

But nothing.

Now you see, three voices melded into each other.

Like before, an invisible force struck Elowan's chest. The air from her lungs lifted. Her neck craned and her vision blurred. Then it flashed and sparked, and with a dramatic breath she was pulled back into the present, her ears rattling from a forceful wind.

Elowan fell forward with her hands braced on the floor. Her vision cleared and beside her, Zala had done the same. Her ice-blue eyes pierced Elowan's, wide in surprise. She must have seen the same thing.

"Now you see," the voices of the two oracles before them said. Their eyes still shut in a meditative state.

"I-I am sorry," Elowan said between heavy breaths. She was. Even though she wasn't there for any of the Elite missions, she was still a part of the machine that sought to kill them and the innocent villagers of the Untold Valley.

"The sins of your forebearers will not wash away, but wade in the waters is where you will stay, unless fates of future are to wash upon the shores, the fall to death will be through blood-red claws . . ." The younger oracle trailed off. Its eyes remained closed, though they flitted around underneath its thin, papery eyelids.

They were speaking in riddles and Elowan was losing her patience. She'd just been sucked into the past and catapulted into the future and they were busy spouting riddles?

Sins of your forebearers . . . the Elite. What they did not long ago in the Western Wastes. That had to be it. Maybe there was a way to make amends? "How can we erase the sins of our forebearers?" Elowan asked with growing urgency.

"You cannot." It was the older oracle who answered.

"Then what can we do? Faery is dying. Its people are without a home. The horrors of Queen Calliea and Terr will know no bounds. We need your help," Elowan moved from the cushion she knelt upon. "Please," she begged.

Zala put a hand on Elowan's shoulder in warning.

Together, the oracles spun another riddle.

"Two soot spires above so high, in its centre has red in the sky. The past in chains to be set free. Now just two, where there used to be three."

Now just two, where there used to be three . . . The voices. There were three in the vision Elowan just had. There were three oracles. And before her now, there were only two. That was it. They needed to find the third oracle.

Two soot spires above so high, in its centre has red in the sky . . . Two soot spires with a red sky in its centre, just like . . .

The answer burned in her chest.

"You want us to find the third oracle?" Elowan hoped to the gods she was right.

"Once two become three, the future of Faery will see. Closer to the end perhaps for some, but close to the sun a war will be won . . ." The oracles hissed, their necks twisted in strange angles for several minutes until, at last, the obsidian creatures opened their eyes.

Smoke began to fill the room again.

"Our Praeteritus has been lost for some time. Bring them back to us and we will be indebted to you. You already know where," the older oracle croaked.

"Praeteritus? Your past?" Zala chimed in.

"Time is of the essence." The younger oracle smiled.

In a plume of black glittering smoke, both oracles disappeared.

Elowan turned to Zala. Zala looked as pale as a ghost, her eyes wide.

"That was Praesens and Relicuus." Zala pointed to the where the oracles had sat. "We just met the very first oracles; Present and Future."

"Mother of Faery . . ."

The vision. The quest. The words all jumbled together but finally, it all made sense. Before them was the present and the future. And they were missing their past.

It was now Elowan and Zala's mission to rescue the past – Praeteritus. If they achieved that, then they'd win the rebellion more allies. Powerful ones. The very first oracles themselves.

Holy shit.

They now had a fighting chance.

Elowan shot up from the ground, snapping her fingers to test if her mana would work. Sparks started to unfurl from her hands.

Yes.

Elowan manifested a portal with a quick flick of her mana.

"Do you know where we're going?" Zala asked as she too shot up from the ground.

"Of course. Two soot spires above so high, in its centre has red in the sky." Elowan paused and smirked. "We're headed back to Castle Terrin, baby."

27

SOPHIE

"You ready?" Ash smiled brightly.

"Yep." She wasn't ready.

After attempting – and failing – to hide her unease, Ash grabbed her hand like they always did when they were young and walked her to the stable of arions. She wondered how his partner would feel if she knew they were holding hands like this. It didn't feel quite right. At the stable, he sought his pure white arion named Lumen, and together they flew to the top of the waterfall where the water that ran in reverse, spilled over the edge . . . in the sky.

The Isle of Deos was a floating island and from her vantage point on top of the waterfall, Sophie could spot other floating islands – three to be exact – much larger than the Isle itself. On the closest floating island, she could spot green rolling hills and shiny tall buildings. The island in the middle was thickly covered in something like golden grass. The farthest, highest island was solely black with a dark volcanic mountain in its centre.

She was on a floating, motherfucking island. It was like a scene out of *Laputa* or even *Avatar*. All that surrounded them was pure blue sky and clouds. Various birds and creatures squawked and flew in formation. The sounds of the waterfall they stood atop roared in unison with the adrenalin that ran through her veins. She thought she'd seen it all . . . but this? This was something she'd never read about or could even imagine. She let out an appreciative scoff and her eyes widened with wonder.

Sophie sat snug on the pure white arion, Ash's front pressed firmly against her back. His muscled thighs held her firmly as she braced her hands against the back of the stallion's neck. There was no saddle to hold onto, only Ash's arms that held firmly on the reins in front.

"Hold on to your horses." Ash smiled, no doubt revelling in the pun.

Big idiot, Sophie thought to herself.

His mouth was so close to Sophie that his breath tickled the shell of her ear, sending chills down her spine and a rush of excitement through her core.

Stop it, Sophie. He's got a partner. She repeated to herself. As much as her mind was screaming and waving red flags for her to keep her distance, her body clearly wanted for someone else – though she wasn't ready to admit who.

With two sharp clicks of his tongue, Lumen, the white arion, leapt into the air with one giant thrust of its enormous wings – almost doubling the size of Ash's. The sun peaked through the clouds, warming their skin as they catapulted through the sky.

The arion floated through the skies for a few seconds before nosediving along the waterfall. The wind whipped passed Sophie at alarming speed. They were travelling so fast that Sophie scrunched her eyes and tensed. Still, Ash held her firmly in place.

"Open your eyes Sofreya!"

"No fucking way!"

"You *need* to see this! I promise you won't regret it!" Ash whooped above the wind that cracked against her ears. Strong hands grabbed hers and eased them out of the arion's mane. Her stomach turned and gravity felt like it no longer existed. Ash intertwined his fingers with hers and opened their arms wide as if they were wings, catching the air. "I've got you. I promise. I've always got you. Open your eyes!" His deep voice ran through her, illuminating all the dark corners of her heart.

She burst her eyes open at the words that did all sorts of things to her tummy. The sun shined happily across her face as she took it all in. They whisked through clouds as they plummeted . . . no, flew through the never-ending skies. This was the Godlands. This was Heaven, in all its meanings and iterations.

Sophie leaned back, her head resting against Ash's bare chest, their hands still intertwined. She looked up at him with absolute awe and wonder, as if to ask, are you seeing what I'm seeing? A laugh worked up and out of Sophie's throat. Her heart filled with pure happiness. In this moment, gone was her heartache and gone was her worry. She was herself. She was whole again. And this – rushing through the air on the back of an ancient arion, with her best friend – was where she wanted to be. Where she was supposed to be. She deserved it.

Sophie let go of all her inhibitions and let out a conquering roar. Ash's deep laugh rumbled through her and he followed suit, letting out his own celebratory caw.

Lumen spiralled up into the clouds again, nickering in pure excitement.

As the arion steadied out, Ash leaned in, an arm now wrapped around Sophie's middle and the other holding the reins tightly. "That never gets old."

"That was . . . amazing!" Sophie leaned her head back onto Ash's chest and looked up at him through her thick lashes. Her cheeks ached from overuse but it didn't stop her from basking in his warmth and calm.

Ash watched her, his eyes searching for something. Sophie could have sworn heat washed over them.

"What?" Sophie was breathless. For multiple reasons. Their lips were mere inches away. If she leaned up just a fraction . . .

"Nothing." Ash shook his head slightly.

He's got a partner, Sophie! She thought to herself. She cleared her throat and snapped out of the trance she found herself in. Perhaps it was the endorphins or the altitude that made her head spin and her inhibitions loose. Sophie righted herself and put a bit of distance between them – as much as she could, riding bareback on an arion.

Ash cleared his throat too and scooted his hips back slightly.

They rose above a thick layer of clouds and before them floated the closest island. Like the Isle of Deos, the island was laden with thick jungle but in the centre, there were tall, white buildings. All around was low-lying yet dense Grecian architecture. It was a city. Four rivers intersected the island and like the Isle of Deos, the water ran freely off the edge of it.

"Welcome to Soul City." Pride lined the ends of his words.

Sophie smiled.

For real this time.

Soul City. The place where souls who passed – of humans, Fae, magical and otherwise – came to live for the rest of eternity. The city was a bustling metropolis compared to the Isle of Deos, with tall white buildings that lined white marble streets. Vendors and stalls echoed with excitement, selling their goods to the fancily dressed souls that strolled the markets.

Ash guided Sophie and Lumen through the busy streets. Souls of all ages stopped to greet Ash, many raking a cautious eye over Sophie. The thin blue film that encased their skin glowed with each movement and curious glance. Ash greeted them kindly but kept his steady pace through the city.

He slowed down as they approached a sandstone building with large golden gates. Grass fields lined the front of the building. Various jungle gyms, swings, see-saws, and sand pits were placed across the field. The muffled sound of children playing rang in the distance.

This must be the day care he picks his kids up from. Sophie stood nervously behind Ash as they approached the large golden arches. Across the arch, large letters in a language she did not recognise were cast in iron. She looked up at the sign, trying to decipher it with a furrowed brow.

"The Home for Lost Children." Ash explained.

"Lost?"

"Orphans, if you will. Children whose parents have yet to pass and enter Soul City. This is where they stay until their parents arrive." Ash grinned as he opened the golden gates, motioning Sophie to head in first.

"You leave your kids at the orphanage? Does your partner not take care of them?" As soon as the words left her mouth, Ash smiled mischievously, his twin dimples and fangs flashing. Something clicked in her brain. Sophie finally put two and two together – her words and his roguish grin. There was nothing she wanted to do more right now, than to melt into the floor and disappear. She'd even let Lumen stomp all over her for good measure.

Ash cackled. He outright cackled, bracing his middle and bending over kind of cackle. And Sophie pretty much died, right then and there.

Goodbye life. It was nice knowing you.

"Hang on, you thought . . ." Ash managed to get out between huffs of laughter.

"Don't even finish that sentence." Sophie stormed ahead.

"Why? A little jealous, are we?"

"Why on earth would I be jealous of someone who'd deign to frolic with an overgrown turtle-dove?" Sophie stomped even louder along the gravel path for effect.

"I don't know, Sofreya. That stomping is telling me a different story."

Sophie didn't need to turn around to see the stupid grin that was most certainly plastered across his handsome face. "Shut it, asshole."

"Your wish is my command, my queen," Ash snorted.

That facetious twat of an angel. Sophie grumbled various profanities underneath her breath as she halted in front of the large oak doors to the orphanage. She felt Ash pull up beside her with Lumen.

"For the record, I don't have a partner. Second, I call them my kids because they could very well spend their entire after-lives here. Not all parents arrive in Soul City. And no matter how old you are or what kind of being you are, you'll always want to belong to someone. So . . . while they're waiting for their parents, they're my kids." Ash cleared his throat.

Sophie's heart filled with a newfound appreciation for her best friend. Not only was he strong and scarily adept with weapons, but he was also compassionate, fair and understanding – a true, admirable leader. She finally understood why the other gods and goddesses were drawn to him and followed him even though he wasn't a god himself. He was an enigma.

She looked at him, his strong jawline and the undercut that accentuated it.

He caught her stare and winked. "I suggest you keep your guard up."

Sophie was about to ask why when the oak doors groaned open to a classroom littered with artwork, desks and toys. A team of children came pouring out, surrounding them both.

"Acki! Acki!" They all shouted with youthful glee.

Dressed in different knitted and crocheted vests and jumpers, the kids swarmed Ash and Lumen – screaming like kids in a candy store.

Ash knelt on the ground so he could greet them all. He pretended to fall on the ground in pain as they jumped at him, clinging onto him for dear life. Lumen bent down to lick the children that came up to pet his majestic coat.

"Help, Princess Sofreya! I'm being attacked by gremlins!" Ash shouted from the floor, his arm dramatically trying to reach for Sophie.

Sophie laughed brightly and if she was being truthful, her ovaries had exploded watching Ash this way. A renowned angel warrior capable of combusting enemies with his lightning, absolutely melted for children and animals – the *Godlands Press* would have a field day if they knew. She could see the headlines now.

At the word, several little girls turned to face Sophie.

"She's a princess?!" They all oohed and aahed and ran up to hug her, sparing Ash a moment to quietly slide away without their notice.

Sophie knelt to greet them.

"She's so pretty!" A little girl screamed as she touched Sophie's silver-purple hair.

Another girl leaned up against her and said, "Princess Sofreya, when I grow up, I want to be as beautiful as you."

Sophie leaned down to the girl. "You know what's better than that?" The girl looked up at Sophie with awe in her eyes. "Growing up and being as curious and confident as you."

The little girl blushed and gave Sophie a tight hug.

The little girls closed in and started whispering, "Lady Sofreya, are you Acki's girlfriend?" Sophie's eyes widened as the girls snickered and giggled.

"Girls! Stop terrorising my pretty princess!" Ash shouted from the other side of the room where he showed the kids surrounding him how to nock an arrow on a wooden bow. The children's toys looked comical in his large warrior hands.

At his words, the girls scattered and squealed in every direction, shouting, "They're going to get married! We're having a royal wedding!" They ran across the classroom, gathering supplies and toys.

Sophie just laughed at their fervour and determination. Oh how lovely would it be to be young again? To run around carefree?

Sophie watched the children play but noticed a Fae female enter the room from what looked like an administration office. The female was graceful. Her features were soft and warm. Her skin was alight with the blue glow of a soul, and she was heading straight for Sophie. On her way over, the female nodded an acknowledgment Ash's way, which prompted a raised hand from Ash. Sophie stood to greet the female.

"You'll have to excuse the children. It's not often they get visitors outside of Acheron's cadre." The female stretched out a hand for Sophie to shake. "Amina."

"Sofreya." Sophie smiled warmly, taking the female's hand in hers. "It's lovely to meet you."

"I take care of the children here at the home. Acheron is noble and patient enough to spend a day here each week so I can go out and gather stores." Amina surveyed the children with warmth and love.

"He's great, isn't he?" Sophie watched as Ash helped the children master their bows and arrows. The master of weapons, in his true element.

Amina nodded in agreement. "You're very lucky to have him." Her eyebrows raised slightly in question.

Sophie arced up. "Oh no, it's not like that."

"Have you seen the way you look at him?" Amina leaned in and teased in one ear. She circled around Sophie's other shoulder and continued, "or better yet, the way he looks at you?" A knowing smile splayed across her warm face. "If you need anything, send word," Amina winked.

Sophie's cheeks warmed as Amina left the room and closed the oak doors behind her. What did Amina mean by that? Sophie wasn't looking at Ash in a particular way nor was Ash looking at her in a particular way. Sometimes she'd catch him with a heated look in his eyes but . . . Sophie shook the thought out of her head. They were friends. That was it.

Sophie re-entered the thrall of happy and loud children, trying her best to not get too close to Ash. They spent the afternoon doing crafts. Some of the girls wanted to set up a royal wedding, lining up the toys they had at the front of the classroom and making an aisle in the middle. The girls commandeered the boys to set up chairs and decorations for their extravagant royal wedding. Ash helped the children onto his shoulders as they pinned up the colourful ribbons across the walls, while Sophie helped get all the stuffed toys in line and dressed up.

It was then Sophie noticed a young human-looking girl with blond curly hair and dark, onyx eyes. She was pouting and visibly upset.

Sophie walked up to the young girl. "Hi. My name is Sophie, what's yours?"

"Tenerife." Her voice was all soft and shy, the r sounding more like a w.

"What a lovely name. Tenerife, can I sit with you?"

The girl rubbed her eyes and nodded, her head bowed.

Sophie pulled out the small chair and faced Tenerife. "You seem a bit sad, is there anything I can do to help, or is there something you want to talk about?"

The girl pouted even further and fiddled with the pencil she held in her small hands. "I don't want Acki to get married." She crossed her arms.

"The wedding is just pretend, Tenerife. It's not for real," Sophie assured the young girl.

"I want to marry Acki! Even if it's just pretend!"

"Well, have you told Acki that?" The nickname rolled of Sophie's tongue. It made her heart squeeze.

Tenerife shook her head. Her blond curls bobbing with the motion.

"It's important that if you want something, you go get it or you go ask for it. Not everyone is a mind-reader, so you need to make your intentions clear," Sophie smiled.

"Can you come with me so I can tell Acki? I know you want to marry him, but I wanted to marry him first." Tenerife looked up at Sophie with her beady onyx eyes and cherub cheeks.

"Of course. Let's go now before all the wedding decorations are finished," Sophie stood up from the chair and held out a hand for Tenerife to hold.

The young, shy girl hid behind Sophie's legs as they walked across the classroom to where Ash sat. A few of the children were dressing him with ribbons and glitter. They insisted that he look the part of the groom.

Ash looked behind Sophie's legs, his face screwed with worry. "What's wrong Tene? Are you okay?"

The girl clung to Sophie's legs harder. Sophie knelt before Ash and pulled Tenerife closer. "Tene here wants to tell you something." Sophie gave the girl a reassuring nod.

The girl leaned in so that only Sophie and Ash could hear. She whispered rather loudly, "Acki, I want to get pretend-married to you instead. I asked Princess Sofreya and she said I could have you."

Ash turned to Sophie. "Did she now?"

Tenerife nodded quickly, her lips pouting.

"Not my words, but sure." Sophie laughed.

"There we have it, folks! A wedding with a new bride!" Ash announced to the classroom.

The kids roared with excitement. Someone had rung the wedding bells – cow bells in place of wedding bells – and the children ran to where the seats were laid out.

Ash scooped Tenerife up in his arms and ran to the end of the aisle.

Sophie joined the rest of the children, forming the congregation to the royal wedding. Ash knelt at the front with a shy Tenerife by him, clinging to one of the ribbons that had been wrapped around his muscled arm.

One of the boys stood upfront – the celebrant.

The classroom of children squealed and clapped as Tenerife and Ash were deemed pretend-husband and pretend-wife for the time limit of two minutes – the celebrant was a stickler for timings and had stated such in his speech.

The children roared with excitement as Ash and Tenerife ran down the aisle laughing.

Ash winked at Sophie as he ran by. His deep laughter filled the room and, unbeknownst to him, Sophie's heart filled too. She didn't think it were possible, but Sophie started to think that . . . she liked him.

28

SOPHIE

"So . . . Acki?" Sophie teased, nudging an elbow into Ash's side. He swatted her away like she was an annoying fly.

"The kids struggled with my name, so I let them call me Acki."

"It's cute," Sophie hummed.

"Please do not use that word to describe me. My enemies could be lurking nearby. They'll see it as a weakness." Ash pretended that his enemies were indeed lurking nearby, scanning the perimeter, but a small side smile soon appeared.

Sophie laughed, breathing in the cool, evening air of Soul City.

Amina had finally come back with supplies for the children and relieved them both of their babysitting duties. They now strolled the quieter marble streets with Lumen in tow.

In the distance, Sophie could her the low thump of dance music and the clinking of glasses emanating from the central business district not too far from where the orphanage was situated. It turned out that Soul City was the mecca of nightlife in the Godlands. If you wanted to party or have a romantic dinner, Soul City was the place to be for both the living and the dead.

Ash suddenly halted, flinging out a hand in front of Sophie who'd clearly been distracted by the sights and sounds of the new city. A loud woosh and thump sounded, and two powerful auras coursed through her. Before them landed Eros – the strawberry-blond angel with white wings – and Deymos – the angel of dread and terror with his dark grey wings. Dust puffed up from where they landed in a superhero crouch.

"That was really unnecessary." Ash crossed his arms and served the most unimpressed flat stare.

"We just wanted to impress the lady is all." Eros nodded in greeting toward Sophie.

"Well, colour me impressed." Sophie put her hands on her hips and nodded appreciatively in Eros and Deymos's direction.

"I'd refrain from complimenting him any further. His head will burst soon enough." The god of dread snickered, pointing to Eros, who looked severely offended.

"Where's Nemy?" Ash closed the distance between the four, pulling in Lumen with them. Sophie followed suit.

"She's with the council," Deymos said.

And like they were two peas in a pod, Eros finished it off. "The council has summoned us, boss." A smirk appeared on his face.

"Well, we can't keep them waiting, can we?" Ash rumbled, clearly annoyed that his evening was cut short.

"It smells like drama!" Eros rubbed his hands together with an unnerving amount of excitement.

Deymos, the vision of death and dread, just rolled his eyes.

"I'll see you tomorrow then," Sophie moved to give them space so the angels could shoot into the air.

Gone was Ash's annoyance and in its place was pure delight. Too eagerly, Ash said, "Not so fast, Sofreya. You're coming with us."

A thread of dread washed through Sophie. She wondered if it was Deymos's power at play or if she just didn't want to be in a room of bland aristocrats and politicians. Who was she kidding? It was most definitely the latter. Sophie began to protest, "I'll just be in the way—"

"I don't have time to drop you off first. You're coming with us." Ash cut her short, smiling, knowing full well she was going to die from boredom if not annoyance while she sat in the council chambers.

"Fine," Sophie grunted. She'd make him pay for this.

Annoying, demanding, turtle-dove, Sophie thought.

Instant regret.

Ash's cadre strolled into the council room back on the Isle of Deos after flying at the speed of light. Sophie had screamed the entire way while Ash laughed – no, bellowed – in her ears. Teasing her. Eros and Deymos had trailed them. They had most likely developed tinnitus given the amount of screaming Sophie had done.

Once they all landed, Sophie gave Ash a mouthful to which the angel warrior just smiled with a tendril of heat in his eyes. The more she verbally throttled him, the more he seemed to like it. It was futile. Big, stupid angel indeed.

At the entrance of the colourless council room stood Ash, his cadre and Sophie. Sophie felt like she was standing behind the damned Avengers and she almost laughed at the thought, if it wasn't for the power that emanated from the males that stood in front of her – the power that made the entire council room fall silent.

"Look who bothered to turn up," a slimy voice sounded from the long table in the centre of the council room.

Sophie rolled her eyes instantly. She didn't even have to see Vestes's face and she already wanted to gag. She stepped out from behind Deymos's dark towering wings and raked a look of disgust at Vestes.

"Half-breeds are not welcome here. This is a council meeting." A nameless council man shot up from his chair – a rotund man with a mop of red hair.

"Is that how you refer to the demigoddess of Faery? You forget your place, Cessair." Ash's deep voice was a knife to the throat. At least for Cessair it was. The red-headed councilman dropped his gaze immediately.

Ash surveyed the room like a true-born commander, his voice boomed, "She is under my guard. Anyone who insults her, insults me."

Sophie watched the entire room.

Everyone looked like they wanted to be anywhere but in the same room as the Godlands's master of weapons – except Diafonia. The goddess of discord was probably curling her toes in excitement. When no one dared to utter another humiliating word for fear of Ash's wrath, he walked to the spare seats at the end of the council table, closest to the fire. "As you were," he stated sharply.

The room seemed to relax at the words.

Eros, Deymos and Sophie followed Ash, the former two looking like honed blades ready to strike. Sophie sat down next to Nemysis, who gave her a curt nod. Ash sat right beside Sophie.

Vestes resumed his speech. "There's been another breach. Sentries along the eastern border detected an interruption in the fabric between Faery and the Godlands not an hour ago."

"Enemy?" Dikastis asked in a bland tone. He clearly didn't want to be here either.

"It has yet to be confirmed. We have it on good authority that an intruder has made it past our borders," Vestes continued. The room broke out into soft murmurs, a few council members raising various concerns. "The eastern border trackers are on it. Given the unrest in Faery we must not treat this lightly."

Cessair nodded fervently like he was Vestes's little lap dog. Sophie noted that and tried not to snarl in disgust.

"Has Zeus weighed in?" Commander Ares chimed in, wearing a rich-red battle cape. Various throwing knives jutted out from the belt he wore across his chest.

"No. We must handle this internally before I can escalate this to His Majesty," Vestes looked to Ash from across the council room. "Commander Ares, get your master of weapons to dispatch his cadre to the eastern border to assist the trackers."

Ash didn't let his commander reply. "I will do no such thing. Not until we have more intel." Ash denied the head of council with a bored tone.

A few members of the council snickered; Sophie included.

Vestes, with his skinny, sharp features, simmered with outrage at Ash's blatant disrespect – until he zeroed in on Sophie with a look of triumph on his face.

"Sofreya . . ." Vestes's voice strung out like a hiss of a snake. ". . . do you not find it a coincidence?"

Here we go.

"Out with it, Vestes," Sophie snapped, trying her hardest to not walk across the room to slap that smug look off his face.

"Your arrival in the Godlands comes at a convenient time. The moment Taranis brings you here, a wall bolstered by centuries worth of power between Faery and Sotera falters. The eastern border of the Godlands, whose walls are impenetrable, detects an interruption with intruders, no doubt." He went in for the kill, or at least tried to. "Sources have confirmed that you are the lover of the Shadow King's spawn. What is his name . . . Kaine?" A saccharine smile splayed across Vestes's face.

The council room quietened at the words. A few members whispered in each other's ears in hushed tones. Few looks of wariness found their way to Sophie.

Sophie flinched at Kaine's name, but she did not cower at the words and what Vestes was insinuating. Not in the slightest. Sophie squared her shoulders. "Correction. *Was* the lover." Sophie stood from where she sat to look down on Vestes. He clearly chose the wrong demigoddess to mess with. "Accuse me all you like. Go ahead. Administer whatever tests you need, to prove yourself right. You'll quickly find that you are irrevocably wrong." Sophie let out an animalistic, Fae snarl. "And when you quickly find that out, I will revel in the sad look on your face when the entire Godlands turns to pity you; the fool."

Ash placed his hand reassuringly on the back of Sophie's leg. If anyone noticed, they did not make it known. Sophie had won the verbal battle with Vestes.

Cessair moved back to face Vestes. "We cannot trust the words of a half-breed. We must administer a truth serum immediately."

"I concur! We must not take this lightly!" Another fear-struck councilman pushed his seat back. A few more council members nodded their agreement.

Sophie felt outnumbered but she thought better of going absolutely feral on everyone present in the room. That wouldn't win her any favours with the council. Sophie had to play this right, and right now she was being cornered. It wasn't an easy feeling to deal with.

Ash skittered his lightning across the room, quietening everyone like a crack of a whip. Some watched him in fear while others watched the cowering council members in absolute delight. Ash stood from where he sat, arms braced on the wooden table before him. "As aforementioned, she is under my guard. You insult her, you insult me." Lightning cracked. A warning from Ash himself.

A few council members jumped in their seats.

The cadre however, were a hair's breadth away from unleashing themselves on the less savoury members of the council, feeding off the energy Ash emanated with his lightning.

Vestes, with his snake-like smile was the first to break the silence. "Careful, Master of Weapons. You wouldn't want to mix business with pleasure," he drawled.

Ash scoffed. "We're leaving." The cadre stood swiftly at the words. "Send word when you have more intel," Ash commanded to no one in particular.

The cadre, including Nemysis stormed out, but not before nodding to their commander, Ares, whose eyes shone with delight and pride.

Sophie walked out behind them, not bothering to look back at the pack of vermin that tried to dim her fire. They'd be fools to forget the day they doubted this demigoddess who at her back had the master of weapons himself – a being who was respected and revered by all the gods and goddesses.

She felt invincible.

29

ELOWAN

Elowan portalled just outside of Castle Terrin – something she hadn't imagined doing again so soon. They had to be quick. In and out. That's all they could afford.

Since Kaine's betrayal and the queen's dirty laundry being aired out for all to see, the castle had emptied out. Gone were all her Elite warriors and staff. All had "disappeared" or left to join the rebellion presumably. All except Kaine and of course the queen's now dwindling platoon of royal guards.

The castle looked darker than it had before, if that were even possible. The two soot-covered spires split into the night sky like two giant knives.

Two soot spires above so high.

Nestled perfectly between the two spires was Queen Calliea's throne room. Its door, walls and ceilings coloured in blood red.

In its centre has red in the sky.

To say that the castle had emptied out wasn't to say that the important rooms like the throne room were left unguarded. If Queen Calliea was hiding Praeteritus – the literal Oracle of the Past – in the throne room, then perhaps security had doubled. There was no way of knowing until they got there.

"My shadows can mask us for a while but if we need mana to break the chains of Praeteritus then something has to give," Zala explained.

"Hopefully it won't come to that," Elowan felt like an idiot for saying the words. Queen Calliea had been hiding an oracle for the years which would take a fair amount of mana to conceal and therefore a fair amount of mana to break.

Without another word, Zala waved her hand around them, cocooning them in a filter of shadow. Like shadows under the cover of night, they moved in silence through Castle Terrin's courtyard. Inside the dark steel gates, the court was quiet. Grey gravel lined the walkways and in the centre a gargoyle fountain that once gurgled, stood quietly, its water covered in algae. Wilted white-rose bushes lined the main path, leading to the throne room.

They needed to take measured bounds here. Before they entered a space, they would need to send their mana in quickly to feel for any traps or triggers. If the Fates were in their favour, it would only be the throne room that contained a spell of sorts, if at all.

They approached the large oak floor-to-ceiling doors of the throne room with trained silence. Elowan watched as Zala placed a gentle hand on the door, sending out a tendril of her shadowy mana to feel for traps. Her eyes narrowed in concentration.

One second.

Two.

Zala pulled her hand away and shook her head. There was nothing. Now that was a surprise. Elowan raised an eyebrow.

Zala shrugged her shoulders.

Too easy, Elowan thought. The queen was smarter than that, right?

Quietly, Elowan and Zala slipped in. The throne room was empty. Completely empty. Not even a bug had deigned to call this place its home for the night. Elowan and Zala parted. One took one side of the room while the other scanned the other side.

Elowan scanned the tapestries, the carpet, the seats – anything that would show signs of disturbance or high foot traffic. Even the way dust settled across the floor would be a sign. There could be a trapdoor or the oracle could be glamoured. It was a meticulous task that required time and patience but here they both were, working against the sands of time with only a few grains left to tick over.

Every few metres Elowan turned around to check on Zala. Operating in silence wasn't easy, but there were small things they could do to keep communication lines open between them.

Elowan scanned high and low, right to left, all the way to the dais. She turned to Zala who had reached the same place across the other side of the dais. Elowan locked eyes with the wraith and shook her head. Zala did the same. Nothing still.

Shit. Time is running out.

They both scanned the sides of the dais, moving swiftly and methodically to its centre.

Elowan circled the throne, scanning for any disturbances. If she were the queen, she'd hide the oracle close by. She scanned the floor around the throne, but there was nothing.

Elowan could feel Zala's proximity. While Zala's shadows kept them invisible and camouflaged for the most part, if you were close enough you could see the ripples of the air that separated them from reality.

Elowan examined the reflections of the throne's shining surface. Perhaps there was a lever, a special button.

It was then Elowan noticed. As Zala moved in the background, her shadows appeared. Then disappeared. Then reappeared.

Elowan turned swiftly, catching Zala in time to signal to her. Elowan held up a hand, halting Zala in place. She pointed to the throne and asked Zala to move back and forth again with a wave of her hand.

Zala obeyed. They repeated the same thing but closer to the throne until Zala's shadows did not register at all against the reflection of the throne.

Got you.

Zala caught on. There was something blocking her shadows, changing its consistency in the air. Something like a glamour. As the realisation struck, so did the sounds of heavy footsteps down the hallway.

Fuck.

Whoever it was, was by themselves.

Zala maintained her shadows while Elowan worked her mana against the glamour. She skipped the niceties, pulling up her sleeve to gather small rivulets of blood with a quick flick of her short spear. With urgency, she drew the ancient-Fae unlocking symbol on the floor next to the throne where she estimated that the glamour sat.

The footsteps outside grew louder. They were only a few steps away from the door of the throne room.

The ancient-Fae symbol with its swirls and curves burned to life, then guttered. The glamour dropped to the floor like a heavy curtain, revealing exactly what they were looking for. Hunched on the ground with two thick chains fastened around its wrists was the oracle, Praeteritus. It was thin and its skin somehow less alive than its siblings. A wheeze escaped the oracle. Was it even alive? Elowan approached it with caution, still under the protection of Zala's shadows.

With a crash, the door of the throne room burst open.

No.

The sweet and spicy scent was a slap to the face, almost making Elowan gag. Zala turned to face the intruder with her feet planted firmly on the floor. His long dark hair, hollow eyes and dark aura were the last thing Elowan wanted to see.

Kaine.

Elowan and Zala stayed impossibly still, every muscle tensed and ready to pounce. The oracle still lay slumped on the floor, unmoving.

Kaine scanned the throne room, not realising that Elowan and Zala were just a few metres away from him, shrouded by a blanket of shadow. His nostrils flared, sniffing about the room.

Shit, my blood.

The smell of her blood betrayed her.

Kaine chuckled. "Ellie, you can't hide from me. I can feel your mana." He sauntered all the way to the dais, standing mere inches away from where Zala and Elowan stood, braced for a fight.

"It's a shame you decided to play enemy. Your power would be useful to the blood throne." Kaine made clicking noises with his tongue, as if she were some sort of dog. He roamed back down the dais with his arms out wide, ready to catch her. How arrogant.

It took every ounce of willpower to not bitch slap Kaine in the face right now, but getting the oracle out the throne room was priority. Elowan nudged Zala on the elbow and motioned to the oracle. Zala nodded.

One.

Two.

Three.

Elowan thrusted her short spear into the space between her and Kaine. It was a speeding bullet with death written all over it, but Kaine was too quick. He ducked and rolled back. Her short spear lodged itself into the throne room door with a *THWACK*.

Kaine still didn't know where she was in the room. Elowan could tell by the way his eyes darted around, scanning.

Zala had dived to free the oracle of its chains. The wraith was more adept at identifying locks and unpicking them with her shadows. And Elowan . . . Well, Elowan just wanted a chance to beat the shit out of Kaine.

That's when Elowan felt it. The shadows that camouflaged Elowan dropped.

Game on.

Elowan let out a battle cry as she charged for Kaine with Cam's short spear in her hand, the gems glinting with light of the lamps surrounding the throne room. They crashed into each other in the centre of the room. Steel bouncing left, right and centre against more steel. Elowan grunted against Kaine's strength. He was so much stronger than when they used to train together. It was unnerving.

Slash. Stab. Hook. None of her blows landed. He parried and dodged with unnatural speed but at least she could still throw him off balance. She kicked out a leg, sending his knee straight for the ground. Elowan took the chance to roll backward and sprinted for the door where her first short spear had lodged itself. She kicked up against the door and jumped high to snatch the short spear out of the wood. As she came down she unleashed her fire, engulfing her entire body in the flames of her mana. She arched back, driving both short spears down onto Kaine. She felt fucking magnificent.

Kaine dodged, sending his own balls of air to quell her fire, throwing her up into the throne room ceiling. He was barely fighting back. Elowan could feel it in the air. He was holding back.

Elowan fell to the ground at an alarming speed but broke free of Kaine's mana in time to duck and roll. If she fell any harder, her shoulder would probably have dislocated. Elowan rolled off the pain throbbing in her shoulder. "Did taking the blood-oath make you weak?" Elowan laughed, panting heavily. She stood up from the ground. They circled one another, like two jungle cats ready to fight.

"Ellie—" Kaine started.

"Don't call me that." Elowan cut him off. That nickname was reserved for the people she loved.

"We could use a strong Fae like you."

"The chance to recruit me for anything died the moment you killed Camrine."

Kaine snarled and spat. "He deserved it, Elowan, you know that. You cannot argue with me on that." His eyes bulged in hatred and he shook his head erratically. He was *insane*.

They continued circling one another in the centre of the blood-red throne room. Elowan couldn't see Zala. The shadow shields around her remained as she worked to free the oracle. It would only be a matter of time.

Come on, Z.

"I will argue until my dying breath when it comes to you, Kaine. You deserve the hell that you buried yourself in."

"I have access to power that Fae like you dream of having. I get to be the hero. I get to save the day and rid all realms of the Tienthan. You could join me."

"You're fucking delusional is what you are, Kaine."

"Don't you see? They've brainwashed you—" Kaine's poor excuse of a speech was cut short with a whip of Zala's shadows.

Elowan ducked, her eyes wide at the display of power. The blade of shadow cracked through the air, striking him through his right shoulder. Her power had shot right through him easily. Too easily.

Kaine groaned, clutching his shoulder, blood already slipping through his fingers.

"Ellie!" Zala shouted from the dais.

Elowan turned to see the oracle had been freed. Its frail body lay limp in Zala's arms. Elowan didn't hesitate. She pulled on her mana, forming a giant whip of vengeful fire. She'd been waiting for an opportunity like this. With a deadly crack, she whipped her mana around Kaine's throat.

He struggled against it, clawing at the flames that singed his hands. There was no release from this.

"I hope the world you love burns to cinders and you with it," Elowan sneered. She yanked her whip down so hard that his face violently smashed against the floor. The crunch of his bones would satisfy her for years to come. Kaine lay still on the ground for just a moment.

Elowan took that second to pull deep down into her mana, opening a portal just beside Zala for her to jump in. Without hesitation, Zala jumped into the portal with the oracle held firmly against her.

Elowan turned to find Kaine groaning and bracing his face as he came to in the centre of the throne room. Elowan sprinted and dived for the portal entrance. As her feet left the ground, she turned midair and faced Kaine one more time.

As Elowan crossed the glittering edges of the portal, she smiled widely and pulled up her two middle fingers, sending one clear and deserved message.

A scowl so foul burned into Kaine's face as the edges of the portal rippled closed.

Fuck you, Kaine.

30

KAINE

Remember who this is all for. Kaine repeated to himself.

Kaine watched as Queen Calliea savaged the entire throne room. She pulled down tapestries and launched chairs between a frenzy of shrieks and heavy breaths. He wanted to be anywhere but here. What a waste of his damned time.

"This is all your fault!" Queen Calliea shrieked and pointed a red, dagger-like finger at him. The sight of the queen like this would have sent enemies' knees shaking, but not Kaine. He stood tall and unfazed at the bottom of the dais.

Queen Calliea stormed up to Kaine and even though she was shorter than him, she somehow looked down her nose at him. Her eyes widened with anger, and her chest rumbled with rage like a rattlesnake ready to attack.

An invisible hand grasped the blood in Kaine's veins, weakening his knees, making him kneel. He hated how the strings of the blood-oath felt. Like a puppet, he succumbed to its ministrations.

Remember who this is all for.

Kaine stayed quiet. He knew this was coming.

Queen Calliea wrapped a spindly hand around his jaw, letting her claws sink into the skin of his cheeks. Any harder and she may as well have ripped his jaw out – but she didn't. "Why didn't you stop them?" her tone softened.

"I had no choice," Kaine strained. Of course, he had a choice.

Her grip tightened and he felt the strings of the blood-oath pulling at his veins again. It squeezed the life from his blood cells. "You had no choice?" Queen Calliea scoffed.

Kaine tried to fight against the admission. "They beat me to it. I held back. I thought I could gain another strong soldier for us—"

"You weren't thinking about *us* when you were holding back, Captain Aaryn. No, you were thinking about *you*. Because if you were thinking about the blood throne, you would have slaughtered them without hesitation," Queen Calliea seethed.

"She is strong—"

A piercing slap landed across his face. It left Kaine speechless. Blood began to well on his face. He could feel a drop of blood slowly dripping as his cheek burned and the sting alone ebbed into his eyes.

"What did I say about talking back?"

Another slap landed across his face.

And then another.

The raging animal inside him simmered to the surface of his skin. He couldn't hurt her. As much as he wanted to, the blood-oath restricted him. This was all Elowan's fault. If only she stopped being so stubborn, he would have been able to help her see that the blood throne was the side to swear allegiance to. They had the power to take on any enemy. She called him insane. *She* was insane for not seeing clearly. And mother of Faery, the next time he saw her, he would have her head. His blood and this embarrassment lay on her hands alone.

"You wanted my trust? You want to *share* my power?" She paused. "Well consider your chances squandered." Queen Calliea pushed his head back with a soul-crushing hand to his face. He fell to his ass, sprawled across the floor like a damned imbecile.

A growl started in Kaine's chest. He'd done so much for this female. He'd taken the blood-oath, he'd won the allegiance of several courts and entered into a marriage for this female. Hell, he was only helping her out and making her look good. She was a measly detour for what his end goal was, and still, it wasn't enough for her?

Queen Calliea stalked to her throne. Though she stilled as an electricity of sorts skittered through the room. The ground hummed and rumbled with power. Thunder boomed outside. A rip in the seams of reality appeared behind Queen Calliea. They both stopped to watch.

Ominous blue light seeped through the seams of the ragged portal, unlike anything Kaine had seen before. The smell of decay billowed through. Smoke, grey and opaque, spilled through the entrance. Kaine held his breath, his short spear already out and poised to attack.

"At last . . ." A deep booming voice echoed from the portal.

Shivers scurried down Kaine's spine like tiny spiders. His throat dried and his hands grew cold.

Immediately, Queen Calliea was on her knees. The *queen* was on her knees.

What in Faery is going on? Kaine was obliged to do the same, but he was torn between attacking what was about to come through, protecting the queen and protecting himself.

From the portal, a figure, eight-foot tall, stood, its silhouette highlighted by the blue light. Muscles bulged in places Kaine thought no male of this world could ever possess. Horns protruded and curled from its forehead. The being stepped into full view. His skin was an unorthodox blue. Bright blue flames for hair spilled down to his shoulders. His eyes were entirely red. His teeth razor-sharp and his dark blue lips curled in a wicked grin. The only thing covering the god of the underworld was a dark blue loin cloth. And in his hand, a staff skewered with several skulls towered over him. It rattled with every step he took.

It was Terr, the Shadow Realm King, in all his might and glory.

Kaine gulped and moved swiftly to his knees, his breath growing colder as the king neared. The unfettered power that emanated from the underworld god was nothing like Kaine had ever experienced in all his life. The power shrunk his mana to a tiny marble. And if Terr so much as flinched or moved, Kaine was sure that his own mana would run away squeaking like a terrified mouse.

Gods be damned, this male is powerful . . . and I need it all.

". . . we meet." Terr stood with his arms out in welcome, a mischievous grin plastered wide across his face.

Kaine bowed his head lower.

The queen shot up from where she knelt. "Darling, I wasn't expecting yo—"

"Leave usss." Terr's voice boomed and hissed at the same time, sending shivers all over Kaine's body.

The queen looked torn. She shot her eyes to Kaine's, trying to decipher what was unfolding before her. Whatever this interaction was, it had caught her off guard. But Calliea was smart, she knew heeding Terr's words was probably the better choice. She picked up the skirts of her blood-red gown and walked swiftly to and out the throne room doors. Was that fear that ran through her eyes?

Kaine maintained his bowed form, his eyes fixed upon the ground again. Kaine could feel the eyes of Terr upon him. Like a hot knife being held to the back of his neck.

The throne room door clicked shut.

"Ahhh, my pet has spoken highly of youu . . ." Terr's voice hissed and purred as he surveyed Kaine. With each step he took, his skull-adorned staff clattered with the rattles of death. An invisible hand drew Kaine's head back, craning his neck to look at Terr, right in the eyes. "Let me see, let me seeee . . ."

Kaine had to admit that Terr, the devil, was handsome. A strong jawline, clean-shaven, otherworldly cheekbones and those blood-red eyes that could haunt someone for days. His power and essence it felt . . . familiar.

"Eyes of green, eyes of greennn and your powerrr"—the Shadow Realm king, with preternatural speed, pulled Kaine's hair back and took a deep breath in along Kaine's throat. It was oddly intimate, but Kaine wasn't about to deny the devil. Terr pulled back, a low maniacal laughter leaving his throat.

The invisible grip that held Kaine's head back relented. He massaged his neck and with determination, he addressed the king, "Your Majesty. It's an honour."

Remember who this is all for.

"Oh where have they been hiding youuu?" A deep chuckle left Terr's throat. "The honour is mine, Breaker of Realmssss . . ." A saccharine smile etched across Terr's face.

Breaker of Realms?

On a whim of his mana, Terr manifested a throne of storm clouds to sit upon. The room turned dark, and the walls of the throne room turned black. It was like they had transported to another realm.

"Let me guess, you wish to commandeer my army of the dead, for what pray tellll . . . ?"

Was there even a point in speaking?

"To defeat the Tienthan of the Godlands. They have stolen what is truly and rightfully mine. For that they will pay."

"Ahhh, your soulmate." Terr leaned back into his cloud throne and laughed. "A favour like that has a steep price not many are willing to payyy."

"Name your price. I'll do what it takes." Kaine squared his shoulders, embodying the confident captain of the Elite and Faery's strongest warrior again. This was his chance, handed to him on a damned silver platter. Whatever it was, Kaine would do it. His Sophie was waiting in the Godlands. She was waiting for him, and time was wasting away.

In a blink, Terr's cloud throne came closer. Kaine now knelt at Terr's feet. It was an uncomfortable place to be. Terr leaned over and whispered something in Kaine's ear.

At the words, Kaine's eyes widened but only for a second. He schooled his face back into neutrality. He would do it. He needed to.

Remember who this is all for. He uttered these words until they became a holy hymn, the words marring his skin for lifetimes to come.

Terr sat back into his cloud throne. "You could have it allll. Your full strength has yet to unleassshh itself. Do this and I will allow you access to my armyyy"—he took in a sharp breath—"I will teach you all you need to knowww." Terr paused and smirked. "My Breaker of Realmssss."

The Fleeting Forest was quieter, darker and staler than the last time he'd been here several weeks ago. The blight running rampant through Faery had finally hit the western edges of Soxis and the results were devastating. The once full-of-life forest was now grey and dull. With a thunderous storm pounding down from above, it painted the perfect picture for the crime Kaine was about to willingly commit.

It wasn't long after naming his price that Terr had portalled himself back to the Shadow Realm. In the mist and wake of his leaving, he left something. A flute. It was small, the size of Kaine's palm, and carved from bone. It drew him in and smelled of blood and darkness. Its smooth, cool surface was bone-chillingly cold in his hands.

Kaine had found a large enough clearing in the Fleeting Forest. What he was about to do was a small sacrifice for the greater good but still, something ate away at his conscience. What would Sophie say? Would his soulmate agree to this?

Kaine shook his head. Of course Sophie would want this. She would want her soulmate to find her by whatever means necessary. Kaine knew deep in his tattered soul that she would do the same for him. He knew it. Just like how he knew that even after the darkest of nights, the sun would rise.

Kaine sat on the forest floor, the wet grass beneath him crunching and sliding. He was surrounded by large thick oak trees. And above, the Faery double-ringed moon sat, watching him, playing witness. Slowly, he pulled the flute to his lips. The touch of it was cold at first but slowly it warmed. He pulled his mana from the pit in his stomach and blew softly. It rattled to life with a few eerie dissonant notes.

He paused, then blew into the flute again. This time with a bit more gusto. His fingers flew across the instrument, taking on a life of their own. With that, the magic of the flute began. A menacing melody lifted into the air, bounding and jumping, dancing its way through the forest. From the corner of his eyes, Kaine could see where the melody danced. The trees of the forest flinched and bent out of its way to avoid the siren song. He hoped the melody reached its rightful listeners. Minutes had passed and the melody had turned into a harrowing, mournful song. His fingers slowed, stretched and bowed as they flew across the flute.

There, a rustle of a branch in the corner of his eye.

Then another.

Then another.

It was working. Slowly, the little figures made their way toward him. Their eyes glazed over like the walking dead. The rain poured but it did not matter. It did not faze them. The ominous melody had lulled and lured them here, to this very spot where Kaine sat in the rain. Right where he wanted them.

The children of Faery, from the courts of Wrenntia, Soxis and Fyllera, inched closer and closer to him. Into the clearing. Kaine had found out that Wrenntia and Fyllera had sought refuge in Soxis after the blight had rendered their land unliveable. It was the perfect puzzle piece to the jigsaw that was his plans. Kaine continued the melody for a few minutes more. Until there were enough.

Forty, rain-soaked children of all ages sat silently in front of him. Their legs crossed and their eyes unblinking. Lightning cracked and thunder boomed overhead. As the sound of the angry sky ebbed, the sound of rustling leaves and the heavy thudding of feet cut through the air. Kaine's ears twitched toward the noise. He sniffed the air.

Checkmate.

With his Fae speed, Kaine fixed the flute away and whisked a giant dome of impenetrable air around the children. With the melody of the flute no longer infiltrating their minds, the children began to stir.

He turned to face his new guest. "It's been a while."

"Indeed," Regin breathed.

The blond-haired blacksmith stood at the edge of the clearing. His white-blond hair clung to his face and his light-purple eyes shone with panic, darting back and forth between Kaine and the children trapped behind him. Regin pulled his arms up in front of him – an attempt to calm Kaine. But the funny thing was, Kaine was already calm. His heart was a steady beating drum and his breaths borderline still. The power he longed for was at the tips of his fingers. He just needed to reach out to have it all. He only had one thing to do.

"What are you planning to do with them?" Regin flicked his chin toward the children.

Kaine smirked. "Nothing." An obvious lie.

Another voice sounded from the lip of the clearing. "Let them go," said Lady Ollette, High Lady of Soxis. Her voice was delicate but strong. Powerful. Other Fae lined up beside her. Some weeping and others downright angry. The parents of the children then.

Kaine scoffed. His neck and jaw twitching just the slightest. "I'll let them go, if he can break through my wind shield." Kaine smiled and pointed at Regin. He knew Regin wouldn't be able to. Anyone in Faery, barring the queen and Terr, wouldn't be able to. Regin was just a lowly Fae, a blacksmith at that, and Kaine wanted to make sure he knew his place. Especially after what Elowan had done to embarrass Kaine. Payback was sweet.

A tick started in Regin's jaw. He did not move. The children began to cry. Some even tried to claw their way out of the shield. Kaine wouldn't have it. With a twist of his fist, he restricted the oxygen in his shield, making it thicker. The children stilled, sensing the change. The parents stilled too. An older male ran toward the children. With a push of his mana, Kaine threw him backward. The male landed with a harrumph, groaning in pain as he tried to right himself.

"Let them go," Lady Ollette demanded again, stepping forward ahead of the crowd.

"As I said, not unless he"—Kaine pointed to Regin again—"breaks the shield."

"You of all people know that I do not possess the mana to break your shield. You're asking the impossible." Regin simmered, but stood tall, fists bunched up beside him.

There was something about how the words left Regin's lips that cracked the dam holding back Kaine's anger. The way he stood, unwavering defiance despite his obvious shortcomings. *FLASH.* Kaine rushed to Regin. His incisors mere centimetres from ripping the blacksmith's face off.

Regin did not budge.

"You're not even going to try? Not even for the children?" Kaine egged him on.

Regin pushed Kaine out of his space with his muscled arms. The blacksmith had strength and gall, Kaine would give him that.

Lady Ollette powered ahead of the crowd and stood in front of Regin, shielding him from Kaine. "You are on Soxis soil. You must do as I say. Let the children go or else." She braced her tanned hands in front of her, ready to strike Kaine with her earth mana.

"Or else what?" Kaine twisted his hands, making the shield around the children shrink. The children screamed as they crushed against one another.

Regin pushed forward ready to attack but Lady Ollette caught him by the back of his shirt. Regin let out a furious growl.

Kaine laughed. *Elowan chose to be with him? Despicable.* "If you will not even attempt to break the shield to free the children of these hard-working, fair Fae folk here,"—Kaine pointed to group of parents who pierced him with glares—"then perhaps . . ."

"Out with it, you bastard," Regin sneered.

"Then perhaps you can kneel"—Kaine crossed his arms—"to me." The rain poured down as the words left his mouth. In this very moment, Kaine felt indestructible. A group of Fae and a high lady of the courts stood before him with fear struck in their bones.

Regin screwed his face and spat on the ground at Kaine's feet.

Kaine tightened his grip around the children again, stealing their air. He could hear some of them fainting. The parents screamed.

"I'll never fucking kneel to you," Regin spat at Kaine's feet again.

"Is that so?" From behind Kaine, the children sounded.

"Help! He's taking our air, Mama!" a little boy screamed.

"Papa, please help us!" a little girl shouted from the group.

Regin shook his head. Closed his eyes. What was that? Resolve? Determination? He opened his eyes again and it was unmistakable. His eyes wished death upon Kaine – an all-too-familiar look that Kaine often used on his enemies. The torment on Regin's face only made Kaine happier.

Regin stepped a foot forward, the rain battering him, whipping him . . . and he began his descent. The movement was slow. Every inch of his being fighting against it.

Just as his knee was to kiss the ground, Lady Ollette dragged Regin up by the scruff of his neck and pushed him back behind a wall of earth she had pulled from the ground. The high lady of Soxis stepped closer to Kaine. "We will not kneel to a tyrant. If you do this, you will have defied the essence of what it means to be Fae. You will have *destroyed* lives, and you will never reach the Elysian Fields. Your soul will wander the Resting Ruins and gods be damned, you will deserve every single hell it serves you," Lady Ollette spat, her teeth bared.

The words twisted in all the wrong ways and unleashed the beast that prowled underneath Kaine's skin. Darkness clouded his vision. With a good measure of mana, he sent Lady Ollette flying back into the crowd of angered Fae with a gust of his air. She screamed. Regin charged at him. Kaine let him close enough to slam him with a wall of air, then sauntered over to the male who now lay flat on the grass. And with ease, as if he were a feather, Kaine picked Regin up with one hand wrapped around his thick neck.

Regin struggled against Kaine's grip, spitting in his face. The dollop of spit felt warm against his rain-slicked skin.

Kaine let it slide down his face. As it blended into the cold rain, he smiled a wide, toothy grin. "Send Elowan my regards, will you?" With a twist of his hand, Kaine closed the air shield he had around the children and misted them into meagre droplets of blood. Once living and breathing, now gone.

Just. Like. That.

Kaine watched with unbridled satisfaction as Regin's eyes widened, registering what had transpired within a fraction of second.

"You son of a—" Regin started but Kaine threw him on a gust of wind before he could finish, slamming him into the parents that wailed and pined for their lost children.

Kaine turned back to where the children were. So much blood painted the grass. A beautiful nightmare.

Kaine tilted his head. His hands glowed as he used his mana to collect all the drops of blood. He suspended the large mass into the air and held it there for just a moment. Soaking in the moment for what it was. So much power and potential lived inside this blood. This blood meant more than just power; it represented freedom. It represented winning.

Remember who this is all for.

Kaine released his mana. The mass of blood dropped ceremoniously to the ground into a roaring sea of red, forming an ancient-Fae symbol. The symbol glowed and glittered despite the rain.

Then it burned.

Kaine breathed in the scent, hot and acidy.

The trees near the clearing shook with violence. The ground rumbled and cracked. Kaine lifted himself upon a gust of wind and watched as the ground in the clearing fell away. He could no longer hear the screams and shouts of the Fae behind him. It was just Kaine and his very own creation.

Bright red lava-like matter rushed up to the surface and began to swirl in a giant whirlpool. The heat alone almost burned Kaine, but he did not quake in fear. He did not baulk or run. Kaine simply watched as the gateway to the Shadow Realm ripped into the very soil of Faery. The shrieks and cries of

Shadow Realm demons spilled through the gateway. The sounds were a melody that quelled the anger in his veins and invigorated him.

He did it. A permanent gateway to the Shadow Realm. And Kaine was the only Fae strong enough to make it. A smile bright and wild stretched across his face.

Love was a powerful thing. A name in which kings and queens started bloody wars. It was a fire that burned, strong and deadly and, gods be damned, Kaine was burning in it.

"This is all for you," he finally whispered.

31

ELOWAN

Elowan tumbled through the portal, landing in a crouch in the oracles' tent.

Zala was on her knees, watching Relicuus and Praesens hover over their long-lost sibling. They chanted feverishly in another language as their hands waved all about. Smoke and shadows danced around Praeteritus, its body lying flat on a bed of cushions.

Elowan stood from her crouch and rested a gentle hand on Zala's shoulder. The wraith looked up at Elowan but said nothing.

They both watched in silence as the two oracles revived the third.

It was far more intimate than Elowan felt comfortable with. The world around her quietened, and perhaps Faery itself was waiting to see what happened.

In a blink, the oracles before them disappeared in a plume of black smoke.

"I'm going to take that as a sign to leave . . ." Elowan had no idea what just happened. The oracles were working like madmen and then they weren't there at all.

Zala nodded, standing swiftly on silent feet.

As they moved out of the tent, soft murmurs from outside the tent sounded. It was the villagers. They were stirring.

Elowan moved swiftly through the flaps of the tent to see what the commotion was.

Children squealed in excitement. Others chattered, while others gasped. They all congregated to the centre of the village, where the three oracles stood.

Standing together like that, with their backs to one another, painted a holy divine image that would be burned into Elowan's memory for all time.

Together the past, present and future stood.

The secret village of peace that they wrought in the fires of despair and uncertainty, crowded around them. Hugging them. Crying.

It sparked a morsel of envy in Elowan. She thought back to the peace she'd found in Regin and his family, and she longed to feel that peace again.

"Now what?" Zala asked watching the village, now whole.

"Once two become three, the future of Faery will see . . . I don't know what the oracle meant but perhaps it's just a matter of waiting."

Once two become three, the future of Faery will see. Closer to the end perhaps for some, but close to the sun a war will be won.

Elowan tried to make sense of it, but nothing came to mind. It stirred the anxious beast inside her that baulked at the thought of uncertainty.

A female wrapped in tan linen approached them, her eyes soft with a smile. "Come join us. We will gather by the fire and share a meal tonight."

The female did not give them a chance to object.

Elowan turned to Zala.

The wraith shrugged her shoulders and followed the female through the tall grass.

"This is my daughter Sayuri, and my husband Enda," the female that approached them earlier picked her daughter up, holding her on her hip, and placed a loving hand on her husband's shoulder. The female introduced herself as Anya.

They were all wrapped up in warm-coloured linen, with just their eyes on show.

"How long has your family been living here in the Untold Valley?" Elowan asked, grabbing a potato from the sack of vegetables, peeling it.

Zala stood just a few paces away, standing above a cauldron and stirring it occasionally. The fire underneath it crackled and popped. Embers flew into the cool night air.

"Many generations. My great grandparents were the first to move here from the mainland," Anya relayed as she moved about the camp, setting her daughter down into a cot just outside her tent. "Is this the first time you've been to the Western Wastes?"

It felt like a loaded question.

"It's our first time," Elowan pointed between Zala and herself.

"And how are you finding it?"

Elowan thought on it for a moment, and landed on, "Peaceful."

Anya laughed.

Her husband Enda had moved to the cauldron to assist Zala in loading all the vegetables they had been peeling.

Anya pulled up next to Elowan, sitting upon a wooden stool. She pushed up the sleeves of her linen blouse, revealing golden tan skin. She picked up a knife and began to peel the remaining potatoes.

"You'll find that some people here are not overly welcoming of strangers. As a village, we've been deeply hurt. It's why we hide. To protect ourselves and our way of life."

"It seems like a way of life worth protecting."

"The oracles do not seek power, they seek balance and understanding. It's why our forebears moved to the Western Wastes. If that is what you seek then there's a home for you here among us. Only if you wish." Anya smiled, the corners of her brown eyes lifting with warmth.

Elowan paused for a moment. "I'd like that."

Together, they carried the final peeled vegetables to the cauldron.

"So this is what peace feels like." Zala sighed as she lay on the grass, watching the Faery stars above as they danced to a happy song.

Elowan finished the final dredges of the rich vegetable soup they had shared with the villagers of the Untold Valley. The beautiful voice of a young female sounded throughout the camp, supported by the melodious plucks of a lyre. She sang a song of hope.

"Once this shitshow is over, I'm moving here. I don't care what you say." Elowan laughed.

Zala laughed too. "Take me with you."

This sliver of quiet and serenity was a breath they needed to take. Between finding allies and fighting former allies, they hadn't had a chance to recharge.

Sitting under the moon with the fresh night air felt like they were back in Faery before the whole ordeal with Queen Calliea came to light. Back when they were a family who trained and ate together. There was no threat of looming war. It was a time of peace.

A low, soft whisper carried through the air. It wasn't the young female that sang a hopeful song for everyone. The voice was feminine still, but older.

Elowan sat up fully and looked around.

Zala didn't seem fazed at all. She even had her eyes closed, with her hands braced behind her head.

The low, softer whisper sounded again.

This time, Zala jolted up from where she lay. She looked around, searching for the source.

"Did you hear that?" Elowan asked.

Zala nodded and moved swiftly to her feet. Elowan followed. They skirted around the villagers who ate and shared hushed conversations by the fire.

Together, Elowan and Zala followed the soft whispers. It led them to the oracles' tent, the flaps of its entrance billowing in welcome. They walked inside and like before, the room was shrouded in thick smoke. Elowan shielded her face and felt for a cushion to kneel upon.

With a hiss and a click, the black smoke receded to reveal the three oracles. Relicuus sat on the left, Praesens sat in the middle, and sitting on the right was Praeteritus – restored to perfectly good health. Its skin was less paper-like, and its green eyes were full of life.

"We are grateful . . ."—Praesens paused—"our two has at last, become three," its voice croaked.

"Our word is all you will have. We have no blood to spill and bind," Relicuus explained.

"As a token of appreciation and a symbol of our word, we give you an opportunity," Praeteritus continued, its voice sounding weathered and oldest of the three oracles.

They all spoke one after another, as if they finished each other's thoughts and sentences.

Without warning, the oracles threw back their heads, possessed, their green eyes rolled back to show only the whites of their eyes. The room began to spin, turning black and dark. The interior of the tent disappeared completely and now they hovered in a black and empty space. Elowan recognised the glittery particles that floated in the air. They were in the Between.

Elowan's heart began to race and her breath echoed into the nothingness. She turned to Zala who looked equally confused.

The three oracles before them intertwined their hands and lifted them in the air.

A violent wind picked up through the confines of the black space, whipping Elowan's red hair all around.

Together, the oracles spoke. It was a melody of voices; young, mature and old. "The war will spill beyond two realms, as the pot of power overwhelms. The connections you seek, they can be won. Find the flaming purple heart, who lays with the sun."

As the last word left their blackened lips, the oracles craned their necks in strange angles, like they did before. With a breath of relief, their eyes turned green again.

It was a sight Elowan didn't think she'd ever get used to.

With a wave of their hands, they conjured a plume of black smoke in the centre of the dark room. The light that shone directly above them was the only source of illumination.

The glittery plume of smoke dissipated to reveal a relic of ancient Faery.

Elowan and Zala gasped.

It was a Wayfinder. An ancient bridge that connected Faery to the Godlands. Its rainbow, iridescent centre, glittered and glowed against the intense light above them.

"The answers you seek are not here. But as a sign of trust, we give you this," Relicuus broke the silence.

"The Wayfinder," Praesens followed.

"An opportunity," Praeteritus rounded them off.

"What do we do?" Elowan asked from where she knelt, no longer on a cushion but on the cold, dark flooring of whatever pocket of space they were in.

"Place your hands upon the Wayfinder and hear the call of the Godlands. The Wayfinder will take you there," Relicuus explained.

It sounded simple enough.

Never in her immortal life did she imagine travelling to the Godlands upon a Wayfinder. They were rumoured to have been destroyed, yet right in front of them, stood the ancient gateway, tucked away into the gaps of reality.

"Find the flaming purple heart, who lays with the sun," Praesens reminded them.

"How will I know when I find them?" Elowan asked, but her mind snagged at the word purple. Then her mana snagged at the words "flaming heart", just like the golden necklace that Sophie always wore around her neck.

Praeteritus stole the words out of her mouth. "You already know her." It smiled.

Elowan turned to Zala, who observed in reverence. Her face schooled into a cool mask, no doubt calculating their next best steps.

Zala nodded.

That was all Elowan needed.

Together they rose from the cool ground and approached the glittering Wayfinder.

Together they laid a hand upon the glassy surface of it, the sounds of a harp-filled melody rushing through their ears. Elowan closed her eyes, heeding the call of the Godlands.

Then she felt it.

A force so strong pulled them from the ground.

For a moment, all she felt was weightlessness and all she could see was light.

PART II THE FALL

The thing about walls is that no one sees the foundations they are built upon. Are they strong, wrought from metal and stone? Or are they built upon paper legs, the foundation flimsy and fickle? Whether of stone or paper, with time, no matter how high they are built, walls often come crumbling down.

32

SOPHIE

It had been a week since that council meeting. The one where Sophie had gone a little over the top with threats against Vestes. A little? Maybe a lot over the top. She was just *impossibly* tired of all the politics. The dry-as-a-wall characters that often made up council members. Why were they always old . . . and annoying?

The cool water of Sophie's courtyard pool surrounded her in a perfect cocoon of calm. She stayed underneath the surface of the water for just a moment before lifting herself up, floating freely on her back. It was a tiny pool, but it was the perfect place to be when the sun burned bright, and the air was thick with humidity.

A knock rapped against her front door. The sharp sounds bolted her upright. Quickly, Sophie sent a tendril of her mana to the front door but found no one there. The hairs on the back of her neck stood up.

Sophie pulled herself out of the pool and quickly dried herself with a wave of her mana. Ever since Ash shared his memory of her father with her, mana came much easier. Sure, the remnants of Kaine still stuck around making her wince every now and then, but her mana was hers, and hers alone.

She jogged to her front door and pulled it open. On the floor lay a golden envelope. Sophie stepped out for just a second to survey the pathways surrounding her villa. There wasn't a trace of disturbance in any direction.

Weird.

Cautiously, she opened the envelope and pulled out the letter. Black ink painted across the piece of parchment.

Shit.

It was a letter from the council. Flustered, Sophie speed read its contents.

Double shit.

Sophie thought the whole idea of her being an infiltrating spy had blown over. Evidently not. Even worse, they wanted her to take a truth serum before the entire council to "make sure" she was not a threat to the Godlands. Today. In two hours.

"And to think I was going to spend the entire day sunbaking and bathing," Sophie muttered. She took a moment to take measured breaths and calmed herself. Then she looked up to the sky, damning all the Fates. Heck, she wasn't sure if looking up to the sky was even relevant anymore given that the Fates lived somewhere in the Godlands . . . she'd have to find them and give them a mouthful for the lousy cards they dealt her in this lifetime.

Moving swiftly to her room, she donned a loose-fitting linen jumpsuit. Pants would be the wiser choice today – in case any fights broke loose. Sophie rushed out the door with the council letter in hand and ran to the black-doored villa just three doors down from hers.

She rapidly knocked on the door, sweating from the humidity that hung in the air and the nervousness the letter had triggered.

Come on. Please be home. Please be home.

"It's my day off, Sofreya, leave me—" Ash started but then noticed the golden envelope Sophie held out in front of her. He eyed it. Then he eyed her, his smoking eyes burning a trail of heat wherever they went. He took the envelope from her hands, stepped aside and held the door open for her. He wore white linen pants and no shirt, his six pack on full display along with a tattoo of intricate swirls that extended from his arms down and across his chest. The sight added another point to the list of things that were making Sophie nervous right now.

Ash quickly shut the door behind him.

Cal jumped up from the couch with his tongue lolling out the side of his mouth. His flaming tail wagged furiously as he waited for Sophie to greet him.

Sophie quickly obliged the hellhound before turning back to Ash. "Read it," Sophie said, as she paced across his living room.

Ash pulled out the letter, his face expressing no emotion whatsoever. When he was done, he looked back up at Sophie.

"What do you think I should do?" Sophie started biting the bottom of her lip. Of course, she was a mess of anxiety, nervousness and annoyance. Fine, the council wanted her to take a truth serum but what questions did they have planned for her? How were they going to spin it their way? Vestes was a slimy slug at best, and there was no doubt in her mind that he had something malicious planned – the slimy types always did.

Cal joined Sophie in her pacing. He was prancing like some sort of show horse with his beady loving eyes looking up at her. "Buddy, we're meant to be angry right now. Not happy." Sophie sighed, looking at the pup and wringing her hands through her hair.

Cal huffed a puff of smoke, narrowed his eyes and continued pacing with Sophie a little more angrily.

Ash scoffed at his hellhound. "At least we know where his loyalties lie." Ash shoved the letter back in the envelope and tossed it on a small table he had by the door as if it were junk mail. He moved to a small bar he had with assortments of alcohol atop it. As he passed Sophie, his white wings bristled.

Sophie's heart fluttered at his proximity.

Ash proceeded to pull out two glasses, pouring an amber liquid in both. He turned, handing one to Sophie before clinking their glasses. He took a sip. Sophie followed suit.

This isn't looking too good.

Sophie perched herself on the edge of the couch, Cal following her every move. Ash had his hip leaning against the bar, pants hanging devastatingly low, showcasing a sinful V of muscles.

Is it getting hotter in here?

"Look. I'm not going to lie. It's going to hurt a little *but*, the more you lean into the truth serum, the less painful it will be." Ash shrugged his shoulders, taking another sip of his drink.

"Painful? What do you mean *painful*?" Sophie gaped.

"Veritas, the truth serum, is the burning sword of truth. It'll rip through your memories to extract the truth and it'll leave you nauseous for a little while. Nothing major."

"Have you tried it before?"

"Yep." The *p* popped as Ash paused. "And I'll do everything in my power to never be exposed to it again."

"You call that *nothing major*?!" Sophie jumped up from where she perched and began pacing again. A spark of fear flashed in her chest. If Ash was a war-hammer hulking god who *never* wanted to be exposed to Veritas again, then what did that spell for Sophie?

"Like I said, lean into it and it won't hurt so bad." Ash put his glass of whiskey down and moved to Sophie, placing two sure hands on her shoulders. "It's not like you've got something to hide, Sofreya." He smiled showing off his two damning dimples, really pulling out the charm to make her feel better. It didn't.

Sophie's eyes widened. She was so not ready to be laid bare in front of a group of grumpy old males. Well, Diafonia and Dikastis weren't old but that wasn't the point. "You're right. I shouldn't be scared. I have nothing to hide," Sophie said, a little too panicked as she pressed her lips into a thin line.

Ash leaned back and folded his arms. He raised a brow. "Wait, why did you say that like you actually have something to hide?"

"I *don't* have anything to hide! Can't you just pull rank and tell them to fuck off?"

"I can, but they'll be on your tail until Vestes gets what he wants."

Ash was right. Damn it. "Fine. I'll rip off the Band-Aid." Sophie sighed, gnawing at her bottom lip. She paused in her tracks. She turned to Ash again who now wore a devilish smile. He was *revelling* in her nervousness and worry.

The audacity of this overgrown pigeon. Sophie narrowed her eyes at him.

"Come on, I'll take you there." Ash reached out with his hand for her to hold.

Sophie pouted her lips, resigning to the fact that the council's request was not really a request but an unavoidable order that would be more beneficial for her than detrimental – as annoying and inconvenient as it may be. She took Ash's hand, and he pulled her toward the front door. As they walked out of his villa, he manifested his white loin-cloth uniform to replace his long linen pants. Sophie swore she caught a flash of butt cheek as he did.

"If I were you, I'd try to stop drooling. The council already thinks you're a spy, let's not add sexual deviant to that list," Ash said all too calmly.

Sophie gasped. Before she could muster a smart remark, he wrapped his arms around her waist and catapulted them into the air.

They landed on the other side of the Isle of Deos before the council building. On the outside, it looked like a white marble courthouse. The scales of justice were sculpted into its front, and giant marble pillars lined the entrance. Marble statues of gods from all realms lined the top of the building.

Sophie ran her fingers through her purple hair, taming it into something presentable after having flown via carrier pigeon. Sophie snickered to herself at her new description of Ash.

Ash raised an eyebrow. "What?"

Sophie tried to hide her smile. "Nothing."

Ash shook his head at her before leading the way to the interrogation room. They walked side by side, through a hallway featuring elaborate painted portraits of generations worth of head of councils and their families. They stopped in front of black double doors. A golden plaque above the door stated, *Interview Room A*.

A knot of nervousness lodged itself in Sophie's chest. She looked up to Ash to find his turquoise smoking eyes dancing with mischief. He'd managed to keep her laughing and groaning in annoyance the whole way here and she appreciated it. "Wish me luck," Sophie sighed. She'd need luck and more to survive this torture, she thought.

"I'll be waiting outside for you." Ash smiled, leaning into the space between them. Subconsciously, Sophie began to lean in too. It was like they were two magnets being pulled closer and closer. Before she knew it, Ash pulled back, opting to give her an awkward punch on the shoulder as if to say, *Good luck, buddy. Go get 'em, tiger.*

Sophie raised an eyebrow at the awkward exchange but before she could say anything, the door to the interrogation room opened on a phantom wind. With her head held high, Sophie marched into the room. It was circular. Tables circled the entirety of the room, fashioned like an amphitheatre. In the centre sat a lone chair. The councilmen sat all around the closest circle of tables.

Sophie scanned the occupants and immediately regretted making eye contact with Vestes.

Fucking hell.

A sneaky, slimy smile plastered itself across his wrinkly pointed face and next to him sat Cessair, the rotund councilman who supported Vestes's idea to interrogate her. All around sat another eight council members who Sophie didn't care to learn the names of. Diafonia and Dikastis weren't present.

Great, the only council members that have their heads screwed on right aren't here.

"You are five minutes late," Vestes drawled. "Sit." He pointed to the lone chair that sat in the middle of the room.

Sophie obeyed, though not without glowering at everyone present in the room to show them how annoyed she truly was.

"Ahem, Taranis, leaving so soon?" Vestes was absolutely delighted with himself.

Sophie whipped her head to the door where Ash stood, his back slightly turned as if he was about to leave. Ash turned slowly back to the room and Sophie swore the air grew thinner as if all the moisture in it had been sucked away. Gone was the playful Ash that carried her across the Isle. In his place was the being that everyone feared.

Sophie examined the room carefully. Everyone except Vestes averted their eyes. Afraid. She couldn't help but let out a small smile.

"I am not needed here," Ash stated, his deep voice rumbling in the room.

Without a word, Vestes sent a small rolled up piece of parchment across the room toward Ash. Her best friend snatched the parchment out of the air and let out an annoyed growl.

"Zeus has requested a member of the Tienthan be seated at this hearing should important information regarding the borders between realms come to light," Vestes said a little too quickly.

Sophie rolled her eyes. *This day cannot get any worse.*

"Get on with it then." Ash stalked down the aisle, his steps measured and painfully slow as he planted himself among the first ring of seats with the council members. A predator. The council member directly next to him looked downright uncomfortable.

Fucking fantastic. Not only did Sophie have to sit through an interrogation with these sad sacks, she had to lay herself bare in front of Ash and while she felt safe with him, she had no idea how Vestes would spin the narrative.

Vestes smiled conspiratorially and cleared his throat. "Sofreya Brighid Taliesin, daughter of Danna Taliesin"—her mother's name came out with a hiss—"you are brought forth before the council today to speak your truth. The answers we seek to pull from you, can and will be used against you in this realm and any realm beyond. Do you understand this?"

"Yes," Sophie said, her voice firm and confident, though her knee trembled just the slightest. She wouldn't let them on to how nervous she really was. She pulled her chin up just a little higher and she swore a spark of challenge lighted in Vestes's eyes.

"By the power of Veritas and the gods that be, the words before me shall only be spoken truthfully," Vestes announced. He waved his hand and a small glass cup appeared in Sophie's hand. In it sat a shot of glittery black liquid. Sophie lifted it to her nose. It smelled sweet and sour all at the same time.

Bottoms up. Sophie gulped down the black glittery truth serum. Veritas, Ash had called it. The grit of it travelled down Sophie's throat, cooling everything inside her.

Oh, it's not so bad.

False. It was bad. Really bad.

A burning sensation that rivalled molten lava started at Sophie's throat then worked its way into every single fibre of Sophie's being. The Veritas burned like a phoenix, twisting through her blood, seizing her throat until it became numb. Sophie sputtered and coughed violently. It took her a few seconds, but she managed to right herself in the chair, staring at Vestes with as much hatred she could possibly muster. Perhaps if she stared hard enough, he would feel the burn of Veritas too.

"We will commence with a few standard questions for calibration purposes," Vestes smiled. He pulled out a piece of paper and began to read. "Are you the daughter of Danna Taliesin and Lou Taliesin?"

"Yes." The words flew out of Sophie before she could even think about what she was going to say.

What the fuck?

"Does that then make you a half-breed, of the Godlands and of Faery?"

So it's going to be like this, huh?

"Yes," Sophie gritted. Half-breed wasn't her preferred term for it, but sure.

From the corner of her eyes, Sophie spotted Ash. He moved onto the next tier of seats to sit directly behind Vestes. His face glowering, promising pain like a storm cloud waiting to strike.

The head of council pulled at the collar of his shirt with a trembling hand and shifted the list of questions closer to his chest. Satisfied with her answers, Vestes continued his line of questioning. "Why did you come to the Godlands?"

Sophie's skin was now on fire, and she wasn't even resisting the effects of Veritas. "I was brought here by Acheron. He heard my call for help."

"And now that you are here in the Godlands, what are your intentions?"

"I have no ill intentions. I'm here to harness my powers and will return to Faery once I do."

Vestes took his time to write down a few notes. "Are you aware of someone named Kaine Dormarth Aaryn? And if so, what relation does he have to you?"

Sophie had a sinking feeling that she was falling straight into the clutches of a very meticulously laid-out trap. She looked to Ash, managing to find him in the chaotic burn of her skin. His face was stern, watching her intently. What was he thinking?

Lean into the truth. That's what Ash had said.

A flicker of hesitation was all it cost to launch her into a coughing fit before she answered between breaths, "I am aware of Kaine. We had a brief relationship during my time in Faery. I once thought we were fated." The words felt like cinders leaving her mouth. Rigid, dry and bitter.

"Are you also aware that he is the prophesised Breaker of Realms?"

Sophie's eyes flicked to Ash's. His wings bristled the slightest as he sat back in his chair with his arms crossed, looking angry as fuck. Did he know this too?

Fuck.

The truth serum pierced a burning hot lance down her throat as Sophie fought against the next few words. "Yes, I am aware that he is the Breaker of Realms."

Shit. Shit. Shit.

It was only a recent revelation. If she had known back in Faery, then perhaps she would have been able to stop him. She would have. She was sure of it.

A murmur erupted from the council room.

Sophie swallowed deeply, trying her best to lean into the ways of the truth serum. The more she tried, the more the invisible daggers that prettily lined her neck seemed to close in. The blades were sharp. The pinch of their tips against her delicate skin, torturous.

Vestes paused to write more notes down. "Are you aware that there has been a breach along the eastern borders of the Godlands?"

"Yes, I am aware." She was telling the truth, but it felt like her own lips were betraying her.

"Given your intimacy with the Breaker of Realms, would you say he has the power and capability of infiltrating the Godlands?"

Sophie ground her teeth, hot tears starting to well in her eyes. She knew what picture this was painting, and she hated every ounce of Vestes for it. She spat out, "He is blood-oathed to Queen Calliea and may have connections to the Shadow Realm through her. He is strong. With his new blood-oath he may be capable." The thing was, she didn't know for sure. She knew how strong he was but had no idea how his powers had progressed since she left Faery.

"Now, the council are aware of the situation that has transpired in Faery and the throne's connections to the Shadow Realm. Given this, why has the Breaker of Realms taken the blood-oath?"

"To gain more power."

"Why?"

"To start a war."

"Why? Or rather for who?"

Sophie took in a deep breath. Vestes wasn't playing fair. He fucking had her *exactly* where he wanted her. And Sophie, in all her stubbornness, fought against the truth serum with every single piece of mana inside her. She wouldn't let Vestes win. No fucking way.

That's when Sophie landed in a different realm of pain. Needles piled haphazardly into her stomach pierced through the organ walls, splitting cell by bloody cell. Her skin ripped apart as the needles wormed their way through her pores. This was the effect of Veritas. The effect of telling the truth. Sophie tried to push through the pain, and she knew she was wailing now. Pained, whole-body-convulsing sort of cries. Had she just fallen off the chair? She couldn't tell. The chokehold of pain stopped for just a second, just enough time for her words to tumble out on a pained whisper, "For . . ."—Sophie sniffled—". . . me."

The room erupted.

"Spy!" A plain-faced councilman stood from his seat, pointing an accusatory finger at Sophie.

She could only see their outlines from where she knelt on the ground. This was the ground right?

"Traitor!" another councilman shouted above the raucous that had set ablaze across the room.

No. No. No.

"Settle down!" Vestes roared above the pandemonium.

CRACK. Thunder, loud and deafening, shook the room – Ash's warning. Sophie pushed herself farther into the ground, hands cradling her ears. Loud. So loud.

A moment passed before the soft murmurs of the council returned. They had already drawn their conclusions. She was a traitor in their eyes. To them, she was well aware of Kaine's powers and capability. To them, she already knew he was the Breaker of Realms and that she of all people, his lover, was the one who beckoned him to wage a war against the Godlands.

Sophie dared to lift her head from the ground, forcing her eyes open through the pain.

"Answer me this. Do you still care for this Kaine Dormarth Aaryn?" Vestes's serpentine smile brought upon the dawn of a dark violence Sophie never knew she possessed. If it wasn't for the truth serum that seemed to hold her in place, she would have gone hell for leather. She would have launched herself at him, a possessed demon, ripping his head off by the might of her own teeth. Consequences be damned.

"You're skating on thin ice, Vestes." Ash's voice was low. Threatening. His arms were crossed as he stood a few paces behind Vestes.

With a dismissive wave of his hand, the head of council warned, "I'd be careful if I were you, Taranis. It might look like you *care* for the enemy."

Vestes was right. Damn him. Sophie tried to meet Ash's eyes, but he was avoiding hers. Instead, Ash let out a strike of lighting. Nothing but simmering anger and annoyance upon his face as the room flashed brightly.

"So, Miss Taliesin, do you or do you not still care for the prophesied Breaker of Realms?" Vestes continued smugly, leaning back into his chair, clasping his hands together.

The council members stirred in their seats but waited eagerly for Sophie to answer the question. Sophie knew the answer that would tumble out of her mouth unwillingly. She hated Kaine with every atom she was made of, but somehow, the tiniest morsel of her still cared for him. That tiniest morsel in her still believed that Kaine was salvageable. That tiny morsel was convinced that she *must* have seen something good in him. It was a tiny, insignificant morsel, but the truth serum couldn't tell the difference, could it?

Sophie let out a gut-wrenching wail, her back arching terribly, as the invisible needles passed through her skin. Sophie let the pain ebb away before she breathed in deeply, wiping the snot from her face. She hung her head in defeat. "I do." As the words left her mouth, she only cared to find Ash. She looked up to see him standing very still, his arms crossed and his face a stern mask. She tried to speak again, to explain, but there an invisible force that held her jaw in a vice. It had to be Vestes. It *had* to be. Someone wasn't playing fair here – not that fair was a term that could ever be used in this room.

Sophie tried to pry her mouth apart again, but all that escaped was a garbled cry.

What was Ash thinking? Sophie wiped her tears with back of her hand. She so badly wanted to yell out that she didn't care for Kaine like *that*.

"Then answer me this, *demigoddess*." The word was poison on his tongue. "Are you . . . his spy?" Vestes was barely holding back a triumphant smile.

The pressure on Sophie's jaw ceased, allowing her to rasp, "No."

A confusion of murmurs flooded the room.

Sophie started again, breaths dry and ragged. "N-" She gripped the arms of the chair again as the invisible vice wrapped around her jaw, sealing it shut.

Vestes quickly stood, his eyes scrunched in confusion for just a millisecond. He wasn't expecting her to say no. He thought he had her. He *really* thought he had her.

Not that it mattered.

With a poise that only came with perfect practise, Vestes righted his bony shoulders and plastered on a sickening smile. "Well, well. It looks like the Veritas has worn off." His voice was a guillotine through the room. "I think we have enough to mark you as a reasonable suspect. As it is not hard evidence as such, we will be keeping a close eye on you. You have been warned, Miss Taliesin." Vestes neatened up his stack of papers as a smug smile appeared on his pointed face. "The truth has set you free."

A small glass of clear glittering liquid manifested before Sophie. An antidote. She fumbled for it like a crazed animal and downed it. Splashes of the antidote dripped down the sides of her mouth. The vice grip that the truth serum had over Sophie's body relented. Sweating, fear-struck and nauseous, Sophie fell to the ground with a soul-cleaving cry, her face scratching against the carpeted floor. She felt like absolute shit, as if she'd been trampled over by a thousand arions. Her stomach lurched. Her vomit spraying across the interrogation room floor in chunks. Wiping the remnants of bile from her mouth, Sophie looked up and locked eyes with Vestes, promising him that he would suffer the most gruelling, torturous death by her hands and her hands alone.

Fucking cunt.

Vestes's smug smile faltered just the slightest before switching his gaze to the rest of the room. The councillors had already begun to leave. He gathered his papers hurriedly and rushed out of the room without so much as another glance in Sophie's direction.

Sophie lay on the floor for a while longer, trying to catch her shaky breath. Her limbs were leaden, her head was spinning uncontrollably. Though through her tilting world, she heard the beat of his strong wings before she saw him crouched before her, mere inches away. Sophie averted her gaze, embarrassed and unsure, tucking into a tight, messy ball of a being. She didn't want him to see her like this.

With warm fingers, Ash brushed the sweat, tear and bile-slicked hair away from her face. The light of the room washed over her eyelids the same time her skin washed over with the anticipation of what he was going to do next.

To her surprise, he traced her jawline with a gentleness that no warrior should possess. It only made her shy away, scrunching her eyes as if she could make him disappear.

I don't want you to see me like this.

But it seemed that Ash *did*. He lifted her chin, brushing the pad of his thumb in encouragement. "Sofreya." His voice was soft, hushed. He waited for her. He waited until her eyes softened and fluttered open to look at him.

There Ash was. A glint of concern in his eyes. He let go of her chin. "Can I please take you home?"

The polite, patient, *please* broke her. Of course he could. Sophie tried to speak but all she could muster was a pouted nod as tears found their way down her face again.

Without another word, he moved to pull her into his arms, held her tight against his chest and carried her out of the interrogation room.

33

ACHERON

Ash wanted to skin the entire council alive.

The interrogation they had planned for Sophie was pointless. It did nothing but paint her as someone who could not be trusted, just as they wanted it to. He should have fought against it when Sophie suggested that he pull rank, but he didn't think Vestes would be so cruel. By the time she ingested the serum, it was too late. They had to see the interrogation through.

That's my fault for wanting to see the good in people. I should have known.

And now, Sofreya lay shivering in his arms as he flew across the Isle. The look in her eyes, of shame and fear, haunted him. She'd come so far since arriving in the Godlands, he hoped that he had not set her up for failure by letting her run into the damned interrogation room with no defence.

Please be okay. Ash moved quickly into his villa, shoving his front door open with a whip of his powers. Cal jumped up from where he lay on the couch, a whimper escaping his lips.

"Make room, buddy, she's not feeling too well," Ash said quietly, as to not rouse Sophie. She had fallen asleep a few seconds into their flight, the truth serum leaving her drained and dry. Gently, he lay her down on his brown leather couch, heaping blankets around her to make her comfortable.

More blankets maybe?

She stirred. "Ugh, I'm going to be sick," Sophie groaned, turning farther into the blankets he'd cocooned her in.

Acheron moved quickly to his kitchen, pulling together a concoction of herbs, berries and ginger to help with the nausea. He crushed the ingredients with a push of magic and poured it into a cup. He moved back to sit on the coffee table, just by Sophie's head, careful not to knock anything over with his wings. "Drink this. It'll help with the nausea." Ash held the cup out for her.

Sophie fluttered her eyes open and propped herself up on one elbow, a little hazy and slow but much better than when they were in the interrogation room.

She took the cup with trembling hands and took a few sips before handing it back to Ash. He set the cup down on the coffee table so she could reach for it when she needed to.

"Thanks," she muttered before lying back down.

"Oh, I didn't do this for you. I just don't want you projectile vomiting all over my expensive leather couch." Ash smirked.

Sophie's eyes flew open and narrowed on him. If looks could kill . . .

"I take it back, you giant carrier pigeon," Sophie groaned, a little more angrily this time. She huffed into her blankets but after a few seconds, a small smile grew.

The whole flight home, Ash swore he forgot how to breathe. Seeing her so distraught, almost curling away from his touch, did something to his chest. He never wanted to feel that again. He thought he'd brought her to the slaughter. Broken her. But here she was. His Sofreya. His starlight. She did not break after all.

Two hours passed as Sophie lay on his couch, recovering from the effects of Veritas. Ash had spent the entire two hours stress-crocheting – a task he wholly threw himself into. He learnt how to crochet a few years ago to manage his stress and channel his anger. Deymos and Eros had teased him when he first started, but he managed to get them into it too. The thing about crocheting was that it brought them into the present, ways away from the past where their minds often lingered and lost control.

Ash was halfway through a pink and purple jumper he promised to crochet for Tenerife when a knock rapped at his bedroom door. He didn't have time to stow away his hooks and the half-done jumper when Sophie pushed the door open. She paused and she took him in, her starlight hair mussed and her mouth slightly ajar.

Fuck.

Ash realised all too late that he was sitting in his rocking chair, shirtless, feet propped up on an ottoman surrounded by a rainbow of yarn. His enemies would pay a hefty sum for this sort of information.

Quicker than a flash of lightning, Ash threw the jumper and hooks into the air, not caring where they landed and rushed to the door. He pushed Sophie back into the living room, quickly shutting the bedroom door behind him.

Sophie took a step back, her face still pulled into confusion. "Wait, wait. What did I just see?"

"Nothing. You saw nothing." Ash felt stupid saying it.

Sophie crossed her arms, a huge grin on her face and she looked up at him with brightness in her purple eyes.

By the Fates, I'm never going to see the end of this.

Sophie closed in on him, pushing a finger into his bare chest. She was wearing one of his t-shirts. It fell just short of her knees. In his shirt, she looked like his and Fates be damned, it sent him into a possessive arousal.

"First, it was the spicy book collection and now this . . ." she almost hissed. "You, my friend, are keeping dirty secrets." She smirked.

Ash couldn't stop his roguish grin as he, instead of swatting her hand away, pulled her arm closer. She wasn't expecting it so she fell into him. Their bodies perfectly and sinfully lined up with just the fabric of her shirt keeping distance between them.

Ash watched her intently as her throat bobbed. He leaned down, pulling her closer so that he could whisper in her delicately pointed ear. "Glad to see you're awake." Ash smiled. He swiftly skirted around her. The place where she'd been perfectly lined up instantly fell cold and he so badly wanted to pull her back.

Clean slate, Ash reminded himself. Rustling his wings, he shook off the arousal as best as he could. He needed to busy his hands. He needed to focus on anything else but Sophie and how she looked in his shirt, bare faced and sleepy eyed.

Cal. Food. That's right, I'll fix a bowl of food for Cal. He moved to the kitchen. Wait. What was he doing? He was the lieutenant of the fucking Tienthan. "Hey, I was thinking . . ."—Ash poured in some dog food and fresh vegetables into a bowl—"if you're up for it, maybe we could go for an adventure this evening?"

Fates fucking help him, Ash was nervous. Not even the council or being in the presence of Zeus himself made Ash nervous. Yet, there Sophie stood, five-foot-nothing and full of attitude. She had Ash quaking at the knees.

Ash popped his head out from the kitchen when a beat passed, and Sophie did not answer. She was leaning on the edge of the couch, her hands beside her and his shirt slightly hitched up on her thigh. There was softness in her face. It honestly looked like she was going to cry.

"You're the one that crocheted me all those things, aren't you? The sun, little Calypso and the two draekins," she said softly.

Ash did not say anything. He just watched her, waiting to see how she would react.

"And the kids at the Home for Lost Children . . . they all had knitted jumpers."

"Well, that was a team effort between Eros, Deymos and I—"

"Thank you," Sophie breathed, her eyes watering just the slightest. She ran across the room to hug him around the middle. Her movements were so quick it stunned Ash into place. He was still flying half-mast and holding Calypso's food in his hands for Fates' sake.

Shit.

"Who knew such a brooding angel full of bravado was actually just a big ol' softie?" she said into his chest. He could feel her cheeks pushing up against his skin in a stupid smile that knocked the wind out of him more than he wanted to admit.

Softie?! It was not a word he would *ever* use to describe himself. She looked up at him, nuzzling into him with a silly grin. Ash gently pushed her hair away from her eyes, memorising every line of her face before he pushed her away abruptly with his palm on her forehead. The sound of her protest was all he needed to rumble into laughter.

"Get dressed! We're going on an adventure!" Ash howled, popping Cal's bowl of food down for him to devour. Calypso spun around in circles, his flaming tail wagging furiously before digging into his food.

"Asshole!" Sophie called after Ash. It only made him chuckle more.

With a flick of the wrist, Ash dressed himself in a dark, loose-fitting shirt and pants – perfect for flying in the evening summer sky. "I'll be back in five minutes. If you're not ready, I'm throwing you over my shoulder!" Ash smiled, making his way out the front door.

Clean slate, Ash reminded himself again, but he knew all too well that he was powerless when it came to Sophie. She had him by the balls and she didn't even know it.

34

SOPHIE

The thought of being thrown over Ash's shoulder was looking more and more appealing as the days rolled by. Rushing back to Ash's brown leather couch, Sophie pulled on the black jumpsuit he had kindly washed for her. Cal, with his tongue out, moved from paw to paw, waiting for her in the doorway. Ever the impatient pup.

The golden sunset light washed over the living room and Sophie's skin as she moved quickly through the front door, Cal glued to her side. They waited a few beats in the cooling summer breeze before the sounds of giant flapping wings descended upon them. It was Ash on the back of Lumen, hovering just above the ground. The sight of a real arion still made Sophie's insides jostle. To think the myths and legends she obsessed over in school were real. Better yet, she was living it! She was in the Godlands, living and breathing among other gods. This was all too messed up but in the best way possible.

With a firm grip, Ash pulled Sophie up onto Lumen, nestling her between his thighs.

Calypso whined. "Up you get, buddy." Ash laughed as Cal made a face that said *How dare you take my seat.* Sophie laughed too as the hellhound leaned back and launched himself into Sophie's lap. He landed with a quick lick of Sophie's face as if to say *Fine, I'll forgive you.*

Sophie held the hellhound firmly in her arms, feeling the consistent tap of his flaming tail against her thigh. Her back was flush against Ash's torso. Leaning back, she looked up at him. "Where are we off to?" She smiled.

Ash leaned down to whisper in her ear. "I wouldn't want to ruin the surprise for you, Starlight."

Did he just— Is my chest tightening? Wait. WAIT.

Before she could say anything, Ash launched them all into the sky, winding up and up. The air brushed harshly against her skin as they careened past the waterfall on the Isle, and instead of plummeting down like they did before, they spiralled up. As they flowed through the orangey-pink sunset sky, Sophie stretched out a hand so she could rake her fingers through the clouds as they passed.

"Do you think you'll ever get tired of this?" Sophie's voice was all light, airy.

As she leaned back again, Ash sighed with content, pushing even closer with his thighs and chest. He looked down at her, his expression soft and simply said, "Never."

"The Elysian Fields," Ash informed.

They circled just above the Elysian Fields – an expanse of golden grass and trees upon a floating island. Through its centre, a lake of golden water flowed, spilling over the island's edges. Sophie spotted small boats carrying transparent souls across the water. From their vantage point, they watched as boats docked momentarily, allowing the souls to corporealise and move onto the surrounding fields. Through its own volition, the unmanned boats moved across the water, flowing over the other end of the lake. The process continued effortlessly with the steadiness of a ticking clock.

"It's where the souls of those who die come to rest, right?" Sophie asked as she watched as souls continue through the lake.

"Just the worthy ones," Ash corrected. He banked left, carrying them away from the Elysian Fields.

"Oh, we're not heading down there?"

"Nope." Again, he popped that *p*.

There. Coming into view was a smaller floating island, only a few hundred metres wide. Overlooking the Elysian Fields, the smaller island had the same golden grass. In the centre, crested upon a small hill and in the shape of crescent moon, sat a cluster of golden trees. Ash guided Lumen down onto the small island, slowly spiralling downward. They landed softly, Lumen's body jolting them a little. Lumen trotted to a halt as they landed on top of the hill, shaking his pure white wings, before stretching them high. With grace and years of practise, Ash slid off the side of Lumen. Sophie followed, hiking a leg over and sliding down one side of the arion with no grace whatsoever. She hung onto Lumen like a frazzled possum as her feet dangled in the air. Before she knew it, Ash's strong hands braced her hips and gently guided her to the ground.

"Thanks," Sophie murmured.

Cal interrupted the exchange with a loud, impatient bark. "Go on then." Ash smiled, pointing down the hill. Cal obeyed his master's command and bolted across the island in a serious case of zoomies.

Sophie let out a small laugh, watching him. She'd have to find a way to steal Calypso from Ash, that was for sure. Cal was too darned cute. Sophie looked around, taking in the golden grass, the way the soft breeze danced over it. It was quiet, the reverent kind. "Where are we?" Sophie felt like she needed to whisper.

"Officially, the Meadow of Mainn or the Meadow of Yearning . . ." Ash said, looking down the golden hill over to the Elysian Fields. "Unofficially, my secret sanctuary." Ash turned to Sophie, grinning.

Sophie didn't realise when it happened, but she was standing so close to Ash. The back of her arm grazing his chest. She took a half-measured step back.

Clean slate.

The sun had finally set, leaving a pink-and-orange glow in the sky. The sky around them was cloudless and the heat of the Godlands summer had cooled. Without a word, Ash started to move down the hill.

"Wait, where are you going?" Sophie called out.

"Come sit with me." He looked back at her with a handsome smile, his hand reaching out to her.

Sophie eyed his hand suspiciously and walked past him, a smirk upon her face.

"Oh, above chivalry, are we?" Ash shook his head, a small laugh escaping those perfect lips.

Perfect lips? Just lips. Normal lips. Very normal lips.

"Something like that." It was meant to sound snarky but instead it came out somewhere between a strangled cry and a squeak. It was the sound of her resolve quaking at the knees and it most *certainly* had nothing to do with the fact that Ash carried her in his hulking arms across the city, cocooned her in blankets and made her a damned nausea tonic. Or the way he had, since the very moment she arrived in the Godlands, been thoughtful. It was Ash the entire time. Cute, crocheted gifts. Food appearing at the most *impeccable* time. Snacks, placed swiftly in her hand before she even knew she wanted food. A fireplace that replenished magically. Words of encouragement when training felt a little too hard. Well, the term encouragement was a loose term but still, it was Ash the entire *fucking* time.

Sophie plopped herself onto the soft, golden grass, leaning back on her hands. Ash followed closely, leaving just enough space between them. Together, they watched as the boats carrying souls worked their way through the lake – up, over and off the floating island. Up, over, off. What a breathtaking, unobstructed view of the Elysian Fields.

After a few beats of silence, Sophie asked, "How did you happen upon this place? Your little sanctuary." She dared look at Ash. He was leaning back on one hand, one knee propped up on the grass and his other elbow resting across it. His dark shirt showcased a sliver of his muscled chest, his white wings rested high above him and his dark hair blew on the softest of breezes. A dark angel upon golden grass. He was a piece of art that belonged in the damned Sistine Chapel.

That is so unfair. No one's allowed to look that good.

"This place . . ." Ash struggled to find the right words. "It's a bittersweet place. You can only step foot on the Elysian Fields if you are soul *but*, if you're another being, you cannot. You're forced to watch the souls of your loved ones arrive in the fields from afar. From here, in the Meadow of Yearning."

"Hence the name." Sophie paused. "So you can't just see your loved one in Soul City?"

"Not every soul wants to leave the Elysian Fields. Perhaps they're waiting for someone else to arrive and didn't want to chance missing them. Perhaps they enjoy the peaceful afterlife there and can't be swayed by the contemporary afterlife in Soul City."

"So over time people just forgot about this place, and what, gave up waiting for their loved ones?"

"Precisely." With a heavy sigh, Ash laid back onto the ground, his hands casually resting underneath his head.

"That's sad," Sophie said softly.

"Isn't it . . ." Ash agreed.

Sophie looked at Ash. She really looked at him. And she scoffed. Just a little tiny one. On one hand, Ash was a fear-inducing, war-hammer wielding, take-shit-from-no-one godly being. And on the other hand, Ash was a sweet angel emo-boy who found solace in the bittersweetness of yearning. She wanted to scruff his hair and tease laughter from him, knowing underneath his steely exterior was a soft side. He made her feel warm, he made her feel . . . Sophie didn't want to finish the thought. Instead, she opted for an age-old game that stoked the nostalgia in her. "Last one to the bottom of the hill is a rotten egg! No wings or it's cheating!" Sophie cawed, a bright burst of laughter coming out.

She launched herself off the grass and pushed her legs. They felt strong. Stronger than they'd ever been.

"You—" Ash didn't finish as he pushed himself off the grass, sprinting after Sophie.

She could feel the steady beat of his feet, pounding on the earth below. The air was crisp and the view ahead was unbelievable. She was here in the freaking Godlands and her heart was soaring. It finally felt like she belonged somewhere, and it was here. That much she knew.

Ash whisked passed her without any effort, his wings firmly tucked behind him. He turned back to smirk at Sophie as he passed her.

Oh, no you won't.

Sophie sped up, not wanting to lose the race. Who said she was going to play nice? Sophie leapt up, using her mana to propel her into the air. She crashed into Ash's back, taking a hold of his broad shoulders and dragged him down with her. With unrestrained laughter, they tumbled down the hill – a mess of limbs and linen. They came to a soft stop at the base of the hill. The moon turned brightly in the sky above them, casting a divine glow on Ash as Sophie landed firmly on top of him. She quickly rolled off him, lying just by his side in the curve of his outstretched wing, breathless.

"Beat you," Ash breathed.

"Did not!" Sophie laughed between breaths.

"I hit the ground first. You just landed on top of me. It's a clear win."

They both watched the night sky above, not daring to look at one another as their breaths slowly stabilised.

The magnet inside her, the one that was drawn to Ash, pulled her onto her side. Ash remained looking up in the sky, a small content smile across his face. The moonlight glow caressed every angle of his face, and Sophie found herself envious. To touch every perfect angle, every nook, every bump? How lucky.

"Thank you," Sophie said softly.

"For what?" Ash was looking at Sophie now. His burning gaze stirred the magnet inside her again.

"For sitting through that interrogation and for taking care of me from the moment you found me in Faery. I know it was all you."

Ash turned on his back, contemplating, it looked like he was holding back. His words fighting to get out just behind his teeth.

"Listen, what Kaine and I shared was a momentary lapse in judgement made by the broken version of myself. It decimated me. I won't lie. But a part of me is still trying to make sense of it. A tiny morsel of me is hanging onto the salvageable pieces I saw in him. Surely— Surely, I saw *something* in him. Something good. I had to have. I think that's what the truth serum brought forward . . ."

Ash turned to face her again. His eyes, softening. "Sofreya, you don't have to explain yourself to me. Ever. What I see is someone who sees the good in people. What I see is you and . . ." Ash trailed off.

The air between them frayed with electricity.

"And?" Sophie's voice was soft and small, hanging on the air between them desperately. Did he feel the magnet too?

A moment passed.

"And you're crushing my wing." Ash smirked, holding back a laugh.

Sophie gasped and sat up, purposefully pushing herself against his wing as she did.

"You stupid,"—Sophie whacked him across the arm—"giant"—then she poked him in the stomach—"turtle-dove. I was being *vulnerable* and you ruined it." Sophie went in for the kill, moving to poke him in the chest when he grabbed her wrist and pulled her closer so that her head rested upon his chest and her legs intertwined with his.

Her breath had escaped her entirely as she lay against his expanse of muscles. Sophie looked up, a question waiting to be asked on the tip of her tongue.

"I'm calling in the favour you owe me." Ash didn't look at her, instead he watched the night sky.

He tapped his chest. The sound running through her. She knew what he was asking. Sophie laid back down on his chest, her hand upon his beating heart. She had almost forgotten about it. The favour she owed him for letting her train with the Tienthan.

"And what would that be?" Sophie asked softly, joining Ash in watching the revelry of the night sky.

"Stay with me. Just for a little while."

35

SOPHIE

The afternoon sun blazed down on the Gardens of Incrementum. The faint sounds of the Isle's waterfall gurgled away in the air. Sophie sat on the crisp grass, blooming all sorts of flowers and vines. The goddess side of her power came a little easier now and with Danna present beside her, showing off the same powers, it was like a festival of flowers had decided to impose itself on the Isle.

"Since you've got the pretty side of your power down pat, I think it's about time you start learning how to unlock its darker side," Danna said, a hint of pride shining through. Her long silver hair was bound up into a bun to abate the heat.

"Finally!" Sophie groaned. She was finally making headway. One step closer to controlling her power that would one day beat the shit out of Kaine, Queen Calliea and Terr. With her goddess power, she could create, but she could also destroy.

Truth be told, Sophie had already practiced her offence powers. Late at night before bed, or early in the morning just after breakfast, she practised using the nature around her to form different-shaped weapons then coating them in the Fae elements she'd mastered. Her favourite combination was a giant flaming flower sword. It made no sense, but gods was it good to swing it around. She was living her childhood fantasy and *finally* she had a chance to test her mettle against someone or something.

As Sophie got up from the ground, ready to move onto more strenuous work, a puff of white smoke appeared between her and her mother.

From the smoke, the strawberry-blond Eros materialised, floating softly to the ground, flexing every single muscle until he formed what Sophie could only describe as Arnold Schwarzenegger's double bicep and back pose. Sophie blinked her eyes in a little bit of surprise, but mostly confusion.

"'Tis I—" the god began dramatically, his white wings spanning out slowly.

"Eros, what on earth are you doing?" Sophie crossed her arms, not the least bit impressed, but a smile broke from her lips.

Eros let out a little whine of annoyance and huffed, crossing his arms. "Ash said you wouldn't be impressed. Guess he was right." Eros stood there, blowing a curl from out of his face with an exasperated breath.

"Oh did he? Well in that case colour me impressed because that was . . . that was really *something*." Sophie fought a laugh.

Eros's furrowed brows quickly turned into a bright smile. "You hear that, Ash! She said she was thoroughly impressed!" Eros crowed between his cupped hands.

Not my words, but sure.

Sophie turned to find Ash with a nasty scowl across his face. He only broke the scowl to greet Sophie's mother.

"Danna," Ash nodded curtly before returning to scowl at Eros.

Deymos, all dark and gloomy, landed in the fray with a loud boom. His darkness flowing around him in tendrils. He nodded to both Sophie and Danna.

"Sophie!" Nemysis called from behind. Sophie turned in time to receive a forceful pat on the shoulder from Nemy. Her chestnut-coloured wings were extra shiny today.

"Good to see you, Nemy," Sophie responded, putting a hand to the angel's shoulder. They hadn't seen much of each other outside of training, but thankfully, Nemy had dialled down her thirst for retribution, quickly making them training partners.

Danna was in full conversation mode with Eros, exchanging fits of laughter. Nemy moved to greet the goddess of all lands.

To Sophie's surprise it was Deymos who moved closer to her. His grey wings coiled tight behind his back as he leaned into Sophie's ear to whisper something. Except, he didn't whisper at all. "Ash, the grand master of weapons wanted to see you before we left," he teased. Move over terror and dread, Deymos was clearly a comedian.

Eros oohed from across the garden, stoking the fire that now burned in Ash's smoking eyes. Lightning skittered into the air.

Deymos, unfazed by Ash's turbulent power, turned to the master of weapons and butt-tapped him. Literally, butt-tapped him. The sound was sharp. "Don't get too riled up Ash, I was only joking." He smiled before running over to Danna to kiss her cheek in greeting.

Sophie could no longer hold on to her laugh. These angels were so *human* it wasn't even funny. "Ah, it's always a good time when they're around," Sophie sighed happily.

Ash muttered profanities under his breath before clearing his throat. "Sorry, they can get out of hand sometimes."

"Don't be sorry. I like the teasing." Sophie smiled. "So . . . what's up?"

What's up? Fucking hell. Sophie didn't know what to do with her arms, or her entire body for that matter. She was as nervous as a bag of cats at a greyhound meet and it was all because of the moment they shared last night in the Meadow of Yearning. Nothing else really happened after that but they were teetering on a tightrope of friendship and as each day passed, the more the tightrope was bowing and bouncing out of control.

Ash's smirk snapped Sophie back into reality. He could tell she was nervous. And he *liked* it. Sophie immediately went back to hating the arrogant angel.

"We just received a mission. The Tienthan have been tasked to clear the surrounds of a portal that has just opened in Faery." Ash paused. "As their demigoddess, I thought it was best that you know . . . The portal opens to the Shadow Realm and it looks like it's there to stay."

Sophie's gut sank.

"Who opened it?" Sophie asked, a little panicked.

"Kaine."

"And what about the people of Faery?"

"It's something we'll assess when we get there," Ash said with a grim look on his face.

Fear struck itself in Sophie's chest for a little bit, but after a brief pause and breath, the fear abated and, in its wake, came the feeling of fury. Sophie was stronger. Wiser. Better. And she had a target aimed straight at Kaine's head.

"Let me know what you find," Sophie said more confidently.

"I'll keep you updated."

"How long will you be?"

"A day or two. I'm not too sure."

"Well good luck then. Don't let those miscreants make your head explode." Sophie grinned, pointing to Eros, Deymos and Nemysis. They were still in a deep conversation with Danna.

Ash moved a touch closer.

Sophie's heart beat a little faster.

It was as if he was about to embrace her, but he didn't. He stopped just a short distance away. "I know I'm your only friend here, so try not to miss me, alright?" Ash grinned, earning a narrowed look from Sophie.

He sparked into a hearty laugh. He baited her. It was exactly what he wanted.

Idiot, Sophie thought as Ash walked away toward his friends.

With curt nods and quick waves, they all blasted into the air – the picture of divinity at its finest. Except Eros, who instead of propelling himself into the air with a mighty push of his majestic wings, conjured a little nimbus cloud, hopped on it like it was a bed and proceeded to draw in little tendrils of white smoke, a love heart with the initials A + S in the middle of it. He even had the audacity to wink as he ascended into the air.

Sophie just shook her head as he disappeared into the brightness of the sun.

"So, want to tell me what that was all about?" Danna wagged her brows. Her skin was glowing just a bit extra after that encounter.

"Absolutely not—"

"Tell her about what?" a deep male voice cut in.

Sophie startled and snapped her head to the voice that came in from the side of the garden. It was Commander Ares. He emerged from a rose bush, with his battered wings, tanned skin and golden hair.

This whole appearing out of nowhere thing is extremely exhausting. Sophie let out a frustrated breath.

"You're late." Danna frowned with a hit of a smile.

"Apologies."

"Late for what?" It was Sophie's turn to chime in.

"He volunteered to help you with your offensive tactics. What greater opponent than the god of courage and war himself?" Danna beamed.

If Sophie could melt away into the ground and somehow slither out of this situation, she would. Sure, she was ready to up the ante with her powers, but she wasn't ready to face *the* god of war.

Sophie turned on her heel quickly and groaned. "Fine. Let's get this over and done with."

"Was it something I said?" Ares said under his breath.

Dash. Slice. Throw.

The mana buried deep inside Sophie seemed to have no end. The more she threw out her mana, the more her well filled back up again. She was getting stronger, and her body was thrumming from the adrenalin of it all. With speed, Sophie launched herself into the air using a mound of dirt. She tumbled on a whisper of wind and came crashing down, collecting variants of vines and flowers to form a longsword that burned to life. She rained a downpour upon Ares before striking down with her flower-encrusted blade of fire. She felt invincible like this, weaving her elemental Fae magic and her core powers as a demigoddess.

Ares, donning his infamous golden helmet and spear, quickly whisked away the water with a swipe of this spear. He jumped up to meet Sophie and they clashed in a flurry of strikes and hits. Sophie landed few strikes, her floral sword falling away with each impact. The sword had some kick to it despite being made of flowers. Ares, being centuries old, had the skill and dexterity to outmanoeuvre Sophie. He wasn't tired by any means, but he was panting just a little and that was enough of a win for Sophie.

They landed on the ground and almost cracked the earth beneath them. Sophie crouched low, breaking away her flower sword to pull out her favoured rope dart. She hadn't had much practise with it, but it called to her in this very moment. With a flick of her wrist, she encased the rope dart with her favourite fire and shot it out, aiming for Ares's jugular. Sophie tunnel visioned as she saw the sharp blade of her rope dart fall short and nick his bicep instead, drawing the tiniest gash of blood.

Sophie gulped. In an instant, Ares's golden spear tip was pressed firmly onto Sophie's neck. If she moved, she'd be done for.

Sophie's rope dart fell unceremoniously to the ground with a clatter. Her body as still as stone as Ares's spear drew tiny rivulets of blood from her neck. Ares was as still as a predator in the jungle. His face unmoving and all serious. It was only after a beat of silence that he pulled back, wiping the blood that dripped down his bicep and healed it all in one motion.

Sophie pulled back too. Standing from the crouch, she placed a hand upon the tiny cut the spear had made upon her neck. She channelled her healing powers to it. With a slight tingle, the bleeding stopped, and her skin was new. Sophie dared to look up. Had she just royally pissed off the god of war?

Oh.

Ares stood with his arms stretched out wide and a proud smile on his face. In all accounts of history, the god of war was cruel and punishing but in all the times Sophie interacted with him, he was nice. She expected a call for blood or her instant death by spear, not him standing there looking like a proud father.

A smile broke from her lips.

Ares threw his spear into the air. It disappeared into an invisible abyss as he drew his hands together and clapped. "Bravo, Sofreya. You've got grit and you've clearly got the power. It's not often anyone draws blood from me. Dare I say that rope dart is as slippery as a hydra," Ares claimed, moving forward to clasp Sophie on the shoulder.

"Really?" Sophie was wide-eyed now.

"Really. Don't let it get to your head though." Ares winked before turning, heading toward the refreshment table.

As his back turned, Sophie let out a silent *yes*, fisting her hand and pumping it in the air several times, before righting herself and heading for the refreshment table too. Sophie grabbed a glass of water and perched on the table beside Ares.

"A rope dart is possibly one of the hardest weapons to master. I'm surprised you handled it so well, especially wrapping it with your elemental fire. Very clever." Ares lifted his cup to Sophie in a salute of sorts.

"I haven't mastered it as such, but I guess having a great teacher helps in any case," Sophie explained.

"Acheron." Ares scoffed. "I swear by the Fates that the boy needs to just look at a weapon to master it. The man, I should say. He's been through a lot . . ." Ares moved into a state of reflection, his eyes glazing over as if peering in the not-too-distant past.

Sophie didn't want to pry. It didn't seem like it was her place to do so. What happened in the time that they were torn apart in Faery?

Ares sighed heavily and pushed off the table. "Anyway, let's do another—" He was cut short as a small, levitating scrolled appeared beside him on a puff of smoke. He snatched the scroll from the air and read it with a huff.

Curious, Sophie asked, "Is something the matter?"

Ares disintegrated the scroll in the air and pulled out his spear from the invisible pocket of reality he'd managed to tuck it away into. "It's from Acheron. One of the Tienthan have gone AWOL in Faery. I'll need to handle it. Perhaps we can reconvene in a few days. You are strong, Sofreya, and I'd like to see your power honed into a dauntless reckoning. Keep up the good work." Ares nodded before disappearing into thin air.

The compliment made Sophie beam and her cheeks flush. It was the confidence boost she never knew she needed. Against Kaine, Queen Calliea and Terr, Sophie actually stood a chance.

36

ACHERON

I t had only been a few hours, but Ash's hands were *itching* to send a message to Sofreya. What was she thinking? What was she doing? What did she think about last night? The questions rolled endlessly to the point where he was distracted. Ash never got distracted. Ever.

"Taranis," the deep voice of Pallas, God of Battle and Warcraft, pulled Ash from the hamster wheel of thoughts he didn't remember jumping on.

They stood a few steps away from the edge of the portal that Kaine had created. It reeked of sulphur and the screeches that echoed through it made the hairs on Ash's arms stand up. There was nothing good about the Shadow Realm. There was undeniably nothing good about the four-hundred-metre-wide portal in the Spring Court of Faery that led straight to it. It would have taken copious amounts of blood and power to have wrought such devastation. The soil had turned black and the trees around the portal had petrified. Ash had never seen anything like it.

"Pallas." Ash acknowledged the god with a firm hand on his shoulder. As soon as he touched him, Ash could sense the anger that consumed him.

"It's Artemis." Pallas looked like he was going to split someone's head open. His long grey hair practically levitated off him.

Ash quickly looked over Pallas's shoulder in search of Artemis, Goddess of the Hunt, and the peaks of her dark red wings.

"She jumped into the portal." Pallas's face was pure anger.

Ash moved past Pallas, storming to where Achlys stood. The god of eternal night, with his dark skin and hair, peered over the edge of the bright red portal, a wash of concern on his face.

"Was she hunting something?" Ash asked Achlys.

"She murmured something about a voice calling her. One moment she was checking the perimeter and then next . . ." Achlys stood up, brushing the dirt away from his knees.

"By the Fates . . ." Ash took a moment to reel in his thoughts. He pulled the small messenger scroll he had tucked away in his sandal and scrawled a message to Ares. He shot the message through the Between where it would head straight to Ares. It disappeared on a puff of smoke. Ash turned back to Achlys and Pallas who patiently waited on orders. "Achlys, Pallas. Find Ares. Tell him everything. As you saw it." Ash's voice was steady, but he didn't like the odds of this at all. The Tienthan had never ventured into the Shadow Realm and for good reason. The place was the literal underworld, and they had no business being there.

Fuck. This isn't how I expected the day to go.

The two gods nodded and quickly shot up into the sky.

Ash let out a loud wolf whistle, pulling the focus of Deymos and Nemy from across the portal. He beckoned them over. They sped around the perimeter of the portal in case anything decided to claw its way out. The blackened soil around them kicked up as they landed swiftly next to Ash.

"Achlys and Pallas think Artemis went in," Ash growled.

"We would have heard her," Nemysis pointed out.

"She's right. The surface would have burned her alive," Deymos added.

"It's a portal that only allows things to come out. Anything that tries to go in, burns." Nemy picked up a stick and threw it into the portal to prove a point. The stick disintegrated from the heat before it even touched the surface.

It made sense, but it didn't sit right with Ash at all. The whole thing reeked of foul play. "They said she heard voices. We can't rule it out."

Deymos swore under his breath.

Ash moved a little closer to the edges of the red portal. Perhaps the voices would speak to him if he was patient enough. One of the Tienthan was in there. For all intents and purposes, Artemis was his sister, and he would never leave a family member behind. Ash took in a deep breath. "There's only one way to find out. Tether me and if I don't come back in five minutes, pull me out."

Deymos and Nemy didn't protest. Deymos conjured a dark glittering rope and lassoed it around Ash's waist. Nemy stood behind Deymos, a supporting hand on his shoulder. When everything was in place, they nodded.

"Five minutes," Ash reminded them.

Ash turned back to the portal, washing himself over with a protective layer of magic in case the portal burned him. *Fates be kind.* Without a moment's hesitation, he dived in. The portal surface sizzled as it met his layer of magic. No damage. Good. As Ash moved through, the portal turned darker and darker. Sulphur burned his nostrils as he catapulted through the Between. *FWOOM.* There it was. Thick air snapped into place, stifling his breath. His wings dragged against the thickness of its a barrier and an almost deafening sucking sound filled his ears. He'd made it to the other side. Ash shot his wings out, pulling himself into a swift stop.

By the Fates.

It was bloodier, darker than he assumed it would be. The Shadow Realm.

Soot floated through the air, clinging to his wings as the smell of burning filled his nostrils. Looming black mountains painted the entire landscape before him. The Shadow Realm was a giant crater of shadow and foreboding. The screams. Fates, the screams and shrieks of demons and creatures made of pure nightmares were debilitating. Ash had to layer another protective coat of magic over his ears to dull the sound.

Four minutes.

Ash advanced with precision, scanning the dark flat land he landed in, Deymos's glittering rope still tied firmly around his waist. Large boulders scattered all around. He scanned, right to left. There. A set of tracks. Two feet. The size too large to have been Artemis's. He followed the track regardless. If it wasn't Artemis, then perhaps it would lead him to her.

The sound of yelps and howls sounded the more Ash followed the tracks. He took cover behind a large boulder, his shoulder resting upon its warm surface as he angled his head to peek around it.

Three minutes.

From the corner of his eyes, Ash spotted a pack of hellhounds much larger than Calypso. Some rested while others looked like they were taking orders from someone, moving around in various formations. Ash shifted farther away from the boulder so he could get a better view.

Who is that?

A male, with long black hair stood in the centre of the pack. He commanded them with various clicks of his tongue and hand signals. The hellhounds obeyed.

What the? Ash stepped back, dirt beneath his boots crunched, giving his position away. A miscalculated step on his end.

The male ahead snapped his head to the sound.

It was as if all sound, all feeling and all control over his mind was razed to the ground by a deadly fire. And all that remained beneath the embers was pure, deadly rage. Ash stepped out from the behind the boulder and faced the male. He'd seen the likeness before in his own mirror.

Kaine.

"It's you." Ash's voice was deep, calm as he flowed into his fighting stance. Arms braced. Legs slightly apart.

"*You*," Kaine seethed, his eyes narrowed on Ash. There was rage there. A rage that he had no right to feel.

"I'd wipe that look off your fucking face." Ash didn't hesitate. His mighty wings pushed out. With a powerful thrust, he shot up into the air, unhooking his war hammer from the waist. Lethe. Kaine. Whatever he deigned to call himself, he would pay for what he'd done to Sofreya and the Faery Realm.

Two minutes left.

Ash roared as he funnelled all his power into his flame-engraved war hammer. Lightning and thunder crackled into the air as he swung for Kaine. *CRACK.* A narrow miss. This guy was fast. Too fast. Kaine rolled himself back in time using his mana, forcing the hellhounds back behind a shield of air. They clawed, barked, and scratched at the shield their master had put up, adding to the pandemonium.

"Don't be so sure of yourself." Kaine shot out two giant blades of mana. The air rippled and sharpened. Dust kicked up, shrouding them both as Ash pulled back swiftly, shooting up into the air, away from the grasp of Kaine's mana.

Damnit, he's stronger than I expected.

"You stole her from me. You stole MY soulmate!" Kaine closed the distance between them, shooting out blocks of air to step and manoeuvre off, a nasty snarl across his face.

The word soulmate twisted Ash's insides. This guy was insane. Ash threw a lightning bolt at Kaine, smashing him into the ground. *CRACK.* His head smashed upon a rock but as if he were more than Fae, Kaine shot back up, shaking his head. He quickly recovered. Too quickly.

What the fuck?

"Sofreya is not something to own. She's not something to be stolen. You forfeited your chances with her the moment you laid a hand on her!" Ash pointed his war hammer into the air, filling it with raw lightning again. Thunderclouds rolled all around him as he hovered just above the darkened dirt of the Shadow Lands.

This is going to feel so good.

Ash pointed his war hammer at Kaine. The edges of it glowed and electricity flitting across its surface. "May you never reach the—" Ash was cut off by the strong tug of Deymos's rope around his waist.

Fuck.

Ash flew back to the portal at pace, completely out of control and by the whim of Deymos's rope. His wings rustled against the speed as he careened to the edge of the portal.

Kaine pushed himself into the air, a fierce snarl across his face as he gave chase. "You are wrong, angel." He let out a maniacal laugh. "It is I that runs through her mind when she uses her mana. It is I that runs through her mind when she looks upon your face. My face. MY fucking eyes. *You* stole my identity. *You* stole my soulmate. And you will do well to remember that, angel. Whenever you think her gaze softens for you, remember that it was *me*. Me who claimed her first. Me that will claim her *always.*"

The words were all twisted. Vile. All fucking wrong.

Enough.

Ash shot out the lightning from his war hammer at the last minute. Kaine dodged it, rolled midair, grabbing a fist full of Ash's wing. Pain lanced through his wing, sending sharp pain down his back. Ash twisted in the air, fighting against the hold, but it was futile. As the threshold of the portal tingled against his skin, he felt the sharp pain of his feathers being ripped out.

Shit.

The last thing Ash saw before he disappeared into the Between was Kaine's satisfied smile as he held several plumes of Ash's feathers, coated in blood. The portal to the Shadow Realm closed in on Ash as he swiftly flew through the Between and out of the portal into Faery. He landed with a crash on the dry soil of Soxis, breathing heavily.

What the fuck was that?

Deymos and Nemy were at his side immediately, pulling him up from the ground. Deymos vanquished the rope around Ash's waist.

Ash watched the portal as if Kaine was about to burst out from it. He stared and stared, but the Breaker of Realms did not give chase. The snapped hollow shafts of Ash's feathers stung as the Soxis breeze hit them. Ash let out a soft grimace.

Nemy moved to quickly stop the blood that dripped from his wing. The wound would heal soon enough but the feathers would take a bit of time before growing back.

Deymos and Nemy stared at Ash, waiting for an explanation.

"It's worse than I feared." Ash brushed a hand through his hair.

"Did you find any trace of Artemis?" Deymos asked.

"No, but the Breaker of Realms has a hold on Terr's hellhounds and who knows what else." Ash paused. "And he's a lot more powerful than I expected. His power could easily match any of ours."

Deymos swore under his breath.

Ash hated to admit it but when his magic brushed up next to Kaine's, there was a challenge there. He was so much stronger than a Fae. His power felt like a god's. Something had changed since they crossed paths in Faery. That much was true.

"We could take him on, right?" Nemy asked.

A beat of silence passed between them all.

"I'm not so sure."

37

ACHERON

Kaine's words planted little seeds of doubt in Ash's mind. Did looking upon his face bring her pain?

Surely not.

Ash surveyed the town of Soxis with a deep sadness in his heart. Its buildings were worn, the ground gritty and dry. The air was no longer fresh. The people however, still had a brightness to them, despite their faces being gaunter than he'd seen any Fae before. The blight plaguing Faery had reached the Spring Court not long ago and it was clear the effects were devastating.

As Ash, Deymos and Nemy walked through the town centre, Fae from various courts moved to watch them. This was the part of being a guardian angel that Ash felt most uncomfortable with. He didn't think he'd ever get used to it. The townspeople gawked and pointed at the wings the Tienthan bore. Some even muttered prayers while others came up to them, thanking Ash and his friends for taking time out of their day to visit. Ash gave a small smile to those he passed as they moved toward Asteria Hold where Eros had asked them to meet him. A mixture of fear and hope washed over the eyes of the people of Faery the closer they got to the Spring Court's centre.

They finally reached the green wooden door to Asteria Hold's receiving room. Its golden handles were carved in the shape of fern leaves and flecks of gold scattered throughout the green paint. It opened before them on a silent wind.

Ash was first to move across the grass, the evening sun shining a golden light into the circular skylight fixed above them.

Ash spotted Eros first. The god of love knelt on the grass, both of his hands holding that of a delicate, tanned-skinned Fae female. Her eyes were washed with concern and it looked like Eros was comforting her. "Lady Ollette wanted to meet you all. She is the High Lady of Soxis." Eros smiled back at Ash.

Ash gave a polite nod.

Around Lady Ollette sat another Fae female with raven hair and olive skin. Eros moved from the grass to her. "This is Lady Firtha, High Lady of Wrenntia." He pointed to a Fae male with silky, dark maroon hair and dark brown skin, "This is Lord Fern, High Lord of Fyllera." Eros then pointed to the last Fae male with long, blond hair and light-purple eyes. "And this is Regin Taliesin, blacksmith by trade and for lack of a better term, leader of the rebellion against the blood throne."

Ash's heart rate spiked at the mention of Regin's last name. He was related to Sofreya then.

Regin watched Ash with a cautious eye, no doubt having a visceral reaction to his outward appearance and how similar it was to Kaine's. Ash didn't blame him. The sight of Kaine before him was the strangest thing he'd ever experienced too. Ash shook off the unease that coiled in his feathers.

"Thank you for welcoming us," Ash said with a hand on his bare chest.

"It is us who needs to give thanks. The portal and the power it holds is beyond us." Lady Ollette circled a finger around the group surrounding her. "Kind Eros here has assured us that the Tienthan are willing to help." She moved from the grass, taking slow steps toward Ash as if he were . . . some sort of holy being.

I guess I am, but I'm not that intimidating, am I?

Lady Ollette, with sure hands took a hold of Ash's. She looked up at him with hope in her eyes. "So, thank you. Our people are suffering, but if we have the mighty Tienthan by our side then there is hope yet. Hope that we will be able to stop the blood throne's treachery."

"We will put an end to this, one way or another," Nemy chimed in from behind. Thank the Fates for that, because Ash always found it difficult to navigate gratitude. He never needed it. Nor did he need praise. Growing up alone did that to him.

Lady Ollette turned to squeeze Nemysis's hands. The rest of the high Fae watched on with hope in their eyes.

Eros moved to join Ash. "We'll be in contact, Lady Ollette." Eros dipped his head, spreading his pure white wings behind him.

"And we'll send down some supplies, rations and water for you." Ash nodded before ushering out his closest circle of friends. Ash was about to close the receiving room door behind him when heavy footfalls sounded, inching closer to him. Ash turned to find Regin with a worried look on his face.

The blond blacksmith with eyes like Sofreya's looked at Ash, then noted his swirling tattoos that sprawled on his right arm, with a pointed look. Ash instinctively pulled his right arm out of view.

"How is she?" Regin whispered.

Ash blinked in surprise. He knew exactly who Regin was referring to. The thought of her alone made his heart sing. "She's happy."

"Good. Take care of her." Regin smiled, clapping a hand to Ash's shoulder.

The reaction made Ash feel warm inside. Ash gave the blacksmith a curt nod before joining his cadre who waited patiently outside.

"What was that?" Eros cooed.

"Nothing," Ash groaned.

"Was it about someone who rhymes with trophy?"

"Shut it." Without another word Ash rushed into the sky. He didn't wait to see if his friends followed.

Ash landed back on the Isle of Deos, greeted by its thick summery air. He let out a sigh of relief as he opened the door to his villa. The day did not go according to plan. They were sent down to scope out the portal, gather intel and observe how the Fae population surrounding it were faring. It ended up with an accidental trip to the Shadow Realm, a press tour in Faery's dying Spring Court and most importantly . . . Artemis was missing.

I need a drink.

Ash wished away his sandals and cleaned himself up with a flick of his magic. He'd deal with the deep layer of dirt that only a shower could get rid of, later. He sunk into the brown leather couch and wished to the Fates that he wouldn't have to get up for several days. Calypso was nowhere to be found. He was probably nuzzling against Sofreya.

Sofreya.

Should I? No, I shouldn't.

She was probably resting after her training session earlier today. He could just see her tomorrow, but he could also send a message to her now. It wouldn't hurt right? Or perhaps the words of Kaine hit much closer to home than he thought.

Ash sat up quickly with a frown upon his face. Why on earth was he acting like a prepubescent boy with a giant crush on the girl next door? Well technically, the girl three doors down. Ash shook his head to clear it. He was a full-grown male for Fates' sake.

Fuck it.

He pulled a piece of parchment from the table and scrawled a message.

Acheron:

What are you doing this evening?

Ash sent it off on a puff of smoke. He felt his hands warm, and he shook his knee in anticipation. He waited for a moment but grew impatient when nothing puffed back in response. He stormed to his shower in a huff. Shedding off his uniform, he stepped inside the black marble shower and let the cold water run through his wings, being sure to keep the patch of broken feathers out of the water's way so they didn't get wet. He rested his head upon the cool tiles. The situation between Faery and the Shadow Realm was escalating and given the dire state that the rebel side of Faery were in, he wasn't sure how they'd survive. It made Ash angry; it made him want to—

A messenger scroll puffed into the shower with a pop.

Ash snatched it from the air with a growl.

Sophie:

Is this some sort of booty call? Not impressed.

You've interrupted Cal and I's backyard yoga session.

Ash bit his lip. He didn't know whether it was the adrenalin crash or the pain from the chunk of feathers that was missing from his fate-forsaken wing, but the thought of Sofreya in shorts, doing yoga poses in the summer heat, sweat slicking her body was doing all sorts of things to him. Sorts of things that needed to be sorted. Immediately.

Ash scribbled a message in response. Then crossed it out. Then scribbled it back on. Frustrated, he ended his cold shower, dried himself with his magic and flopped onto his bed.

Acheron:

Not a booty call. Unless . . .

Ash sent the message before he could stop himself. He was smiling like an idiot. An idiot who was *definitely* not meant to be crossing the best-friendship line, but here he was kicking it with his toe, seeing if it would budge.

A beat passed.

Sofreya:

Get your head out of the gutter you smut-loving angel . . .
Heard you had a bit of a rough day.
Want to come by and talk about it? And binge watch Twilight after? It'll make
you feel better, I promise.

Ash let out a laugh. His heart did that squeezing thing that he dared not acknowledge. He could almost see her, with her starlight hair and the little scrunch on her nose as she took a jibe at him.

Acheron:

Talk, yes. Twilight? Maybe you can convince me after a couple of drinks. Soul City?
I can pick you up in about thirty minutes.

Ash sent off the piece of parchment. Clasping his hands over his stomach, he waited patiently for what felt like an eternity. Sofreya's response puffed into existence right above his face. Ash quickly unfurled it with a silly grin.

Sofreya:
It's a date.

Ash sputtered at the words that scrawled across the piece of parchment. He had to sit up, clear his vision with several blinks, before reading it again. *It's a date.* Wait, was it a date? What did these words mean? Was this permission? A green light to forego the whole best-friend, clean-slate deal and act upon the undoubted, inseparable, gravity-defying connection they had?

Ash dropped back onto his bed, groaning. The Fates were testing him. There was no other explanation for this turmoil he found himself in.

38

SOPHIE

Sophie ran across her room in a panic. She was slicked with sweat from the hot yoga session she was doing with Cal.

Shit. What do I wear? Should I wear some make-up? Why did I say it was a date?!

Sophie's heart hammered as she went to work like a madwoman. She blasted the shower, rinsing off as much sweat and dirt as she could before jumping out within minutes and drying herself with a whip of her air mana. She bolted to the wardrobe where Calypso sat with several dresses in his mouth. Slobber had started to seep through the linen. Sophie gingerly pried the moist dresses out of Cal's jaw, earning herself a little whine.

"Oh buddy, thanks but I think mama needs something a bit more . . ." Sophie trailed off as she surveyed the options in her closet. She pulled out a dress she bought at one of the Isle market stalls. It was a tight fitting, maxi length lilac dress. Its straps were thin and all over were shiny, purple sequins. It matched her hair perfectly and it wasn't too casual, nor was it too dressy. It was just right for this date that wasn't *really* a date she was about to go on with Ash.

Sophie slipped on the dress and rushed to the mirror in the bathroom, spinning a tendril of mana through her long hair so that it curled and waved effortlessly. She added the last touches to her outfit, straightening the golden, flaming heart necklace she had never taken off since coming to the Godlands.

She hadn't looked in a mirror for so long that she barely recognised who stood before her. She was wearing *colour* for fuck's sake. Her curves were accentuated by the tightness of the dress and her skin practically glowed from the amount of sun she'd been exposed to. She looked healthy. She looked happy. She *was* happy.

I like this look on you, Sophie. Happiness really suits you.

She breathed in all the excitement and nervousness that coursed through her veins and smiled to herself.

Knock. Knock.

"I'll be out in a sec!" Sophie shouted from the bathroom. She quickly applied some clear lip gloss and bronzer before slipping into some sandals and bolting for the front door.

Cal looked at her with a slight tilt of his head from one of the white chaises.

"I'll be back soon, love you, buddy," Sophie quickly said to the hound, who in response huffed a puff of black smoke from his nostrils before burrowing himself into a blanket.

Sophie pulled the front door open and stepped out.

Ash had his back facing her, his white wings pulled tightly against himself as he held Lumen's reins. He wore a loose-fitting white tunic, black slacks and sandals. Casual. "Took your time . . ." Ash didn't have the nerve to continue as he turned and spotted Sophie in a splash of colour.

Sophie watched Ash's gaze burn into molten lava, hot enough to melt away her dress.

He gulped.

Sophie did the exact same thing. Her throat was as dry as godsdamned chips as she spied Ash's muscled form, his long black hair with a tuft of white falling over his shoulders, fresh from a shower. He belonged on a period romance novel cover, and it made her think of *terrible* things. Terribly carnal things she wanted to do with him. Sophie swore her heart was about to leap out of her chest and perform some form of gymnastics routine before guttering out and dying on the steps of her villa. The electricity that had always existed between them sparked in delight as they stayed quiet for just a moment.

"Hi," Ash breathed.

"Hi," Sophie couldn't help but smile.

Lumen's neigh echoed around them, jolting them both from the magic spell they were under.

Ash stretched out a hand for Sophie and she took it as she descended the very few steps from her villa. He let go of her hand briefly to lift her up onto Lumen with ease.

"The stars are wary tonight," Ash hummed.

"Why is that?" Sophie adjusted herself on Lumen's back. Because her dress was tight around the hips and legs, she had to sit sideways. Her legs dangled off the arion's side.

Ash pulled himself up and over Lumen, adjusting Sophie's legs so that they draped across his hard thigh. He locked her in the confines of his arms as he grabbed Lumen's reins. "Because you outshine them," Ash said into her ear. His deep voice rumbled through her and Sophie swore he almost purred.

Sophie's breathing hitched. Is this how she was going to die? From swooning too hard? It seemed like a probable cause and given the way his woodsy scent was holding her captive; it didn't seem like a bad way to go either.

"It's a new dress." Sophie smiled, looking up to his smoking eyes.

"I didn't say anything about the dress." He pulled Lumen into the sky with a giant leap.

Yep. I've gone into cardiac arrest and now I'm dead.

Sophie smiled shyly and jabbed Ash playfully with an elbow, not sure what to say. Her cheeks burned profusely, and her words eluded her as they flew across the Isle toward the waterfall.

Ash pulled her closer to him so that she could lean her head comfortably in the space between his shoulders and neck. All the nervousness she felt caved, making way for something full and warm. It felt like home here, with Ash. It felt like they were back in Faery – young and impressionable with no other worries in the world. They were two of a kind. Where one pushed, the other pulled.

The Isle's waterfall roared beneath them as Ash slowed Lumen down for just a moment.

"Both arms around my neck at all times, okay?"

"Is that permission to strangle you?" Sophie joked. She couldn't help but smile brightly as the knowledge of what was to come sent a ribbon of excitement through her.

"That smart mouth of yours . . ." Ash shook his head and smirked as Lumen charged over the Isle's waterfall with a joyful whinny.

They were airborne. Light. Weightless. Sophie felt invincible as they spiralled through the night sky like a falling star. She stretched out her hand just the slightest to rake her fingers through the clouds as they descended.

Ash wrapped an arm around her back, holding her tighter. Sophie could feel her resolve melting with every day, every laugh and every jibe. She could stay like this. She really could.

Ash led Sophie down a black set of marble stairs behind the main strip of Soul City.

"This place looks fancy, are you sure I'll be able to get in wearing this?" Sophie asked as she looked up at the sign carved in white marble. It read *Archi's*.

"Of course, come." Ash grabbed her hand and for once Sophie didn't pull back, she let him guide her completely.

There was something inside her that tingled, watching Ash with his towering form lead the way, his large hand enveloping hers.

They ventured down a dark corridor as the sound of revelry echoed and surrounded them. They came to the end of the corridor but there was no door or entrance in sight. That was until Ash walked straight through the damn wall. As Sophie followed suit, the cooling sensation of the walk-through wall swept over her skin. On the other side, everyone cheered for joy.

Most of the revellers were angels of the Tienthan. In fact, all of them were. Sophie recognised most of them from training and in the corner of a sunken lounge area, she spotted Eros, Deymos and Nemy waving their hands, beckoning them to come and join them. Well, Eros and Nemy were waving ecstatically. Deymos however, looked like he was going to kill someone, and he'd happily do it right here.

Everyone in the room got up to greet Ash and Sophie. All the angels looked casual in various forms of linen, but no one could mistake the power that vibrated in the room.

Is there an off button for this shit? I'm going to hurl.

This was a place they came to relax in private it seemed. As Ash made his way through the room he didn't let go of her hand. Not until the flock of angels swarmed in on Sophie, kissing her cheeks and asking how she was faring.

A dark-skinned male angel came up to Sophie with a wide smile, his arms open wide. He kissed both her cheeks in greeting. "You haven't met me yet, the name's Morpheus."

Morpheus, God of Dreams and Sleep, slung an arm around Sophie like they were the best of friends. He pulled Sophie forward, so he could introduce her to another angel she hadn't met yet.

"This is my darling Nyx." The goddess of night smiled before rushing to Morpheus's side. They were surprisingly anything but dark. Their stark white hair, porcelain skin and white dress were the exact opposite. They were the moon personified, if anything.

Sophie could sense a theme with all the angels. Their powers were all dark and deadly.

"How long have you been together for?" Nyx smiled sweetly between Sophie and Ash.

Sophie sputtered. Panicked even. "Ugh no, we're just friends, right, Ash?" Sophie snapped her eyes to Ash, and he looked like his soul had left his entire body.

"Totally," Ash agreed with a weird, pained grin. It wasn't very convincing.

Nyx's eyes widened, clearly embarrassed by the assumption they'd made.

Morpheus barked. He literally barked, "Oh don't be silly. I mean maybe you two are just friends, but not for long, eh?" The dark-skinned god clapped Ash across the arm.

Nyx pulled back their partner with eyes of warning. They looked back at Ash and Sophie and said, "We'll leave you to it." The goddess smiled sweetly before turning back to Morpheus with a deadly glare and muttering something about embarrassment underneath their breath.

Sophie loosed a breath, watching the pair disappear into the other side of the room and disappear into another rippling wall.

That went well.

Half the room in Archi's bar was a large, sunken lounge where the angels lazed and conversed. In the middle of the sunken lounge space was a fireplace.

To the left of the room was a well-stocked bar and a bartender, dressed smartly in a grey, pinstriped vest and a matching flat cap.

Sophie sighed. "I think I need some wine."

"I second that." Ash whisked away to the bar, ordering two glasses of wine and returning to Sophie in record time.

They walked over to the corner of the sunken lounge where Ash's cadre lazed.

Eros sat up, raising a glass he toasted, "To better days."

They all clinked their glasses together, Sophie included, before taking a long sip.

Sophie took a seat right next to Nemy, while Ash took a seat on the floor, his back resting next to Sophie's legs. Her thigh and calf brushed against his thick shoulder and muscled arms. Ash's wings rested next to her, occasionally brushing against her arm.

Nemy turned to Sophie. "I heard Ares gave you a bit of a run for your money this afternoon."

"He did a little at first, but I think by the end of it I earned my stripes." Sophie smiled shyly into her wine glass. It was a win from today for sure.

"Watch out, Nemy, you might have someone gunning for your spot on the Tienthan," Deymos teased, poking Nemy on her side. He earned a deserved pinch on the arm from the goddess of retribution herself.

"How was everyone else's day?" Sophie smiled.

Silence swept through the group.

"Well, Artemis is potentially missing, but we hope she just got too worked up in hunting a cute animal in the Faery forest," Eros said it as if it were nothing, but long gulp of his cup told Sophie otherwise.

"Oh, and Ash accidentally went to the Shadow Realm," Deymos offered.

Sophie's eyes widened.

"Yep. I accidentally went to the Shadow Realm," Ash confirmed it as if it were merely an unimportant speck of dirt on his shirt.

"Sorry, you what?!" Sophie looked like a fish out of water.

Ash, the ever-brooding angel then had the gall to shrug.

"He even lost a couple of feathers," Nemy pointed out to the patch of missing feathers, the pink skin looking sore.

"Yeah, Kaine did that to him." Eros took a sip from his cup. "The Breaker of Realms," he mocked in an annoying voice.

"Omg Ash, what the fuck? Why didn't you tell me?" Sophie gasped, instinctively examining the patch of missing feathers. Barbs stuck out but it looked like it was healed well. It would just be a matter of growing the feathers back.

"I was *going* to until these assholes beat me to it," Ash complained, taking a sip from his cup. He turned to Sophie with a devilish grin.

Oh gods, what's he going to say now? Sophie could feel an impending eye roll start at the back of her eyelids.

"Worried about me, are you?" Ash smirked. And there it was. Ash. The giant carrier pigeon.

"Ugh," Sophie groaned, rolling her eyes and downed the entire wine glass. As she put it back down to rest on her knee, the glass filled back up as if enchanted. Sophie marvelled at it, and looked to the bartender who gave her a small nod.

This is going to get messy.

"Don't worry, Sophie, his pretty wings will grow back in no time." Deymos winked.

Eros put his glass down on the ledge behind him. He leaned into the circle, his elbow upon his knees, his hands serving as a pretty seat for his chin. He looked downright mischievous, as he asked, "Tell me, Soph, has Ash told you about how he got his wings?"

Ash let out a groan of annoyance, pinching the space between his brows. "They only tell this story to remind me how powerless I used to be. Don't buy into it, Sofreya."

Whatever the story was, it clearly annoyed Ash which made Sophie lean farther into the circle with a conspirator's grin. "No, he *hasn't* told me the story. It sounds ever so interesting, please do tell," Sophie said sweetly as she looked down at Ash who gave her an offended look as if to say *How could you?*

Sucker. Sophie grinned, resting a hand on Ash's neck as she buckled in for the story to come. The touch was second nature.

"When Ash landed in the Godlands, he was a wee baby Fae," Eros pouted his lips as he conjured a little cloud figure, in the shape of a boy. "Baby Ash cried a lot," he continued as little cloud tears fell from the small cloud Ash.

Why was he crying a lot? What happened when he departed Faery? The questions echoed in Sophie's head as a pang of sorrow filled her. She squeezed Ash's neck in comfort. She doubted he needed it, but still. Ash leaned in closer to her legs, the movement bringing her warmth again.

"Then one day, he spotted us training in the ring," Eros continued. He conjured a tiny training ring with three angels fighting one another. The little cloud Ash was crouched underneath a table, spying on them.

Deymos scoffed. "He followed us around like a lost puppy. Day and night."

"Come on, I was not a lost puppy," Ash argued.

"Don't listen to him, Sophie, he was. He even had a little chip on his shoulder and everything. I've never seen such a sad little thing before." Nemy held up a hand in front of Ash's face to shush his arguing.

Sophie smiled at the little exchanges they had. They were like squabbling siblings.

"We told him to go home when we found him sleeping in the training ring, but he wouldn't leave. So, we put him to work." Eros conjured a little cloud Ash, a little older now, who practised various weapons as the cloud angels watched over him.

It was really sweet but where did Cerri fit into this? Afterall, she was meant to take care of him in exchange for her son's protection.

"He grew up big and strong, but he had no wings. How could he keep up?" The cloud angels flew away as little cloud Ash chased them.

"The little bugger had guts though." Deymos smirked, lifting his glass to Ash before downing his drink.

"That's right. When the Hrabrost Trials rolled around, he followed us there too. Only fifteen years old at that point." Eros arced his hands wide, to create a big mountain out of his clouds.

Nemy leaned into whisper into Sophie's ear. "The courage trials. An annual test for us Tienthan to make sure we've got what it takes to stay in the Aerial Legion," she explained.

Sophie raised her eyebrows and nodded. *Interesting.*

"We were so angry with him, Sophie. He followed us to the Hrabrost Trials, for Fates' sake. Once you're in, you can't get out without completing it." Deymos shook his head in disbelief.

"And so we dragged him with us for the *entire* trial. He was a nuisance. Always complaining. Always brooding and carrying around his little war hammer thinking he was some warrior." Eros made a face to say that he was annoyed and disgusted at the same time. The cloud angels climbed the mountain with a little cloud Ash among them.

Ash laughed, as if the thought sparked a fond memory.

Sophie smiled a little at that.

Eros's voice turned serious. "When we reached Mount Gehenna, the largest monster we'd ever seen came spilling out of it, sending rocks crashing around us." Cloud rocks dropped down the mountain and the cloud angels dodged them, carrying little cloud Ash by the scruff of his neck.

Sophie laughed at the clouds. They looked so darned cute.

Nemy chimed in with a laugh. "Deymos's leg got crushed by one of them." She poked her tongue out at Deymos, who snarled back.

"And we were stuck. With the end of the Hrabrost Trials mere inches away," Eros said solemnly. The cloud angels looked frantic, trying to pull out cloud Deymos from the rock.

Deymos leaned in, a look of sadness upon his face. The entire room quietened, as if they too were listening to the story.

"Fifteen-year-old Acheron Taranis, with the bravery of a thousand soldiers, climbed upon one of the rocks and called to the lightning above us with his war hammer." Eros paused as he conjured little lightning strikes around the scene. "He channelled the lightning above and struck the monster, stopping the onslaught of rock and debris falling from the mountain top."

"He saved us." Deymos watched the cloud formations, though his eyes were a little distant.

"And he fried his entire body doing it," Nemy added.

Sophie's hand squeezed tighter on Ash's neck. His cheek was leaning on her thigh now and she became all too aware of where their skin met. Poor Ash. To go through something like that at such a young age.

"I mean I got some cool hair to go along with it, didn't I?" Ash tried to make light of the conversation, earning him a scowl from Eros for interrupting.

Sophie let out a soft smile. She absentmindedly ran her fingers through Ash's pure white strands. Softer than that of his inky hair.

"When we found him, he was a hair's breadth away from the clutches of death." The cloud angels swarmed around the lifeless cloud Ash. "So we imbued our powers in him. Whatever we could give, we gave," Eros said the last part with a smile, as if proud to have given a part of himself to his friend. "Zeus was watching the trial from afar. For Ash's gallantry, Zeus offered his own power too."

Sophie's eyes widened. In her mind, Zeus was an overzealous, power-hungry bully, but she was starting to think that it was worth putting her preconceived notions aside. Just for this one act of kindness.

Sophie replayed the words in her head again. *Zeus offered his own power too. His power of lightning . . .*

Sophie almost wanted to step back from Ash. He had the power of four gods within him and not just any god, Zeus's power coursed through his veins.

Holy shit.

"When he came to, he was granted his wings by Ares," Eros marvelled. Little wings appeared on cloud Ash.

Nemy smiled. "The youngest to ever achieve it."

Eros vanished his cloud display with a click of his fingers. Gone was his solemn, reminiscent tone and back in its place was his playfulness. "So, what did you think of the story, Soph?"

"It sounded like Ash saved your asses, which, by the way you set up this story was *not* where I was expecting it to go. I thought you were going to roast his ass until kingdom come." Sophie made a face of disappointment.

"Ah darling, you forget that I am the god of love living among the dark and deadly. I just made you fall in love with him," Eros stated as a matter of fact, his lips pouted as he leaned back into the lounge as if to say *Hook, line and sinker.*

Sophie gaped. "Why you little—" Sophie made to lunge at Eros.

Deymos barked in laughter while Nemy tried her best to hold hers in.

Ash groaned, facepalming himself.

Eros curled away defensively. "Just admit it, you *love* each other!" Eros teased with the silliest grin Sophie had ever seen on a god of any kind.

"We're JUST FRIENDS!" Ash and Sophie screamed at the same time, their hands shooting up in unison.

"Ah, the beautiful sounds of denial. The first step to true love they say." Eros sighed romantically, fanning himself with his hand as if he were about to swoon.

"By the Fates,"—Ash pushed himself off the ground—"I'm getting a stronger drink." He trudged away, a cloud of lightning following in his wake.

Sophie leaned back into her seat, taking another long sip of her wine.

Eros caught her eye and winked.

Sophie couldn't help but smile. She enjoyed his teasing *way* too much.

39

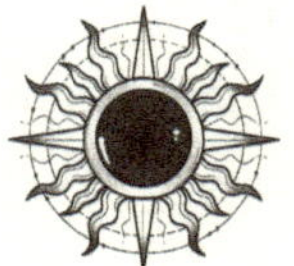

ACHERON

The Ephemeral Eclipse was fast approaching.

Every three years, for three days, the Godlands would stop to celebrate life and love. The legends had it that the sun and the moon were lovers, cursed to chase each other in the sky for all eternity. The Fates had felt sorry for them, so with their powers, they granted the sun and moon three days to stand still. Three days to bask in something other than the chase, forever destined to live their lives apart in the sky.

On the first night, the eclipse would appear. On the second night, while the sun and moon stilled, the stars would come down to rest in the Godlands. And on the third night, the stars would rise again, shooting back to their rightful positions in the night sky.

Ash had never paid much attention to the Ephemeral Eclipse until this year.

He fidgeted as he held the bouquet of purple flowers he had picked up from the market earlier in the morning. The sun was approaching its peak in the sky now, and the heat of the Godlands had started to settle in.

He practised the lines over and over again as he walked down to Sofreya's villa. And when the lines jumbled and mashed up in his angel brain, he turned and walked back to his place. Ash had burned a trail on the ground.

"Starlight, would you please do me—" Ash huffed.

Do me? She's going to slap me if I say it like that.

He slowly moved toward the door of her villa. "Starlight, please be my date—" Ash growled. Date? What date? They were just friends. At least that's what Sofreya wanted, and he would honour that. He couldn't risk— He shook his head, trying to stay on track.

Ash climbed the three steps and halted before her front door. He mumbled under his breath one more time, to get the words right. "Starlight, the Ephemeral Ball is in two days and the only person I want to celebrate with is you. Will you go to the ball with me?" he whispered.

That was good. A little lengthy, but good.

Ash psyched himself up, letting out a sharp breath and shaking out the nervousness in his wings. He righted himself before lifting his hand to knock against the door. But before he could knock, Sofreya pulled the door open and leaned on the doorframe looking as smug as a bug in a rug.

Fuck.

"Did you hear all—" Ash started.

"Oh, I heard *allll* of that. Everything starting . . ." Sofreya paused, lifting her wrist as if to look at a watch. She didn't even have a watch on. She continued, "about thirty minutes ago."

Ash in all his twenty-seven years of life had never felt his power and life essence drain from him in one fell swoop. Until now. Sophie was grinning like she'd just gotten away with murder and if it weren't for his utter embarrassment, he would be right there with her grinning. Instead, he shoved the bouquet of purple flowers in her hands and stormed off. Briskly. At pace. Anything to retrieve his soul as it whisked away on a wind of humiliation. He opened his wings, ready to thrust into the air.

"Wait!" Sophie shouted.

Ash snapped his wings back. Her voice pulled at him. He turned on his heel to find her still in her doorway with a bright smile on her face.

He instantly melted. Only she could do this to him.

"It's a date," she said, lifting the bouquet up in the air.

Ash smiled to himself and concluded that those very words would torment him for the rest of his life.

It was a custom in the Godlands. A custom made long ago that the person who asked, would find something for their date to wear to the Ephemeral Ball. So here Ash was, standing in front of a tucked-away dress shop in Soul City. Its display windows were draped in black velvet and a white sign painted with red cursive hung above the door. *Night Blossom's Eveningwear.*

Ash felt unequivocally out of his depth. Give him a sword, a spear or a rare weapon and he'd master it seconds. This? He didn't know where to start. That's why he enlisted the help and support of his older brother, for all intents and purposes, Deymos.

Ash looked up at the white sign, a touch nervous but he'd heard from the other Tienthan that this was the place to go for all evening wear.

Deymos clasped a hand on Ash's shoulder in reassurance. "You've got this, baby bro," Deymos said, his voice deep and stern as if he were about to go to battle.

Ash gave him a tense smile.

"Oh my god *dress shopping*!!" Eros sung right in Ash's ears.

Ash winced. He also clearly remembered asking only Deymos for help. Turns out Eros had as much of a penchant for eavesdropping as he did delivering love letters. Who was Ash to turn away the god of love? Now, Ash and Deymos were paying the ultimate price.

Eros linked his arms with a sullen-faced Ash and dragged him to the store door. Deymos followed closely behind, his shadows billowing around him. As they opened the door, the doorbell rang with a crystal clearness. The chime conjured a female being whose skin glimmered gold, as with her hair. "Welcome to Night Blossom's. I am Night and I'll be of service to you today," she smiled, bowing her head reverently. She was a golden statue – stoic and still.

Ash stepped forward upon the black carpet. It felt like they were in a black velvet portal. "I am after a dress for my date to the Ephemeral Ball."

Night assessed Ash with bored face. "You've left it a bit late, haven't you, angel?"

Eros chimed in. "Oh, please excuse him. It's his first time at the ball!" He clasped his hands in excitement and bounced on the spot.

Ash growled in warning as dark clouds began to plume around him. He had granted Eros permission to join them on the condition that he kept calm and collected. Whatever this was, it was not calm and collected.

Eros made a noise under his breath that sounded like he was sorry, but the tone was full of attitude.

Night lifted her hand for Ash to take. He obliged, manifesting his favourite moments with Sofreya. He could see Night's eyes flicker with warmth and happiness as she watched Ash's memories unfold.

"What a beauty," Night breathed.

Ash couldn't agree more.

"Do you have any dresses left?" Ash asked.

"I have a few in mind. Just a moment." Night whisked away behind the black curtains of the store.

The three angels of the Tienthan turned around, busying themselves, taking a look at the suits and dresses that were on display. Some were gaudy and bedazzled. While others were elegant and reserved. Ash noticed how Deymos's shadows were out in full force today. Which meant his shadows were restless, speaking to him and urging him to do things. Ash never really understood how Deymos's shadows worked, but he was glad he did not have to deal with such a power. Right now, it looked like he was sifting through his shadows, trying to find something.

"Lost something, have you?" Ash asked.

Deymos shook his head to clear it and smirked. "Something like that."

It seemed like Night was taking her time finding dress options for Sofreya.

"So, you've asked Soph to be your date for the Ephemeral Ball, does that mean you've told her?" Eros asked too excitedly. Ash could almost hear the stupid grin on Eros's face.

Ash turned to find Eros with his arms draped around a tall, sturdy mannequin in a dark purple suit. His heel was popped as if he were receiving his first foot-popping kiss. Lightning struck inside the black velvet room. "No," Ash growled lowly.

Eros rushed to Ash in despair, his hands upon his face. "Oh come on, Ash. Don't leave the poor girl hanging!"

"He's right, baby bro. You've got to tell her," Deymos added, bristling his grey wings behind him.

"Hey! Whose side are you on, Deymy?" Ash pointed at Deymos.

"With this"—Deymos circled his arm over Ash's general vicinity then pointed at Eros who stood with his arms crossed— "I'm with Eros. You can't leave the girl hanging with something as important as this."

"I'm not leaving her hanging. If anything, she's leaving me hanging. She has her memories blocked and unless she accidentally strolls into the Stagnum De Memoria, my hands are completely tied." They weren't technically tied. No. But Ash didn't want to risk it. He'd only *just* found her and if telling her would push her away . . . well, it was a pain he didn't want to live with. As selfish as that made him.

"You know you could just tell her, right?" Eros wagged his eyebrows.

"Absolutely not. She wants a clean slate. I'll be honouring that . . . as torturous as it may be." Ash almost whispered the last part.

He would go to the ends of time for her. Ever since he held her almost lifeless body in his arms in that fate-forsaken temple in Faery, he knew couldn't let her go. He wouldn't. Never again. He'd been doing well in keeping things platonic but when they ran down the hill in the Meadow of Mainn, nostalgia ignited a spark in him. A spark that transported him back to their days in Faery and by the Fates did he want her to remember it all. He wanted it so badly that his chest ached for days. Every shared moment that she'd forgotten, he wanted to tell her. Wrap them in a warmth and kindness that she deserved to feel again. He wanted to be selfish, but he couldn't tell her. He wouldn't. They were her memories and if she wanted to start over again, what was he going to do? Tell her otherwise? Force it upon her? And risk losing her? No way in all the realms would he risk that. So that night in the Meadow of Yearning, he did the next, most selfish thing. He called in the favour she owed him, just so he could hold her under the stars. A moment of selfishness that he would tuck away for safe keeping. He shouldn't have done it. It stirred up an addiction so viral, visceral and deeply rooted that he didn't know where he started and where his need for

Sofreya ended. He needed her as much as a wayfinding warrior needed the stars to guide him home.

Eros looked at Ash, thrumming his fingers against his arm with a sort of side smile. The look only meant one thing.

"By the Fates, Eros, don't you dare meddle with this," Ash sighed.

Eros raised his eyebrows and shot his hands up defensively, as if to say that he wasn't going to agree to anything.

"Promise me, Eros, that you won't interfere," Ash pleaded.

"Okay, fine." Eros relented, kicking the carpet with his head hung low, as if he were a kicked puppy.

Night reappeared from behind the curtain with perfect timing.

"I have three options for you," Night sang out.

Ash shook out his feathers and stepped forward, surveying the three dresses that Night had sprung into the air with her mana. The dresses danced in between them all, showing off the movement in their skirts.

"Oooh, I like the red one," Eros cooed.

The red dress looked like a living flame. Strapless with a full skirt. It was a lovely dress, but it didn't scream Sofreya. The second dress was a blueish purple dress with a halter neck that wished and washed around. It looked like water, spilling over endlessly. Again, it was beautiful, but not something Sofreya would wear. Ash didn't think so at least. It was the third dress that caught Ash's eye and held his attention. It wasn't the most glamorous of the three. It didn't have mana imbued into its skirts, but it was perfect for Sofreya. Tiny silver beads and crystals lined the entire dress and the skirt flowed endlessly like a galaxy of stars.

"I'll take this one," Ash picked the flowing dress out of the air. The other two dresses flew behind the black curtains again.

"A wise choice." Night smiled before rushing away behind a glass counter, preparing the dress.

Deymos moved to Ash to scruff his hair. He smiled as he ducked out of the storefront, the bell chiming as he did.

"We'll meet you outside," Eros smiled.

Ash moved to the counter where Night had wrapped up the dress and placed it in a black box. "You can charge it to my last name."

Night nodded with a thanks.

"Thank you so much." He dipped his head, took the box and headed out the door.

Deymos grinned, raking a hand through his short silver hair, while Eros looked like he could barely keep it together. His lips and eyes brimmed with excitement. The god was basically vibrating.

Ash rolled his eyes. "Alright, go on. Let it out," he groaned.

"BY THE FATES I JUST LOVE LOVE SO MUCH!" Eros cried through the streets of Soul City.

Ash laughed and for once, he enjoyed the teasing, because a part of him loved love too.

Ash lay in his bed, restless.

His mind wandered to Sofreya far too often. He watched the dark ceiling, trying to count sheep. As the sheep bounced happily over the fence, they'd form constellations in the night sky, then they sparkled, forming a bright constellation in the shape of Sofreya. Eros was right. Ash should tell her. Everything. And it would be up to her, whether they continued their friendship or not. She had the right to know.

Ash turned to his bedside table and fished out a bracelet he'd been gifted long ago. As he flipped over each bead, it calmed him. Cal whined as he curled up next to Ash, laying his furry chin on Ash's stomach. He looked at Ash with concerned eyes.

Ash sighed heavily. "I'll tell her after the ball," he said to Cal, scratching his friend's furry ears as he did.

Cal let out a long tendril of smoke from his nostrils – an approval.

40

SOPHIE

The Ephemeral Eclipse was to start in an hour and Sophie would be spending the first night of it in the company of angels, gods and goddesses. *Who woulda thunk?*

Sophie's mother had told her all about it. Three days of night, to celebrate love and life. It turns out all her bookish dreams were coming true, but the nagging sensation in the back of her head also told her that all her bookish nightmares were about to come true too. Sophie had been warring against herself over the past day, seeming to have forgotten why she was staying in the Godlands in the first place. She'd gotten stronger and had grown her power. It was probably time that she made her way to Faery, though a few more days in ignorant bliss surely wouldn't hurt.

Sophie opted for a black halter-neck maxi dress for tonight's celebrations. Completely backless and flowing, it was perfect for staving off the summery night. She tied her purple hair up into a high ponytail and finished everything off with a touch of clear lip gloss. She already knew who was at the door before they knocked. "I'm in the bedroom, Mum!" Sophie called out.

The warmth of her mother's golden mana washed over her as Danna entered the room, a bright smile on her face. "You look absolutely stunning, darling!" She hugged Sophie as tight as possible.

"You too, Mum." Sophie pulled back, noticing that her mum had a bit of make-up on. Danna never wore make-up. Ever.

Sophie's eyes widened, ready to gasp dramatically for full effect. "Mum, you're wearing make-up." Sophie pointed a finger at her mum. It was an accusation.

Danna, with her long silver hair and golden eyes, stuttered but righted herself just as quickly. "So what if I am?" She turned to start toward the front door.

Sophie followed, a wolfish grin on her face. "It's Ares isn't it? You're seeing him."

Danna pushed out the front door with her head held high. Sophie locked her front door behind them. Before them stood a pearl-coated arion with blond wings. "Thanks for waiting, Spirit." Danna ran her hand across the arion's neck before pulling herself up with ease. She reached back, lending a hand to Sophie who pushed up and over Spirit, seating herself behind Danna.

Sophie embraced her mother. It'd been a while since she'd done it. Ever since Danna had admitted to shielding Sophie's memories, it felt like there was a wedge between them. A wedge that was tall and intimidating. Sure, a part of her was angry but there was also a part of her that was tired and ready to move on. The road ahead for them wasn't going to be smooth, but at least there would be one.

Danna made a sharp clicking sound and the arion boosted into the air. Sophie could feel the tension in her mother, her back tense. "He makes me feel safe, Sophie," Danna said lowly. A taste of reservation and guilt hung around her words.

Sophie tucked her chin onto her mother's shoulder, feeling the mana that calmed her through childhood and even now in moments like this. "That's what matters most, Mum. You shouldn't feel guilty either. If father was the way you had described him, a good male, then he'd be happy knowing you'd found happiness. I'm certain of it," Sophie offered.

Danna remained quiet for some time. The only sound breaking their silence was the beating of the Spirit's wings and the gush of air around them as they soared over the Isle of Deos.

Danna's voice was soft again. Solemn. "I looked for him. From the Meadows of Mainn. It all happened so long ago. I thought, maybe there's a slim chance he's there by the river, waiting for me. I even searched Soul City"—Danna scoffed—"The thing with most souls in the Elysian Fields, is that they find peace. And I know that if I found peace, I wouldn't want to leave it either." She let out a long breath. The type that only a heavy heart could muster. "He was a good male."

Sophie smiled. "Then be happy, Mum. You deserve it."

Danna's body softened at the words. They remained that way for the remainder of the flight. Sophie with her arms around her mother's waist, and Danna leaning back into Sophie.

Sophie followed behind Danna as they pushed into the golden doors of Ares's home. Correction, mansion. The white marble house could easily fit ten of Sophie's villas. Ancient weapons, shields and armour lined every single wall as if it were a museum. The click of their sandals on the pristine floor echoed as they walked down the hallway. Sophie had to pick her jaw up from the floor as she spotted a large shield and sword, encased in glass. The plaque below it read *Achilles.*

She was in the freaking Greek god of war's home. The actual son of Zeus and Hera, who had freaking ancient Greek artifacts that no human had ever laid eyes upon. Artifacts that were on display in his home as if they were random golf trophies. What was Sophie's life right now?

Danna resorted to dragging Sophie by her neck because she couldn't stop gawking, fawning and silent squealing from artifact to artifact down the hall.

They stopped before a set of large golden doors. Pushing them with her magic, Danna grabbed Sophie's hand and together they walked over the threshold.

The doors opened to a large, circular dining room etched out of marble. Golden tapestry lined the entire wall. Towering marble columns surrounded the sunken dining area where a long table sat in the middle, laden with fruits and starters. Ares stood up to greet them. Deymos, Eros and Nemy did the same, but Sophie's vision simmered and tunnelled in on one person only.

Her mouth instantly fell dry.

Ash. *Ash.*

His long hair was slicked back into a tight bun so that part of his undercut was on display. A thin golden diadem with a small angel wing beside his temples painted him the image of a perfect pious angel. A golden sash covered parts of his chest and wrapped tightly around his waist. His dark tattoos popped out against the warm tones of his clothes and Sophie never felt so powerless. Her knees quaked and her heart hammered like a fool. He was an angel. A perfect fucking angel and he was her damned date for the Ephemeral Ball. How had she managed that?

Ash grinned his bright, gummy smile she knew he only reserved for her. Sophie's ovaries self-detonated. Her will and resolve dissolved into nothingness and her throat . . . so, so dry.

Someone please get me some water. Girl dying from thirst here. Sophie made a squeaking noise that was a mixture of gushing and terror.

Ash walked over to Sophie, and she swore time itself died just so she could savour every moment of this. His thick, corded, muscled thighs peeked through the golden sash he wore as he moved closer. He grabbed Sophie's hand with confidence and bent low, placing a chaste kiss on the back of her hand. His large white wings, no longer patchy, spread out behind him, encompassing her entire field of vision. Those turquoise smoking eyes burned into her and didn't dare leave. He mouthed a greeting, but Sophie's couldn't hear through the roaring in her ears.

What was happening? Why did it feel like the entire world was spinning away and the only thing that survived the chaos was Ash? Why did it feel like her stomach had been sucker punched into another realm and at the same time, her heart was soaring in the clouds? It was a confounding conundrum of emotions but what Sophie knew for sure, was that she wanted to feel this high forever. Whatever it was, she'd take it.

Sophie gulped.

The sound of Danna clearing her throat snapped Sophie back to reality quicker than a rubber band. Sophie gave Ash a light, breathy smile. She probably looked like she was off with the fairies, but she didn't care.

Sophie turned to find Ares with his arms outstretched, waiting to greet her. "Hi Ares, how are you?" Sophie laughed, stepping into the Ares's embrace. He hugged her like she was his child and it made Sophie feel all sorts of warm.

"Very well." Ares guffawed, his laughter vibrating through Sophie. "Happy Ephemeral Eclipse." He let her go to greet everyone else in the room.

Deymos, Eros and Nemy swarmed around Sophie, offering their Ephemeral Eclipse wishes. They all wore similar sashes to Ash. Deymos wore all grey, while Eros wore white. Nemy wore a beautiful green chiton, embellished with gold leaves. It complemented her chestnut hair and wings perfectly.

Beyond the dining table was a wide balcony. Three large marble arches encased the balcony, which overlooked the dense jungle of the Isle. Above in the night sky, the moon shined with fervour as the eclipse slowly took its place. The sounds of insects buzzing and singing made its way through the dining room and everything, for once, felt at peace.

Ares moved to the head of the table with Danna in tow, her hand gently placed in the crook of his arm. She moved to his left, standing behind her seat. Sophie moved to sit next to her mother. Deymos took a seat to Ares's right. Nemy slotted in next to him with Eros on the end. It left Ash sitting right next to Sophie.

They all shared warm smiles across the table, and it honestly felt like a perfect Australian Christmas. Not that Sophie had ever had one, but this was as close as it was going to get. The only thing she was missing was Elowan, Zala . . . and Cam.

Ares cleared his throat. "Thank you all for coming. My children,"—Ares pointed to the angels in the room—"my light"—he then pointed to Danna—"and the new force to be reckoned with." Ares gave Sophie a wink. "Every three years, we come together to celebrate life and love under the eclipse of the moon. And this year, we are blessed with additions to our found family." From the folds of the Between, Ares manifested what looked like a snow globe. In its centre spun a replica of the moon. He held it between his two hands and shot a sprout of his power into it. The golden sparkling power danced happily around the moon. He passed it around the table, each person imbuing the globe with a shot of their power.

As it reached Nemy, Ash leaned in closer to Sophie, his wing coming to wrap around her, but not quite touching her. "It's a tradition of ours. Each eclipse, we put a tendril of our power in the globe to perfectly encapsulate who was here and how we felt," he explained.

Sophie craned her neck to look up at Ash. "Like a little time capsule?"

Ash nodded as he took the globe from Eros. He quickly shot his power into it. The globe was now full of energy that danced around the little moon that was inside. Ash gently passed it to Sophie who marvelled at the little time capsule of power. She pushed a tiny piece of her mana into the globe, and she could see the purple magic twist and shout around the moon, among the other pieces of power that lived in there.

There was something special about all of this. Not once had Sophie felt so full of warm love. Her childhood was always cold and distant, as if she was never really there. This felt real.

Sophie passed the globe to her mother who repeated the process with a tender smile across her face. Ares moved to take the globe from Danna. Sophie's eyes caught at how he purposefully brushed his fingers across hers, stealing moments wherever he could.

Ares levitated the globe and placed it in the centre of the table. "Let the feast begin!" With a click of his fingers, food appeared. Roasts, seafood and hearty vegetables lay across the table. Everyone dived into conversation as soft classical music spilled into the room.

They spoke about their childhood, their favourite battles and the funny moments spread out in between. Ares was basically a walking encyclopedia and Sophie was eager to listen. Her heart was full and so was her belly – from laughter and food. She didn't even have enough room for dessert and that was a first.

Ares leaned back into his seat, his wings stretching out behind him. "Acheron, I heard you're heading to the ball. Who's the lucky lass?"

Nemy gasped. "It's Chronos isn't it? That sneaky angel has *finally* worn you down."

Ares leaned in, eating up the gossip with a smirk. He pointed a finger at Ash who had storm clouds brewing around him. Sophie laughed, happy to not save Ash from this embarrassment. Though a pang of jealousy made its way through Sophie's chest at the name of another female who sought Ash's attention.

"She has always been persistent. She is a quite a good match for—" Ares didn't get to finish the words as Sophie let out a warning growl. A full-blown, territorial-Fae growl. She didn't mean to. Sophie blanched.

Did I just growl like a fucking territorial Fae bastard?

Sophie cleared her throat, grabbed her goblet of wine and stood abruptly. "If anyone needs me, I'll be on the balcony watching the eclipse." Sophie's smile was more of a grimace.

Sophie passed Danna, who gave an amused, knowing smile. Ares however, looked severely apologetic. Of course, he hadn't known that Ash had asked her to the Ephemeral Ball, not when every chance she could, Sophie would refer to Ash as her best friend and nothing more. But there was no denying how she felt now. The warning growl was proof enough that even the fibres of her being knew where she wanted to be when it came to Ash. Even if her brain and heart hadn't really caught up. It was a startling revelation and made her feel a little uneasy.

Sophie climbed onto the balustrade of one of the balcony arches, careful not to spill her wine as she did. The moon was almost fully eclipsed and the jungle before her was darker than she'd ever seen it before. It made the stars burn brighter in the sky.

A rustle of wings sounded behind her, and Sophie turned to find Ash, holding back a smirk. Sophie rolled her eyes but patted the space next to her so he could sit. He obeyed, lifting himself up with a flutter of his wings to gently sit down beside her. They said nothing for a while. All they could do was stare at each other. Unspoken words lay heavily between them. Sophie wished upon every star in the sky that they would be spoken but something like fear wrapped around her throat. She'd let the steel walls around her heart down before, and well, that didn't turn out too great, did it?

It was Ash who broke first. "Listen, I—" He didn't finish his words as the rest of the dinner party came tumbling out of the dining room, loud and unruly.

Deymos levitated over to Ash, clasping a strong hand on Ash's shoulder. He moved to kiss Sophie's cheek. "Happy first Ephemeral Eclipse, Sophie." Deymos beamed. His shadows weren't out on display today.

Danna moved to Sophie and hugged her close. "Happy Ephemeral Eclipse, my darling."

"You too, Mum." Sophie squished herself against her mother.

Danna moved to Ares who stood just behind the others, watching the moon with content in his eyes. Deymos, Nemy and Eros climbed onto the balustrade, next to Ash. Ash scooched over just the slightest to give them room, his wing gently brushing Sophie's back.

Sophie laughed as Eros fought to sit beside Ash, but Deymos wouldn't let him. They pushed each other around like pups in a pack.

A moment later, the group fell silent, watching the moon as it became fully eclipsed. Sophie leaned back on her hands, letting her feet dangle over the edge. She breathed it all in. The Godlands washed over in darkness, and it felt like everyone had let loose a breath.

From the corner of her eye, Sophie noticed Ash leaning back on his hands too. The smallest, tension-filled space separated their hands. And Sophie's hand burned to touch his. They'd held hands before, but this was different. This was all consuming. A moment before the flood gates opened, but could she cross the line with her best friend? Sophie didn't dare look at Ash. What if he didn't feel the same way she did? Would their friendship ever be the same if they did cross the line from best friend to something more?

The stars above rattled to life, dancing around to a waltz that Sophie could not hear but felt in her soul. She'd seen this before. Her eyes widened just a fraction. The Ephemeral Lights, made of blue-and-green swirls, from the night she had escaped Faery with her mother. Tears stung behind her eyes. She committed this to memory. She had dreamt of and thought of these lights for all her life. They kept her grounded and they kept her calm. And suddenly she remembered why she had committed these to memory. Even though she was young, she never wanted to forget the tether that had been torn to shreds as she left Faery. The tether whose other end belonged to Ash.

The dinner party whooped and cheered, but Sophie and Ash didn't. They continued watching the night sky come to life. She was wondering if he too was remembering that fateful night they parted ways.

As if in answer, Sophie felt a feather light touch on the back of her hand.

Still, she did not look at him. She was scared to. She worried about how hard her heart was beating. Singing. The warmth of his skin was like a lullaby that soothed the fire burning inside her.

He was seeking permission. And by the Fates, for Sophie, it was a yes. For one night at least. She could do that right?

Softly, gingerly, with all the care in the world, she flipped her hand over, letting him intertwine his hand with hers.

Together, they watched the night sky.

Two halves of a whole.

41

SOPHIE

Sophie woke to a soft knock on her front door. She sent out her mana to feel who it was, but nothing reached back. She rushed to the door, opening it ever so slightly hoping Ash would be there, but he wasn't.

After last night, Sophie felt strange. Like she was stuck between two realms. Like a piece of her was stuck in Faery, and for what it was worth, a part of her truly was. There was unfinished business with Kaine and the maelstrom of a prophecy that they had momentarily been swept up in. There were her memories tied into her identity that had escaped her for so long, kept hidden by her mother. Without those things being put to rest, she felt a little empty and guilty if anything, for giving into the pull that existed with Ash. The last time she let her heart open she'd been burned and broken by Kaine. She knew it felt different with Ash. It was a soul-destroying yearning she'd felt her entire life, and it was caused by him. She knew it. Though the fear in her heart sunk its teeth deep into her skin. She had yet to learn how to bite back.

Sophie looked to the floor and found a black box with a large black ribbon tied around it. The smell of Ash's woody scent lingered there for a moment.

So, it *was* him.

Sophie picked up the box and moved back inside, unfastening the ribbon as she did. She opened it to find a letter from Ash sitting on top.

Starlight,
The stars were once wary, but tonight they will burn with envy.
Yours.

Sophie bit her lip and her heart squeezed. The nickname. His sign off. *Yours.* Oh it made her heart stupidly giddy.

She placed the note back in the box, cheeks flushed, only to find a dress forged by the stars themselves.

You are kidding me.

She moved to her bedroom and laid the dress onto her bed. The strapless bodice was covered in silver crystals, diamonds and sequins. A see-through skirt cascaded effortlessly as it split at the waist to showcase a thigh. The train stretched out for a while and the hovering shoulder pads were encrusted with diamonds, that would spill over down her arms like raindrops. From the shoulder caps, an almost invisible string attached itself to a thick diamond choker. It would showcase her tattoos and the mana markings on her chest perfectly. This dress was made for her.

Sophie placed her hand on her throat, her heart light and fluttery. This dress was heavenly. She couldn't even begin to fathom what it would have cost – a fortune at the very least.

Shit. He's going to be here in forty-five minutes.

Judging be the opulence of the dress, it was going to be a fancy ball.

Sophie rushed around to the bathroom, blowing a wind of mana through her hair so that it sat completely straightened. She slicked it back with a bit of water and gel before freezing water particles with her air mana. They formed little sparkling stars that shone in the galaxy of her purple hair. Winged eyeliner and frosted water droplets upon the inner corner of her eyes were the final step.

Sophie stepped back from the mirror with a satisfied smile. *That should do it.*

It turned out that applying make-up had taken much longer than anticipated. Sophie only had a minute until Ash arrived.

She rushed for the dress that lay on her bed. It was incredibly light despite being covered in crystals and diamonds. Unzipping it, Sophie stepped into it and managed to fasten the choker into place before a knock sounded at her front door.

Sophie huffed. *Of course he's early. Shit, I can't zip up the damn dress.* "I'm in the bedroom. Ugh, I think I'm going to need a little help!" Sophie called out. She felt his will-bending mana and smelled him before he stepped foot into her room. Velvety. Woodsy.

Sophie had her back to the door and was about to turn around when warm fingers found their way to the zipper of her dress. Slowly, excruciatingly, as if he had all the time in the world, Ash zipped her up. Though somehow, it felt like he was doing the exact opposite. Ash's hand remained at the top of her dress. Perfectly still. She could feel the burn of where his fingers had softly brushed her skin. Gone was her fluster. Rising in its place was pure, unbridled heat. Her hands started to shake, and her stomach filled with butterflies as she slowly turned.

There he was.

Acheron Taranis. In all his unbothered, divine glory. His unbound inky hair was pushed back behind his delicately pointed ears, falling onto a body covered in silver scaled armour. His tattoos peeked just above the high collar and from under his silver sleeves. His wings were decorated in the same light silver armour that ran all over his chest and legs. He was a muscular, brooding, intimidating version of Baz Luhrmann's Romeo and Sophie was Juliet, dressed in white, eager to find him. She could not blink. She could not breathe. She simply could not function.

It wasn't just in the way he looked, but the way he looked at her. His sweet plump lips slightly apart. His breathing unsteady. His pupils dilated and searing with an intensity that burned brighter than any flame she'd seen. He stared at her like she was his. To have and to hold. And as the silence between them grew, there was only one word Sophie wanted to growl and caw at the top of her lungs so that everyone knew what Ash was to her.

Mine.

But the word did not come out. She was still heady, gripped firmly under Ash's spell. Sophie tried to blink her vision clear, but it only made her dizzier. At some point her body had stopped receiving oxygen and it was only Ash that she was breathing in. Not air. It was just him and his woodsy scent and Sophie was quite content in drowning in it for the rest of the night.

"We should probably get going . . ." Sophie swallowed dryly. "If we don't want to miss the Ephemeral Cascade."

Smooth.

It was the second night of the Ephemeral Eclipse, and the stars would be falling to the Godlands to rest. Sophie was starting to think it was a better idea to skip the natural phenomenon altogether and spend the night here with Ash instead. A pull in her mana told her it was something she would regret missing though.

Ash's chest rumbled with the beginnings of a Fae growl. "We should," he breathed.

But neither of them moved.

It was like gravity had pinned them down. Like the universe was trying to make them stay in place. But somehow, Sophie broke free of the hold, lifting her hand to Ash's and laced her fingers with his. It felt simply and truly right. Whatever it was they had.

Sophie pulled Ash with her, leading him through the front door. And he let her, following her like a lost puppy. She could still feel the heat and hunger of his gaze without looking back.

A smirk found its way to Sophie's face knowing that while he was more powerful than her, she still had a hold over him. She chewed her bottom lip, feeling a little out of her depth but dared to turn back to Ash. As soon as she did, he pulled her to a stop as she reached the bottom of her villa stairs. He already towered her, but with the steps separating them now, it looked like he was about to take flight. A guardian angel, reaching down to lend a helping hand. That's what he looked like.

Ash smiled brightly, his smoking turquoise eyes dancing with mischief. "It's an official date then?"

Sophie paused for a moment. Her heart beating faster than she'd ever felt it before. His charm had slithered its way into her heart and for all the times he was there for her, lending her a hand from out of the dark, she knew he was worth giving a chance. With her hand intertwined with his, Sophie jumped off the tightrope of friendship and into the unknown. Even though fear of being hurt attempted to claw its way back onto the tightrope, Sophie continued to plummet. She knew deep down that she would be okay because the strong tether between them would be there to catch her fall.

"It's an official date." Sophie smiled brightly, almost bursting with laughter.

Something like relief washed over Ash's entire body and his eyes shone with excitement. He paced down the steps and swept Sophie up into his strong arms, swinging them both around in the air.

Sophie bubbled with laughter and so did Ash.

He let her softly onto the ground before kneeling beside Lumen, his arm outstretched dramatically. "Your noble steed awaits." Ash grinned. He was her knight in shining armour. Literally.

"Why thank you, kind sir." Sophie played along, placing her hand into Ash's as he helped her onto the arion's back.

Ash jumped onto Lumen, pushing his entire body flush against Sophie's. With a sharp click of his tongue, Ash launched them all into the air, flying them toward the Isle's waterfall.

As they landed softly atop the backward waterfall, Ash leaned down to whisper into Sophie's ear. His lips grazed her ear lobe, pebbling the skin on her arms. "Thank you, Starlight." He paused, and so did her heart. "For giving me a chance. I know what doing so means for you. I don't care how long I must wait. I don't care if the Fates have someone else planned for me. Because I will defy them with all the strength I have in my blood and bones, and I will *never* let you down. I can promise you that until my dying breath and somehow beyond that."

Ash's whispered declaration sent a chill down Sophie's spine. He meant every single word. And every single word burned her core. The words set alight her heart with fate-binding heat, and she couldn't think of a more pleasurable way to die than in Ash's arms.

There was no denying it now. Sophie was irrevocably, undeniably burning. And the flames she bathed and basked in were only burning for one soul. Ash's.

The stars were still high in the Godlands's sky when they arrived at Soul City's Colosseum. It stood several stories high, hewn from pure white marble, situated in the very centre of Soul City. All kinds of beings – souls, angels, gods and goddesses – milled about in the most decadent evening wear. Flirtatious smiles and hearty greetings were exchanged throughout the crowd, abuzz with excitement.

Sophie gawked and gasped to her heart's content, revelling in the thrum of anticipation that the crowd so clearly felt. This was a freaking Godlands ball, and boy, it did not disappoint. Glowing lanterns decorated streets and the colosseum itself, bathing the entire Soul City in warm light.

"Come on, Deymos and Eros are probably already up there several drinks deep. Don't want to miss out on the action, do we?" Ash grinned, pulling Sophie even closer to him.

Sophie hadn't said much since his declaration, not because she denied it or felt uncomfortable with his declaration. She just couldn't formulate the words that would best describe how she felt inside.

"We *definitely* can't let it slide."

Ash held his hand out, helping her pull up the skirts of the dress so she could grace the stairs accident free. A true gentleman.

Be still my beating heart. Sophie tried not to squeak.

As they climbed the stairs, Sophie felt a tingle at the back of her neck as if someone was watching her. Watching them. Before she could even turn around, Ash's grip was ripped from her hand, and with a grunt, he was tackled to the floor. A blur of red and tan pummelled into him.

What the fuck?

The crowd around them dispersed like the red sea. Lightning struck all around them and seconds later, Ash stood tall, holding the struggling assailant by his neck as if he weighed nothing. A promise of death etched across his perfect angelic face.

"Fuck you, you bastard," the assailant grunted.

Wait a minute. I know that voice.

Sophie, wide-eyed, rushed toward them. She recognised the mop of red hair. She recognised the tanned skin and the tall, athletic frame. "Cam?" Sophie breathed.

Ash snapped his head toward Sophie, his eyes relaxing a touch as he understood the recognition in her voice.

Sophie nodded at Ash to let Cam go. She had no idea how, but he understood her, dropping Cam to the ground in a flash, leaving him unbalanced. "Cam, is it really you?" Sophie held back a sob, though tears had already begun to spill.

As Cam regained his balance, his piercing green eyes shot straight to Sophie. Tears she'd been holding back came gushing out all at once. She rushed to him, embracing him with all her might. The blue film of magic that encased him, separated him as a soul. Cam let out a bit of a laugh, hugging Sophie as tightly as she was holding him. "It's good to see you, Sophie. It's so good to see you."

Sophie sobbed and she wasn't even sure if Cam could understand her. "I'm so sorry"—sniff—"It's all my fault. I shouldn't have let you run"—sniff—"after him. I'm unbelievably sorry, Cam. You deserved so much better," Sophie wailed, pushing her face farther into his chest.

"It's not your fault, Sophie." Cam rubbed her back. "I am a full-grown male, and what I did was my choice completely. It's not your fault. The Fates had decided it was my time. You have nothing to be sorry for." Cam held her close. "Though if I had the chance to go back, I'd beat the shit out of him a bit more." Cam laughed.

Sophie pushed back from his embrace, wiping the tears from her eyes. She needed this. For him to say the words that ate away the guilt that sat in her heart for so long. And here he was, his mischievous self in soul form. "I'm glad you made it to the Elysian Fields. Was the lifestyle a little too slow for you or something?" Sophie poked his arm.

"Eh, I had the option to head to Soul City. You know me, I love to be where all the action is." Cam winked.

Ash cleared his throat from behind Cam.

Cam's eyes widened in response, and he immediately put himself between Ash and Sophie.

Sophie tried to move around Cam, but he wasn't letting it happen.

"Sophie, I know I'm going to sound crazy, and I can't really do much now that I'm a soul with no powers but there's a guy behind me who from afar I'd mistaken as Kaine but upon closer inspection he has wings and somehow looks nicer. The point is, I was mistaken, and a little confused and angry but now I've made *him* angry," Cam whisper-yelled.

Sophie looked back at Ash from around Cam's arm. Ash looked amused but there was no mistaking the storm clouds that had formed around him, the threat of lightning hanging in the air.

"Oh Faery, he's listening, isn't he? Shit. Shit!" Cam took a hold of Sophie's hand in a tight grip. "Okay. We're going to run on three. One. Two—"

Sophie stopped him before he could run away. "Cam, it's fine." Sophie tried her best not to laugh. "I want you to meet someone." Sophie firmly grasped Cam around his arms and he genuinely looked frightened as he turned around to face the angel he'd just assaulted.

"Cam, this is Acheron Taranis, guardian angel in the Tienthan and Weapons Master of the Godlands." Sophie paused to place her tattooed hand on Ash's shoulder, watching Ash. "And Ash, this is Camrine Nahvi, a friend who fought in my name and someone who is dear to me."

Ash lifted his hand to greet Cam.

Cam's eyes were assessing. Cautious, if anything, he took in Ash's hand as if it were coated in poison. Cam looked to Sophie one more time and tilted his head, as if to ask *Are you sure about this?*

"Ash will never hurt me, Cam. He and Kaine are entirely different. I can show you." Sophie lifted her hand, waiting for his consent to fill his vision with her mother's memories and memories of her own.

Cam nodded, his lips twisting with scepticism.

Sophie moved the strands of red hair from his brow, and softly placed her fingers upon his temple. Purple mana started at her fingertips as Cam shut his eyes.

She showed him. Channelled her vivid visions and the undiluted emotions that laced them. Cerri's plea for help. Lethe, the moment he turned into Kaine. Ash, the moment he took Cerri's hand and disappeared. Ash, the moment he picked her up from the ground, slick with despair from the dose of Veritas. Ash, and the vow he uttered upon the Isle's waterfall just moments ago.

Sophie let go.

Cam's eyes fluttered open. The greens of them turning with understanding.

Sophie nodded and smiled in encouragement.

And with that blinding trust, he of all people should not possess, Camrine took Ash's hand in his, taking in the tattoos that swirled to the tips of his fingers.

A small smile appeared on Cam's face as he pulled Ash in for a hug instead. It clearly took Ash by surprise as his wings bristled the way they normally did when he felt uncomfortable.

Her worlds were colliding, and in the funniest of ways. It made her heart so full.

"Try me again, and I'll make sure your soul ends up in Tartarus," Ash growled in Cam's ear.

"Ash!" Sophie gasped.

Cam jumped back with a nervous laugh as the lightning in Ash's storms clouds began to spark. "It was an honest mistake, and I do apologise. Clean slate?" Cam lifted his hand between them.

Ash mumbled something under his breath about why *everyone* wanted a clean slate, but Sophie didn't quite catch it. "Very well." Ash clasped Cam's hand again and they both smiled their handsome smiles.

"I hate to burst the beginnings of a *really* hot bromance, but I believe the cascade is about to start. Ash, shall we head in?" Sophie chirped, taking a hold of Ash's elbow.

Ash nodded but looked at Cam in warning as he walked past him. The look was outrageously territorial, and Sophie couldn't help but curl her toes.

Ash guided her up the stairs without another word. Sophie looked back at Cam one more time, just to make sure he was real. He mouthed *Mother of Faery, he is HOT!* and fanned himself as if the temperature had spiked.

Sophie snorted and shook her head, a pang of nostalgia hitting her chest.

"Save me the first dance, will you?" Cam called after her.

"It's yours!" Sophie laughed, waving him goodbye for now.

Sophie turned back to Ash, who seemed relieved to have her alone again. "Took a bit of a tumble there did you? Never thought I'd see the benevolent master of weapons so easily put on his ass," Sophie jibed.

Ash growled, moving so quickly that Sophie had barely registered it. He placed a hand on the small of her back and bent low to whisper in her ear, "There's only one thing I'd like to tumble, Sofreya."

Sophie smirked, leaning up to feel his breath on her ear and her neck. "And what is that?"

"You'd like to know, wouldn't you?" Ash teased.

She did. She really, really did. Before she could even bite back with her smart mouth, he pulled her up the stairs of the colosseum.

Was it possible to die in Heaven, to then ascend to another level of Heaven? Because that's where Sophie found herself. The marble hallways of Soul City's Colosseum were lined with grazing tables and libations of all assortments along the outer walls. Tall archways lined the inner walls of the colosseum, stretching levels upon levels. There were no balustrades to stop people from falling.

Ash smiled. "This is what I love most about this place." He had a firm grip on Sophie's waist as they stepped closer to the inner edge. Sophie was grateful for it, because as she looked over the lip, her knees wobbled. They were four levels high and the centre of the colosseum, the size of a circular football field, ran through the entire island. Top to bottom. Straight through. When Sophie craned her neck, the Godlands's night sky burned fiercely, the stars ready to fall. And when Sophie looked down, she was met with night sky too. A perfect place for stars to fall and for people to watch. It was no wonder why the Ephemeral Ball was held here.

"Is that . . . are the stars going to fall through here?" Sophie was breathless and she turned to Ash.

He squeezed her waist ever so slightly. "Mhmm," Ash mused. His eyes were bright with excitement and Sophie stole a moment to watch him in his fine armour.

Pinch me.

Sophie made the mistake of staring too long, because Ash turned and flashed her a sneaky grin. He knew she was staring. For sure.

Sophie rolled her eyes.

"Would the lady like some drinks?" Ash held his hands behind his back and rocked on his feet, looking a little nervous. Sophie had to admit she was too. Her heart hadn't stopped hammering since they'd left her villa.

"If the kind gentleman is offering."

"We mustn't leave the lady waiting for her libations then," Ash purred, dipping his head slightly before turning to find them some drinks.

Idiot. Sophie smiled to herself. "I'll grab us some snacks!" she called after him.

Sophie turned toward the grazing stations that had been lined upon the outer walls of the colosseum. Tables were filled with a smorgasbord of fruits, meats and delicacies she'd never seen before. Sophie's mouth watered. She'd barely eaten all day because she was so stinking nervous. Sophie grabbed a glass bowl and filled it with everything that tickled her fancy, of course, snacking while she did it.

A prickle started on the back of Sophie's neck. She stilled her hand, debating whether to turn around but curiosity caved in, and Sophie instantly regretted it. She turned to find Vestes standing beside her. His thin lip was quivering with a smile on his pale, wrinkly face.

Sophie fixed a bored look upon her face and continued munching away on the pretzel that was part way through her mouth. "Who died and let you come to this party?" Sophie deadpanned.

"Demigoddess of Faery, it's a pleasure to see you so delectable . . ." Vestes paused, raking his eyes up and down the length of her body, "for a half-breed."

Yuck. Gross. Is that vomit I taste in the back of my mouth?

Sophie scrunched her face in disgust. "Ew. Just no." Sophie stepped aside, picking at the snacks she had gathered in her bowl.

Vestes stepped in her way. He was dressed in a black chiton with what looked like draekin claws cinching the shoulders. It was by far the worst thing Sophie had ever seen.

"Tsk tsk tsk, the master of weapons wouldn't like his plaything to be so disrespectful, would he?" Vestes's voice slithered closer to Sophie's ear.

"The master of weapons does not control me," Sophie said lowly, a growl starting in her throat. She narrowed her eyes at Vestes, ready to smack his excuse for hair off the top of his wrinkly head.

Vestes dared to lean in, his thin lips almost touching the shell of Sophie's ear. Sophie tried to jerk away but an invisible power held her chin still. Vestes's power. A tick started in Sophie's jaw. There was no way that Vestes, the shrivelled sultana, would rain on her parade. Sophie pulled at her mana with a sharp force, burning through his invisible hold within seconds.

Vestes stepped back in surprise. "She's got a little bit of bite. Just like her mother, it seems," Vestes mused.

"Vestes, do me a huge favour and fuck off." Sophie shook her head, moving back through the crowd to find Ash.

Way to ruin my night.

She could still feel Vestes's slimy eyes upon her.

"What services are you offering him?" Vestes started.

That was enough to make Sophie turn around like a raging bull who just saw red.

He smiled that creepy smile, knowing he'd done well in riling her up. He continued, "Perhaps we can come to an agreement if you could lend some of your—"

Vestes couldn't finish the sentence as thunder and lightning cracked all around him. Ash was there in a split second, hauling Vestes into the air by the scruff of his neck like a freaking ragdoll.

Sophie raised her eyebrows, genuinely impressed by Ash's strength. Vestes wasn't hulking by any means, but the male was tall and spindly. Ash still somehow made him look like a damned toothpick.

"Put me down! This is assault!" Vestes squirmed in Ash's grip, but Ash did not give two shits. He didn't even give one, as he stormed over to one of the large open windows, tossing Vestes through it.

He tossed Vestes through a window.

From the fourth floor.

Like he was a piece of trash.

Not that I condone littering, but I don't mind it on this occasion.

Sophie ran after Ash, looking over the edge of the window where a circle of revellers surrounded Vestes's bent and battered body.

"Holy shit! Is he dead?" Sophie gasped, turning to Ash who looked pissed as all hell.

"No. He'll heal in a few minutes." Ash sounded extremely disappointed.

"Well," Sophie sighed, "that's a shame, isn't it?" Sophie pulled her lips into a thin unimpressed line.

Ash sighed too. "Sucker made me drop the drinks too. Come with me, I'll get us new ones." Ash grunted, turning swiftly as he took Sophie's hand in his.

The annoyance and anger she had felt dissipated. Back in her stomach was the squirming nervousness she felt whenever Ash held her close.

A soft, fairy-like voice began to echo around the colosseum, singing in a language that Sophie didn't understand. She looked around to find the owner of the voice. There. Two levels above them, was a fairy-like female standing in front of a microphone. Her skin was entirely pink and her butterfly-like wings were soft green and translucent. Her mint-coloured hair was tied up in a high ponytail that stretched metres in length.

Ash paused his movements, catching who Sophie was staring at. "That's Aeranya, a famous fairy singer."

Sophie scoffed. "Huh, you don't say?"

Ash pulled them both forward, toward a table laden with drinks. He took two shots of iridescent liquid and handed one to Sophie.

"To your very first Ephemeral Eclipse." Ash raised his shot glass.

"And hopefully not my last." Sophie met his glass with hers, sounding a clink, before guzzling it down. It was sweet, like grape soju, and it tickled her throat. "That was delicious!" Sophie beamed and somehow, she already started to feel a little buzzed. Maybe it was the excitement.

Cam had somehow found them among the crowd. He cleared his throat as he moved around Ash's towering frame.

Sophie's heart squeezed. Seeing Cam again was . . . relieving, even if he was a soul.

Cam stretched out his hand. "As promised?"

Sophie took his hand in hers, looking back at Ash with a smile. He answered by taking another shot and flashing her a grin.

Stringed instruments flowed together with Aeranya's lulling voice, sounding through the entire colosseum. Sophie watched as the stars above burned even brighter, shaking in place, ready to fall at any moment.

Cam pulled Sophie close, and they began to sway in time with the slow music. "You look happy."

Sophie dipped her head, shying away. She was. She was stronger now. She understood more. Sure, she was missing a few bits and pieces but once she executed her plan, she'd be whole, and she'd be sure of who she was. All her secrets, kept from her, would be set free.

Sophie looked back up to Cam's piercing green eyes. He was handsome in his light-grey suit. "I am happy. Truly. A lot can change in six months it seems."

They swayed to the music, dancing close to the arches. Sophie's dress swayed and billowed like stardust and smoke. "Are you happy?" Sophie asked.

"Very much so, Soph. I found my parents in the Elysian Fields. They were waiting for me." Cam looked like he was about to cry, and Sophie was very close in joining him too.

"That's wondrous, Cam. You deserve all the happiness the afterlife can bring you. And for all that it's worth, I'm sorry that I stole your time away from you." Sophie squeezed his hand tighter.

Cam stopped their swaying. "It was never your fault, Soph. It never was, and it never will be. I made the decision all on my own. Please know that. The weight of my death is not yours to wear. Okay?" He shook her shoulders a little, bending down to peer under her tear-soaked lashes.

Sophie bit her lip, biting back tears.

"Okay?" Cam shook her again, a sorry smile across his face.

She mustered a measly nod.

"Good. And promise you'll visit, now that you know I'm here?"

"Name the time and place. I'll be there," Sophie smiled.

Cam pulled Sophie in closer, pulling her into a hug, his hands feeling cold and a little empty. He whispered in her ear. "Try not to drool, alright?"

Sophie looked up at Cam with furrowed brows. One, confused. Two, ready to punch him because she missed that teasing tone so much.

Sophie heard the bristling of Ash's soft wings from behind her. She turned to find Ash, slightly bowed and his hand stretched out waiting for her. His pure white wings were stretched out in show and Sophie's breath caught all over again. She smiled brightly and grabbed his hand without a moment's hesitation. Sophie looked back at Cam. "I'll see you soon."

Cam nodded. His red hair falling into his slightly watering eyes before he turned, disappearing into the throng of people dancing.

Sophie turned her attention back to Ash.

That was when the music paused.

That was when everyone looked up to the stars that began to descend upon the Godlands. Some people clapped, some gasped in awe, while others started tearing up. Sophie was a strong contender in the tearing-up category of revellers, with her hand stuck at her throat.

Above, the stars floated down to them on a magical song, leaving swirls of green and blue in their wake. The eclipsed moon painted the sky in a dark, romantic navy; the perfect backdrop to the cascade of burning starlight that only happened every three years. It was a true celebration of love and life because in this very moment, Sophie was truly grateful for all the things she'd been through. The good, the bad and the ugly. Every single ugly thing that happened to her, had happened for a reason. And now she was here, in the damn Godlands watching this natural phenomenon beautifully unfurl like a rare rose in front of her very eyes. She didn't regret a damn thing. She couldn't if it meant that she was here to watch the Ephemeral Cascade.

Ash's warm hand pressed against the small of Sophie's back. Sophie glanced at him momentarily, a brightness in his eyes as he watched the stars fall toward them.

They shared a smile. A look.

And Sophie didn't need anything else.

The music started again. The light keys of a warm piano sounded through the air. Then full strings that pulled beautiful, elongated notes tumbled into the fray. Every note, every pause and every beat, filled her heart to the brim with a mixture of awe.

Sophie's heart burst at the seams as every single being in the room started into a waltz.

It felt like a dream.

Ash pulled Sophie with him, toward the centre of the colosseum. Sophie went willingly, the sounds of the orchestra carrying her feet. That was until Ash stepped off the edge.

"Wait." Sophie tugged his hand.

Ash turned back, the smoke in his eyes billowing. "Scared?"

"Never." Not with Ash. Sophie paused for a moment before he pulled her up in the air. One moment on sure feet, solid ground. The next, dancing with the stars.

This right here . . . was Heaven.

Stars fell all around them, burning brightly, skittering around the colosseum in joy. It was their moment to rest after years of shining brightly, of course they were rejoicing!

Sophie let out a full-hearted laugh as Ash twirled her around and around in and among the stars. They said nothing, but they didn't need to. Laughter was all they needed. Each other was all they needed. The stars were a bonus as Sophie and Ash danced with wild abandon. He held her close, his arms a harbour she wanted to anchor in for a long while. They spun in endless circles like soft delicate snowflakes upon the surface of new snow. Like autumn leaves upon a gossamer wind. Like bright moonlight dancing upon the leaves of a pine tree.

When the song came to an epic close, a slow, sweet-sounding song took over. Their dancing slowed. Sophie found her head resting on Ash's chest, her senses consumed by his sandalwood scent as they swayed slowly in the air. Ash's thumb burned slow circles on the small of her back. Sophie dared to look up at him. His turquoise smoking eyes, full of . . . what was that? Content? She dared ask, "Why do you call me Starlight?"

Ash scoffed as if the answer was clear, common sense. He lifted an arm to brush his hand through the trails of green and blue swirling light, spreading the star matter into the space between them. They both watched as the star matter, green and blue swirls, glowed and dissipated. All that remained between them were words left unspoken.

It was Ash who moved first. He lifted his hand and held her chin between his fingers. "People spend years waiting for the stars to fall. It leaves them breathless, and it leaves them wanting." His eyes looked down to Sophie's lips, as if trying to remember every detail. "You are my starlight. You take my breath away with each glance, with each word that comes from these bewitching lips." Ash traced Sophie's lips with his fingers and Sophie's heart thundered furiously, completely entranced by the angel before her. "You leave me wanting more no matter the cost, forever chasing the stars. Forever chasing you."

Sophie's eyes fluttered, wanting more than just his fingers upon her lips.

"May I kiss you?" Ash's voice was but a whisper.

Sophie let out a shaky breath and nodded. Where were her words? They had disintegrated along with her resolve into nothing but stardust.

Slowly, achingly, Ash closed in on the tension-filled distance between them, brushing his lips lightly on Sophie's. His breath was warm on her skin, and his scent . . . by the Fates, Sophie wanted to drown in it. But before she could surrender to him, Ash pulled back quickly, as if the words *clean slate* echoed between them. He dropped the hold on her chin, a mixture of need, urgency and acceptance upon on his face.

Sophie watched him, carefully. Did she want to do this? Cross the threshold of friendship and explore the world anew with Ash?

Fuck the clean slate.

Sophie crashed her lips into Ash's on pure, raw instinct. Like two planets falling into each other's gravity, they collided. Her body was a newborn star, rising in heat and pressure, destined to shine brightly for a million years to come. Their lips melded together, turning into a nuclear fusion of want and need. The catalyst? Ash.

They only pulled apart to gather their breaths. Their chests rising and falling to the beat of their own song. Ash held her still, a hand upon her waist and the other holding her neck. He looked into her eyes as if they held the inklings of an undiscovered galaxy. That look alone undid the steely armour that Sophie had moulded around her heart.

Her voice was all breathy. "I've felt a deep chasm in my soul for as long as I can remember." Sophie placed a hand on Ash's cheek, the plains of his face feeling every bit perfect against her hand. "Every part of me ached to find its missing piece. I've been searching for so long." She had been. For years. Through two realms. What felt like an eternity spent searching, looking, *pining* for the other half of her soul. She had the scars to prove it too.

Ash leaned into her hand, a purr starting in his throat. "You can finish with your searching, Sofreya, I am here and I'm waiting to be found."

Of course he was. He was always waiting for her. The words made Sophie's throat ache. Was he even real?

"The moment I heard your voice…" Sophie's mind flew back to the moment she was whisked away in Faery. She cast it to the moments where she lay bed ridden with despair after the loss of Camrine. The moments when the sound of *Ash's* voice lulled her to sleep with beautiful stories of strength. Ash had been there for everything. "I knew I was in trouble. My heart gave in completely, and the thought of someone holding the fate of my heart in their hands, unbound and naked, has me terrified."

That was her truth. She was terrified. What if she was wrong again?

Ash placed his hand on top of hers where she cupped his cheek. "There would be no one stronger or more capable of protecting your heart, Sofreya. You are safe with me always."

And with those words, she knew she couldn't be wrong. Not about this. Home was no longer realms out of arm's reach. It was right here.

But there was one thing she had left to do.

The stars hovered around them, creating a little private space to call their own among the Ephemeral Lights. Sophie's eyes began to water. "I know. I've always known and that's what scares me."

"That's the thing about love." The word made Sophie's heart thunder. "People forget how sharp and ruthless of a blade it can be. It's daunting. Your whole life, everything that matters, everything that makes it shine is concentrated into one point of origin. One wrong move and suddenly you're bleeding. But like a sharp blade, it can bring you comfort knowing your darkest demons lurk nearby. It can protect you, and it can save you all the same. So, I'll have it. Whatever you are willing to give, Sofreya, I'll have it." Ash's hand was firm against her jaw, urging her to look at him.

Her heart. What was this feeling? Like shedding her armour, so that all her soft bits were exposed. She should have been more scared than she was. She should have. But she wasn't.

Sophie leaned into his hold, fluttering her eyes closed. Tears ran down her cheeks as she lifted her chin. And as if it were his second nature, wordlessly, Ash closed the distance between them. They'd spent years apart, pining for each other. Realms apart, even. Now, they were here. Swirling among the stars in each other's embrace. The time that they had spent apart shattered into nothingness. Time itself paused for them – a whirlwind of starlight and armour.

It was in this moment, with their lips never wanting to part, that Sophie had to wonder if her heart had ever truly loved. For Sophie swore, she'd never felt such burning desire, such fierce loyalty, or the irrefutable, deep ache in her soul for anyone until Ash.

42

SOPHIE

Sophie was on the cusp of complete inebriation. Staying up past four in the morning did that. They'd danced the entire night among the stars. Deymos, Eros and Nemy had finally found them and so started the raucous drinking games. Cam even joined in for a few.

Ash, despite the number of shots he'd had, was sensible, knowing he'd have to take Lumen to get them home. The ride back to the Isle of Deos had Sophie screaming. The alcohol had loosened all her inhibitions and Ash had to pull her back onto Lumen with a growl of warning. The stars were so, so pretty. Sophie insisted on taking one home to keep.

Arm in arm, they stumbled to Sophie's villa, feeling like they were kids in Faery again. Sophie ran up the stairs ahead of Ash, bubbling with laughter. She pushed her white marble door open to find Calypso jumping up and down in excitement.

"OH BUDDYYY! We left you for *so* long. Mum and Dad are so sorry," Sophie cried. *Did I just say Mum and Dad? Shit.*

Calypso licked and yelped as he nuzzled Sophie. The hellhound had a habit of letting himself in, alternating nights between Ash's villa and hers, but Sophie wouldn't have it any other way. Calypso barrelled to the front door where Ash stood, jumping into his arms. Ash held him like he was a baby and the sight of it left Sophie's heart twisting in weird ways.

Cal howled in excitement.

"Let's go home, buddy," Ash said, ready to turn down the stairs.

"Where do you think you're going?" Sophie slurred, rushing to the door. Calypso jumped out of Ash's arms and ran inside to a chaise, settling himself down.

Ash turned red. The Godlands's master of weapons turned red. And his wings bristled. His godsdamn wings bristled.

"Stay." Sophie tugged at Ash's hands.

"Sofreya, I—"

"Please."

Ash grinned and nodded before stepping into her villa with his towering frame. He always had to duck before coming in. He closed the door behind him and all of a sudden the room felt so small. Sophie gulped, feeling a little more confident than usual thanks to the alcohol she'd consumed.

"I have some oversized pants that might fit you if you want to change out of your armour. Come with me." Sophie grinned, pulling Ash with her into her closet. He leaned against the doorframe with his arms crossed, a mischievous grin across his face.

Sophie rifled through her clothes looking for her largest, stretchy, black cotton pants and handed it to Ash.

He took them from her. "Thanks."

Sophie pointed to the bathroom. "You can get changed in there."

Ash nodded before moving past her. Sophie turned to watch him with appreciative sigh. He was so stinking handsome that it almost broke her heart.

Sophie turned and tried to shimmy out of her shimmering dress but couldn't quite reach the zip. Before she knew it Ash had come out of the bathroom with his tattooed, muscled torso on display. He still had his armoured pants on but he helped unzip her before moving back into the bathroom. The exchange was wordless. Second nature.

Popping on the oversized shirt, Sophie found that her inebriated mind could not tear away from the fact that an angel was getting naked in her bathroom.

Calm down, Sophie, you freaking horn dog.

She was spiralling. So, so fast. If she didn't rein herself in, she'd be kicking down that door and plastering herself all over him. Sophie shook her head to clear the indecent thoughts, but it only made clear the vision of Ash slowly pulling up pants over those sweet butt cheeks . . . Coffee. She needed coffee, stat. Anything to pull her mind out of the gutter.

"Did you want some tea or coffee?" Sophie called out, moving to the kitchen to fix herself a cup of coffee. No matter what time of day it was, or the level of intoxication she'd found herself in, coffee always made her feel better. There was something about the taste and fullness of it that was so perfectly addictive.

Ash closed the bedroom door behind him, looking sinfully . . . adorable? Was that even the right word? Sophie's long black pants came up to the back of his calves. It was like the angel was wearing some odd three-quarter-length pants – but at least his butt looked cute in it, almost stretching the pants to their limits. He looked very disgruntled as he spied the laugh that was edging out of Sophie's lips.

"Tea would be great," Ash's voice rumbled through the room. He was unimpressed. So unimpressed.

"One cup of tea coming up for the brooding angel. Try not to move, will ya? Not sure if those pants could handle it," Sophie teased.

Sophie let out a tiny gasp of surprise as Ash rushed up to her. He looked like he was going to take a bite out of her, but instead he leaned down with a growl, tucked her hair behind her ear and placed a kiss on her forehead.

It was the softest kiss she'd ever had and Sophie had no idea what to do with it. The kiss had sobered her completely. Who needed coffee? He'd stunned her. Like a stiff legged, spooked goat, Sophie fell still. Ash was clearly the wolf who enjoyed the torment.

Ash leaned back against the white countertop with his arms crossed. He grinned at her. He knew *exactly* what he did to her.

"Asshat," Sophie mumbled with a small smile on her face.

Sophie returned to fixing him a cup of tea and handed it to him, piping hot. Her teacups looked outrageously stupid in his big hands.

"Thanks," Ash said, before taking a sip.

Sophie took her coffee mug in her hands, breathing in the aroma before taking an unhurried sip. She let out a sigh of satisfaction, letting the beans bring her back to life.

"How can you drink that stuff?" Ash asked, genuinely disgusted that she was drinking coffee.

"Coffee? How can you not? It's the nectar of the gods!"

"In what Godlands do you live, Sofreya? That is not the nectar of the gods. You wouldn't *ever* catch me drinking that stuff. It smells horrific."

Sophie gasped dramatically, feeling both offended and amused. "Wait, you've never had coffee?"

Ash shook his head. "We don't grow it here, nor do we need it."

"It's never a need, Ash, it's always a want." Sophie held out her mug for Ash to try. "Take a sip."

He narrowed his eyes, eyeing the cup, unsure what to think of it.

"Come on, a teeny tiny sip. I promise you'll like it." Sophie laughed.

Ash mumbled something under his breath before gingerly taking the mug into his hand. He caught a good whiff of the coffee and gagged.

Sophie laughed.

Ash was ridiculous.

He took a sip, pouting his lips as if he didn't really hate it, but it looked like he didn't really like it either. To Sophie's surprise, he took another sip, this time a little longer.

"So, what do you think?"

"I see why we don't grow it in the Godlands, it tastes like rubbish and it's making my chest buzz. I don't hate it though," Ash said, handing back the mug.

Sophie snatched it away from his grip, "Well, more for me I guess." Sophie grinned, watching Ash watch her.

He hiccupped. The sound echoing into the living room. He braced his abdomen and hiccupped again. "Sofreya, I don't know what's in the cup, but it's . . ."

"By the gods, are you alright?" Sophie tilted her head.

Ash bent over, his hand on his knees as he hiccupped again. The angel before Sophie started giggling. *Giggling.*

Ash stumbled forward but Sophie was there in a split second, catching him before he ate the ground. Sophie pushed him back upright which was a feat within itself. He'd gone all floppy and he looked utterly high.

He hiccupped again. "The coffee makes me feel – feel nice," Ash breathed. He tried to lean back on the counter but missed it by a fraction.

Sophie caught him again, a laugh starting in her throat. "Of course it does. You're higher than a fucking kite and considering you're an angel, that's saying a damned lot."

Ash tried to prop himself onto the counter but started to fall forward as he clearly did not consider the size of his wings. "Woahhhhh."

Sophie was cackling now. Ash was high off coffee. Coffee, for Fates' sake! She caught him by the shoulders and pushed him toward the bedroom, so he could at least lie down and ride out whatever buzz he had.

Cal popped his head up from the chaise they passed, wondering what the hell was going on.

"So pushy, S-S-Starlight. I love it," Ash purred. He kept trying to look back at her as she pushed his hulking body across the room.

"Hey, less surveying the goods. More helping me out, asshole. Keep it moving!" Sophie laughed. She tried her best to make him sit, but Ash just turned around and hugged her so hard she thought her spine was about to burst.

"You are the best smelling thing I've EVER smelled," Ash slurred, taking in a deep breath around her neck. His nose and mouth tickled her endlessly, making her core heat in the most tantalising way.

Sophie swatted him away. "Sit. I'll go get you some water."

Ash sat, looking like someone had stolen his lunch in the playground. He hiccupped, and mother of Faery, it was the cutest thing she'd ever witnessed. His entire tattooed chest rose and fell, and his lips pouted, fighting for control over his hiccups.

"I'll be back," Sophie said, moving toward the door.

She wasn't quick enough. She never was.

Ash pulled her into his embrace from behind. His arms curling around her chest and his front firmly pressed against every curve of her body. Her entire body melted. She was a damned puddle of drool and heat. Her breathing stopped.

With more coordination that she'd anticipated, Ash lifted her up into his arms, breathing her in the entire time. He stumbled a fair bit on the way back to the bed, but he sat her down with such carefulness.

"You're not going anywhereeee." Ash laughed darkly.

Oh, he is absolutely shit-faced.

"You can't tell me what to do." Her small smirk said that he totally could.

Ash knelt before her, placing his hands on either side of her legs. He looked up at her with hooded eyes, strands of his white hair coming loose. Sophie could barely breathe. They were so close. His hands, just grazing the outside of her bare thighs. She watched him carefully as he assessed her, from her face down to every inch of her bare skin.

"I think I'll stay riggghhtt here tonight." Ash flashed a cheesy grin before curling up against her legs and laying his head down on her lap.

"I don't think—" Sophie didn't get to finish, because Ash the guardian angel that struck fear in other gods, had fallen fast asleep in her lap. "Of course, even when you're asleep you're so stinking handsome," Sophie scoffed, moving his inky hair from out of his face. She traced the pointed parts of his ears and his striking jawline. The pads of her fingers burned, and her heart squeezed at the sight of his light scars along his left eye and cheek. The scar he'd gotten when they played chase along the hills of Soxis.

Sophie sat there for a few minutes, not really knowing what to do except admire this beautiful angel before her. *I could get used to this,* Sophie thought.

He began to talk in his sleep, his eyes darting back and forth underneath his eyelids. Sophie brushed her fingers through his hair to calm him and he softened immediately. He was like a little stray puppy she'd taken home, but it wasn't long before his nightmare had come back. He was shouting and slurring all at the same time.

"Stop. STOP!" Ash yelled.

A flash of bright lightning encased the entire room and Sophie felt a sharp pain run up her thighs. She breathed in sharply as the world around her grew bigger and bigger. Her insides felt like they were tossing and turning.

"Starlight! Shit! Holy shit!" Ash shot up from where he had lain sleepy. His eyes were now wide as if he'd seen a ghost.

The room continued to grow bigger and bigger. Sophie looked down to her hands and down to her feet. She was standing on the bed and stood about the height of Ash's kneecaps.

"Did you just FUCKING SHRINK ME?!" Sophie shrieked but it was futile. Her voice was all small and squeaky, and very much nonthreatening. Any heat and softness she felt toward Ash in those endearing moments of slumber were promptly thrown by the wayside.

Ash crashed down to the floor, his eyes wide with concern, terror and confusion. "By the Fates, I have no idea how I did this." Ash looked like he was about to vomit.

"Are you KIDDING ME?!" Sophie threw her hands in the air. She'd been shrunk into a fun-sized version of herself and now she stood completely naked before Ash. The clothes and undergarments she was wearing were clearly not susceptible to whatever spell Ash had just zapped into her.

Ash, still in his too-tight cotton pants stilled for a moment to take a deep breath. He was thinking and it looked like he was coming up short for ideas.

Not good. This is SO not good.

Sophie stood on the bed, her arms crossed and her fingers drumming impatiently. She didn't care if she was naked right now. She was as tall as a freaking ruler and there was nothing remotely cute about this situation. Once Sophie returned to her normal height and size, she'd be walloping Ash until kingdom come.

"Okay, okayyy . . . don't panic," Ash said with both hands raised up, trying his best to calm her while his eyes darted around the room as if the answers to her predicament lay in the damn walls of her villa. He was still slurring. STILL.

"Don't panic?! You're the one panicking, Ash! Turn me back to normal." Sophie gritted her teeth.

Ash stood from where he crouched and ran to the bathroom, tripping on the carpet as he fumbled across the space. Sophie heard him rifle through a few drawers before coming back and producing a tea towel. His giant hand passed it to her, and she all but snatched it out of his grip. Sophie wrapped the tea towel around her like she'd just gotten out of the shower and huffed.

Ash let out a sharp whistle and Cal was instantly beside him. "I need you to run to our library. Find the book of transformation spells." Cal looked at Sophie and a bark started in his throat. "Quick, boy."

Cal whimpered and dashed through Sophie's backyard.

Ash crouched down to Sophie again, almost losing his balance. "I'm so sorry, Starlight. You'll have to come with me. We'll meet Cal at my place. He'll grab the book of transformation spells and we'll somehow undo this."

He held out a hand for her.

To sit on.

"You better remove that *somehow* from your sentence, Ash." Sophie pointed at him with anger. "This is the stupidest first date of my life," Sophie grumbled, but a side smile worked its way onto her face. She stomped all the way to Ash's hand, making sure to stomp on him extra hard, before perching herself on the edge, grabbing a hold of his thumb for support.

Of course on their first date Ash would accidentally get high off his face on coffee and then accidentally shrink her. Peachy. It was just peachy.

Sophie glowered at Ash, whose eyes were brimming with something. "What?" Sophie grunted.

"It's just— It's just that . . ." Ash bit back laughter.

"Spit it out, you overgrown turtle-dove. I'll be beating your sorry ass either way after this whole schemozzle is dealt with," Sophie gripped his thumb tight as he lifted her up to his face.

"It's just that you're so cute," Ash barked out in pure, unrestrained laughter.

"Bite me." Sophie pinched his thumb in anger which only brought on more laughter from the angel.

Asshole.

They walked over to Ash's villa. Sophie insisted he fly over but Ash had protested saying that he was scared to drop her and wouldn't know what to do if he ended up losing her in one of the bushes. He lived three doors down from her. And given her size, she wouldn't be able to get very far, but no. Ash insisted that walking was the best option. So here they were, walking together with Sophie carefully perched upon his calloused hand. Sophie shivered as the wind of the summer morning picked up. It was still dark as they neared the last day of the Ephemeral Eclipse.

"If you were a worm, Starlight, I'd give you the best fruit scraps and make sure that my compost was the best in town, I really would. You have my word on that," Ash blurted out.

Sophie just shook her head and laughed. His slurring had slowed at this point, but now he was extremely chatty. Sophie couldn't help it, her heart squeezed seeing him so at odds with his brooding, intimidating exterior. When he got completely inebriated, he was lippy of all things. It was a side of him that only she got to see, and it warmed her heart that he trusted her enough to let his walls down, even though what spurred him on was a little bit of intoxication. Scrap that, a lot of.

Ash pushed through his front door. Cal was already there with a small tome in his mouth. "Thanks, Cal, I appreciate it." Ash bent low to scruff his best friend's head, taking the tome out of Cal's mouth. Sophie held on tight to Ash as her giant world tipped around her.

Cal stood up on his hind legs to sniff Sophie. He took a breath, then another before jumping around in recognition.

The poor hellhound is probably so confused right now.

Ash quickly busted his bedroom door open, placing Sophie gently on the black silk sheets of his bed. He threw the book filled with transformation spells next to her and frantically read through the pages.

Sophie sat quietly as she watched him concentrate. The deeper he got into the tome, the more it dawned on Sophie that she could possibly stay this size forever. She said nothing, letting Ash concentrate as fear crept up her chest.

Ash thumbed through the final pages before sitting back on his haunches, a look of defeat on him. "Nothing."

"Nothing?" Sophie gulped.

"Nothing."

Fuck.

Sophie wasn't taking nothing for an answer. If he could do it, he could undo it. And by the Fates she would do everything in her power to make it happen. She wasn't going to spend the rest of her life pocket-sized, snuggled up in Ash's pocket – despite how comfortable that sounded.

Ash had moved to the wall of yarn he had in his room, picking out various colours and adding them to a basket. She remembered the day when he brought her back here after she'd taken the truth serum. He tried to hide his little hobby from her but now, it seemed like he didn't care if she saw him for all that he was.

"You hit me with your lightning when you shrunk me. Do it again."

"No, I'm not going to do that again. What if I accidentally kill you?"

"You won't." Sophie moved to the edge of the bed to watch Ash be totally engrossed in what he was doing. He looked stressed out, needing to find a way to channel it and focus again.

Ash moved back to the bed, placed the basket of yarn on the side, sat down next to Sophie and he started crocheting.

He started *crocheting*.

Time was of the essence and Sophie's quality of life lay precariously on the tip of a blade and the man in front of her was crocheting. Sophie had obviously drunk too much and had entered an undiscovered level of inebriation because this was wild.

Sophie was about to rip Ash a new one when he broke from his trance.

"Crocheting helps me concentrate and helps me channel my stress."

Sophie raised her eyebrows in surprise. Who knew Ash, the big burly guy with tattoos and painted fingernails, had a healthy way to manage anger and stress. Sophie wasn't sure if she could even say that much for herself.

Ash made quick work of his hands, producing a tiny tube made of pink and purple yarn.

"Is that what I think it is?" Sophie pointed at the tiny tube that looked awfully like a tiny dress.

"Put it on. You must be so cold being so small. Starlight, I cannot tell you how sorry I am," Ash paused as he tied off another article of miniature clothing. It was a bright yellow jumper. "I will spend forever making it up to you." He started on another article of clothing. It started to form the shape of black loose pants. "I'll carry you around everywhere. I promise." He sounded like he was about to cry.

Sophie stepped out of the tea towel she'd wrapped around herself and shimmied into the purple-and-pink knitted dress that Ash had made for her. The angel was rambling now, the effects of the coffee still firmly gripping his senses. Sophie was thoroughly impressed how he managed to ramble while simultaneously making perfectly sized and fashionable clothes for her.

What is my life right now, honestly?

"The only thing you're allowed to promise me right now, Ash, is getting me back to normal. I don't want to hear this 'I'll carry you everywhere' nonsense," Sophie said.

"Oh, but I'm so tiiiiired." Ash yawned loudly, dropped his crocheting sticks into the basket . . . and began stripping his pants off. His pants that were her pants. Sophie felt whiplashed from the way Ash danced from emotion to stress, through to tiredness. It was a rollercoaster and Sophie was ready to get off.

Ash was wearing a pair of tight grey boxers that accentuated the curves of his booty. His very large booty, among other very large things, now that Sophie was the size of a Bratz doll. He crawled into bed lazily and like before, fell asleep instantly.

Great. I'm going to be pint-sized forever.

Ash began to stir in his sleep, so Sophie, feeling like a bit of a lost cause, moved to soothe him. But then she felt like the world's biggest idiot because her hands were the size of mouse hands, and she was trying to soothe a giant angel with them. Mouse hands! It couldn't get any more comical, and a part of Sophie wanted to dowse herself in the nightmare fuel that it was and set herself alight. "This is the stupidest fucking thing I've ever experienced in my life." Sophie laughed softly. Because if she didn't laugh, she'd surely be bawling her eyes out into her damned mouse-sized hands. One day, they'd look back at this and laugh. Surely.

That's if I turn back to normal size. Otherwise, Sophie would be plotting Ash's death in the confines of her tiny future home.

Sophie sat down next to Ash, leaning her back against his chest. Sophie looked up to the stars and wondered which Fate decided this would be the way their first official date played out. Once she found out which Fate it was, Sophie would be paying them a visit with some stern words and perhaps a little Sophie-branded craziness.

Sophie began to doze off when Ash grabbed her entire body. It sounded like he was arguing with someone in his sleep when he catapulted her into the air and zapped her with a burst of lightning. Sophie let out a yelp and the room stretched and bowed, returning to its normal size. *PHWOOM.* She landed firmly on her ass, with a harrumph. Her hands were normal. Her feet were normal, and she had never been so grateful to be butt naked in Ash's room, perfectly normal-sized. Perhaps the internal threatening of the Fates had worked in her favour and the one Fate that was threatened realised she'd fucked up on this one.

Surprisingly, in and among her crashing to the ground with a yelp, Ash didn't wake from his peaceful slumber.

Sleep peacefully, my little lamb. I've got a world of hurt waiting for you when you wake up. Asshole.

Sophie moved to Ash's closet. Everything was either pure white, grey or black and his scent was encased in this room like nothing else. Sophie picked out a t-shirt and slid it on. Stepping out of the bedroom, she found that Ash had already climbed under his black silk sheets. His relaxed wings spread out behind him as he slept on his side.

Sophie shimmied into the bed like a stiff caterpillar beside him. It turned out that shifting molecule sizes did certain things to your muscles and now she was a little sore. Facing Ash, Sophie left a bit of space between them. As soon as she settled, sleeping Ash reached out to wrap his hand around hers, clutching it to his chest. The movement startled her, and it seemed like he was awake but the soft snores he let out told Sophie that he wasn't. He held her hand like it was the most precious thing and nothing could have made her feel more warm or safe than that gesture alone.

Sophie smiled to herself. She had found a place where she belonged, and it was here with Ash. A place where adventure called, and they answered. A place where they'd always have each other's backs, no matter how big or *small* the issue was.

As the grip of sleep slowly claimed her, Ash's dark sumptuous voice whispered the words she'd never imagined she would hear. She could feel his hot breath on the hand that he held so tightly. "I loved you from the very start, Starlight, and I always will," Ash whispered.

The words were achingly soft, and Sophie was sure she'd dreamt it all.

43

ACHERON

The house that Cerri had brought Ash to was strangely cold and painfully plastered in white. Ash had never seen anything like it before – a home so void of colour and warmth. Cerri, with her long dark red hair sat with her face in her hands. She was distraught and hadn't stopped crying since they arrived in this strange place. Ash, with his small hands, tried to comfort the crying female but as he neared her, the golden glow that encased her burned a touch brighter. She was angry. He could feel it in his bones.

"Ma'am, is there anything I can do to help you?" Ash asked timidly.

Cerri shrieked, flinging her chair across the marble mansion she called her home. "Get out of my sight," she seethed.

Ash could see the venom in her eyes. Sharp. Accusing. Deadly. She meant every single word and he felt every single sting. He didn't know where to go. He'd just arrived at this place and all his mother and father said, was to stay strong and to stay with Cerri. So that's what he would do.

Ash shook his head slightly, feeling the hot prick of tears behind his eyes. This place was so big and so cold.

"I don't care where you go, just get out!" Cerri shouted. She lunged for Ash, grabbing a hold of his ear and twisted it painfully. Ash tried his best to claw free of her grip, but he couldn't. She was strong.

Ash tripped over his own fumbling feet as she threw him out of the front door. He turned quickly, trying to get back inside. He didn't want to be outside. He didn't even know where here was. His stomach toiled and tumbled, and his palms were sweaty. He didn't really know what was happening but all he knew was that he didn't like being here.

Cerri gripped his wrist to make him stand still and Ash tried his best not to cry as his lower lip wobbled.

"You are *not* allowed to cry. You hear me? While you are here, you are to do as I say and if *anyone* sees you, I will throw you out on the streets where you will receive no protection from me." Cerri twisted his wrist harder, looking as if she was expecting him to say something.

"Yes, Ma'am," Ash whispered, he lowered his gaze.

Cerri let go of his wrist to grip his chin, forcing him to look up at her. Her fingernails digging into his soft skin. "Is that all I get?" Her long hair fell off her shoulder creating a curtain.

Ash didn't know what to say. His wrist ached and so did his ear. Mother and Father were going to come back for him, right?

Ash looked up at Cerri, into those dark, endless eyes and said nothing. He was trying his hardest to not cry, but the tears were on the cusp of falling.

Cerri slapped him across the cheek so fast and hard that he barely even blinked. "When a goddess gives up her world to house a lowly Fae boy like you, you grovel at her feet and thank the *Fates* that you're still breathing."

Ash's cheek pulsed with pain and the tears spilled. He couldn't stop them. A panic rose in his chest. He didn't like this at all. "Thank you, Ma'am. I appreciate all that you've done for me." He tried to calm his shaky voice as he sunk to his knees and bowed to the scary woman before him.

She let him stay there for a few moments, the cold marble biting into his knees.

Cerri scoffed. "Get up."

He obeyed, wiping the tears from his eyes.

"Go to your room and do not leave it," Cerri commanded as she disappeared on a puff of smoke.

Ash ran as fast as he could to the small room that Cerri had assigned him. The room could barely fit a single bed, but at least it had a window that Ash could smell the fresh air through. At least he'd have a place to stay dry and warm.

Ash shut the bedroom door behind him and curled up onto the bed. He let the tears fall freely from his face, soaking into the pillow underneath him. Soon. His mother and father would come for him soon.

When Ash ran out of tears to cry, sleep found him.

Though not for long.

Dark shadows edged into his vision. For a moment he felt a hand holding his as his mind suspended between consciousness. His body felt like his again, no longer five years old, but his mind was still stuck – lost in a dream state. But that hand, it gripped his tighter as if to say everything was going to be okay. He squeezed the hand back, hoping it would pull him from his dream state, but it didn't. It couldn't. Because the shadows of his past were back, and they brought him to a place he never wanted to visit again.

It had almost been two years since he'd seen his mother and father. He felt impossibly homesick. He'd started to forget what his parents looked like, what they sounded like and what they felt like. And he was scared to forget completely.

Life with Ma'am was difficult. There were days when she would explode in anger and other days where the soft, sad female moved around the house. A shell. A ghost. He never knew who he would be expecting for the day but had learnt quickly to tread lightly. It was tread lightly and keep quiet, or risk not having food to eat for the night. At the rate Ash was growing, he hungered too quickly, too often. So, he adapted.

Ash had barely left the room for his entire time here, only taking quick trips to the bathroom across the hall to wash or relieve himself. He spent his days looking out the window wondering what it was like to feel the grass between his toes or how dirt would feel beneath his fingernails. He could climb out the window if he truly wanted to, but he didn't want to be whipped or have his food taken away from him.

While Ma'am was difficult most days, there were days where she was nice enough to fulfil his requests. He didn't ask for much, he wanted drawing journals and books to read. It was entertainment enough and he enjoyed escaping to the world of the gods; reading about their wars and the heroes that came with. Heroes. He so badly wanted to be one of them. Clad in armour, strong and free. When he grew up, that's exactly what he wanted to be – unstoppable.

On days like this, where daylight stretched and the weather reminded him of home in Faery, he took to drawing. Drawing his mother. Her soft and kind face. The necklace that he was supposed to protect with his life. He would draw his father, laughing as he wore a crown of gold and colourful gemstones. He would draw his best friend Sofreya and would wonder where she was now and if she was taking Astraea and Orion flying. The last time he saw her she was being rowed away, but Ash had no idea where to. He remembered crying and how Lou, his father's friend, had told him that she was headed somewhere safe. Ash hoped that the safe place Sofreya went to wasn't like the place that Ash was sent to. He was so alone here, but at least he had his drawings and books to escape to.

The door to his bedroom slammed open.

Ash quickly stashed his black drawing diary underneath his pillow and stood up beside his bed, tall and straight.

"What are you *hiding* from me?" Cerri sneered. Ma'am was angry today. Ash could feel it in his bones.

He knew better than to lie to her. He was never good at lying but Ash didn't want her to rip up his drawings. That's what she had done last time she found him drawing his family. She had said it was pointless. That if she wasn't allowed to see her son, then Ash couldn't see his family either, even through drawings.

Ash gulped and bit his lip in anger. He didn't want to do it, but he couldn't risk not eating. His stomach already gnawed at him. He only had two square meals a day.

Ash slowly turned back to his bed and pulled out his drawing diary from underneath his pillow and handed it to Cerri. She was dressed in a dark purple dress and her hair was pulled back tight. It made her look like an evil witch.

Cerri all but snatched the diary from his hands. She flicked it to the last few pages and Ash swore that fumes started to billow from her nose and ears. "What did I tell you about drawing this *nonsense*?"

Ash hung his head low. "You told me to stop drawing them, Ma'am." He was never allowed to look at her directly in the eye when she spoke to him. Even if she stood right in front of his face, screaming, he would have to look through her. Never at her.

"Then how can you explain this?" Cerri turned the book around to show a picture of himself and Sofreya throwing rocks across a river.

"It's nothing, I made that one up. She's not real." Ash knew he shouldn't have lied but he did. He'd spent hours perfecting the way Sofreya's hair bounced in the air, and he was proud of it. It brought him joy.

Before he could stop her, Cerri took the page and ripped it out. He flinched at the ripping sound that sounded awfully like his heart right now. She scrunched it without a care in the world and did the same for the drawings of his mother and father. They fell to the ground unceremoniously.

Ash's throat ached and he tried his best to school his face into neutrality, but his lungs gave way. He was angry. Fuming. He'd worked so hard on those drawings and now they were all wrinkled and torn. Ash rushed for his drawings, but before he could reach them, Cerri set them alight with flames she had manifested.

Ash looked up at her incredulously. In the eyes. And the shocked face he received in return for his defiance was all he needed. He braced himself for what was to come.

Cerri struck him so hard across the face that he crumpled to the floor. But he did not get up. He never did. He'd learnt that if he got up, she would just do it again. Curling up into a ball and letting the world around him fade was the easiest way to cope.

The shadows filled Ash's vision again. Tears wet the sides of his face but the hand holding onto his was still there, providing him warmth. Whoever it was would be there for him always. He knew it. He could feel it. Even through the shadows that fed on him.

It had been seven years. Seven years of staying in this one room, yearning to feel the grass between his toes. Of yearning for his parents, his friends, his *true* home. In the time he'd spent here, he'd grown tall and strong, adding exercise routines he'd seen his father doing in a training ring once. Sit ups, push-ups and pull ups. He'd read about the exercises that soldiers did to keep their fitness up. He'd also learnt how to use a bit of his mana. He didn't know much about what he was doing, but he was able to do small things like conjure a glamour so that he could hide his drawing diaries in an instant. Ma'am had thought he had stopped drawing altogether, growing bored of it in favour of reading textbooks. It meant that he could draw whatever he wanted, whenever he wanted. He drew his family often. His mother and father would be older now so he would draw them with a few finer lines with Ash in the middle and his stronger arms around them both. He drew him and Sofreya learning how to knock a bow and arrow. He had no idea what she looked like now, perhaps her cheeks would be similar, but her bright purple eyes would have remained the same, he knew that much. Drawing made him happy. He made memories he could never have through his drawings, and they were his most prized possessions – not that he had much.

The summer sun beat down on the grass of Cerri's backyard and the birds chirped carelessly. Ash often wondered what it felt like to fly. To be free. Every now and then, when he opened his window to daze, he would spot an angel in the distance. He'd read that they were part of the Godlands Aerial Legion called the Tienthan. Guardian angels they were. They looked so strong and capable. And most of all, they were free. Oh how Ash wished he could be free. Just like the Tienthan.

He had dreamed of what freedom would taste like for years. It would start with him running toward wherever the angels were flying to. He would beg for them to let him join them. Ash didn't have wings, but he was smart. He could draw and he kept as fit as possible. He knew how to listen to orders. He'd done it for almost a decade now. And if they denied him, he would beg even more.

But that was just a dream. Distant and unattainable.

Ash was here, in this one room, eyeing the green grass and how it bristled on the slightest of winds. He could just smell its freshness from his window. Ma'am would be leaving for the day any moment now. He could risk it. He'd just have to time it properly.

As if on cue, the front door slammed shut.

Ash waited a moment. Then another.

When silence echoed back, Ash pushed himself onto the windowsill. Was he really going to do this? It would only be for a second. He would just touch the grass with one foot and then he would climb back up. Today was his birthday after all. He would finally be turning twelve.

Ash began to lower himself from the window, bending his elbows and stretching out his leg. The breeze cooled his skin and the anticipation bubbled up in a smile across his face. He carefully dipped his toe into the grass. Its cooling blades bending and twisting against his foot. Ash let out a whimper. It had been so long since he felt this. So long since he smelled the freshness of it this close. He would run across the yard if he could, but this touch alone was just enough.

Ash lowered his other foot to the ground and before he knew it, he was standing firmly on the grass that served as his torture for seven years. What a day to be alive. What a wondrous feeling. Ash stood there; his hands still latched onto the windowsill as he revelled in the beauty of the green grass. This was the best day of his life. That was for sure.

SLAM.

Ash's bedroom door slammed open with a crash. His heart had never lodged itself in his throat so fast before. In a panic, he scrambled up the side of the house and tumbled onto his bed. He stood straight and tall, like a soldier at attention.

"What did I just *see*?" Cerri growled.

Ash stayed quiet.

"You are a disgrace. You were given direct orders to *never* go outside. What, did you think because it was your birthday that I'd give you leeway? It has been YEARS. You should know by now that the day of your birth means nothing to me." Cerri gritted her teeth and moved to Ash. She breathed furiously, inching closer and closer to his face. But Ash did not falter. He looked just off centre, avoiding her eyes.

"Turn around," she demanded.

He obeyed, taking his shirt of as he did.

Ash didn't have to turn around to know what she had just manifested. The leather of the nine-tailed whip creaked and bowed as she wielded it in her hands.

He'd grown numb to the feeling of the whip ripping his skin apart. In fact, he welcomed it because it was the only feeling he was allowed to fully feel. The rush of adrenalin after his beating had always made it easier to sleep.

His skin prickled in anticipation.

One lash.

Ash held his breath as the sharp edges split his skin open.

Two.

It wasn't too bad today.

Three.

"On your knees," Cerri commanded.

Four.

Five.

Six.

"You are to *never* go outside again."

Seven.

"You are to *never* draw again."

Eight.

"You think I don't see the rubbings or pencil shavings that you try and fail to hide?"

Nine.

"Do you think I'm an imbecile?"

Ten.

"Do you think you can outwit a goddess?"

Eleven.

"You are wrong. You are ungrateful. And no one will ever love you."

Twelve.

"I should have left you in that blasted Faery realm."

An anger so wild swept through Ash's chest. Maybe it was the feeling of the grass, the momentary slice of freedom he felt. A world outside waited for him and if this was to be his reality for the rest of his life then he didn't want any of it. His mother and father were never coming back for him. Cerri would never protect him as she promised. All she was doing was hiding him from the world.

As the blood from his back dripped down to the floor, Ash found himself at a crossroad. Should he stay here, whipped and starved? Or should he run, toward the angels, toward the world that he'd almost forgotten existed? It was just outside his window, waiting for him. He just needed to reach out.

Cerri wound the whip back into the air, it's leather creaking as she did. She posed to strike Ash's raw back.

"Stop . . ." Ash's voice was croaky, weak.

"Are you attempting to defy me?" Cerri scoffed.

Ash stood slowly from the ground. His bloodied back dripping and oozing with the movements. He turned around to Cerri, stared her right in her endless eyes. He promised to hate her eyes for all eternity as he bared his teeth. "Stop. STOP!" Ash screamed and spat.

Cerri took a step back, something like wariness or fear shone across her face.

But as Ash stepped closer, the raging goddess he knew too well bit back. She winded the whip and tried to lash him across the face. He ducked just in time and ran for the journals he'd kept glamoured underneath his bed. He snatched the bag they were in and dived out the window. The feeling of the grass was splendid but marred by the pain of his raw back.

Cerri shrieked after him. "You are EXILED. Never come back. If you do, I will smite you and so will the other gods. You have been warned!"

Ash ran across the backyard, tears streaming down his face. The heat of the summer sun seared onto his flesh, but he ran, following the path he'd seen the angels of the Tienthan take in the sky. He ran as fast as he could. Rocks and debris bit into his feet but he didn't care. He was finally free.

He ducked and weaved through roads he'd never seen before, all the way to a waterfall where in the distance, he saw them. The angels. They were fighting. The sounds of steel, clanging against steel, and their hearty laughter echoed across the cavern.

He rushed as close to them as he could, staying as quiet as possible. He hid behind a large rock, with the satchel of journals in his hand. What was he doing? Did he just run away from home? His only source of food? It was the right thing to do, right? Ash doubted himself, feeling confused and lost.

But as the clangs of steel echoed and reverberated through him, he focused on the angels. They were everything he imagined them to be. Strong. Tall. Fearless. Confident. Ash sat by the rock, admiring them. Tears fell freely on his cheeks. Years of not being able to cry had them gushing out uncontrollably. This was the best birthday he'd ever had.

Ash closed his eyes again, the shadow of nightmares edged into his vision.

Ash groaned. Why did it feel like his head had been stomped on by several arions? He spread out his limbs, feeling like they too had been through the ringer.

"Good morning, you overgrown turtle-dove," Sofreya said. Her voice was layered with the promise of death and as all the memories from last night came flooding through his mind, Ash suddenly remembered why.

Ash sprung awake, finding Sophie seated on his chair, a leg crossed over the other, her hands clasped calmly together. A pillow lay on her lap. She looked at him with a sinister smile.

I'm in trouble.

Ash grinned sheepishly. "I'm sorry?" Ash offered.

"You'll be sorry alright." Sofreya laughed, wielding the pillow like a giant shield. She leapt up from her seat and began her onslaught with maniacal laughter.

Ash grabbed her waist before she could smack him with the pillow and pinned her to the bed. He grabbed a pillow of his own, ready to attack. She slipped out from underneath him, smacking him square across the face as she did.

A growl left his throat as he grabbed one of her ankles to immobilise her, but she was slippery. She pulled her knee upward, making Ash lose his balance. He fell onto his chest. Sofreya quickly turned and pinned him in place, straddling his back. She sounded a triumphant caw as she rained down her pillow attacks.

Ash laughed, feigning he'd been truly hurt.

"Yield!" Sofreya cried with laughter

"I yield! I yield!" Ash laughed with her.

She stopped her onslaught, pulling at his shoulder so he could lie on his back. He obeyed as she straddled his front.

They stared at each other for a moment.

She was wearing his t-shirt and Ash could feel her every curve as she pinned him down underneath her. What did he need to do to wake up like this for the rest of his life?

Sofreya leaned forward, her hands braced beside his head. She looked worried, like she didn't know how to find the words to speak.

"I saw your dreams, Ash. Your memories. I didn't mean to. I'm sorry. You were just so distraught, I didn't know what else to do. I thought maybe if I dipped into your mind for a moment, I could help you. But the pain was too much. I think your little self latched onto my mind . . . I couldn't get back out." Sofreya whispered.

Ash instinctively looked away from her gaze for a second. Calming the beat of his thunderous heart.

She pulled at his chin with the softest touch, making him look at her. "I'm sorry you went through those things. No child should have gone through that. Is there anything I can do for you?"

Ash leaned into her touch, wishing he could stay like this forever. Wishing her touch could burn through the pain and the nightmares so that he could never see them again.

"Just stay," Ash breathed.

Stay because I lost you once. Stay because I can never lose you again.

She lowered herself onto his chest, squeezing him tightly. Ash pulled her closer, savouring her smell and the way she fit into his arms. She was made for him.

"You're still an asshole for shrinking me though," she grumbled against his chest.

Ash let out a hearty laugh.

He loved this. He loved them. He loved her.

The words he spoke last night, knowing she'd been asleep, echoed through his mind. The words could not be truer. He loved her from the very start, and he always would.

44

KAINE

21 YEARS AGO

Lethe had been running for so long now. His little legs burned with urgency, but his mind was clouded and confused. He didn't know where he was running to. The only connection to this different world was the kind-eyed female. The one that pressed the bloodied sleeping-sun necklace into his hands.

Lethe looked down to the necklace in his bloodied hands. It was warm from being held so tightly, and it was splattered with the female's blood.

He looked around the forest. The thick air clung to skin even though the double-ringed moon sat high in the night sky. He pressed himself as close as he could into the trunk of a tree, its bark biting into his skin as he made himself small. He looked up to the sky, hoping that his mother could hear him.

"Mother? I'm ready to go home now," he whimpered.

But Cerri did not answer.

He was alone in this world that she had called Faery, and he didn't know what to do next. His mother had told him that he would be safe with the female and that from this different world he would enter another. But that hadn't happened.

He waited and waited, all alone, hungry and confused, but no one came to find him. As the night grew long and his mother did not respond, he had to wonder if she had lied. She tended to do that. Every time she was crying or angry, she would push it away and said that everything was fine, even when it wasn't. He was a child, but he could tell the difference. Or when she got angry and would lash out at him, she said she loved him. It was all so confusing. Perhaps this was his mother's way of punishing him because he didn't do something right. She tended to do that too.

The longer he waited in the dark with the necklace clung to his chest, the more the feeling of dread rooted itself inside him. Had his mother abandoned him? Had she lied to him? What game was she playing?

All he knew was that he was angry. He used to get upset, seeing other children in the Godlands being held and cared for by their mothers. His mother was never like that with him. There were nights when he so badly just wanted to be held, by anyone. Nowadays, he learnt that being angry was the only way to protect himself.

The sharp crack of a twig snapping sounded in the air.

Lethe whipped his head toward the noise, just a few metres away from him.

A beautiful female, with blood-red hair and skin so white stepped from out of the shadows. Her face was filled with concern as she approached him.

Lethe sunk back into the shadows. It wasn't the female that his mother said would keep him safe. His heart pattered with uncertainty as his mind warred between whether to trust her or not. She seemed nice enough, Lethe thought.

"I won't hurt you," the red-headed female said. Her voice was soft as she moved closer to him. She knew where he was hiding.

Lethe peeked around the tree he was hiding behind.

"There you are," she breathed. "Are you hurt?" The female moved closer to him and crouched down before him. Her eyes were golden yellow and her features sharp.

Lethe shook his head in response.

She held out her hand for him to take but he did not move from his spot against the tree. She pulled back her hand into the red cloak she wore when a few more moments passed. "Are you scared?" she asked.

Lethe nodded.

"I thought so. Take this, it'll calm your heart. You don't want to be scared anymore, do you?" She held out a small vial of purple glittering liquid.

Lethe shook his head. No, he didn't want to be scared anymore but he didn't want to take something from a stranger without knowing what it was.

"Your mother sent me."

Lethe's heart lurched at the words, stepping outside of the shadows just a little to take a better look at the female.

She smiled warmly, extending the small vial of purple liquid between them.

His mother did have a roundabout way of communicating things she wanted. She wasn't always so clear but if the woman before him said that she was sent by his mother, then what other option did he have? He was stuck here all alone.

Lethe reached out to grab the vial of liquid. It felt cold in his hands.

"Once your heart calms, we can get moving. Do you like the sound of that?"

Lethe nodded. He did like the sound of that. And perhaps this female *was* working with his mother. His mother had clearly stated that they were going to go to another world after this one.

Lethe unplugged the vial and downed its contents. It tasted like grape lollies and fizzed down his throat with a bit of magic.

Suddenly, he felt sleepy. Calm. The female was right. He was about to thank her for the reprieve when she yanked him closer by the wrist and snapped his neck back by his hair. The pain of it etched across his scalp, making him wince. Her spindly blood-red nails danced in his vision, as she muttered words he did not understand. He felt the magic run through his head, like a cold wind.

"From this day forth, you are known as Kaine Dormarth Aaryn. You are an orphan born in Summeira. I am your queen and your saviour. You will fight my fights and be a warrior in *my* Elite," the female hissed.

The words she spoke wrapped around his throat and then eased.

"Kaine, are you ready to go back to the castle now?"

"Yes, my queen," Kaine muttered. He didn't understand how he got into the forest. The queen before him looked concerned and there was a feeling that brewed inside of him. Determination. Determination to serve her and whatever she stood for.

She held her hand out for him and he took it with surety, wiping his eyes but not entirely sure why they were wet to begin with.

Together, they walked toward a castle surrounded in a blaze of fire, its two spires piercing into the dark night sky.

45

SOPHIE

It was the last day of the Ephemeral Eclipse. The day where the stars would return to their rightful place high in the sky. The day where the sun and moon, star-crossed lovers doomed to pine after each other for all eternity, would resume their aching chase across the sky once more. Sophie would enjoy tonight, not knowing what tomorrow would uncover for her.

Sophie sat at her desk, looking out into the courtyard. The night air was cool, the sounds of insects buzzing and chirping filled the empty space around her. Ash had asked her if she was up for a training session with the Tienthan but she politely declined, in favour of sorting out her jumbled mind.

She opened her desk drawer, its wooden surface smooth, to find the two throwing knives she thought she had left behind in Faery. Her father's throwing knives and now hers. Sophie smiled softly, running a finger across the pearlescent surface. They represented a past she'd never known. A past that was written into her DNA. It was a reminder that she was about to do the right thing. Tomorrow. It would all change tomorrow.

Sophie returned the throwing knives into their scabbards and pocketed them, returning to the task that she'd set out to accomplish this morning.

Two letters. One that protected her heart. And one that left it open, raw and ready to be obliterated if the person receiving the letter decided to betray her. So much had happened since she had found herself in the Godlands. She hadn't had a chance to organise her thoughts. She found herself at a crossroad again, knowing that her choices had led her here to the Godlands. Where would her next choice lead her?

And so she wrote.

Dear Acheron,

I can't thank you enough for being a friend. You've always been there for me, showing me my limits. You always know how to push them (much to my chagrin).

Sophie laughed, thinking about all the times he knew exactly what to say to rile her up. She shook her head and continued writing.

Our friendship is something that I will value to the end of my days. So I'm writing this to let you know where my heart lies as I fear that lines have been blurred as of late. I've been hurt, Ash. Badly. And my heart will never recover from it. I can feel the irreparable fissure in my flesh, and I simply cannot offer you more of me. If I tried, it would be a disservice to myself, and most of all to you, my dear friend.

I hope in this letter you too find the answer that you've been searching for. I hope that you understand that I will always have your back, as your friend and confidant.

Your friend forevermore, Sofreya.

As Sophie finished the letter, her throat felt sour. The words she'd written were, in part, truth, but they felt so wrong being written into reality. Sophie's mana thrashed against the words too, knowing they were completely false. Her gut told her that. She always trusted her gut. It guided her through everything and so far, it hadn't been wrong. Yes, at times it wasn't clear, but now, it was as clear as moonlight.

Sophie folded the letter, placing it neatly into a black envelope and scrawled Ash's name in golden ink.

She moved back to the writing pad feeling nervous writing this particular letter. The letter that would tell her heart's truth. Sophie took up the pen with a shaky hand and an equally shaky breath.

Here goes nothing.

The words that Sophie longed to voice came spilling out upon the page.

My Acheron,

I told you once how scared I was. My heart had been broken times a plenty, but I find that perhaps my fear with you is not how you'll break my heart but how you'll keep it held together in the palm of your steady hands. That feeling, so whole and true, is something I've never felt before. That unknown is what terrifies me.

But as we spend more time together, as our past and paths continue to unfold and uncover themselves, I can't help but feel that we are destined to walk the unbeaten path – hand in hand. That the stars themselves, the ones that line the sky, had always been lighting a path to you.

I don't know what the future will hold for us. But what I do know is how my troubled heart eases with you around. How my jagged soul softens when you are near. What I do know is how my skin burns for you, and how your touch quells every anxious fibre in my being. I know that whatever our souls are made of, they are the same.

I see you in my memories, my dreams and my future. The point is, despite the times I want to throttle your neck for some smart-ass comment or the times you steal my snacks at training just so I would look at you (do this again and I will kill you), I see us. I see us and no one else. There is no one else for me but you Acheron Taranis.

You are mine and I am yours, forevermore.

Starlight.

The words came too easily. Spilling out onto the page, eager to breathe, eager to live. Sophie teared up, folded the piece of paper, placed it in a red envelope and scrawled Ash's name across it. She held it in her hands for a moment longer with a soft smile on her face. This felt good. Writing it all down felt good. It felt right. Tomorrow, after she did what she needed to do, she would give it to him. Tomorrow.

"What are you doing?" Eros cooed, leaning against a column of her bedroom with a lazy smile.

"AH!—" Sophie shot from her chair, pushing her desk forward, sending her letters and stationary flying. "Godsdamnit, Eros, don't you know how to knock?!"

Sophie blew out a frustrated breath and haphazardly shoved things back into her desk but not before Eros zoomed across the room and plucked the letter out of her hands.

The strawberry-blond god of love, sniffed the envelope and rolled his eyes back into his head as if he'd sniffed the most tantalising drug in the universe.

Sophie tried not to laugh, mainly because she needed that letter back. She crossed her arms and scowled. "Give it back." Sophie laid her hand out expectantly.

Eros snatched it back even farther, a playful grin on his face. His pure white wings bristled with excitement. "Not until you tell me what's inside it."

"By the way you're acting, it looks like you already know."

"It's a love letter then?" Eros wagged his eyebrows.

Sophie sighed. "Yes."

"GAH! THE STARS ARE ALIGNING. LOVE IS IN THE AIR. ITS WOMB PRIMED AND READY TO BE PENETRATED BY THIS VERY LETTER!" Eros cawed like he'd found the damned lost city of Atlantis. He held the letter in the air and Sophie swore there were tears in his loved-up eyes.

"Penetrated? Not sure if that's the right word."

Eros gasped, looking completely offended.

Sophie took that moment to snatch the letter out of his hands, quickly stowing it away in her desk with her Fae speed.

Eros, finally recovering from his outburst, propped his elbows onto Sophie's desk, rested his chin in his hands and started wiggling his butt.

Someone please come and collect this hopeless romantic. ASAP.

"So, when are you going to give it to him?" Eros smirked, drawing outlines of little hearts on her desk with his finger.

Sophie let out shy smile. "Tomorrow. Maybe."

"MAYBE?! With love there is no *maybe*, Soph. You're all in or you're all out. If you don't give it to him, I will." Eros crossed his arms, meaning to look very serious but he couldn't. Not with the heart-shaped smoke puffs he had manifested into the air.

Sophie crossed her arms and narrowed her eyes. "You wouldn't."

Eros stepped closer to her. Defiant. "I would."

"Well good thing I'm giving it to him tomorrow then. I'll save you the trouble."

"Good," Eros huffed.

"Good."

The Ephemeral Rising, the final day of the Ephemeral Eclipse, would forever have a special place in Sophie's heart.

A soft summer breeze swept through the trees and the smell of food wafted into the air. Together with Ash's cadre, Sophie sat among the stars upon a picnic blanket at a local park in Soul City. Who could say, in their right mind, that they sat with the stars? That if she sought to reach out and touch one, she could?

Soul City was aglow with the stars that came to rest. The bright yet warm light of the stars illuminated the happy faces of everyone in the city. A fair, filled with rides and carnival games, had been set up by the townspeople, adding to the magic of the night. Screams and shouts of glee echoed through the park and it made Sophie's heart squeeze.

Gah. This is just so magical, and the stars are going to rise at any moment.

Nemysis had pulled together an extraordinary charcuterie board to share. She lay on her stomach with her brown wings tucked in tightly behind her, as she picked at the fruits and meats. Eros lay next to her, talking about a rom-com he had watched last night. Deymos sat quietly, admiring the stars and the empty night sky. Ash, on the other hand, had run into some children from the Home for Lost Children. The orphans swarmed in on him from a distance, waving to the angels that sat on the picnic blanket before vying for Ash's attention. Amina, the children's caregiver, watched them happily, a young soul in her arms. Sophie laughed as the kids chased Ash around the glowing stars.

His hair was pulled into a tight braid, showing off his undercut. He wore that freaking loose blouse that always sent Sophie's heart a flutter and his dark linen shorts that showed off his tanned quads that she wanted to rest between . . .

Sophie cleared her throat and reached out for a snack to preoccupy her hands.

Soft footfalls sounded on the grass from behind and Sophie looked back to find Cam, a basket of food in his hands. He smiled brightly. "Happy Ephemeral Rising, Sophie." He held out his arms for her.

Sophie shot up from the ground and wrapped her arms around Cam's neck. Sure, he was a soul and his skin felt unbearably cold, but he was alive – sort of anyway. "Happy Ephemeral Rising, Cam!" She squeezed him tight before letting go.

Ash's cadre all shouted their greetings, clapping Cam's hand as he worked his way around the group. When Cam returned to Sophie, she pulled him down to the picnic blanket. They settled down, returning to watch the stars as some of them rumbled awake.

"I can see the appeal," Cam said lowly, nodding to Ash who was now pointing out the stars that rumbled for the children to see. Their eyes widened and marvelled at the movement. Ash beamed in return.

Sophie nudged Cam in the arm with her elbow but didn't say anything. She could totally see the appeal too.

"Do you miss them?" Sophie asked Cam.

"Ellie and Zala?"

Sophie nodded.

"All the time." His eyes were sad, but a bittersweet smile still turned on his face.

"I'll tell them when I see them next." Sophie leaned in, wrapping an arm around his shoulder and squeezing it. She had to head back to Faery soon. She'd have to face Kaine and hopefully stop him from killing Faery entirely. And hopefully she would run into Elowan and Zala.

"Shit, you're headed back to Faery?"

"Soon enough."

"I don't envy you, but I guess it needs to be done." Cam leaned down and grabbed a grape, popping it into his mouth.

"I guess so," Sophie said with a sad smile.

"Do me a favour, Soph. Whatever you do, don't let go of the people that matter to you most." He looked to Ash, then to Ash's cadre as they laughed and went about their conversations. "Tell them you love them every single day, every single second and with every breath that you have to spare. The Fates are ruthless, and they'll rip it all away from you when you least expect it."

Sophie looked at him. The blue film of magic that encased his body was a stark reminder that the Fates were indeed heartless.

"I won't let the Fates win," Sophie said with an air of conviction.

"Good." Cam smiled and paused. "Because if I had *that*"—he pointed to Ash—"waiting for me at home, I'd tell the Fates to fuck off too."

"You salacious soul!" Sophie batted his arm, laughing all the while.

A large, ominous shadow dulled the glow of the stars around her.

"Do we have a problem here?" Ash growled, his wings spread out a little in posturing.

"No! Sophie here was just telling me what a nice ass you have – what a nice asset you are to her life." Cam cleared his throat as he stood up, reaching out a hand for Ash to grab. "Happy Ephemeral Acheron."

Ash took Cam's hand and with a wicked grin said, "Happy Ephemeral." Ash pulled Cam in closer with a tighter grip upon his hand. Sophie swore that Cam squeaked. "Any friend of Sofreya's is a friend of mine." Ash laughed as he clapped Cam on the shoulder hard. Really hard.

"Strong. So strong," Cam groaned, nursing his shoulder.

"Come on, the stars are waking," Ash held out his hand for her and she eagerly grabbed it, lacing her fingers through his. She gave Cam a nod before slipping past him.

The stars, one by one, rumbled to life. Their cores burned bright, ready to catapult themselves into the sky. Everyone in the park stood from their blankets, their hands raised in the air with anticipation.

Like they were possessed with magic, the stars shot up into the sky, just as fast as they'd fallen, leaving trails of blue-and-green swirling light in their wake.

A bright laugh bubbled in Sophie's throat.

This was living.

The stars rushed back to their homes in the night sky, whisking all around in joy.

Ash wrapped an arm around Sophie, pulling her closer. She obliged, leaning into him. Ash's woodsy scent made her heart so full. She looked up to him, into those smoking turquoise eyes and by the Fates, she wanted to squeeze him.

Ash laughed, placing a soft kiss on her forehead, before turning his entire body to stand in front of her. He held out both his hands for her to take. She took them without hesitation, her skin buzzing at the points where they touched. His white wings snapped out, thrusting them into the air.

Sophie let out a little squeal as Ash pulled her closer to his chest, spiralling them through the rising stars. Up and up they went. They floated beyond the stars for a while, having raced ahead of them.

Sophie was completely entranced by Ash. Body and soul. There was no denying it anymore. "Happy Ephemeral, Ash." Sophie grinned, her heart bursting at the seams.

"Happy Ephemeral, Starlight." Ash grinned back.

Like two mirrors, they stared endlessly into each other's eyes before the tension between them sundered and their lips, destined to meet in this lifetime and lifetimes beyond, found each other. Sophie breathed him in fully. His lips. His scent. She knew her soul could not be without his.

And as the stars finally caught up to them, whizzing past, Ash turned in the air and released the tension in his wings so that they were falling. Sophie's stomach turned but as Ash pulled her closer to him, the feeling of weightlessness disappeared without a trace. From point to point, lips to lips, hands to chest, the feeling of Ash overwhelmed Sophie's senses and sense. Her body lay flush against his in the most poetic way, as they plummeted through the stars, locked together in a lover's embrace.

46

ACHERON

"Alright, bottom two with the least points gets kicked out of the running. Got it?" Ash announced.

"Got it," they all responded with determination on their faces. The angels did this every year the Ephemeral Eclipse rolled around. A round robin of carnival games to top off the night and this year, they had two new competitors, Sofreya and Camrine.

The onslaught began. A flurry of baseballs went flying down range. The poor games attendant looked utterly terrified as he squished himself into a corner.

"HEY!" Nemy shouted over the maelstrom.

Camrine laughed. He'd accidentally knocked one of Nemy's balls out of the air when it was bound to land into the one-hundred-point barrel.

Nemy wasn't having a bar of it. She dived for Camrine's stash of baseballs and started tossing them into her own barrels instead.

"That's cheating!" Camrine baulked.

And so the baseball-stealing melee ensued.

Sofreya didn't hesitate, diving straight for Ash's stash and skilfully tossing them into the barrels several metres ahead. "Take that, asshole!"

"Oh no you don't." Ash shoved her aside, pushing her back and making a barricade with his wings so she couldn't get back to her stash.

"This is so unfair!" Eros cried as Deymos covered his baseballs in shadows so no one could get to them.

"All's fair in love and war." Deymos chuckled darkly.

"Don't you dare use the L-word in vain, Deymy!" Eros tried to shove Deymos aside but failed.

Nemy and Cam were still going toe to toe.

Sofreya, ever the sneaky assassin, took the opportunity to swoop in on Deymos's and Eros's stash of baseballs. She feverishly tossed them into her own barrels like a fully-automatic machine gun.

Ash bent over in laughter as Deymos and Eros stood gobsmacked, unable to stop her. "Looks like you've been trumped, lads." Ash crossed his arms across his chest.

"Hey, I thought you were our brother, or perhaps that was before you decided to sleep with the enemy," Deymos smirked.

"What did you say earlier, Deymos? All is fair in love and war?" Sofreya jibed. She leaned back against the counter of the stall with her arms crossed.

Sofreya was a freaking smart-ass, and it took every ounce of willpower to not whisk her away and steal kisses from her underneath the stars.

"Touché." Deymos bowed his head.

"You two are out." The games attendant pointed to Eros and Deymos. Both groaned and complained as Cam was handed a bright green plush frog hat, deeming him the winner of this round.

"To the rifles!" Nemy declared. She was pissed. Probably because Cam had beaten her. They all ran to the game stand, picking up toy rifles. It felt like they were children again, laughing wholeheartedly without a care in the world. This was how Ash wanted to spend the rest of his days. Filled with laughter and filled with love. He'd gone so long without it.

The remaining contenders lined up against the stall, ready to shoot down some metal ducks a metre ahead.

Ash watched as Sofreya lugged the rifle into her shoulder and loaded the weapon with finesse. His throat suddenly ran dry.

Damn. And that's not even a real gun.

Sofreya popped a hip and faced him. "Yippy-ki-yay, motherfucker," she smirked.

Ash had no idea what she was saying, but he was one hundred per cent into it. The way her unbound purple hair glowed and glinted in the starlight had him distracted. The way her bare midriff begged to be touched filled all his senses. Ash couldn't even form any words as the group started firing away without him.

Shit.

Ash came to, pulling his toy gun into his shoulder and started firing with precision. But Sofreya was fast. She was also a really good shot. Damnit, he'd have to work for this.

From the corner of his eye, Ash could see Camrine groaning as Nemy stole every single duck he was aiming for.

Ash leaned into his rifle, taking shot after shot. Sofreya was keeping up without breaking a sweat and damn, if that wasn't the biggest turn on.

"Struggling to keep up, Starlight?" Ash taunted.

"Never. There's one thing you never have to worry about, Ash"—she shot down a duck with precision—"and that's me trying to keep up with you," Sofreya said lowly, just for him to hear.

And by the Fates, did that send Ash's mind spiralling into the depths of a trash-filled gutter.

She shot down a few more ducks as Ash just stared at her. A hunger so violent throbbing through him.

"Time!" the games attendant called. The ducks that swam across the board of the stall stopped. The attendant tallied up the score and pulled down a large heart-shaped plush. He looked like he was going to give it to Ash but at the last minute diverted his path and handed the plush to Sofreya instead.

"Woo!" Sofreya held the heart-shaped plush above her head in triumph, sticking her tongue out at Ash.

Ash crossed his arms and shook his head. She was so frustratingly precious that it almost killed him.

"As the winner of this trial of bravery and tenacity, I'd like to bestow my winnings upon . . ." Sofreya stepped closer to him, her proximity like gravity pulling him closer to her. She grinned. "Eros." Ash's heart sunk.

She quickly turned on her heel and handed the heart-shaped plush to Eros, who appropriately squealed.

I didn't want the stupid plush anyway.

Eros crushed Sophie into a hug, and she patted him away. The Fae parts of him wanted to snarl and snatch her away.

Before Ash could quip, a letter puffed into existence before him. The entire group stopped their merriment.

Ash whipped it out of the air and unfurled the note.

Soon. The trials will begin.

—A

"What is it, boss?" Deymos asked.

"Our official notice period," Ash said calmly, handing the scroll around to the group. "The Hrabrost Trials." Ash looked at Sofreya.

"Do I get to come watch these trials?" Sofreya beamed.

Ash laughed. "I'll make sure you have front-row seats."

Every year, the Tienthan had to undergo retesting to ensure that they had the power, skill, tenacity and most of all courage, to continue their job. It was almost thirteen years ago that Ash had his first trial. The one that earned him his wings. He hoped this year wouldn't be as bloody.

"When does it start?"

"We won't know until the trial starts." Ash took the scroll from Eros and made it disappear. "It could be a day or a week. They like to keep us on our toes to emulate the battlespace."

"I'll be there." Sofreya smiled.

Ash felt those words in his soul. She'd be there for him, through the nightmares. Through his trials. Perhaps through it all. By the Fates, he hoped it was through it all.

47

SOPHIE

The glow of the moon had started to peek into the night sky, the eclipse finally ending. It glowed brighter than any other night Sophie had seen in the Godlands, as if refreshed from its rest.

Soul City had quietened to a soft hum, many people returning to their homes after an evening full of celebrations. Not long after they received the note from Ares, the angels of the Tienthan left for a briefing in preparation for the Hrabrost Trials. Ash had offered Sophie a ride home, but she opted to stay in Soul City to peruse the market stalls for some sweet treats.

In truth Sophie was nervous. Because tomorrow, she would be going to the Stagnum De Memoria. The idea of a clean slate was appealing at first, but it wasn't long before cracks began to form upon the façade. There was so much of herself missing and there was only one way to get those pieces back. Would uncovering her truth make any difference? Would she be relieved? What if all her memories, the ones that had been hidden from her, would only hurt her more? Or perhaps they wouldn't bring the answers she was expecting . . . not that she was expecting much.

Focus. Treats, treats and more treats.

Her thoughts were spiralling. Initially because of the way Ash looked in those linen shorts and how he took her hand at every possible aching moment like he was going to lose her if he wasn't touching her. Shortly after that, her thoughts were spiralling because of where she was going tomorrow.

Sophie stilled as she approached a chocolate brownie stand. The hairs on the back of her neck stood and it felt like she had an invisible target on her back.

Sophie acted as if she hadn't felt eyes on her. She moved closer to look at what type of brownies she wanted to take home with her. "I'll take two plain brownies, please," Sophie said to the stall keeper.

"That's two marks," the lovely rotund soul said.

Sophie handed her two marks in return for the bag of brownies, feeling the eyes of whoever was spying on her even more now.

"Thank you. Happy Ephemeral." Sophie smiled brightly to the stall keeper before heading down a quieter street.

Sophie tucked away the brownies into the bag she brought, feeling for her two throwing knives she'd strapped to her thigh underneath her short skirt.

She plodded along the dark street, her hands relaxed by her side, ready to strike should her stalker dare pounce.

She felt their presence on her side, like a power she hadn't felt in a while. Sophie threw her bag at her stalker and spun backward, pulling out both her throwing knives. She curled her fingers into the loops and braced herself – ready to strike.

The two stalkers held their hands up in the air cautiously. Their cloaks shrouded their faces in darkness.

But Sophie knew that long red hair. She knew those shadows that crept out from underneath a dark cloak.

And her heart burst in a cacophony of relief, happiness, sadness and everything that lay in between.

Sophie rushed to Elowan and Zala, her friends that she missed so much. She crashed into them, pulling both into an unbreakable hug. Sobs of joy left each one of them as all three of them held each other in the moonlight.

Wait a minute.

Sophie pulled back, wiping tears from her eyes. "How are you both even here?" Sophie laughed.

"Long story," Zala said boredly.

Sophie crushed Zala against her again. "I missed you."

"I missed you too, Sophie." The wraith managed to smile a little which made Sophie squeeze her even tighter.

"Is there a safe place nearby we can chat things through?" Elowan chimed in, a hint of worry on her face.

"I know a place." Sophie pulled out a small piece of parchment and pen. She quickly scrawled two notes and sent them off into the ether. "Come with me."

Sophie led them to the white marble doors of Archi's.

Elowan and Zala looked up at the matching sign.

"We'll be safe in here," Sophie explained, walking them down the small steps and into the dark corridor. Elowan and Zala followed quietly all the way through to the secret door.

The cooling sensation of the wall washed over Sophie as she spilled onto the other side. The room was empty barring Achlys, God of Eternal Night, and Athena, Goddess of War and Battle, sharing laughs in the conversation pit. They turned to see Sophie enter, raising their glasses in acknowledgement.

Sophie nodded in their direction. They greeted Zala and Elowan with the same warmth. The gods and goddesses were so . . . lovely.

Sophie moved straight to the bar, ordering three wines that were served in the magically refilling glasses she had last time. She handed them each a glass.

"Looks like you're right at home, Sophie," Elowan observed.

"I am." Sophie beamed. She really was.

Sophie led them to the conversation pit where they settled in for the evening. Elowan and Zala, mainly Elowan, detailed their journey here. From Seaspun Bay, through the Resting Ruins to the Untold Valley where they met the last surviving oracles and saved the third. And how, on the rainbow bridge that was a Wayfinder, they ended up here in the Godlands, on a mission from the oracles to find the flaming purple heart who lays with the sleeping sun. The answer and possibly the solution to win the war against the blood throne. Elowan believed it was Sophie.

And Sophie believed it too. She knew deep down that in the fate of Faery, she was written in it some way and somehow. Whether it was a prophecy or by happenstance, it didn't matter. The demigoddess of Faery needed to return to her lands and would need to deal with the cards that the Fates had dealt her. It was her responsibility.

"Well shit . . ." Sophie sat there for a moment, digesting all the information that had been dropped on her.

"You're the common denominator in all of this, Sophie," Elowan said firmly.

"Well, about that . . . turns out I'm the demigoddess of Faery," Sophie grimaced.

Elowan choked on her wine.

Zala's face went impossibly still.

Sophie explained it all. How her mother was the goddess of all lands, how they managed to escape Queen Calliea many years ago. She left out all the parts about Ash thinking it would be better explained when they met him in person.

"You somehow keep surprising me, Sophie." Zala shook her head, a small smile creeping upon her face. As soon as Sophie spotted it, it disappeared.

"Speaking of surprises"—Sophie shot up from the couch—"stay right here."

Elowan blinked several times, trying to keep up with Sophie. It looked like she was going to argue when Sophie didn't give her a chance. She shot straight for the door, running through the corridor to the entry way where her favourite soul in the Godlands waited for her.

"They're inside?" Camrine said, a little nervous.

Sophie nodded. "Ready?"

"As I'll ever be," he breathed.

Sophie took Cam's hand and pulled him through the corridor. They ran down the hallway, squealing.

The power of the door washed over Sophie.

"Ta da!" Sophie pulled out her best jazz hands to show off Cam.

"Mother of Faery," Zala gasped.

Elowan made a choking noise as they both threw their glasses down and sprinted to Cam. They bowled into him, almost knocking him over.

Elowan was sobbing while Zala surveyed the blue tinted film that coloured his skin.

"Ladies, ladies, ladies. Please. One at a time." Cam laughed.

"Cousin," Elowan breathed, another sob rounding out in her throat. She crushed into him, her red hair matching his.

"It's good to see you. Are you okay?" Cam held her by the shoulders.

Elowan smiled. "I'm holding on."

"And my favourite wraith. My only wraith." Cam held out his arms for Zala who scoffed and gave him a big hug.

"Good to see you alive, sort of." Zala pointed out the blue film.

"Compliments my skin tone, doesn't it?" Elowan and Zala both rolled their eyes and it felt like they were all back in Faery again. Finally, they were all together. They would be returning to Faery, but one of them wasn't.

Sophie felt him from a mile away.

The electricity in the air sizzled before the door rippled to life. Ellie, Cam and Zala stilled, their attention turning to the rippling door.

Ash, with his long inky hair, the white parts of it draping over his shoulder, stepped into the room and Sophie swore the air stilled to watch as well.

A beat passed.

Elowan shot a fire ball in Ash's direction so fast Sophie barely even registered it. The fireball puffed into smoke inches away from Ash's face, shrouding him in an ominous dark grey cloud of smoke. His lightning skittered across the room.

Sophie stood between them all, a reassuring hand on Elowan's shoulder. She managed to calm her friend's rage.

"I'm sensing a trend here," Ash growled.

The smoke dissipated, slowly revealing his devastating white wings and the storm clouds that seemed to trail him everywhere.

Godsdamn. Sophie let out a breath.

Cam let out a low whistle while Elowan and Zala looked between Sophie and Ash in confusion.

"Elowan, Zala"—she looked to her friends from Faery then to the turquoise smoking eyes that consumed her dreams—"meet Acheron Taranis, angel of the Tienthan and Weapons Master of the Godlands."

A feeling so bright and whole shot through Sophie's chest. It was pride. Unbridled pride as she looked to Ash.

Mine.

"Did you know this was here?" Sophie asked Ash. They all stood in the Shrine of Remembrance. A place to honour the fallen angels, gods and goddesses who had died protecting the Godlands and its interests. The shrine was almost forgotten, covered in vines in a less populated corner of Soul City.

"I always thought it was just a glass statue," Ash murmured, looking up to a glass statue, hewn into a shape of an angel. Neither feminine or masculine, the angel stood with its wings tucked neatly behind it, its head bowed and its hands resting upon a flaming sword that pierced the ground before it. It was magnificent yet wrought from sadness.

"This is where the Wayfinder dumped us and we'll be able to head back to Faery from here," Elowan assured.

They had spent a better part of the evening catching each other up on everything that had transpired. Sophie explained Ash and who he really was, the true son of King Gydeon and Riviera. Which explained who Kaine was too, the son of Cerri and Terr, the Breaker of Realms. Elowan detailed the status of Faery and what the oracles had explained. Ash retold his encounter with Kaine and the power that he felt emanate from him. Together they formulated a plan. Sophie would join them in Faery in a few days in hopes to draw out Kaine. Ash would bring his cadre in support, and they would take it from there. Much to Elowan's dismay, the full strength of the mighty Tienthan could not be deployed without Ares's or Zeus's approval. They'd have to make do with just a few angels to help.

"I'll see you in a few days." Sophie smiled, pulling Elowan and Zala into a hug.

They turned to hug Camrine. "Good luck," he said to them, squeezing them both tight. Who knew when he was going to see them next? He was a soul. He was stuck in the Godlands.

Elowan turned to Ash, holding out a hand for him to clasp. Ash obliged and firmly shook her hand, but Elowan did not let go. She pulled him in closer, crushing his hand and growling. Ash did not falter. "You so much hurt a hair on her head or get her the wrong fucking cookie from the bakery, I will fucking break you." Elowan bared her sharp Fae fangs.

"I'd rather sell my soul to Typhon than hurt her, Red. You can bet on it." Ash grinned. His declaration did all sorts of funny things to Sophie's insides.

Elowan and Zala moved to touch the glass flaming sword with a string of rainbow light running through its middle.

"May the gods guide you," Sophie said, her voice shining with pride and joy. Her friends were alive. Sure, war loomed over their heads, but they were alive, and they'd come here to get her to join in on the fray. There was no one else she'd rather do this with.

"To where we're destined to be," Elowan and Zala said in unison before flashing out of existence. The air where they stood rippled and settled, dust falling to the ground in the sliver of moonlight.

Sophie would see them soon. In Faery.

48

SOPHIE

Sophie was a ball of anxiety, spending the entire day in her villa turning thought over thought. Who knew time flew when you were on the verge of a panic attack?

Sophie fiddled with the heartfelt letter she'd written for Ash as she waited on a white chaise in her villa.

I'm fine. It's fine. I'm fine . . . right?

She felt fine. Mostly. Though her palms were sweating, her knees were weak, and she felt like she had a freaking furball stuck in her throat.

A knock rapped on her door, pulling her from the spiralling clutches of her own thoughts.

She quickly pocketed Ash's letter into her free-flowing pants. The ones Ash wore not a few days ago when he decided to shrink her.

Sophie bolted for the door and pulled it open. The cool evening air rushed into her villa. Her sunshine-kissed mother stood there in all her goddess glory.

"Mum." Sophie breathed in her mother's fresh strawberry scent and pulled her into a tight hug.

"How are you feeling?" Danna said, pulling back from Sophie's embrace. Her silver hair was pulled into a loose braid, and she wore a long, white linen sundress.

Sophie moved through the front door and pulled it closed behind her, linking her arm with her mother's. "Somewhere between vomiting and elation." Sophie laughed nervously.

"I'm sure it'll be quick," Danna assured.

"Oh, had your memories wiped for the better part of your life, have you?" Sophie quipped. She knew it probably twisted the knife a little when it came to her mother's guilt, but hey, Sophie was hurting too.

Danna clicked her tongue as she let go of Sophie to pull herself up onto Spirit, the pearl-coated arion. Sophie followed suit, swinging her leg over the mythical horse.

Danna clicked her tongue sharply, leaping them into the air. She waited until they soared gently across the Isle of Deos.

"Listen, Sophie." Danna leaned back slightly. "I'm truly sorry. I know what I did wasn't right." She swallowed deeply. "At the time, I thought I was protecting you, but I can see how my actions have impacted you. I hope that one day you'll forgive me, Sophie. Just don't shut me out, okay?" Danna looked back over her shoulder to Sophie.

The words her mother spoke patched up a tiny part of her heart, but were they enough? Only time would tell, but one thing was certain. She would never shut her mother out. "I won't. I promise," Sophie said softly, leaning her chin onto her mother's shoulder. They flew across the Isle in comfortable silence.

The Stagnum De Memoria.

The Pool of Memory, as Danna had called it, was situated on the edge of the Isle. To access it, one had to work through a hedge maze but once you got through . . . Sophie was left utterly breathless.

Eight gargantuan marble columns stood tall behind a deep pool. They lined up to create a crescent shape that hugged the edges of the bioluminescent water. The stars shone brightly above, making the water itself glitter. Beyond the columns lay the edge of the Isle. Nothing but pure, night sky.

Four beings, with the skin of marble, stood along the grassed path to the pool. They had elongated elf ears, their eyes were all milky white and they wore golden chains that clinked and sashayed as they moved to greet Sophie and Danna.

"Welcome," one of them said in a soft, monotone voice.

The rest said nothing. They wordlessly handed Sophie a white dress similar to theirs. The four mysterious beings looked to Danna with expectation.

"I'll see you outside when you're done." Danna smiled sweetly at Sophie, pointing to the other side of the hedge maze. "Good luck," she said, before swiftly moving back to where they'd come from.

The four beings before Sophie remained silent as they reached out to grab a hold of Sophie's hands and arms.

They ushered her behind a hedge with the white dress in her hands. Sophie obeyed, quietly moving behind the hedge to find a mirror. Her skin was numb, and her head felt like it had been shoved into a glass bowl. She was moving, she was breathing, but she felt like she was barely there. Sophie mindlessly shed the pants and top she wore and slipped into the dress the beings had given her.

The white dress was stark against her tanned skin. She looked at herself in the mirror. She was taller than she was over a year ago. Wiser than she was. More whole. More at peace. The last missing piece to the puzzle to who she was, was just within reach. Half goddess. Fae. Human. Sure, she was all these things but deep down she was merely Sophie – a girl from Melbourne who loved her books, her friends and her family.

Sophie sighed, nervous for what was about to unveil itself.

She moved quickly out of the hedges, back to where the four white-marbled beings were waiting for her. The one that spoke guided her to the edge of the glowing pool, while the others moved reverently around it. Fountains, carved into celestial figures like the moon, the sun and the stars, spurted the luminescent water into the crescent pool. Flower petals of blue, white and purple floated serenely on the water's surface. A soft, harp-filled melody echoed through the air, calming Sophie's furiously beating heart.

"The Stagnum De Memoria will bring to light what has been locked away," the being said.

Sophie swallowed, finding her throat a touch dry. "Will it hurt?"

"Physically? No."

"How long will it take?" Sophie now stood on the edge of the pool. Small incremental steps led down to the depths of the water.

"As long as you need."

The being that spoke left Sophie's side to join the others, standing directly across from Sophie.

"We will begin our song for the moon and when you are ready, submerge yourself in the water. Float on your back and close your eyes."

And so they began to sing. Their four angel-like voices melded together in an entrancing hymn. A song for the moon, they said.

Sophie let out a shaky breath.

This is it.

She dipped her toe into the edge of the pool. The water was piercing cold and where it rippled, the water glowed brighter.

The haunting hymn continued.

Slowly, Sophie descended into the water. Chills ran across her arms and through her entire body. She hoped to the Fates that she was doing the right thing here and that this blessed pool would give her the answers she desperately needed.

When the water reached her neck, Sophie leaned back as instructed and floated among the flowers, their fragrance spilling into her nostrils and their soft petals caressing her skin. The voices of the four beings amplified into the water as her ears filled. Their calming tones eased the fire that surged through her veins.

Sophie's eyes fluttered closed, heavy with the burden of a past unknown. A high-pitched chime sounded through the water, to crescendo in her ears. And where the glow of the water around her seeped into the skin of her eyelids, darkness claimed them and guttered them out.

The hymn of the four beings ceased, and suddenly, Sophie was all alone.

Sophie's eyes opened to a soft, kind voice. Riviera's. The memory was clear and crisp as if Sophie were really there.

"When you put these together like this"—Riviera showed how the sleeping sun pierced the centre of the flaming heart, unlocking with a small click—"you'll find this." She fished out the fragment of multicoloured stone. Streaks of emerald, ruby, amethyst and citrine swirled throughout it. Sophie could feel her young self marvel at the shining stone as she sat next to a younger Ash. Sophie's heart squeezed. He was so much clearer now. Gone were his hazy edges.

Riviera placed the fragment back into the flaming-heart necklace. "And when you're old enough, you will wield the power hidden inside. Together." Riviera placed the flaming heart necklace over Sophie's neck and then moved to place the sleeping sun necklace over Ash's.

"It's the key to Father's power, isn't it, Mama?" Ash asked, his little face screwed into worry.

Riviera gently brushed the dark hair off his face. "That's right."

"But doesn't your father need it? He's the king. Kings are super powerful," Sophie pointed out.

Riviera smiled sadly and knelt in front of them. Her long dark hair spilled over her shoulder. She cleared her throat. "When someone has that much power, bad people often try to take it."

"But we can make the bad people go away right, Mama?" Ash asked, a little urgently.

"You're right. We need to make sure we don't *ever* let the bad people take your father's power, so we put it in something like this." Riviera touched the necklaces that lay on each of their chests. "A part of the power lies safe and hidden. While the other part is kept in Sofreya's necklace." She turned to put a hand on Ash's shoulder. "And the key to the missing part is your necklace, Acki." Riviera leaned back on her haunches. "This way, the only people that can get to it, are you two. Our beloved heir"—she squeezed Ash's cheek—"and our little princess." She turned to caress Sophie's cheek.

Sophie leaned into the warm touch. A mother's touch.

"We promise to take care of these with our *lives*, Mama."

Sophie nodded feverishly.

"Good." Riviera stood up, sighed heavily, then put her hands on her hips. "How do you both feel about going on an adventure?"

"Now?" Sophie beamed.

Riviera nodded.

"Yes!" Ash and Sophie shouted.

"Well, you better be quick then!" Riviera teased as she ran out the front door. Sophie and Ash ran after her in a flurry of giggles.

Sophie dashed down the few steps to the cottage, the summer heat thick in the air. She waited as Ash turned to lock the front door. She knew that front door. She'd been here before. Not in her memories but more recently.

Sophie almost gagged as she figured out where this memory had brought her. To Kaine's cottage.

Ash turned to smile at her, grabbing her hand as he rushed past. Sophie could feel her little self absolutely giddy with joy. They ran into the Summeiran forest without a care as the memory faded along the edges and Sophie found herself floating in the empty darkness again.

Her chest ached and tears were on the verge of spilling as another memory glittered into view.

Her throat was raw as she was wrenched into the arms of her mother. "Sophie, stop, we need to go."

She knew this memory. She'd seen it before, except there was sound here.

"We need to take Acki! We need to take him with us!" Sophie screamed and kicked. Her heart ached painfully as the distance between herself and her best friend grew.

"Sophie, stop." Sophie was abruptly put back onto the ground. Her mother wrapped a blanket tightly around her. "Listen, Sophie. Acheron is going to a safe place. He will be okay and maybe one day you will see each other again. He will be safe, Sophie. I know it hurts, but we need to get onto the boat. Can you do that for Mummy?" Danna said.

Sophie nodded wearily, trying to stifle her sobs.

She looked back to her best friend again, he was screaming and running for her but Sophie's father, Lou, held him back. Sophie could *just* hear Ash's words.

"Come back, Sofreya! Come *BACK!*" he screamed with all his might as he was wrenched away.

She needed to touch his hand one more time. Just so she wouldn't forget. Just one more time. Sophie ran for Acheron across the grassy knoll, but strong hands lifted her away. The memory faded back into darkness.

The memories that the Pool of Memory unlocked seemed to hasten, crashing into each other like a chaotic sea storm.

Sophie opened her eyes again to find herself at Flinders Street Station in Melbourne. It was dark and the train platforms were crowded. Everyone was wearing coloured football scarves as their warm breaths billowed out into the cold. Sophie stood with her mother, waiting for a train. She was still much shorter than her mother, perhaps ten years old.

In the distance, down in the depths of a train tunnel, Sophie spotted something glowing and purple. It was only for a second, but Sophie saw it flicker twice. She scrunched her eyes and tried to focus.

There it was again.

"Hey Mum," Sophie said, tugging on her mother's hand, "do you see that purple glowing light?" Sophie pointed down the tunnel.

Danna leaned down to try and spot what Sophie was pointing at. She hummed. "Hmm, I don't see anything, honey."

The purple light sparkled again.

"There! Did you see that one?" Sophie turned to face her mother.

Danna moved down to Sophie's level and brushed a hand across Sophie's forehead. The faintest glow danced into Sophie's vision. "It must be some railway workers fixing something. What do you think?"

A pang of confusion shot through Sophie. "Yeah . . . it must be." Sophie looked back down the tunnel and found darkness.

The memory faded out.

Holy shit.

She'd seen the portal to Faery when she was just ten and her mother withdrew it from her memories.

Before she could even begin to digest the memory, another memory danced into Sophie's periphery.

Sophie was standing in her childhood home kitchen in Melbourne. The sound of cicadas barrelled into the room on a hot summer's day.

Her father . . . who wasn't her father, propped down to her level. The greying ringlets of hair bounced down to frame his face. His features were much sharper than she had remembered. He had a tattoo on his neck that looked like small claw marks. Sophie hadn't remembered that either.

"Stay safe, kiddo," he muttered sadly as he mussed her hair before turning to exit the kitchen through the security door.

It clanged to a close.

Sophie looked to Danna with an emptiness so profound. Danna looked defeated, her silver hair tied into a messy bun and her tear-stained cheeks bright red. She didn't say anything. She didn't explain anything. She just turned and walked down the hallway.

As darkness pulled the memory away, Sophie could feel the deep ache of her throat as tears spilled from her own eyes.

And when she opened her eyes, she was dressed in her high school uniform, waiting in front of the principal's office. She could just overhear what her mother and the principal were saying.

"I'm so sorry, Mrs Gilfeather, she's just a teenager you know," Danna said apologetically.

"Teenager, sure, but this level of aggression is borderline criminal. She *burned* the girl's hair to a crisp. We do not allow lighters or flammable substances at school." Mrs Gilfeather's voice was high and shrilly.

"Then what's your policy around bullying? Is the other girl going to get punished for this?"

"That's not something I can discuss with you, Mrs Taliesin. I'm sure you can understand."

"Fine," Danna said firmly. The sound of a chair screeching backward spilled into the waiting room. Sophie could hear her mother's stomps as she almost pulled the principal's office door apart.

Sophie stood as her mother stormed toward her. She hadn't ever seen her mother this angry before.

"I'm so sorry, Mum. I don't know what happened. She called me an alien because of my eyes and then kept saying how Dad left because I was an ugly alien. I just got so angry. The next thing I know . . ."

Danna grabbed Sophie's wrist, pulling her out of the hallway. "It's not your fault, honey. Trust me."

The memory sucked away from her vision and was instantly replaced with another.

She was at Flinders Street Station again.

"See you later guys!" Sophie's voice was obnoxiously loud, given how late it was in the night. She stepped back into the train, holding on to one of the handles for dear life. She stuck her head out as her friends waved her goodbye.

"Happy eighteenth, bitch!" they shouted over the various beeps and announcements at the train station.

Sophie laughed to herself before taking a seat and popping on her headphones. She leaned against the glass window, drumming her fingers to her current favourite song. She was slightly inebriated. Slightly? No. Completely inebriated.

Getting lost in the music, she drummed and sang away, with no one else in the carriage to judge her. When she opened her eyes again, a flash of a sky with green-and-blue swirling lights danced in her vision.

What was that?

49

ACHERON

NINE YEARS AGO

Ash had been tracking the hellhounds for days now. They'd spent days terrorising innocent Faery folk. As to who summoned them, Ash did not know. He'd been waiting for them to gather at night to sleep, so he could send them back to the Shadow Realm as a pack. He managed to track down their camp along the edge of Red Oak Forest, beside Summeira – the Summer Court.

The hellhounds were tricky beasts that covered their scent with their flaming tails. Using various shadows, they camouflaged themselves. The Summeiran weather didn't help at all, in fact it stifled their scents. It was warm, hot and humid just like the Shadow Realm. They were in their element.

Ash perched high on a treetop with his white wings tucked tightly behind him, balancing him so that he almost hovered. His silver vambraces covered his muscled forearms and his black hair loosely billowed in the wind. His favourite war hammer, with blazing flames carved into its side, was strapped across his bare torso, ready for action.

The hellhounds had finally settled for the night. The last of them had returned from wreaking havoc in the surrounding Faery villages. As they passed through the centre of the pack, they taunted the one hellhound that lay weak. Someone had clearly tied it down and the other hellhounds were revelling in it. It was the runt of the litter. A pup.

Ash hadn't seen anything like it before. It was so much smaller than the other hounds, much younger and skinnier, though its flaming tail still burned bright.

How did I not notice the pup before?

The pup whimpered as the older hellhounds nipped at its patchy fur, leaving blood to pool at the sites they taunted. What had the pup done to warrant this torture from its pack, Ash wondered.

The surrounding forest hushed. The bristling leaves and branches stilled and the air itself grew stale. Unmoving.

A small figure covered head to toe in dirt and leaves, sprinted for the centre of the hellhound pack, a makeshift dagger carved from wood in its hand.

"What in the blazing . . ." Ash muttered from his observation point. His eyes locked on the fast-moving figure. He floated quietly down to perch on a tree closer to where the pack lay asleep. He needed to take a closer look.

The figure – a petite female, Ash realised – ran straight for the pup that lay dead centre in the pack. Wielding the makeshift dagger purposefully, she cut through the several ropes that bound the hellpup in one swift movement and scooped up the hellhound in both her arms. The pup was too big to be held in one.

Ash's jaw fell open as he watched the spectacle unfold before him. Not a sane soul in the immortal world would have had the gall to face death itself by the jaws of heathen hellhounds, all to save a pup. Not a single soul.

He laughed at the scene unfolding before him, admiring her bravery.

Once securing the pup in her arms, the female figure sprinted her way across the pack to the other side of the forest entrance, rousing the older hellhounds as she did. The hellpup bounced and flopped in her arms as she ran for her life.

Oh shit.

Ash snapped out of his trance and leapt off the tree from where he perched. He dived toward the dirt-covered female. She was fast. Deadly fast. She'd already reached the other side of the opening, but Ash flew faster.

His wings tapered in closer to his body, propelling him.

His wings flew open dramatically with a woosh as he cut across the pack of angry hellhounds that were ready to maul the female to shreds. The female who just stole from them one of their own.

Ash hovered midair, extending his palms toward the pack that yipped and barked. He swept his arms wide, one going anticlockwise and the other moving clockwise. He whispered beneath his breath the words of the origin spell. A spell that would send the hellhounds to the world they came from.

The tones of the hellhounds changed then.

They whimpered knowing full well that their bloody rampage through the Faery realm would end here. Ash clasped his hands together in prayer, finalising the spell. Blinding bright white light shot through his hands, enveloping the entire pack of hellhounds.

He twisted his palms, locking the hellhounds in – sending them straight to the Shadow Realm with a crack of his power. His lightning.

With a flash, the yelping was no longer. The rabid pack of hellhounds had disappeared to the hole they had crept out of.

Ash turned swiftly in the air with a push of his wings, knowing there was one hellhound left to send back. He weaved through the trees like they were nothing.

He heard her then, the female, panting but still moving.

He found her dirt-covered figure leaning up against a tree, fighting to gain her breath. The injured pup lay curled in her embrace, its head resting in the space between her neck and shoulder.

Ash tried his best not to startle her, ruffling his wings so she could hear his approach. But still . . .

"AH!" the female screamed, jumping from the surprise. The hellpup in her arms startled at the sudden noise and movement. Its ears perked, facing Ash as he slowly landed on his feet, white wings tucked in before the female.

"I didn't mean to scare you," Ash said apologetically. Hands up in surrender, Ash tried his best to show her that he meant no harm. He approached the female and pup, his feet inching cautiously forward. "I think you may have something that doesn't belong to you." Ash pointed at the pup.

She scuttled back farther into the tree that she rested upon. It wasn't fear that showed in her face, but something like determination.

She yanked the pup back, shielding it so that her body stood between it and Ash.

"I promise I won't hurt it. I need to send it back to where it belongs. It is a creature of evil, you see." Ash stopped his slow approach. Perhaps explaining his way through this would help convince the female to hand the hellhound back over to him safely. "The hellhounds have been slaughtering innocent Faery folk. I need to make sure they all go back to where they came from. That's all," he said softly.

The shadows of the forest hid her well.

The moonlight peeking through here and there didn't help him much. Ash could barely see her, save for the flaming tail that wagged happily in her arms. It didn't hurt her. It didn't want to hurt her, he realised.

"Not this one," the female said low in her voice, standing her ground.

Ash stepped closer to the female. "The faster we return the creature to its home, the safer everyone will be. The happier it will surely be."

"No."

"What do you mean no?"

"No." The female walked out of the dark shadows of the forest. Most of the dirt had flung off her face in her desperate flee from the hellhounds.

Ash's throat constricted.

His heart hung uncomfortably in his throat, and he swore his stomach had started to lurch back and forth.

His skin began to buzz.

For once in his life, Ash was stunned into silence.

The female was human. She was divine. Her long black hair was pulled back into a braid. Loose tendrils shaped her face like how the sea hugged the shores. She had to be about eighteen. The same age as he was.

Her bright purple eyes did something to his heart. Twisting it. Warming it. Floating it. Her eyes reminded him of the catmints that were planted around his home in the Godlands. Her sunset-dipped lips were full, and he unabashedly wondered how they would feel against his. Dirt was splattered across her tan, dimpled cheeks and the way his heart squeezed in that moment was so unearthly.

Ash felt like he was about to drop to his immortal knees if it weren't for the hellpup she held that would surely jump out and hang by his jugular if Ash dared inch closer.

With her arms braced across the furry back of the hellpup, the female moved closer to Ash, daring him. "I will not allow you to do that. He is injured. His packmates are the cause of these injuries. I will not allow you to send him back there. Beast or not." She stood her ground. The hellpup nestled in her neck farther as if completely agreeing with her.

"He may be injured, but what is to happen once he is healed? He will surely ravage the towns, tearing through citizens," Ash argued.

"No. Evil is made. Not born. He is still a pup and with that, he has a lot to learn. He's endured much from his pack and yet he does not bite or harm me." She moved the hand resting against the hellpup's back to his flaming tail, picking it up with her bare hand to prove her point.

The pup huffed, letting out tendrils of smoke from its nostrils as if to say, "I told you so."

Ash laughed at that.

Then he laughed at himself.

He was arguing with a human, who was holding a hellpup as if it were her only child, in Faery. She had a good point though, Ash had to admit. The hound, despite being a creature of evil as legends had it, did not hurt her.

This human intrigued him. Not only did she face what no immortal dared, she challenged him to see and think differently. And because of that intrigue, he relented.

Ash crossed his muscled tan arms and said, "I tell you what. I won't send the hellpup back to the Shadow Realm for now, only if you tell me about your world."

She looked at him, puzzled. He pointed to his own ears that were delicately pointed.

A blush rose to her cheeks, realising that her perfectly round ears were a dead giveaway. She was a human.

She narrowed her eyes, "You said 'for now'. What's to say you won't send him to the Shadow Realm in the next two minutes?" She shielded the pup farther away from Ash.

"Let me rephrase. We will let him heal from his injuries and if he decides he is a good pup, and not born of evil, he can stay. But if he so much barks in the wrong direction, I will send him back immediately." Ash compromised – a skill he did not exercise often.

"Deal." She stretched out an arm between them.

A deal.

"The name is Ash." He stretched out his hand to meet hers.

"Sophie." She smiled. Ash could faintly see his own swirling turquoise eyes dancing in the reflection of her purple eyes.

She took his hand in hers. Ash's much larger hand enveloped her petite one – covered in speckles of dirt, but they were soft and delicate.

The moment they touched, a spark of electricity shot through Ash's hand. It felt like he'd been punched in the gut, or he was free falling. The sensation was odd, sending him into a tiny dizzy spell.

They both flinched back from the spark, shaking their hands free of the sensation. Ash's mana swirled in joy, and a bond he hadn't felt for a long while snapped to life, awakening from its dark slumber.

He snapped his gaze to her enchanting eyes, the moonlight highlighting them. He tilted his head, wondering if she felt the same thing. She tilted hers too. They were like mirrors. The same, but different. Part of the same story. Cut from the same cloth.

She cleared her throat. "I've named him Calypso." She grinned widely.

Ash's knees wobbled. He couldn't help but plaster on a mischievous smile in return. He shook his head swiftly though, finally registering what Sophie had said. "We are not naming him," Ash argued. The last thing he needed was to get attached to something he knew he was going to have to send back to the Shadow Realm.

"We already have. His name is Calypso," she said firmly, tickling the little beast's belly, careful not to graze any of its existing lacerations.

The hellpup wriggled in her arms with happiness, its flaming tail wagging furiously side to side. Ash grinned at the wholesome sight.

"But Calypso is a female name. He's a boy."

"And since when were you so wrapped up in gender norms and stereotypes? If you haven't realised, you're the one wearing a skirt. Not me." She laughed, pointing at his loincloth.

Calypso huffed with her, tendrils of smoke trailing from his nostrils in laughter.

It's a damned loincloth, not a skirt. Reminder: Don't wear a loincloth on missions ever again.

"You have a point. Calypso it is." Ash shot his hands up in mock surrender. He laughed, shaking his head. This was ridiculous.

Life in the Tienthan was tough and gruelling, especially under the command of Ares. If Ash were to climb the ranks, he'd make a change in the culture but for now, he was a lowly soldier. "How about we rest for the night. I can heal his wounds and you can tell me all about Sotera while I do it," Ash offered.

Sophie nodded and motioned him to lead the way through the dark forest with a quick nod. The hellpup settled back into her arms for a nap. Calypso nuzzled her neck and gave little licks as he settled. Ash didn't know what a melting heart felt like until this very moment. Had he completely lost his mind? Shaking his head, he offered her his hand. She hesitated, unsure whether to take it.

"Well, we're certainly not going to walk there. Perks of having these." Ash pointed at his large white feathered wings, grinning.

Sophie beamed right back, with a flash of a bright white smile. "Well, there's always a first for everything right?" She laughed, placing her hand in his.

Ash swung around her, lifting her with an arm behind her legs and the other supporting her torso. Calypso clung tightly to her chest at the sudden movement. Ash's wings burst open, casting an enormous shadow on the forest floor.

Sophie gasped. "You're . . ." Her hands reached behind his shoulder to caress one of his feathers. He shuddered at the sensation, almost dropping her.

"Careful, fair lady. They're very sensitive." Ash laughed deeply.

"Sensitive?" She tilted her head adorably.

"Sensitive." Ash wriggled his eyebrows.

She grasped her hand over her mouth. "I am so sorry! I didn't mean to—"

"It's fine." He cut her short, assuring her it was truly okay. Angels rarely permitted anyone to touch their wings, sometimes not even their lovers. They were gifts from the gods and were treated as such. Sacred.

On that note, he leapt into the sky above the forest canopy with one big thrust of his wings.

Sophie let out a breath of unfiltered awe. The stars above rejoiced in their flight, cheering them on with quick flickers of light.

Ash flew the three of them to a large hollowed-out red oak tree he sighted earlier during his observations. Its opening was large enough to accommodate his wings.

"Your world doesn't seem as beautiful as I imagined," Ash said with Calypso curled up in his lap.

When they settled in the hollowed-out oak tree, Sophie started a fire while Ash healed Calypso with his powers. The pup healed quickly and fell asleep immediately in his lap. Though the pup was healed, Calypso was still strung out and skinny from being starved.

"Climate change, the patriarchy and racism aside, it is beautiful. The small moments are at the very least," Sophie said longingly, staring into the fire.

Ash had never been to Sotera. He hadn't reached the rank of lieutenant yet. Only lieutenants were allowed across the three realms – The Godlands, Faery and Sotera. As a private, he was assigned Faery and only a small portion at that.

"Do you miss your family?" he asked while petting Calypso softly across his furry back.

"My mother to be precise, and very much so." She smiled.

"You'll see her soon enough," Ash reassured her.

They sat next to each other to keep warm by the fire. Sophie had told him of her world, of how she ended up in Faery and how she snuck away from the Fae that were trying to help her get back to her home world. The group that led her through the tunnels of Faery to the departing train at Northern Helm. He respected her confidence and her bravery in wanting to see Faery in the flesh, even if it meant sneaking away from the only group of Fae that could protect her. Silly and stupid, some may have called it, but he couldn't complain. He was completely entranced by her.

"Can you tell me a story? Maybe when you were younger and how you joined the ranks of the Tienthan?" she asked, legs crossed, reaching over to sooth Calypso as he stirred from a nightmare.

Ash smiled. He didn't know why this story rushed to the forefront of his mind. Maybe it was because her presence and aura reminded him so much of his long-lost friend.

"I can tell you how I got this," Ash pointed to the scar running through his left brow, all the way down to his upper cheek.

She grimaced at the scar and asked, "Do I even want to know?"

"The story isn't as sinister as you think." He laughed, careful not to stir Calypso from his slumber.

Ash's wings rested behind him, strewn gently across the ground, giving him the perfect balance. Then he told her. Of his first love. His best friend. His princess with purple and silver hair. How they snuck down to the river to duel with the swords they stole from her father's armoury. Despite her much smaller size, she beat him fair and square, and as she did, he slipped on a rock, falling face first into the river. He spoke of how they laughed and laughed and how they kept it all a secret from their parents.

Sophie smiled softly, longingly at the story he shared with such fondness. "And where is the princess now?"

"She was taken away. To this day, I'm not sure where," Ash said sadly, his hand idly petting Calypso. Remnants of the lost princess danced through his vision. Flashes of her bright purple hair and the eyes to match haunted him.

"And you love her still?" Sophie rested her head against her knees, watching Ash.

He paused. Unsure.

"Don't fight it. It's written all over your face," she laughed softly.

"She took my heart with her. I still have hers. Here." He nodded, patting a hand against his broad tanned chest.

Sophie scoffed. "Ugh. It's like you're waiting for her to return! Eck, you make me sick!" She poked her tongue in disgust.

Ash laughed at that. "Say what you will, but love is powerful. People have started wars in its name," he defended.

The following evening Ash flew Sophie and Calypso closer to Northern Helm station so she could meet up with the Fae group escorting the few humans back to Sotera. He landed softly on a grassy knoll that overlooked the scaffolding-covered station. The open platform was covered in fog and lit by moonlight. The departing train was docked, prepped and ready to go.

Sophie turned to Ash as he set Calypso down on the grass. The hellhound velcroed himself onto Sophie's leg immediately, not wanting to say goodbye.

"You're a good boy. No matter what that insufferable angel says," Sophie whispered, scratching Calypso behind his ear.

The hellpup whimpered.

Ash crossed his arms. "You know I can hear you."

"I know. I just wanted to get one more laugh out of your old and cranky immortal soul."

"We're literally the same age," Ash pointed out.

"See? Cranky." She pointed at Ash, while speaking to Calypso.

Ash let out a loud cackle. Sophie made him laugh. He enjoyed her wit and company. He'd miss it, that was certain.

"Well, are you just going to stand there or are you going to give this measly human a big old goodbye hug?"

Ash opened his arms and his wings, an offering. Sophie laughed. It was music to his ears. She walked straight to him, wrapping her petite arms around his waist. Her head leaned softly on his chest. He enveloped them both in his arms and wings.

They stood there for a while. Calypso whined with impatience just behind them.

Breaking from the hug, Sophie paused to pull something off her wrist.

It was a colourful bracelet, with beads in various shapes, sizes, fruits and flowers. Nothing could juxtapose Ash – a lethal angel warrior – more.

"I want you to have this. It's not a family heirloom nor was it forged by immortals, but it is something dear to me," she said, head tilted up to meet his eyes.

Ash didn't even have the chance to object when she quickly grabbed his wrist and clasped the bracelet on. It barely fit around his wrist. Gaudy as it was, he appreciated it.

"I won't remember you, but at least with this, you'll remember me." She smiled brightly.

He smiled right back and took her hand that lingered on his wrist. Bowing deeply, widening his wings behind him, he raised her hand to his lips in gratitude.

A blush formed on her cheeks. It made Ash smile even more as he bowed before her.

He let go of her hand reluctantly and called for Calypso to stay by his side. The hellpup obeyed, though whimpered in Sophie's direction.

"Farewell, fair Sophie. Perhaps we'll meet again." He bowed his head again as she started down the grassy knoll.

Sophie walked down, halfway across the knoll when she suddenly paused and turned around. "Take care of him, will you? I think you and I both know he doesn't belong down there." She pointed down to the ground, to the Shadow Realm.

"I promise." Ash grinned, waving as she turned around again and jogged the rest of the distance toward the tunnel entrance just before the station.

As soon as she jumped into the tunnel entrance, Ash sat down on the grassy knoll, Calypso jumping right into his lap. He consoled the hellpup as it whimpered and whined for Sophie. "It's okay buddy, I've got you."

The train tooted its horn, signalling its departure. The sound echoed all the way across the grass surrounding Northern Helm station.

Ash looked to his wrist where the colourful bracelet stood out from his tan skin. It was brazen. It was endearing. It summed up Sophie perfectly.

He scoffed at the thought of a mighty angel of the Godlands wearing such a thing. For Sophie, he would. He knew then that there was room in his heart for more. For someone else. Maybe someone like Sophie.

Ash toyed with the beads of the bracelet, flipping them over. Bead by bead, letters revealed themselves.

And as each letter began to form a name he'd long burned into his memories, it felt like acid was rising in his chest. And as the acid finally seized his throat, all that was left in its wake was unadulterated panic.

T.A.L.I.E.S.I.N, the bracelet spelled.

Sophie was . . . his long-lost princess. She had to be.

And he was about to lose her. Again.

It was something only the Fates could orchestrate.

Like lightning, Ash bolted up. His eyes fixing on the departing train just in time to see Sophie pop her head up in the carriage. She was waving him goodbye, the foolish girl.

The train started forward with a jolt.

He ran for her. *"Wait!"*

He burst into the air with a powerful beat of his wings, his arm stretching out in front of him, doing anything he could to get closer.

But as the distance between them closed, a burning sensation washed over his right arm underneath his vambrace, sending him crashing to the ground.

No.

Ash tried to right himself, but the pain was too much. A film of white light engulfed his entire forearm. He grimaced at the light, yanking off the vambrace. In place of it was an intricate tattoo, starting from the crook of his elbow all the way down to his index finger. It was made of complex Faery symbology and at the tip of his finger was the shape of a lock.

It was the soulmate bond, seared into his flesh.

That panic he felt before? It was nothing compared to this.

It felt like he'd been struck by lightning, several times over.

Ash tried to get back up again. He cradled his stinging arm as he tried to push into the air. He could still see her in the distance. Sophie, who was bracing her now tattooed left arm. Eyes wide. In shock. He knew he had the same expression written all over his face.

With a woosh, the train disappeared into the portal heading for Sotera.

Ash looked back at the bracelet Sophie gave him.

Taliesin. Sofreya Brighid Taliesin. His first love. His long-lost princess with purple hair and purple eyes.

Sophie's eyes.

His *soulmate.*

Ash fell to his knees.

What hurt the most wasn't that the breath from his lungs had ceased to cooperate. It wasn't that he was only given a moment with Sophie, when all he wanted were moments and many more. It wasn't that he was so preoccupied with his past that he failed to see the present. What hurt the most was that Sophie wouldn't even remember him.

50

SOPHIE

Sophie gasped awake, water spilling into her mouth. She coughed roughly as she tried to find her bearings. The smell of flowers filled her senses and the bright moon shone above her.

Holy shit.

The four beings of the Stagnum De Memoria stood by the pool. Their skin had hardened to stone and their breathing, non-existent. They were freaking statues.

Sophie's mind was reeling. She pulled her left arm out of the water, examining her tattoos. The ones she mysteriously received on her eighteenth birthday. The ones that were in truth, her soulmate bond seared into her flesh by the Fates themselves. The one that she shared with Ash The one that swirled from the crook of her elbow all the way down to her finger to form a key.

Sophie wanted to vomit. She wanted to scream. She wanted to shout and rejoice all at the same time as the truth of her past finally set her free.

Sophie sobbed as she rushed out of the water, her chest heaving. The evening sky pooled with moisture. A storm was coming, Sophie could smell it in the air but that didn't stop her from running from the Pool of Memory and drying herself with a whip of her air mana.

She tossed all her clothes back on, making sure the letter she had written for Ash was safely in her pocket.

Sophie needed to find him.

Sophie sprinted to the hedge maze like a wild cat, bouncing left and right with a fiery urgency. She collided into her mother with her words already spilling out into a tumbling mess. "Mum, I love you. I get why you needed to do it." She pressed a kiss to her mother's cheek. Danna looked outright frazzled. "But our conversation can wait. I need to find Ash. I need to find him *now*." Sophie was practically vibrating, and she probably looked equally crazed. Her hair was undoubtedly knotted. Did she even put her shirt on the right way?

Sophie placed another kiss on her mother's cheek before sprinting toward her mother's arion. "I'm taking Spirit, SORRY MUM!" Sophie shouted behind her.

"It's fine. Just ride safely!" Danna called out.

Sophie sprinted to the pearl-coated arion, jumping onto its back like a crazed banshee. With two quick clicks of her tongue, she leapt up in the air, pulling the arion by its reins. She barely knew how to ride one but for Fates' sake, she didn't give a single shit.

Sophie careened through the air like it wasn't her first rodeo.

Ash was her *soulmate.* And she painfully, carelessly even, slapped on a clean slate clause since her return. He knew they were soulmates. He'd always known and yet, why didn't he tell her? Was it because of the boundaries she'd set on him, prior to knowing her truth? And holy fucking shit, they'd reunited before, when she was eighteen. Years of not seeing each other. Years after being ripped apart, they reunited and neither of them managed to figure it out until it was too late. Oh, the suffering Ash must have felt. To have known that his long-lost friend was *alive,* that she was his soulmate and not being able to find her again until . . . now.

Sophie pulled Spirit to an abrupt stop, sliding off the horse in a way that would have her legs aching tomorrow.

The heavy rain that hung in the air poured down from the sky. Sophie was sopping wet, but she did not care. She ran up the steps of Ash's villa, pounding on the door. Her hand pulsed with ferocity on each impact.

"Ash, it's me!" Sophie shouted above the pouring rain. No answer. Maybe he was in his library.

She laid a palm on his door, sending out her mana in search of his. Nothing came back, though she felt Cal's presence.

Sophie propelled herself over Ash's hedge and into his backyard. Lightning struck above and the storm angered. She ran into the cover that would lead to Ash's bedroom and opened it for Cal to come out.

The hellhound came barrelling out the door, jumping up to lick Sophie.

"My boy!" Sophie squealed. Her pup. The hellhound she'd saved in Faery. The hellhound that she made Ash promise to take care of. And look at him now; nine years old, big, strong, smart and kind. Sophie could almost cry. Ash had kept his promise to her this whole time.

"Where's your dad?" Sophie asked the hellhound.

Cal did his adorable spin before he pointed toward the north.

"The training ring?" Sophie asked.

Cal whimpered. A no.

"The waterfall?"

Cal shot out a puff of smoke from his nostrils before jumping around in excitement.

"You're the best!" Sophie bent down to kiss his noggin, earning herself a few licks to the face. "We'll be home soon, okay? You know where the food is. Stay inside. It's too wet out." Cal obeyed, running back into the bedroom.

Sophie launched herself back over the hedge and sprinted for the waterfall.

The rain was unrelenting. It was pouring down in droves so much that she could barely see ahead of her. But Sophie knew the path. She had walked it what felt like hundreds of times.

Sophie ran hard and fast. The beat of her feet almost matching the pace of her heart.

She needed to feel him. Touch him. Tell him most of all how he made her feel. He was the moments just before the fall of dusk and the rise of dawn. He filled her with anticipation, excitement and awe. He was everything that mattered to her. The truth of it all made everything fall into place. It made everything make sense. Sophie could finally stop her search for the other half of her soul because she'd already found him. It was Ash.

A dark figure appeared in front of her, closer to the waterfall.

Sophie tried to shield her eyes from the onslaught of the rain.

"Ash!" Sophie shouted above the cacophony. She was already crying. "Ash!" But he didn't answer. Sophie stopped in her tracks. That wasn't Ash.

A firm hand from behind her, pressed a cloth to her face so suddenly she didn't have the time to react. The smell on the cloth was sharp enough to send her eyes rolling back and her body limp.

Fuck.

51

ACHERON

Ash sat on top of the Isle's waterfall. Its backward running water lightly sprayed his skin as it spilled over the edge of the floating island. Ash swung his legs carelessly over the rocky edge as he breathed in the thick evening air, watching the pink-kissed sunset. Ash sighed. He would never tire of this view. Ever. This was freedom.

"So does she know yet?" Deymos asked, leaning back on his hands as he too watched the sunset beside Ash.

Ash shook his head, letting out another sigh. "Nope." He leaned back, letting the last of the sunshine caress his bare torso, bringing warmth to his wings.

Deymos shifted his weight and grey wings to face Ash. The god of dread and terror looked at Ash sideways. "Dude."

"Don't, *dude* me," Ash scoffed.

"I can *dude* you all I want. You spent years searching for her. *Years*, Ash. And now that she's here you're getting cold feet?" Deymos looked at Ash as if he were the biggest idiot.

Maybe I am the biggest idiot.

"She slapped the biggest 'friend-zone' sticker on my forehead the moment she realised who I was. Clean slate. That's what she asked for. What am I supposed to do?"

"You have the power of *several* gods, little bro. You don't ask for anything. You don't even have to wait for anything. You take it. So, what's holding you back?"

It wasn't in Ash to just take. He respected Sofreya and her boundaries but there was something holding him back. It was true.

Ash groaned as he eased onto the ground, closing his eyes. He stewed on his words a little longer. "I fear that . . . I could lose her again if I push too hard. That she'll disappear again and by the Fates, anything with her, platonic friendship or otherwise, is better than nothing at all."

Deymos sighed. "She's not made of glass you know?" Ash could hear the god lie down on the ground as well.

"I know." Ash knew that to his core. She was forged by fire with a resilience that left him in awe. He declared his intentions to her before the ball but now he was just waiting. Waiting for what? He knew the way her eyes lit up when she looked at him. How her heart paced when he neared. He knew the way she had kissed him wasn't for naught. It meant something. He meant something to her, and he knew it deep in his bones. He just . . . he just wanted to hear it from her. He wanted to hear her say it.

Ash opened his eyes and gazed at the sky longingly, hoping the Fates could hear his desperate plea. "Fates, if you are listening, please give me a sign. Anything."

A beat passed.

"Cause I'm your laaadyyyy and you are my maannnnn," Eros's singing voice shot through the air.

By the Fates.

"I wonder what song he's obsessed with this week." Deymos laughed.

Ash groaned before he sat up, watching Eros and his strawberry-blond mop of a head fly over to them. The god of love floated down slowly, his white wings spread wide. Above his head he held a small black envelope as if it were the damned holy bible.

"Whatever song it is, I'm sure we'll want to drown ourselves by the end of the week," Ash mumbled underneath his breath.

"Bright suns, my brothers." Eros popped himself down next to Ash.

"What have you got for us, Eros?" Deymos pointed at the black envelope.

"Oh, this?" Eros feigned surprised. Suffice to say, the god of love had zero acting skills. Eros held the letter delicately between his fingers. "It's a letter . . ." He dangled it right in front of Ash's face. "That Sophie wrote." Eros wagged his eyebrows and his mouth screwed into a cheeky smile, *bursting* to say something.

Ash narrowed his eyes. "I told you to stay out of it, Eros."

"Are you accusing me of meddling? I did no such thing! She wrote this through her own volition." Eros thrusted the black envelope toward Ash and grinned mischievously. "Well, aren't you going to open it?"

"Absolutely not." Ash stood, taking a few measured paces back from Eros and crossed his arms.

"But, Ash, it's got your name scrawled on it." Deymos pointed out the gold writing.

"Hey, I thought you were on my side," Ash complained.

"I'm Switzerland. I don't have a side, but I *do* want to know what that letter says." Deymos chuckled.

"See? It's two against one! You must open it, Ash," Eros pleaded.

"I don't *have* to do shit. If Sofreya wrote that, then she's the one that needs to give it to me."

"What would you say if she told me she was going to give it to you but then I gave her an ultimatum and a timeframe of which she *clearly* did not adhere to and now, as a result, I'm the only one in possession of the letter that she so heartfeltly wrote for you and *therefore* I'm the only person that is able to deliver to you?"

Ash's heart stuttered. Of course, he wanted to know what the letter said. But it felt wrong to open it at all, if Sophie wasn't the one giving it to him. It felt like he was going behind her back.

"She wanted to give it to you, Ash. She told me so." Eros pushed, shoving the letter closer to Ash.

Ash growled, shaking his head. This felt wrong but the kernel of hope in him agonised over not knowing the letters contents. "Fine," Ash gritted as he stepped forward, snatching the black envelope out of Eros's hands.

Eros squealed with excitement, clutching Deymos's arms in anticipation.

"Don't get too excited Eros. It's not like I'm going to read it out loud for you."

Eros let out a noise of disappointment.

Ash turned around, moving farther away from where Deymos and Eros sat. The letter's of his name had never excited him more. He felt like a giddy kid, waiting to unfurl the handwritten love letter from his childhood crush.

Ash held his breath as he pushed open the envelope. His heart beat uncontrollably as he fished the letter out and unfolded it.

And he never regretted anything more in his entire immortal life.

Dear Acheron,

I can't thank you enough for being a friend. You've always been there for me, showing me my limits. You always know how to push them (much to my chagrin). Our friendship is something that I will value to the end of my days. So I'm writing this to let you know where my heart lies as I fear that lines have been blurred as of late. I've been hurt, Ash. Badly. And my heart will never recover from it. I can feel the irreparable fissure in my flesh, and I simply cannot offer you more of me. If I tried, it would be a disservice to myself, and most of all to you, my dear friend.

I hope in this letter you too find the answer that you've been searching for. I hope that you understand that I will always have your back, as your friend and confidant.

Your friend forevermore, Sofreya.

Ash's heart was sinking. It was unbelievably heavy, and he wasn't sure how to breathe anymore. His heart was melting, but not in the normal way a heart melted. It was dying a silent, painful death. It was caving in on itself and nothing could staunch the blood flow.

He folded the letter, placed it back in the envelope and pocketed it. His hands were numb and so was his now hollowed chest. He needed to go. Anywhere but here. It felt like time itself had died and nothing existed but the harrowing affliction of his breaking heart. He didn't even have the strength to look up nor the strength to call upon his lightning to soothe him.

"Ash, wait . . ." Eros's sorrowful voice followed him.

Ash didn't wait, he kept walking with his head bowed until a force so powerful struck him backward. As Ash fell onto his ass, Ares stepped out from behind a puff of smoke.

"It's go time." The god of war smirked.

Shit.

Ares's clap boomed across the waterfall, sending all three angels down to the ground. A bright light filled Ash's eyes and suddenly, he was nothing.

52

KAINE

The Shadow Realm was his home now. Kaine's lungs had taken to the hot and humid climate with ease and he no longer longed for the sun. It was all darkness here, just the way he liked it.

It'd been weeks since he opened the portal to the Shadow Realm. Weeks spent gaining Terr's trust, weeks in commanding his hellhounds and soon enough, his army of the undead. He was so close now. Close to reaching the Godlands and saving his Sophie.

He just had one last thing to do before all hell broke loose.

Kaine breathed in the stale Soxis air, just outside the portal he'd created. The dirt was blackened and the once thick, lively trees were sullen and grey. The sunlight, however, was bright enough to make him hiss. He stalked toward Asteria Hold, a pack of hellhounds behind his back. They listened to his every command and because he'd starved them for a few days, they were foaming at the mouth for fresh flesh.

The streets of Soxis's town were emptier and dirtier than he'd last seen it. Once teeming with Fae from Wrenntia, Fyllera and Soxis, it was now a shell. Debris flitted through the town on a soft wind. It was too empty.

Kaine stopped in his tracks, focusing on his hearing to find any signs of life. The barks and yips of the twenty hellhounds behind him became too overbearing. "Quiet!" Kaine demanded. The hounds whimpered but quietened immediately.

What was going on? Where was everyone?

Kaine let out a sharp whistle. All the hounds stood at attention, their ears perked up, waiting for a command. "Search the town. Kill anyone you find. Go." The hounds bounded in hunger and anger, casting a wide net to capture any loose ends.

Kaine had come here to collect. Collect what he needed to open another portal, one that led to the Godlands. With Terr's dark power on his side, he could open something devastating. And all he needed was more blood. Children's blood.

No screams or shouts sounded in the air, just the growls of his hellhounds. Anger built up in Kaine's chest like a hot fire and these days, he never held it back. Kaine splintered the broken-down wooden stalls that sat idly. He ground his teeth. No one was here. The people of Faery, the rebels and sympathisers had moved camp, but to where?

Kaine stormed through the streets of Soxis, his hounds returning to his side as they too came up empty. He looked for traces of movement and disturbances in the dirt, any sign that would clue him in on where they had disappeared to.

But nothing. The dirt was undisturbed. Only the paw prints of his hounds showed. No residual scents of magic hung in the air. It was like they'd just vanished.

Kaine ground his teeth. Terr would be angry, that much was certain. And what it meant was that his timelines would be pushed back and now more than ever he wanted to kill the damning angel that shared his face. Kaine imagined all the depraved things he was doing to Sophie. His Sophie.

With a growl so deadly, Kaine let out a burst of his mana, pushing his hounds out of his personal space. He was going to kill that blasted angel, and he would kill him dead.

The heat of the Shadow Realm caressed Kaine's skin, a welcome warmth. He stormed down the path he'd walked hundreds of times now. The path leading to the deadly mountain Terr had called home for centuries. Desperation's Maw.

The blackened mountain loomed over everything in the Shadow Realm. Its mouth lay open, glowing with molten lava. Inside was a latticework of caves and cages that housed Terr's terrors. It was a place of torture, experimentation and nightmares Terr planned on releasing into realms beyond his own: to conquer with fear.

Kaine walked through the main hall. Each wall was lined with cages, some bolted to the ground while others hung high in the air. Creatures, winged and webbed, skittered and screeched as he walked by. The first time he ever walked through the halls of Desperation's Maw, chills ran rampant down his spine. He'd never been equally disgusted and intrigued at the same time. Now, he walked through the halls without so much as blinking.

He halted before the room Terr liked to call his experimentation room, knocking twice before entering.

The smell of fresh blood assaulted his nostrils.

Terr, with his bouldering muscles and unorthodox blue skin stood in front of a being strapped to a chair. Kaine couldn't see past Terr, but he knew whatever creature the Shadow King had captured was the one bleeding.

The room was dark except for the bright downlight Terr had centred upon his experiment. Terr turned to face Kaine with a sickly smile filled with razor-sharp teeth. "I have sssomething for youuu," he breathed. Terr wiped down a blade covered in blood across the front of his apron; an excited grin swept across his demon face.

Kaine stepped around Terr, a small smile working up on his own face. He saw the blood, dark yet glittering. Anticipation raced across his skin. They'd been talking about this for a while, ever since Kaine was taken under Terr's wing.

Underneath the harsh spotlight sat an angel, her blonde hair mussed with blood as it stuck to her skull. Her head drooped as she murmured, in a state of delirium. A thrill of excitement shot through Kaine. This was his chance. A sure-fire way to make sure the angel that stole his Sophie would stay dead.

"Hereee," Terr hissed, handing Kaine the blade he'd used to mutilate the angel before him. Terr moved to the stump of flesh that oozed from the angel's back. Blood spurted as Terr pointed out the place where a dark red feathered wing used to be. "The ssshadow blade is the only thing that worksss."

Kaine examined the blade Terr had handed to him. Its handle was carved of the blackest stone, moulded perfectly for anyone's grip. The blade itself was onyx, and as he pulled it closer to his face for inspection, a magic hummed across its surface. Shadows laced the entire blade.

Kaine moved toward the angel, her breathing was shallow but even in her closeness to death, she tried to get away from him, no doubt sensing his intention.

With precision and patience, Kaine slowly dragged the tip of the shadow blade into the bleeding stump of a wing. It sliced perfectly, allowing another gush of ruby red, glittery blood to fall to the ground. The angel whimpered.

Kaine looked to the table beside him. Strewn across the top were different blades and weapons used for torture. He picked a blade that was plain-looking and made another incision across the bleeding stump. Her lightly tanned skin healed where he made the cut. And that was proof enough. The shadow blade would work.

"What isss an angel without its wingsss?" Terr hissed in his low voice. He wrenched the angel's head back with a death grip on her hair. Small, shallow gasps left her throat as her honey-brown eyes watched him. Still, there was contempt in her eyes. Defiance.

The rage monster inside of Kaine surged. How dare she sit there, covered in her own blood and mess, on the brink of death and deign to laugh in the face of hell itself? The Tienthan were disgusting pigs. They'd taken everything good in his life away, yet arrogance even oozed out of her in this instance. She had no right. They had no right. Not when each waking moment of Kaine's life was spent empty and alone. The only light in his life *stolen* from him.

Worthless. Spineless . . . wingless. As Kaine formed the words in his head, the angel spat a mouthful of blood into Terr's face.

"Fuck you," she hissed.

Terr stood tall, unfazed that he had vile angel blood running down his face. He tsked. "Worthlessss is the anssswer." He smirked, his eyes narrowing onto the angel's last standing wing. Without even blinking, he snapped the angel's wing. It sagged unhappily on her back as bone protruded and blood oozed. She wailed in pain. "Clean thisss up and use it as a warninggg." Terr snapped his blue fingers and disappeared from the room.

Kaine moved to the table that donned all the weapons and began cleaning the blades he'd used. Oiling them as he went so that they remained sharp.

"Why . . . why are you doing this? You're Fae, aren't you?" the angel rasped.

Kaine scoffed. "Do not assume to know me." He continued cleaning the blades.

"He's going to kill everyone in Faery. Anyone that doesn't obey"—she breathed heavily—"aren't Fae meant to create life, not destroy it?"

Kaine placed the blade down with deadly silence. He looked over his shoulder at the angel. She'd grown pale from the blood loss but still, there was defiance in her.

As their eyes met, recognition washed over her eyes.

"You . . . you look like someone I know," she breathed.

Kaine knew who she was referring to and there was no one he hated more.

Kaine shot to the blonde angel in the room. "We may share the same face, but we are not the same person." He wrenched her head back, looking deep into her honey brown eyes, with a snarl on his face. He inched closer and closer to her quivering lips. "I am the Breaker of Realms, and you just wasted your last breath."

Kaine seized the air from her lungs with his mana and reached above her head. He grabbed the ill-shaped wing and hacked it off her body with a swift slice of the shadow blade. The force of his attack knocked her entire chair backward and she landed on the floor in a slump.

53

SOPHIE

An incessant *tap, tap, tap* stirred Sophie awake.

Her world was wobbly and waving all about. The sound of water, lapping up and around her crashed into her ears. The smell of sea spray hung in the air and mother of Faery was it cold.

Sophie sat up slowly, her head pulsed with a ferocious headache and the back of her throat was oddly sore. She blinked to clear her vision. Then blinked again.

You've got to be kidding me. . .

She was on some piss-poor wooden dinghy in the middle of some forgotten ocean. A fine mist of rain began to coat her skin, heavy with the threat of a more tumultuous downpour. The sky was dull, cloudy and grey and all around her was nothing but the open sea. She was all alone.

Shit.

Someone had kidnapped her and dumped her here. Sophie didn't even know where *here* was. There were no notable landmarks there was just sea, stretching for miles and miles.

As Sophie stood to survey the small boat, a small piece of parchment slipped from underneath her crop top. Sophie picked it up, her fingers numb from the cold and wet from the rain.

She unfurled the small note.

Filthy half-breed. Traitor. There is no place for you amongst the gods.

Sophie scrunched the note and incinerated it with her fire mana. Rage coursed through her veins. The choice of words and ill wishes only pointed to one person.

Vestes.

When Sophie figured out how to get off this stupid boat and back to the Godlands, she was going to flay Vestes alive, and she would make sure every soul and being in the damn Godlands was there to watch and laugh at how pathetic he was.

Sophie let herself simmer in rage for a moment before taking three deep breaths, stilling her mind and her heart. Shredding Vestes into tiny little pieces would have to wait. She would figure this out. She had no choice.

In the distance, the sound of a horn blared through the air. The sound was loud, jarring and its source was unknown. The clouds that hung close to the dark, choppy water cleared to reveal a gargantuan, black mountain in the distance. Its peak glowed with red-hot lava and all around it were, from what Sophie could see, sand dunes. Sand dunes that then rolled and dipped to the outer edges of a forest. The forest was met with the sands of a beach. A golden beacon of light glowed on the outer rim of the island, calling to her.

Sophie gulped.

She had an inkling. She felt like she knew what sort of place she'd been dumped into. A chill ran down her spine and for once, Sophie feared for her life.

She had been unceremoniously dropped into the freaking Hrabrost Trials. It had to be.

The trials meant for angels of Zeus's Aerial Legion. The courage trials meant to test their mettle, and quite frankly, Sophie was nowhere near qualified to even be here.

Ash hadn't explained much about the trials. Sophie knew there would be a swim involved, but the rest was completely up to whoever was running the trial that year. The monsters released and the schedule of tests was randomised, lasting an entire week. No weapons. No wings. Just magic and willpower.

Sophie shook out the fear that crept up her arms and focused on the golden beacon of light in the distance.

"Game on, moles."

She hoped to the gods that Vestes was watching her. Because she'd be burning a trail of fury throughout this entire trial. And by the end of it, she would be the dauntless reckoning he wished he never knew.

Sophie dived into the dark water of the angry sea before her. The water bit into her skin so cold and so fast, she almost lost her breath. She pushed her arms and legs to a steady pace. The rain above her pelted her skin as she swam through the choppy waters. Occasionally she would look up to make sure that she didn't lose her path toward the golden beacon.

She swam hundreds of metres, using bits of her water mana to propel her, before resting in place. The island didn't look any closer but when she'd turned around, the dinghy she'd jumped off was but a speck in the distance. What sort of hell was this?

"You can't be serious," she breathed heavily.

Her legs were aching, and she wasn't any closer to getting out of the blasted water. The cold was biting into her and if she stayed any longer, she'd be going down with hypothermia. As Sophie treaded water to regain energy, a slithery tentacle brushed past her leg.

Nope. Nope. Nope.

Sophie broke into a frantic swim.

She didn't dare look underneath the water, focusing solely on the beacon of light ahead of her. She pushed as hard as she could, but it felt like she was going nowhere.

The dark water grew thicker and harder to push through. Sophie dared not use too much of her mana, saving it for the rest of the trial. But suddenly, she was moving backward. No, she was being sucked into a fucking whirlpool.

Sophie whipped about in the water, sputtering as she tried keep her head afloat. Water assaulted her eyes and ears. The force of the whirlpool pulled her under and what she saw underneath nearly dispelled all the air from her lungs.

Yellow, slitted eyes, bigger than her entire body, blinked at her.

Sophie pushed up, trying to break the surface of the water, but the giant squid's blackened tentacle caught her before her fingers could scrape the surface. Sophie let out an unintentional yelp that cost her the minimal air in her lungs.

Sophie fumbled, trying to feel for the throwing knives she hoped to the gods were still strapped to her thighs.

The squid tightened around her leg in a death grip, spinning her as it dragged her down into the depths of the sea. Sophie let out a scream, but continued to fumble her way to the throwing knifes. The force of the creature's pull continued to knock her about.

By the will of the Fates, her throwing knives were still there. Disorientated as she was, Sophie stabbed at the tentacle frantically. As her blades pierced the squid's thick skin, it shrieked. The sound was deafening, but it gave Sophie an opportunity to break free.

She kicked and kicked, breaking through the surface with a desperate gulp of air. She didn't stop. She didn't have the time.

Sophie swam toward the beacon of light that thankfully seemed closer. But the murderous roar of the giant squid rumbled through the water, sending a string of fear so furious through her body. Sophie didn't want to look back. She could see the water before her turn darker and darker. The barely there light provided by the grey sky turned into darkness and the waves around her turned more violent.

The water surged into a massive wave as the giant squid shrieked, aiming straight for Sophie.

She swam as fast as she could, riding the wave until giant squid tentacles came crashing down on her, pulling her down into the depths of the dark sea again. She was surrounded by tentacles. Everywhere she turned, its crater-like suckers swarmed around her.

There was no way out.

Fuck this shit.

Sophie dived deep into her frantic mana and pulled. She let her favourite fire wash through her veins and out through her fingertips. She blasted the squid, and its tentacles flinched from the barricade of fire she'd created under the water.

It roared again in pain.

But Sophie roared harder.

She swam up and up, encasing her entire body with her air mana. When she broke the surface, she pulled herself higher and higher into the air. Quickly, she pulled at her mana again, shooting a hot red beam of fire straight into the squid's eye.

It flailed, diving deep into the water to get away from Sophie. As soon as it disappeared into the water, Sophie broke free of her air bubble and fell freely. She had to reserve as much mana as she could and what she'd just done had cost her a fair amount. The smell of fried fish grew stronger as she neared the surface of the water.

This time when she dived in, no tentacles or giant yellow eyes neared her. Not that she could see much anyway. She didn't let complacency get the better of her. Sophie righted herself again, focusing on the golden beacon of light ahead, now only a few hundred metres away from her.

The adrenalin pumping through her veins warmed her enough, but her extremities were growing painfully useless. She pumped a small amount of mana to her fingertips as she pushed for the shore.

It was so fucking cold, and her body was numb, but Sophie pushed and pushed until the island neared. She spotted the edges of thick jungle and the dark black sands before it.

Closer and closer she swam.

Sophie was on the verge of tears as she finally felt the sandbank underneath her boots. The grit of the sand was a welcome sound and feeling. She fought against the waves with a whimper. The smell of frying fish hung in the air as she crashed onto the shore with a sob.

Land. Oh beautiful land, I will never take you for granted again. Sophie kissed the black sand beneath her, thanking the Fates that she was alive.

"Ahem," a male voice sounded from above her.

Sophie looked up with her sand-covered lips to find Morpheus, the dark-skinned, white-winged god of sleep towering over her.

"What the fuck are you doing in Tartarus?" he snarled.

54

SOPHIE

"Tartarus?" Sophie spat out the word. The angels had failed to tell her that the Hrabrost Trials were held on freaking Tartarus. *Bastards.*

Tartarus. The place where the ancient gods locked up the most depraved creatures and their deadliest enemies. It was a place worse than hell. It was hell for the beings that belonged in hell itself.

Sophie gulped.

Morpheus's eyes danced with amusement, taking in Sophie's reaction.

"It was Vestes," Sophie groaned, rolling onto her back as the water lapped up onto her legs.

"Vestes?" Morpheus asked.

"That shit-eating wrinkled worm thought to punish me for being a half-breed. Oh and apparently I'm a traitor too." Sophie scoffed. Vestes was a fucking idiot because not only would she get through this trial, but he'd also unwittingly made it to the top of her damned hit list. Not that she'd ever had one before, but she *definitely* had one now.

Morpheus whistled low.

"Tell me about it." Sophie sat up from the ground and surveyed the dark seas before her. She just escaped a giant squid. A giant squid!

"Is that your doing?" Morpheus pointed to a giant floating form, peeking above the surface of the water.

Sophie narrowed her eyes, focusing her sight. The bumps and ridges of the giant squid's purple-y black skin bobbed close to the water's surface, a few hundred metres from the shore. It was awfully still. "Huh . . . I guess it is." Sophie looked at her hands, she hadn't realised her fire was so . . . capable.

"I'm impressed." Morpheus pouted his bottom lip and nodded.

Sophie looked up at him from where she sat and beamed. "Fried calamari, anyone?"

Morpheus guffawed. "More like fried Charybdis," he added before, lending Sophie a hand.

Charybdis. So that's what the creature is called.

Sophie took Morpheus' hand without hesitation. He pulled her up with ease and trudged ahead of her. The sound of the gritty sand squelched underneath his boots. "Chronos made it to the shore as well," Morpheus explained as they walked. "We'll rest along the edges of Baba's Forest tonight. I take it you weren't given a proper briefing for the trials?" He paused his steps, turning slightly so that Sophie could catch up.

Being five foot two on a good day did not give her any advantages. For every one of Morpheus's steps, Sophie had to take two. Three, if there was a slight uphill.

"Nope," Sophie sighed.

"The rules are simple. You come in with nothing but the clothes on your back. No wings"—Morpheus motioned to the red clips that had been attached to the tips of his wings—"just magic. Four trials. One week. Then it's back to reality."

"Well, shit." Sophie couldn't imagine it. Having the freedom of flight taken away. Even if it was just for a week. "Can we at least make weapons?"

"To your heart's content."

Good. Sophie couldn't just rely on her two throwing knives and her mana. She needed to be more resourceful, especially if she needed to manage her mana for what was to come.

"And four trials?"

"Well, you already *fried* the first one. There should be three more. That's if they don't surprise us." Morpheus winked as they neared the edge of the forest.

The god of sleep swiped his broad hand in a circle before him. The air rippled to reveal another angel sitting by a small fire. The flames' orange glow was a stark contrast to the darkness that surrounded them, Sophie had to squint her eyes a little.

The angel that sat quietly by the fire narrowed her pitch-black eyes upon Sophie. Her white hair was wet and clung to her head. Champagne-coloured wings fastened with the same flight-inhibiting red clips as Morpheus, towered over her. Her paper-white skin was covered in black inky veins. She was devastating yet eery.

Sophie moved closer to the flames of the small campfire, its heat warming her icy skin. "You must be Chronos." Sophie held a hand out to the angel. "My name is Sophie, demigoddess of—"

"I know who you are." Chronos's voice was like the weather, icy. Disdain accented each of her words.

Geez, what's up her ass?

Sophie let her hand drop between them. "Nice to meet you too," she mumbled beneath her breath. It was most certainly *not* nice to meet her. Clearly, the goddess of time had no time for Sophie.

Chronos returned to watch the flames, her brows knitted into frustration.

A palpable tension rose in the air.

"Take whatever spot you like, Sophie. There's also some fresh drinking water if you like," Morpheus cut the tension in half as he pointed to a small jerry can.

"Thanks." Sophie gave him a soft smile.

He shot a quick glance at Chronos who seemed keen to focus on the flames and turned back to Sophie with an apologetic smile.

Sophie guessed being the goddess of time, the very thing that people wished they could stop, fast-forward or outwardly resented, was a tough gig.

Lifting the jerry can, Sophie poured a handful of water into her cupped hand. There wasn't much water, so rationing seemed like the right thing to do. Sophie wet her mouth before swallowing.

Morpheus made a little pillow out of a log and lazed on the ground. Sophie joined him, sitting cross-legged and warming her fingers by the fire. "How many trials have you done?"

Morpheus counted his fingers. "This would be my fortieth. I'm a bit of a late comer compared to Chronos over here. What number are you up to, Chro?"

Sophie looked to the alabaster angel with black abysses for eyes.

An uncomfortable silence stretched between them all when Chronos didn't even bother acknowledging Morpheus's question.

I thought they were all friends. This is so fucking awkward.

A moment passed before Chronos stood up abruptly and huffed. She looked down her rim-rod nose at Sophie. "Slow us down and I'll make sure time for you is painful." She sneered before taking off, farther into the forest.

Sophie blinked, watching the goddess disappear into the brush.

"Yikes, who spat in her coffee?" Sophie asked, widening her eyes. Chronos seemed as friendly as a caged lion.

Morpheus let out a laugh and then sighed. "I'm not so sure you want to know."

55

SOPHIE

"Do not look at them in the eyes. Look straight ahead, less you want your soul eternally damned in Tartarus," Morpheus warned.

This was Baba Yaga's forest, and in her forest she let loose the wrath of her wailing witches. Vengeful women once scorned and burned at the stake, who reincarnated themselves through dark magic to haunt and feast on souls. If you looked at them in the eyes, they would paralyse you and steal your soul through the sharp tips of their spindly fingers.

No thank you. Sophie was at her wit's end with creepy shit.

The forest air was thick with heat. The canopy so dense that barely any light seeped through. Sophie looked to Morpheus who seemed equally as fed up as herself. Chronos, who stood beside Morpheus, looked like she still had a stick firmly lodged up her ass.

"Scared, kid?" Morpheus asked Sophie.

"A little." Sophie shrugged a shoulder. More like a lot.

Together, they advanced through the forest. Sophie wielded her blades in both her hands ready to attack if a wailing witch decided to tempt fate. They moved in pairs through the forest. While one moved, the other watched their backs.

The sound of a snapping twig tried to pull Sophie's attention, but she shook it off, focusing on the eerie forest ahead of her.

Then the wailing started.

The sound of several women crying and howling in pain echoed and layered in the air through the trees, sending chills down Sophie's back. The branches above them shook with ferocity as they moved through the forest. The wailing witches jumped from tree to tree, following them. Sophie hadn't laid eyes on one yet, but she sure as hell didn't want to.

Morpheus, currently leading the group, quickened his pace. Sophie followed but she was still fatigued from the swim they had yesterday.

Sofreya, a female voice whispered.

"Keep moving, kid," Morpheus ordered from ahead. Did Morpheus hear that too? It sounded like the voice was just in Sophie's head, but perhaps they could all hear it.

Morpheus had warned her about this. To ensnare their prey, the wailing witches would mimic certain sounds – calls for help, the cry of a baby. It would voice your deepest desires and your deepest fears, in hopes that its prey would stop, look and listen.

The movement in the trees above them grew more panicked, as the group quickened their pace. They were being chased.

Sophie pushed her legs harder, working doubly as hard to keep up with the two angels.

"Morpheus, help!" Nyx's voice cried out. It sounded exactly like them.

Morpheus knew better. He charged forward without a glance in any direction but ahead, toward the slight glow of the beacon that marked their next checkpoint. Sophie was a few paces behind him while Chronos ran behind Sophie.

As they ran through the forest, branches snapped back and forth. Sophie's face was numb with tiny little cuts over her cheeks.

"Chronos, stop!" a deep male voice shouted.

Sophie's heart lurched in her chest, because she knew that voice like the back of her hand.

The sounds of Chronos's steady run grinded to a halt. Defying all logic and rules of Baba's Forest, Chronos had stopped.

Shit.

Sophie turned to find Chronos looking up into the canopy. Her head craned all the way back. Her arms limp beside her. The small knife she'd been carrying lay carelessly on the ground.

"Sophie, cover your fucking eyes!" Morpheus was running back toward her.

In Sophie's periphery, a woman-like creature crawled down from the tree closest to Chronos.

A wailing witch.

Sophie didn't have to even look at the creature in the eyes for her soul to leave her body. It was the stuff of nightmares.

The witch's skin was a ghastly greyish blue. Her long black hair was wet and glued to her skin. It looked like she'd just crawled out from a river. Like in the damned *Exorcist*, the wailing witch scurried to Chronos with preternatural speed. The witch reached out a spindly black talon and began to pull at Chronos's soul. Sophie could see a faint glow leaving Chronos's chest.

"I've always wanted you, Chronos." The wailing witch moved its lips, but it was Ash's voice that came tumbling through.

What the fuck is happening?

Chronos, with her abyss eyes, was completely entranced. Her eyes filled with irrefutable desire. Her face almost touching the wailing witch's as her soul was wrenched from her.

Sophie wasn't even thinking.

Half struck with fear and the other half with adrenalin, she spear tackled Chronos at the waist, sending them both crashing down into dirt.

Chronos woke from her trance with a desperate gasp of air.

Sophie tried to get up but was quickly knocked onto her back by an invisible force. She could feel Morpheus's warm hand trying to pull her up, but it was too late.

Yellow and red eyes dived deep into Sophie's soul. The wailing witch's blackened teeth bared a spine-chilling smile.

Sophie's body stilled, and her vision grew blurry.

"Why would I be with someone like *you*," Ash's voiced pierced her ears. Each word dripped with disgust. They stung for a bit, but Sophie knew that the words were not true. They were impossible. They were the words of a wailing witch.

Sophie pushed her mana through her veins, willing the earth and air around her. She rushed past the powerful restraints of the wailing witch's power like a mad bull in a shop. She let out a war cry as dirt catapulted into the creature, knocking it back as Sophie's air mana brought her to her feet.

The other wailing witches came scurrying down from the trees as their sister cried in pain. Six of them. Sophie dared not look one in the eye, but it was hard. Their stares were pinned on Sophie.

One by one, they started to drop. They looked . . . sleepy.

Strong hands took Sophie by the scruff of her neck and propelled her forward.

"MOVE!" Morpheus commanded. He'd put them to sleep. All six of the wailing witches.

Sophie obeyed, running as fast as she could through the dark forest. She could see a blur of alabaster to her left. Chronos.

The beacon ahead of them shined brighter.

They were almost at the edge of Baba's Forest.

Metres away.

The sound of wailing started again.

Almost there.

Inches now.

Sophie came crashing through the edge of the forest into a wide clearing. The thick heat of Tartarus air stifled her breath as the bright light of the beacon almost blinded her.

"Shit!" Sophie shielded her eyes, it felt like her corneas were burning as she stumbled into the grass clearing.

"Don't look at the fucking beacon, kid!" Morpheus spun her around.

Sophie blinked to clear her vision. Morpheus had tiny scratches on his face. He was a touch breathless but overall, he seemed fine.

Chronos was on all fours, trying to regain her breath.

"You alright?" Morpheus asked, his tone much softer now.

"Yeah." Sophie nodded, her breath heavy. She was as alright as she could be. Which was good, considering they'd just run what felt like a ten kilometre sprint, being chased by undead witches.

"Good. That's trial two over with. Just two more to go." Morpheus winked.

"Thanks for the save back there." Sophie smiled.

"Thanks for stopping"—he pointed discreetly to Chronos—"I'm sure she'd appreciate it."

"I'm not so sure about that," Sophie mumbled.

Morpheus laughed deeply and sighed. "I'll go start the fire. Good luck." He patted her on the shoulder before walking away.

Sophie let out a deep breath.

Sophie knew what she had heard. The voice of Ash not only calling to herself when she was stuck under the witch's spell, but she'd also heard his voice calling to Chronos.

The witch had called to Sophie's biggest fear, not that it worked, and it called to Chronos's biggest . . . desire.

This explains the animosity.

But it wasn't an excuse for it.

Sophie walked over to Chronos, who now sat quietly, facing the forest they'd just left.

Sophie didn't utter a word as she sat down next to Chronos. "Are you alright?"

"I'm fine," Chronos bit out. Her tone was a touch softer than when they first met.

Sophie picked at the grass beside her. "I just wanted to clear the air." She cleared her throat and faced the goddess. "I know what I heard in the forest." Chronos tried to butt in, but Sophie held out a hand to stop her. "My relationship with Acheron may bother you, but that's no excuse to treat me like shit. I've done nothing wrong to you nor do I wish anything untoward upon you. How about we start over?"

They'd be spending the entire week together and because Chronos was in the Tienthan, they'd be crossing paths for however long they both lived. It would be easier if they could start again. Preferably with a little less animosity.

Chronos spat on the ground. "I cannot begin to fathom what he sees in you."

Sophie blinked in surprise. *This is totally not going the way I saw it.*

Sophie moved to crouch before Chronos. "Where I'm from, Chronos, there's this saying. 'Talk shit, get hit.' If you insult me and my own, if you so even *think* about Ash, I will fucking *bury* you." Sophie smiled the sweetest smile she could muster before standing up and sauntering off.

She honestly didn't even know where that came from. Perhaps it was the territorial-Fae side of her coming out, or perhaps she was finally embracing her demigoddess-hood, but fuck did it feel good to draw a boundary and put Chronos in her place. The freaking goddess of time.

She felt like a straight up badass.

56

ACHERON

Ash panted heavily as he crash-landed into the grassy clearing. They were much closer to Mount Gehenna now. Only two trials left to go.

He'd swum the stretch of the Forgotten Sea with ease, dodging the Charybdis as best as he could. A few of the giant squid's suckers had crushed his feathers, but he was mostly fine. Baba's Forest was something else though. He knew it was all because of that damned letter. The letter that currently burned a hole in his pocket. It was most likely destroyed from all the water, but Ash could still feel its heaviness resting against his thigh.

The wailing witches had probably smelled his hurt from a distance, and they tried everything. The screams of Sofreya in pain, the scream of her pleasures, her desire for him as well as her disgust for him. Every sound of her stung his skin, but he managed to push through the run with minor scratches.

Eros's head slowly poked into Ash's view of the grey evening sky. At least he thought it was evening. Time didn't really exist on Tartarus. The place just . . . existed.

"What?" Ash growled, heaving himself up from the ground to look at Eros.

As he reached the shores of the Forgotten Sea, Ash found Eros sunbathing. He looked as unbothered as a damned sea turtle, on the shores of Tartarus. Not to mention the fact that there was barely any sun.

"I just wanted to check in on how you were feeling. I know you haven't necessarily told me the exact contents of the letter or the wording she used. And it must hurt having your heart chewed up and spat out but—"

"Eros. Please shut up." Ash let out an exasperated breath. Not that he blamed his older brother for it. He was just the messenger, but it was becoming increasingly difficult not to shoot the messenger when the messenger was devoid of the ability to shut up.

"Ash, maybe if you just tell him, he'll hopefully start talking about something else," Nyx chimed in. Their brow was slick with sweat and a few whisps of their white hair had come free of their battle braid.

Eros hadn't stopped asking about Sophie and her letter. Not even when the freakish wailing witches chased them through Baba's Forest.

Eros sat down on the grass next to Ash looking like someone had kicked his dog. His lips pouting and his eyes, watery.

By the Fates. Ash closed his eyes. He was starting to feel bad for his love-obsessed brother.

Ash could feel the presence of Nyx to his left. Together, they faced Baba's Forest, their backs turned against the beacon of light they had been following.

Two beacons were currently lit up, shooting a thick ray of light into the sky above. One just behind them, and there would be another on the other side of Mount Gehenna, drawing in the other half of the Tienthan.

Ash sighed. "Fine."

Eros's eyes were brimming with tears and Ash knew he was holding back a squeal. Eros made a motion to zip his lips together before throwing away the imaginary key.

And so, Ash told Eros and Nyx of the letter that had decimated his heart. They both listened carefully, with no judgement or ill-intent. They simply listened.

"That must be very difficult, Ash." Nyx rested a soft hand on his forearm.

Ash gave them a wry smile. It was all he could muster.

"Hmmm . . ." Eros stroked his chin and narrowed his eyes. "Interesting."

"Ash is heartbroken, Eros. What could possibly be so interesting about that?" Nyx asked, placing a worried glance over Ash.

"Well, she mentioned the word 'friend', and its variations a total of five times. Altogether . . ." Eros paused to conjure a small whiteboard.

"Did you seriously bring a whiteboard with you?" Ash gaped.

"Yes. I thought it would come in handy if we needed to draw up a game plan or something, but *back* to what I was saying. Sophie wrote the word 'friend' including its variations five times." Eros wrote the number down. "And altogether, she wrote nine sentences." He scrawled the number nine circling it over and over until it was bold. He added a colon between the two numbers. "That's a five to nine ratio, little brother!" Eros exclaimed with a hopeful smile.

"Yes . . . thank you for pointing out how much she adores our *friendship* to the point where she'll mention it in more than half the sentences she's written." Ash crossed his arms and grumbled.

"No, no, no. *IF* she really thought you both were better off just friends, if that was how she truly feels then at a *maximum* she would have mentioned friendship twice."

"Eros, there is no science or sense behind what you're saying."

"But *there is,* Ash. I've read thousands of love letters in my lifetime. Heralded them even. I can spot a fake letter, one written by means of protecting one's own heart, when I see it. She's trying to bombard you with the foul word of friendship to hide. Parts of her letter are true. She is deeply hurt, and she is scared, but she loves you. I've seen it with my very own eyes." Eros now had a far-off look in his eyes. The look he often had when he was thinking about love.

Fates, please get me out of this nightmare.

"He does have a point . . ." Nyx said thoughtfully.

"By the Fates, not you too." Ash facepalmed himself. "How about we focus on the trials? I think I'd much prefer that." Ash stood, taking a few paces to stretch out his legs.

Eros's words ate away at him. Maybe she had written the letter to protect her own heart. The parts of Ash that agonised over Sophie groaned awake, a little more hopeful than they were before.

He needed to focus on the Hrabrost Trials first and as soon as it was all done, he'd go running to her. Sweeping her into his arms. And with every waking minute he spent alive, he'd prove to her that he was capable of protecting her heart.

"Help!" Deymos's deep voice sliced through the edge of the forest.

Ash whipped his head toward his brother's voice.

Between Deymos and Pallas was Erebus, the primordial god of darkness. His wavy red hair and white wings sagged. His normally tanned skin had a grey pallor to it.

Shit.

Ash bolted across the clearing to assist. Both Eros and Nyx followed suit.

Quickly, Ash replaced Deymos, carefully pulling Erebus to the ground. Deymos collapsed to the side, regaining his breath as Pallas did the same. Eros took his place in assisting Erebus to the ground too.

"What happened?" Ash asked as he quickly raked Erebus for any catastrophic haemorrhages. Erebus was barely lucid.

"He collapsed halfway," Deymos breathed heavily.

"He got pierced through the side by the Charybdis in trial one. He said he healed it, but maybe there's still some ink trapped in him," Pallas explained as he lay on the grass.

Ash pushed Erebus onto his side as Eros took the god's pulse and checked his breathing.

"His pulse is weak," Eros stated.

Ash pressed his fingers into the shiny scar on Erebus's side. Newly healed. He shot out his mana to assess the wound. He wasn't able to feel anything, but he pushed harder, almost barrelling into Erebus's magic. A tangy darkness bit back. It felt slippery and oily against his own mana.

"He's got ink stuck in him," Ash confirmed.

"Shit," Pallas swore underneath his breath.

"When did he collapse?" Eros asked.

"About an hour ago. We were chased the entire time. We couldn't even stop." Deymos started to get worked up.

"It's alright. Pallas, Deymos, head up the hill with Nyx. Recon a camp for tonight and stay hydrated. Eros, you're with me."

All the angels moved at their best pace, leaving room for Eros and Ash to work on Erebus.

"Okay, Ere, stay with us." Ash said it more to himself than poor Erebus.

Eros moved to kneel beside Erebus's head, cradling the red-headed angel's head and neck so that his airway remained clear. "Ready."

Without a word, Ash pulled out a knife he had carved from a shell on their first night in Tartarus. He pulled at his lightning and zapped it. The knife came out sizzling with heat, making it easier to slice through skin.

"Sorry, Ere," Ash took in a deep breath as he pinned down Erebus's arm and wing with a knee and sliced into his side, where the shiny scar was. He pushed more of his power through the blade to hold Erebus's skin open for long enough to fish out the obstruction.

Erebus's other arm came flying right for Ash's face, but Eros was quick enough to pull it back down.

Ash continued to slice through his skin. It wasn't an easy job.

Erebus murmured and thrashed in pain, but it was clear the poison ink had seeped into his blood. Blood poured out from his wound, much darker than usual.

Ash counted to ten, letting the infected blood run for a moment.

Erebus's movements calmed and his skin turned a touch warmer.

Good. Ash then pulled at his mana, casting a hand over the wound and began to draw out the ink. Like little leeches, the black ink rushed out of the wound. Ash continued until he could no longer feel the oiliness of the Charybdis' ink and slowly, he began to patch up the god's skin.

"How are his vitals?" Ash asked.

"Stable and within standard range," Eros said. He let Erebus rest his head on his lap as he pushed calming magic into Erebus's mind. The faint white glow on his fingers shone in the night.

Erebus stirred awake. "What . . ."

"Hey, Ere, welcome back. Heard you had a bit of a run-in with the Charybdis," Ash teased.

Erebus groaned, raking his hands through his red hair and over his tanned face. "What happened?" He propped onto his elbows, surveying the blood that covered himself and Ash.

"You're alive is what." Ash didn't know what he would have done if Erebus died. He had been so close to it too. Ash had felt the unmistakable ragged edges of death on the tips of his fingers.

57

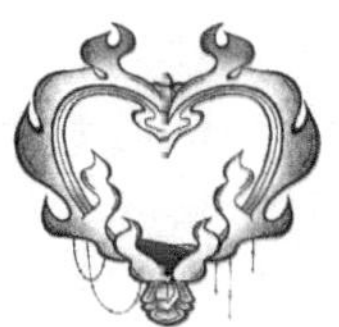

SOPHIE

Sophie rolled onto her side using the base of a tree to support her back. The air was still thick with heat, making it difficult to fall asleep. Not to mention the gaping hole in her stomach. It had been two full days without any food. They had water, thankfully, but the pain in her stomach was becoming excruciating. Distracting even. She felt weak and drained.

I'm going to kill Vestes after this bullshit.

Sophie tossed onto her other side for what felt like the tenth time tonight.

Morpheus had mentioned that other Tienthan angels were to meet up with them before the next trial started, but no one had showed. Chronos had wisely kept to herself the entire evening. No remarks or snide comments were made.

Frustrated, Sophie opened her eyes and sat up. Maybe sleeping in the clearing would be a better choice.

The rustling of leaves and the beat of several footfalls captured her attention. Morpheus and Chronos sat up straight from their slumber as well.

Sophie sat still, listening to the sounds of whatever was fast approaching them. Her Fae ears twitched with each movement.

"It's the others," Morpheus said as he launched himself into a run toward the footfalls.

Sophie pushed herself from the ground and ran after him. So did Chronos.

As they reached the edge of Baba's Forest, Nemy, Achlys and Athena came crashing through the trees. They tumbled and collapsed in a heap, huffing and puffing.

"What in the Tartarus took you so long?" Morpheus admonished. He quickly checked them over for any injuries.

Achlys, God of Eternal Night, was bent over, his hands braced on his knees. "Athena got swallowed by the Charybdis, it took what felt like a lifetime to get her out." He breathed heavily, pointing in Athena's general direction.

Nemy lay on the grass beside Achlys, her arms covering her eyes, her chest heaving. "Yeah, it's why she smells like absolute shit." She laughed.

Athena, with her beautifully brown skin, dark curly hair and pure white wings was on all fours. Her breathing was laboured but she seemed okay enough to bite back. "Hey! Achlys is the one who decided to sprain his ankle the moment we stepped into Baba's Forest." She shot an accusatory glare toward Achlys, poking her tongue out.

Sophie stood a few steps away, watching the amusing exchanges.

Morpheus stood from where he had crouched between the three of them. "We only have an hour before we need to leave for trial three. Come on, let's get some rest." He beckoned them farther up the clearing.

Athena was the first to stand, dusting off her hands casually. Her voice was small and sweet. "Oh, hey Soph— WAIT A MINUTE—"

Nemy and Achlys whipped their heads toward Sophie, their eyes wide. "WHAT ARE YOU DOING HERE, SOPHIE?" all three angels exclaimed in unison.

Sophie wiggled her fingers and grimaced. "Hey . . . everyone. Good to see you too." Sophie laughed nervously.

The Sands of Sorrow.

With its rolling, giant sand dunes, the Sands of Sorrow were impossibly hot. Where the rest of Tartarus had no sun, the Sands of Sorrow were awash with it. The sun and its heat reflected off the sand, making Sophie's feet burn even through her boots.

They had only walked a hundred metres and Sophie had already had enough.

Why is it always some sad, ominous name and never The Sands Where We Get Food and Water and Shipped Home? What the fuck?

Fresh jerry cans of water were magically deposited by the beacon of light by the time they woke up. Six waterskins were laid out, ready to be filled and used. Still, there was no food.

The leather strap holding the waterskin dug into Sophie's shoulder as she crested a smaller sand dune.

Just three whole days of this. Three. No sleeping. No stopping. Just walking. Sophie had felt like crying since waking up. Her body was drained and there was little physical strength left to utilise her mana. The steep sand dunes made her legs ache terribly. All she wanted to do was roll down one of the sand dunes, all the way back to the damned Godlands.

After three days of hell on hell, they would only have one more trial to go. The biggest yet; conquering Mount Gehenna.

The six of them – Morpheus, Chronos, Achlys, Athena, Nemysis and Sophie – walked in a single file. Each had a waterskin and the makeshift weapons they'd made along the way. Sophie spent a good portion of yesterday afternoon re-creating her rope dart out of sharp rocks and vines she'd found on the edge of the forest. It was possibly the most DIY job she'd ever seen, but it would be an extra resource she could use. Who knew what they would come across in the Sands of Sorrow?

"How are you holding up?" Nemy asked from behind Sophie.

"There's sand in places where sand shouldn't be, Nemy. That's how I'm holding up." Sophie sighed, keeping a steady pace of steps. As the shortest person, she was leading the charge. They would all work at her pace, so they could stick together. This part of the trial, as Morpheus had so kindly explained, was focused on teamwork as a small group.

The second day in the Sands of Sorrow brought on a new kind of hell.

Sophie's feet were riddled with blisters. Her thighs chafed. Her cheeks were raw from the sand that pelted her face. Her lips were cracked. With minimal food and rest, her body struggled to heal itself at the rate it normally would. She'd surpassed the pangs of hunger and the group, initially chirpy – save for Chronos – was now quiet. The sounds of their footfalls were the only thing she'd heard for the last forty hours.

Ahead, the ferocity of the heat made the air ripple, and it was in these moments that the sleep and food deprivation got to Sophie. She thought she saw the very base of a giant black mountain. She blinked again and it disappeared. She turned around to see if anyone else had seen it. But no one was there.

"Guys?" she asked weakly.

Sophie felt her lips crack as she spoke. Shaking the waterskin that sat around her shoulder, she found that there was only a tiny bit of water left.

Shit. She needed to save it for their final day across the Sands of Sorrow.

Sophie crested another sand dune. Did she somehow lose the group?

Panic started to set in.

The world around her began to shake.

She lost her footing within seconds, tumbling down a sand dune. She tried to claw herself upright but her world kept tumbling.

A sharp pain lanced across her face.

Once.

Twice.

Sophie came to with a gasp.

Nemy, with her chestnut brown hair and wings, was in front of her, baring her teeth. She was screaming something, but Sophie couldn't hear it over the ringing in her ears. She could barely muster any words, as she took in what was aiming for them. Fear shot through her heart like a hot lance.

A giant sandworm, several hundred metres in length and height, with bubbly brown-looking skin and thousands of razor-sharp teeth opened its jaw behind Nemy. Sophie could feel the weight of it rumble through the sand.

Without even thinking, Sophie pushed Nemy to the side.

"What the fuck!" Nemy went tumbling down the side of a sand dune, taking Sophie with her.

The sandworm bit down with a mighty chomp. The sound of it reverberated through the air as its foul breath assaulted Sophie's lungs.

You've got to be kidding me!

Nemy and Sophie were a tangle of limbs as they slid down the sand dune, coming to a crash at the very bottom.

Sophie and Nemy, stood quickly, covered in sand. They ran. Where to? Neither of them knew but they ran as fast as their weak bodies would take them as the giant worm careened for them.

"Where are the others?" Sophie asked breathlessly.

"I don't know. I looked back for just a second and they were gone!" Nemy grunted as she ran up a steep sand dune.

Sophie followed.

They crested a sand dune. There. In the distance. It was Morpheus and Achlys, going head on with another sandworm. Chronos and Athena were nowhere to be seen.

The foul breath of the sandworm behind them was the only warning.

Sophie and Nemy screamed as darkness consumed them. Razor-sharp teeth pierced their skin. Mouldy, rotten breath attacked their senses. Sophie cast a feeble air bubble around herself and Nemy. It wasn't much but it would be enough.

"Grab onto the sides!" Nemy shouted, pulling Sophie toward her.

They were inside a fucking worm.

Sophie latched her fingers into the sides of the worm. Its flesh was slick with mucus but rough enough to grab hold of. The beast roared as their fingernails dug in.

"We need to get out before we suffocate!" Nemy shouted.

Sophie grabbed a knife from her thigh and started stabbing the lining of the worm. The sound of Nemy's grunts beside her told Sophie that the goddess was doing the same thing. Sophie stabbed and stabbed, blood and gore ricocheting on her face. Her hands were slick with bodily matter, but she did not care. She needed to get out of this hellhole. Their choices were limited. It was either hurt the worm enough for it to open its mouth, or somehow get outside, from inside. Neither were looking like achievable options.

Sophie screamed like a damned madwoman as she threw her entire body weight into the dagger she held, while trying to keep herself latched onto the worm's inner walls.

The beast rolled and rolled, jostling them, turning their worlds upside down.

Nemy let out a scream.

"Nemy!" Sophie shouted, pulling away from her stabbing for a moment to reach out for the goddess. She managed to grab a hold of her shirt. "Hold on!"

Nemy grunted, swinging up to latch onto Sophie's hand with her own.

The worm rolled again, sending Nemy crashing straight into Sophie. The air left her lungs entirely. The air mana bubble around them burst, sending Sophie straight into the razor-sharp teeth, the full weight of Nemy bearing down on her.

Nemy wasn't moving.

"Nemy, wake up!" Sophie shouted. She tried to get up, but the worm rolled again. Nemy fell away. Sophie tried to reach for her but missed entirely. The strap of Sophie's waterskin came loose and wrapped around her neck. And as she fell, the strap snapped taught, having caught on something above her. Sophie bounced from her weight, almost cracking her neck as she hung midair.

Sophie clawed at her neck as the waterskin strap grew tighter and tighter. She let out pained grunts. Her lungs were empty. The pressure on her throat insurmountable. Her knife was still looped into her finger. She blindly swiped up, catching the strap with the sharp end of her knife. She tried to saw it off, but she could feel herself becoming more and more lightheaded.

Please. Not like this. Please.

Sophie thought of Ash, her mother, her friends. Her life. This wasn't the way she wanted to leave the land of the living. There was still so much to do.

With the last morsel of strength she had, Sophie swung her hips and swiped the knife down, cutting the waterskin strap free. That was the last of her water, but boy did the freedom around her neck feel good. Sophie came crashing down on the worm's razor-sharp teeth. Her wounds stung as mucus mixed with her blood.

The beast roared again, letting in a moment of light.

Nemy. She had to find Nemy.

"Nemy!" Sophie shouted. More like cried. When did she start crying?

"I'm here! I'm fine!" Nemy shouted.

Sophie tumbled and climbed her way toward Nemy's voice. When the outlines of Nemy's wings came into view, Sophie's heart released the tension it had been holding so closely. The angel looked worse for wear. Her hair was tangled, and her face was marred with oozing cuts that bubbled with mucus.

"Hold on to my hand and don't let go!" Sophie shouted through her tears. She grabbed a hold of Nemy's hand. "Do you trust me?"

"I trust you." The goddess clasped Sophie's hand.

"Then let go of the wall," Sophie breathed.

They let go.

And together they fell into the abyss of the worm's stomach.

Sophie pulled her arms around Nemy, encasing them in the final dredges of her mana. And screamed.

Sophie felt Nemy's arms tighten around her, but she didn't let it distract her. She screamed and screamed as every morsel of mana left her body, smashing into the darkness that surrounded them. She didn't care if she had no mana after this. She needed there to be an "after this". That's all that mattered.

Bright light washed through Sophie's eyelids as she held on to Nemy with her dear life. The Sands of Sorrow sun set her skin ablaze with hope as they crash landed onto the burning sand.

Sophie sputtered a mixture of blood, mucus and sand as she pushed herself up. Nemy was right beside her, panting.

"By the Fates, Sophie, you exploded a fucking worm," Nemy breathed heavily.

Sophie looked up.

Clumps of rotting flesh, bones, skin and teeth lay haphazardly across the desert sands.

"Thank. Fuck." Sophie collapsed onto her back.

They'd made it out. Her water was gone. Her skin stung. And she swore a rib or two had cracked when Nemy fell on top of her. But she'd made it to "after this". They'd both made it, and by the gods did that feel amazing.

It had been hours since the sandworm attack. Had it been hours? Or had it been minutes? It was hard to tell when the Sands of Sorrow sun stayed in the exact same godsforsaken place in the sky at all times. It was near three full days without sleep. Sophie had reached a point where she was just breathing. No thoughts consumed her. They had all run out of water, lost to the worm attack.

"Come on, get up," Achlys gritted. His black hair and black wings were covered in sand, an arm wrapped around Chronos's middle. The goddess was ducking in and out of consciousness, having lost blood during the worm attacks.

Morpheus had the most energy of them all, so was guiding them through the desert.

Nemy had begun mumbling to herself.

Athena was limping badly.

Sophie had stopped talking altogether.

It was hard to know if they were walking in circles. Sand stretched out for miles. Was Sophie even alive? Or had she slipped into the clutches of death unknowingly? Was this her Hell?

Sophie spotted it then. A change in the shape of the sand dunes. It looked like a giant wave of red rock and on top of it, grass . . . then the beginning of a forest. Behind that, a colossal dark mountain.

"Morpheus," Sophie croaked.

He had his head down and didn't hear her.

"Morpheus," Sophie said, stronger this time.

His reaction was slow. He turned to look at Sophie with agitation. The heat, sleep and food deprivation had gotten to him. Sophie could tell he was putting on a brave face. The others, Sophie included, were worse off.

"Look." Sophie pointed feebly at the wave rock.

He looked ahead, noticing it too.

His eyes widened. "We made it." He started laughing. It was croaky at first. Soft even, but then it grew thunderous and contagious. He sounded like a madman.

Even though Sophie's throat was as dry as the sand she'd been walking on for three days, she too started laughing.

Chronos collapsed onto her knees.

Nemy stopped her muttering.

Athena let out a sob of relief.

It was only Achlys who voiced what they were all thinking. "Thank the fucking Fates."

They all broke into hysteria even though nothing about this entire situation was funny.

Morpheus cleared his throat. "Let's get moving. I'll take the rear. Athena, Achlys, help Chronos. Sophie, Nemysis, you head up first. We'll meet you by Wave Rock."

"I can do it myself," Chronos whispered, though she looked impossibly pale.

"Stop being a hero, Chro. We'll be here forever if we let you do this by yourself," Achlys reminded her.

She said nothing in return.

Sophie took Nemy's hand, and they walked the last stretch of sand together. Nemy squeezed Sophie's hand, pulling her attention.

"You had the chance to jump out of the worm's mouth, but you didn't. You turned around to find me. Why?" Nemysis asked.

"Who's going to strike fear of retribution in my enemies?" Sophie laughed.

"You hide behind that humour of yours too often." Nemy shook her head slightly, then smiled. "Either way, I'm thankful."

Sophie didn't say anything back. She didn't know if she had the right words to perfectly capture how she felt about the Tienthan. About Ash and his inner circle. She loved them all dearly, and the Hrabrost Trials, at least so far, had brought them all closer.

Sophie and Nemy approached the bottom of the wave rock. It stood ten metres tall, its lip hanging over them like a wave on the cusp of crashing. Sophie could just make out the tiny blades of grass that decorated the edge.

Morpheus, Athena, Achlys and Chronos approached from behind them.

"I'll get up and pull you guys up," Morpheus said firmly. He jumped up, gripping onto the tiny lips of rocks that jutted out and began to scale the wave-shaped rock. As he neared the top, he jumped out and hung freely. His legs dangled for a moment before he pulled himself up with impressive upper body strength.

Sophie's mouth fell open. *There's no fucking way I can do that.*

"Alright send her up!" Morpheus shouted from above. He hung over the edge, his arm stretched toward them.

As if they'd practiced it a million times, Achlys and Nemy took up positions just underneath where Morpheus hovered. They took a knee each and Chronos stepped forward.

The alabaster angel moved forward with an unsteadiness. She planted a foot on Nemy's knee. Then climbed to Achlys's shoulder. Her foot found purchase on Nemy's shoulder next.

They counted to three before pushing up on to their feet in unison, launching Chronos's a third of the way up the ten metre wall. Chronos scaled the remainder of the distance with shaking legs and by the will of the Fates, managed to jump far enough to catch Morpheus's hand. She barked a grunt of pain and anger as she was hauled up the edge.

Nemy stumbled forward. Sweat beading on her forehead and her face, awfully pale.

Sophie rushed to her. "Are you alright?"

"I don't think . . ." Nemy didn't finish the sentence before she hurled up bile.

"She'll need to go next," Sophie said to Achlys.

He nodded.

"Nemy, we need to get you up there. We'll push you but you've just got to climb a little bit. Can you do that?" Sophie rubbed her hand on Nemy's back as the goddess hurled one more time.

Nemy nodded, wiping the back of her hand across her mouth.

"I'll climb with her in case she falls," Athena offered. Sophie nodded, giving the goddess a thankful smile.

Moving swiftly, Sophie copied the movements she'd seen Achlys and Nemy do earlier. Her shoulder barked in pain as Nemy's full weight pressed on top. Her lungs felt like they were about to cave in.

"When you're ready, on three," Achlys stated.

Sophie nodded. "One, two, three!"

Sophie pushed with all the strength she had in her legs and looked up as Nemy was launched into the air. She managed to grip a hold of a rock that jutted out. She cried out as one of her hands slipped.

Athena quickly followed suit, grunting in pain as she launched closer to Nemy.

"Come on, Nemy! Get your ass up there!" Sophie shouted from below. She hoped to the Fates that her friend did not fall.

Nemy held on tight with one hand, swung wide and brushed the edges of Morpheus's hands. Like two ships passing in the night, their fingertips missed each other.

Sophie's breath caught in her throat.

Nemy started to fall, almost knocking Athena off the wall as well.

And she would have hit the ground if Chronos hadn't come in from the side, grabbing Nemy's wrist just in time.

So the goddess of time isn't always a douche.

Nemy climbed over the edge with a cry of relief.

Morpheus ran over to Athena, pulling her up by the scruff of her neck. The tan-skinned angel let out a sob of relief as she cleared the edge.

The sound sprung hope in Sophie's chest. Trial three was over with. She just had to climb this freaking wall.

Achlys turned to Sophie and flashed a dark smile. "Together?"

Sophie smiled back. "Together." She nodded.

Sophie looked up at the ten metre wall.

That's a long way to fall.

Sophie shook out the nervousness in her hands and chest. She was so close. So close to finishing the stupid trial. She just had to climb this stupid wall to get there.

With newfound determination, Sophie jumped up on the wall. Her hands were burning immediately. The rock was hot and the surface, jagged. She hung as close to the wall as possible, using her legs to push herself up and up. Her sides barked in pain, and she was losing her grip with every climb.

They were halfway there when her foot slipped.

Her heart lodged itself in her throat

"Sophie!" Achlys yelled from just above her.

Sophie let out a yelp.

She righted herself, clinging on the wall. She could no longer feel her hands, but she gripped with all her might. "I'm alright, I'm alright! Keep going!"

His dark eyes found hers and he nodded firmly.

She'd need to do this on her own. She needed to prove that she didn't need anyone's help. Anyone's saving.

Sophie looked above, the edge so close.

She pushed and pushed.

She climbed and climbed.

A cool, fresh breeze just grazed her fingernails as she grasped the edge of Wave Rock. Morpheus was there within seconds.

"Well done, kid," he breathed as he roughly pulled her over the edge.

Sophie looked across to see Achlys up on the edge, lying on his back and panting, his dark skin flush with sweat.

Sophie let out a laugh, then she started sobbing. The feeling of the grass underneath her was something she'd never take for granted again. She looked to her hands. They were bleeding and bloodied. Her pinky finger sat in an odd direction. But she just didn't care. There was grass here. There was fresh air here.

Sophie curled up into a ball and let out all the emotions. Relief flooded through her. All her hard work was not for naught.

Sophie danced in and out of consciousness. Her head felt awfully light, and her body was fighting to grip onto reality.

She heard Nemy shouting through the haziness. "Ash! Wait!"

The sound of heavy footfalls approached their group. Like a tsunami, his power came crashing through the threshold of the forest just a few metres ahead of them.

"NOBODY FUCKING TOUCH HER!" Ash bellowed, lightning struck above her, and the air stirred.

It brought her comfort.

It eased her soul.

He eased her soul.

Firm hands and arms picked up her from the soft, soft grass. She loved being here. In these arms. In his arms. She wouldn't trade it for the world.

58

SOPHIE

Sophie could hear people rushing past her. The sounds of clanging metal rung into the air. Soft murmurs filled the space around her but what stayed constant was the warmth that held her hands.

Her eyes fluttered open to see Ash. His inky hair was pulled back into a braid, the white strands dipping in and out of it, like a lightning bolt striking in the dead of night. Bruises marred his skin, and scars, freshly healed, marred his arms and chest. Some of his feathers had been broken off. The red flight-inhibiting clips were still firmly in place.

"Took you long enough." He smiled, placing a soft kiss on the back of her hand.

Sophie let out a soft chuckle. He had said the exact same thing when she figured out who he was. What he meant to her.

Tears started in her eyes. "You stupid turtle-dove." She smiled, squeezing his hand.

Her body felt . . . fresh. Healed and hydrated. Her lips didn't feel like they'd cracked. She could breathe properly. Sophie sat up slowly.

She was in some sort of tent with medical supplies. She could see Chronos lying down on a stretcher, unconscious. A medic working on her with healing magic. Next to her stretched out on a litter was Deymos. She would recognise those grey wings anywhere.

"What happened to Deymos?" Sophie whispered.

Ash leaned in close, brushing the hair out of her face in way that made her heart tingle. He didn't let go of her hand.

"A worm tooth severed his femoral artery. We noticed a bit too late so had to heal the entire leg with the tooth inside. The medics just fished it out."

"Shit."

"Doc said you had three cracked ribs, two broken fingers all while suffering heat stroke."

No wonder why it had been so hard to breathe. And no wonder why the last climb up the wave rock was excruciating.

Sophie stretched, revelling in the ease that her muscles and bones moved with. They were nowhere near a hundred per cent, but they were healed. "What can I say? All in a day's work." Sophie winked at Ash.

He shook his head. "Smart-ass."

A moment passed between them.

He looked at her as if he were about to say something.

Sophie herself had so many words, left unsaid.

Electricity filled the silent space separating them.

Sophie hadn't forgotten. She'd safely tucked the thoughts away as she completed the trials but now that he was here before her . . . the full force of what she'd learnt in the Stagnum De Memoria came crashing into her. Her memories. Him. Them. Their soulmate bond seared into their flesh.

She felt a little hot. It had only been a few days since she was running through the blasted downpour. She was trying to find him and here he was. Right in front of her.

She looked down at their tattoos. Ash's were far more intricate as the design climbed up his arms. It looked like he'd added more to it. But the designs on their hands were almost identical. Where hers ended in a key, his ended in a lock. The Fates had chosen for them to be together. And for once, Sophie felt like the Fates were right. Heck, she'd choose Ash for herself, over and over and defy the Fates if they denied her.

Sophie looked up to those turquoise smoking eyes and the scar across his brow. "We need to talk," she whispered.

Hurt danced across his eyes and his jaw ticked. "Come. I know a place." Then and only then did he let go of her hand.

They sat by a small river, just behind the medical tent, away from prying eyes and ears. Their boots were pushed to the side as their legs and feet revelled in the coolness of the water.

The Tartarus sky was still its ominous grey and the sun had disappeared altogether. Not that Sophie was complaining. Three days of unrelenting sun had probably altered her brain chemistry in ways she didn't want to know.

Ash was shirtless. His wings relaxed behind him. A knee propped up onto the bank while his other foot dangled into the cooling river.

Sophie splashed some water in his face. "You're moping."

"Am not." Ash retaliated, kicking a wallop of water into Sophie, drenching her entirely.

Sophie gasped.

Without even thinking, Sophie launched herself at Ash, grabbing a hold of his hands, and pulled him into the river.

His hands found her waist as they pushed up to the surface. Their laughter bubbled all around, bouncing off the surface of the river and the trees that surrounded them. Sophie threw her arms around Ash's thick neck, wrapped her legs around his waist, and squeezed as hard as she could.

"Help! She's trying to kill me!" Ash feigned.

"Oh shush, die quietly, will you?" Sophie laughed, pulling back to look him in the eyes. Every curve and plain of their bodies were flush against each other. Their lips, mere centimetres away. "I went to the Stagnum De Memoria," Sophie said quietly.

Ash stilled.

"And I learnt something," Sophie continued. Her heart was beating wildly. She let go of Ash's neck and pulled herself off him, trailing a hand down his tattooed shoulder. The tips of her fingertips burned as their skin met.

He watched the movement of her fingers the whole time.

Sophie continued tracing the swirls of patterns down his arm. When they disappeared under the water, Sophie pulled his hand up from underneath.

Tracing each line, each detail, each edge until their fingers met. They stood in the river, palm to palm. Tattooed hand, to tattooed hand. And nothing could be sweeter. Nothing could be more whole. Like two mirror images, they stood.

She intertwined her fingers with his. "We are fated," Sophie said simply.

Ash swallowed hard.

Sophie's lips started to wobble, and her eyes started to water. She let out a whimper. "I'm sorry, you had to wait for so long."

Without warning, Ash crashed his lips into hers. His kisses, urgent, demanding, consuming and possessive. Sophie kissed right back, growing breathless with every movement, but she didn't care anymore. Ash was the only oxygen she needed.

Ash pulled back, emotion washing his voice. "I would wait a thousand lifetimes for you, Starlight. An infinity sun cycles. A million Ephemeral Eclipses. However long you needed. However long it would take for you to come back to me, I would have waited."

Sophie was sobbing now. She didn't deserve him. She kissed him urgently. Perhaps it was the Hrabrost Trials, and the agony of knowing one's truth rolled into one hot mess, but Sophie couldn't think of anything but Ash.

Ash. Ash. Ash.

Mine. Mine. Mine.

"I love you." Sophie smiled through her tears, her hand resting on his strong jaw. Her thumb caressing the scars across the left side of his face. This was what love felt like. She had found it at last.

Ash blushed. Literally blushed as he nuzzled into her hand.

"I, wait"—Ash shook his head slightly—"but what about the letter?"

"What letter?" Sophie furrowed her brows and tilted her head.

"It was in a black envelope . . . you said you wanted to remain friends." A sadness laced his deep voice.

Sophie's gut dropped. That letter. The one where she harped on about being friends and a close confidant. The one where she wrote the word friend a suspicious number of times so he would get the point but in actuality, she never felt that way. She was just trying to protect herself. But how did he get that letter?

Her mind rewound to the point in time where Eros, the heart-shape-eyed snoop, had infiltrated her room and gave her an ultimatum. It felt like a lifetime ago.

"*Eros,*" Sophie groaned.

"*EROS,*" Ash repeated murderously.

Sophie gripped his jaw. "Fuck the letter, Ash." She climbed on to him, her hands on both sides of his handsome face and her legs wrapped around his waist.

He wrapped his arms around her and that feeling.

Ugh, this feeling.

It sent her soaring even though she'd barely left the ground.

Her eyes started to water again, as she let the flood gates open. The gates that had held back the full brunt of her emotions. "I'm falling. I've fallen, Ash." He wiped a tear from her eyes. "And it's all consuming. It terrifies me. I don't know whether I'm shining or burning. With you, perhaps . . . perhaps I'm a little bit of both." Sophie laughed softly. "Loving, hurting"—she kissed him on his cheek—"shining, burning"—she kissed him on his other cheek—"in pure ecstasy when I'm with you and utter agony when I'm not." She kissed him on the lips, savouring his woodsy scent and the addictiveness of his essence. "But what I now know for sure, is that the stars that line the sky have always been lighting a path to you." She lightly traced the scar, like a lightning strike across his brow and cheek. "My Ash. I love you. Only you." She leaned her forehead on his. Her chest bursting with a swell of emotions.

Ash kissed her deeply, taking in a full breath as their lips joined. He held her firmly, so that she couldn't look away from his burning, smoking eyes. "I will hold you close until all the realms turn into the dusts of time, protect you until the fires of Hell burn over my very skin and I will fucking love you until the rattle of death is the only sound I hear. Forever and beyond that, Starlight, I am yours and you are mine. I love you, Sofreya. Only you."

Their kiss was slow. Aching. Binding. Soul crushing. Twenty years it took. By the Fates they were going to savour this.

Water lapped all around them, but they did not care.

Their kisses grew hurried. She needed him now. Heck, she needed him years ago. His words were the salve to mend her irreparable heart. His touch, his actions, his kisses were the flames that forged a shatterproof heart.

Ash grabbed her thighs, tightening them around him. She could feel every movement of muscles across his abdomen. It lit her core on fire as they hungrily kissed and moaned.

She would never get enough of this.

He pushed her to the bank of the river and reverently lay her down. Her legs and feet were still in the water. Rocks and grass bit into her back as he trailed kisses all over her neck and down her chest.

Sophie arched her back and opened her eyes to find . . . Eros.

"AHHH! EROS, WHAT THE FUCK ARE YOU DOING HERE, YOU FUCKING CREEP?!" Sophie shrieked, pulling her wet blouse up.

Lightning struck the ground behind them.

Sophie didn't even notice Ash move from on top of her.

Eros was on the verge of tears as he held a bag of marshmallows and chocolate in his hands.

Sophie scrambled to her feet, dodging the small storm clouds that brewed around Ash's wings and shoulders. Ash grabbed her hand, pulling her closer to him. He snarled at the god of love, promising death and more.

Eros ran to them with open arms, dropping the bag of marshmallows and chocolate to the ground. He was sobbing. "I AM SO HAPPY FOR YOU GUYS!" He crashed into Sophie, pushing her back into the solid mass of Ash. Eros held them hostage in an awkward, three-person hug. Vice grip, rather.

All Sophie could see was chest and muscle as Eros squished her, pulling in Ash for a hug too.

I'm in a freaking angel-sandwich. It could be worse I guess . . .

"Eros," Sophie murmured, trying to get him off her.

"I thought I altered the will of the Fates by giving Ash that silly letter, Sophie. Why didn't you tell me you wrote a fake letter? If only I knew! I wouldn't have given it to him in the first place. I thought I was doing you a favour. He was so sad. So broody. He pouted the entire time we were in Tartarus and it was all my fault and—"

"EROS. You're crushing me," Sophie groaned.

"Oh." Eros eased his grip.

Sophie righted herself and smiled. "It's fine, Eros." She turned back to Ash who still looked like he was about to raise hell. "We're fine."

Lightning struck again.

"I say we burn all his rom-com blu-rays for interrupting us," Ash threatened.

Sophie narrowed her eyes on Eros and grinned mischievously. "Better yet, we should block him from our streaming accounts so that he has to pay for his *own* subscriptions."

Eros gasped. "You would never!"

"Oh, but I would. You wanted to watch season three of Emily in Paris, didn't you, Eros?" Ash's grin was positively murderous. "Well, too bad."

Eros yelped, letting out a horrified sound as he grabbed the befallen marshmallows and chocolate, scurrying away from them in pure terror.

They spent the better part of the day resting for what was to be their last leg of the Hrabrost Trials. By tomorrow morning, they would have conquered Mount Gehenna, locked away the monsters that lived inside it and, hopefully, lived to tell the tale.

The entire Tienthan sat by a fire, toasting marshmallows. Eros had started his own s'more-making station. He insisted that the chocolate had to be smeared in a love-heart shape before they were eaten to let everyone in the group know that they were loved.

They were all in the middle of a gruelling test of mettle and teamwork. Gods and goddesses in their own right. Eating s'mores. By a fire. In Tartarus.

This is by far the weirdest thing I've ever experienced.

Sophie smiled to herself. She wouldn't have it any other way.

The medical tent had disbanded and the medical team with it, leaving the Tienthan to themselves with a bottle of water each and a hot meal for the cooler evening. Deymos was awake, though he had lost a considerable amount of strength in his left leg. Chronos had also returned to her normal pallor.

With less of an attitude too.

They were sharing stories of the trial so far.

"Athena was literally dangling from its beak with its putrid ink all over her." Nemy laughed.

"And we had to deal with her stinky ass for days. The absolute worst," Achlys joined in.

Athena smacked him across the arm. "At least I didn't trip over a twig and accidentally look into the eyes of a wailing witch."

"You tripped over a twig?" Pallas barked a laugh.

"Mate, thinking about Pallas too much, were you?" Erebus teased Achlys, earning himself a rock to the head.

Eros cooed. Naturally.

Together they all laughed.

Morpheus had his arm around Nyx.

And Sophie was safely tucked in between Ash's legs. She leaned back into his broad chest as he mindlessly fed her marshmallow after marshmallow.

This is living.

"Well, I'm going to turn in. Rest well everyone," Deymos declared with a stretch of his wings and back.

With that, they all mumbled their goodnights before peeling off. Some of the angels took to the trees while others moved to a small clearing with padded grass, leaving Sophie and Ash to their own devices by the fire.

"Did you want to stay by the fire or move to the grass over there?" Ash whispered in her ear. It sent chills down her back.

Sophie leaned back, smirking. "Seeking some privacy, are you? You dirty, smut-loving angel."

"Hey, you said they were your favourite books," he said, kissing her lightly on the forehead.

She did say that. When they'd been reunited at the age of eighteen in Faery. She'd told him that they were worth a read and that she wished she could read them for the first time again. If only she could.

Sophie's heart warmed. "You got them for me?"

"Of course. And I'd buy you a million copies if it makes you look at me like that. In hardback too."

Sophie chuckled. "Ah, you do know the way into a woman's heart." Sophie kissed him on the lips again. She would never tire of the feeling. Like two jigsaw pieces, they fit perfectly together. "But we do need to rest."

"I'll rest when I'm dead." Ash tried to catch her lips, but Sophie pulled back.

"But you'll be dead tomorrow if you don't rest." Sophie pressed a finger onto his lips, pushing him back, earning herself a growl of frustration.

"Fine."

"When we get back to the Godlands, Ash, we're going to spend an entire week alone. Closed off to the world. You can do *whatever* your smut-loving heart wants to me." She leaned in to whisper in his ear, *"Anything."*

Ash purred. Literally purred. And if that noise didn't make Sophie's toes curl.

"I hope tomorrow comes sooner then." Ash kissed her, pulling back to look at her.

He pulled her down onto the patchy grass by the fire and pulled her into his arms. Her back flush against his chest. He placed his palm on her bare stomach and sighed. "Goodnight, Starlight."

Sophie intertwined her fingers with his. "Goodnight, my storm."

Upon those words, Ash cocooned them both in the safety of his wings.

Sophie could hardly sleep. While Ash's warmth lulled her eyes closed, knowing they were about to embark on the most difficult trial of all within a few hours made her jolt awake every few minutes.

She could feel Ash's steady breaths on the back of her neck. His face was buried into her hair as he held her. Sophie shifted in his arms, trying to find a new position in the safety of his wings.

Ash stirred at her movements. "What's wrong?" he asked softly, his voice thick with sleep.

"I can't sleep."

"Are you worried about tomorrow?"

"Yeah." Sophie let out a frustrated breath as she turned to face him. His eyes were sleepy, hooded.

"I can help you sleep?" He held her face with a strong hand and placed a soft kiss on her lips.

Sophie nodded sleepily. She would accept anything to help her sleep at this point.

Without a word, he turned her in his arms so that her back was flush against his chest again. The feeling of their bodies so close, instantly pulled her focus. Suddenly, all her senses were consumed by a soft kiss on her neck. Then a soft kiss on her shoulder. They were painfully patient and devastatingly delicate. The kind that made her heart squeeze, her stomach flutter, and her legs tense. As his hand found its way up her blouse . . . well. Sophie wasn't thinking about tomorrow anymore.

Ash's thumbs drew intoxicating circles along her bare stomach, driving her into a hazed, sleepy madness. She held her breath, lying in agonising wait, wondering where his hand would go next.

Ash pulled her closer to him with the arm she was laying on. His forearm lay across her chest, binding her to him. His warm breath tickled her ear as he whispered, "Relax." That deep sound. That word. How could she do anything but?

Slowly, painfully, he moved his hand lower. The delicious circling of his fingers made Sophie's breath hitch, her back arch, wanting exactly what he was offering.

He placed another distracting kiss on her neck as he lowered his hand past the band of her pants. Her mind fought against itself, not knowing whether to focus on his sweet kisses, or the way his hand moved closer and closer to the place she really wanted it to be.

Were they going to do this?

"Ash," Sophie rasped. It was a warning. A plea.

"Relax," he breathed into her ear again. And it was his words, his lips brushing against the shell of her ear and the warmth he provided that was her undoing. He nudged his knee between her legs, urging her to open for him, and she obeyed. Eager for his touch. She melted into his arms as he drew closer and closer. He breathed in deeply and as he sank his fingers into her. They moaned in unison.

By the fucking stars.

He explored every curve and every line of her as if she were a fucking map, before settling where X marked the spot. His fingers drew delirious circles. She'd die here. Happily. In Tartarus, with the realm's most deplorable demons listening in.

His fingers were slow at first, occasionally dipping in and out of her as desire built. With each stroke, with each circle, her desire came in droves, forming a cliff edge she'd joyously fling herself off. Every breathy moan that escaped her lips earned her an encouraging growl from Ash's throat. An increase in pressure. A quickening of his fingers. All of which drove her to the edge. She was equal parts need and madness now. On the precipice. Impatient as hell. Her hands clutched hungrily onto his muscled arm and her hips unabashedly lifted, trying to get closer. Her moans grew louder and louder.

"That's my girl," Ash purred.

The words sent her into another fucking dimension. Several dimensions parallel to this one. She was dripping for him. Begging for him.

He gave it to her. He never denied her. And when she was about to spill over, he stopped.

Sophie whimpered, her heart galloping in her chest, her legs weak and sweaty. She turned her head to face him. "Why are you stopping?" She panted.

Ash said nothing as he lifted his hand, sank his two fingers past the softness of his full lips and tasted her. His eyes fluttered closed as he moaned with feral satisfaction.

Sophie's lips parted, her throat becoming awfully dry as her eyes traced every line of his face and the angelic perfection of it. It were as if he had just tasted the most delicious thing in his life.

That is so fucking hot.

Ash let out a little chuckle as if he'd read her mind, before moving his hand back down to her. Ash moved to kiss her deeply. She could taste herself on him. On his tongue. On his lips. He loved the way she tasted and, by the Fates, she swore she could come from that thought alone. And when her kisses grew impatient, when she was grinding mindlessly upon his hand, he didn't hold back.

He groaned and moaned as much as she did.

He circled her. He worked her. He pleasured her until she was sinfully soaked, clutching onto his arm for dear life and claiming his lips like they would be ripped from her in any moment.

She was going to come.

Her entire body tense, electrified.

She couldn't hold on to this cliff edge any longer.

"Come for me," Ash whispered.

His words were her undoing. She cried out as she spilled over the edge of ecstasy. With every pulse, he pulled her tighter against him. She came so hard that every part of her body was shaking. Every curve of her body, fit and flush against his. He showered her with kisses. His fingers stayed, buried inside her, drinking up the last of her climax.

She felt like she was walking on air. She was putty. Her heart raced in her ears, and she could hear his heart doing the same.

Ash kissed her softly on the shoulder before wrapping his arms around her middle again. "Sleep, Starlight. You need to."

And so she did.

59

ACHERON

A bloodcurdling scream jolted him awake. Sending his heart into panic and his body, falling back on years of training. He'd barely opened his eyes before he moved to shield Sofreya's body with his. Ash whipped his head up with laser focus, surveying their surrounds.

An ear-shattering rumble shook the ground.

"Holy fucking shit." Sofreya sprung awake.

"We need to move!" Ash shouted above the maelstrom.

Giant boulders were raining from the dark Tartarus sky. They were burning red hot. The smell of smoke was thick in the air. The last trial had begun. Earlier than expected. Today, they would be conquering Mount Gehenna.

Ash pulled Sophie up from the ground and ran. The only focus right now was to protect her.

Another bloodcurdling scream sounded. It was Nyx.

Pallas, Chronos and Nemy came barrelling toward them.

"It's Nyxy. It's not good, Ash," Pallas panted.

Fuck. There was no medical evacuation for the last trial either.

Ash nodded. "You three"—he pointed to the three angels—"recon a path for us. Sofreya, you're with me." He wasn't letting her out of his sight.

The three angels sprinted away toward Mount Gehenna.

Ash pulled Sofreya with him, running toward the sounds of Nyx's pained cries.

Shit.

As they neared, flashbacks to his first trial where Deymos was crushed by a boulder edged into his vision. At least for Deymos it was just his legs. Nyx didn't have that kind of privilege. A bolder had crushed their entire lower body and all he could see was their chest and arms.

Blood. So much blood.

Their cries of pain were haunting, hollowing. The vision of a visibly distraught Morpheus who held onto his lover's hands left a sinking feeling in Ash's chest.

"Stay with me, Nyxy, stay with me," Morpheus repeated. His face was pale, all drained of colour. He was going into shock.

"Brother." Ash placed a hand on Morpheus shoulder. "I need you to step back, and I need you to focus. We need to get this off them, okay? We need to keep moving. Can you do that?"

Morpheus swallowed hard and nodded. "I can do that. I can do that." He was shaking.

Years of training, years of trials had made Ash numb to gruesome situations like this. His body was on full autopilot. Ash pursed his lips and did what he did best.

"Eros, Athena. As soon as this fucking thing budges, I need you to start healing. They're losing blood and can't afford to lose any more. Got it?"

"Roger." Eros and Athena nodded, kneeling beside Nyx who was moving in and out of consciousness. Eros and Athena were the best healers in the Tienthan. If anyone could do it, it was them.

"Everyone else, we're pushing this motherfucker off."

The boulder was at least six metres in diameter, and the worst part? They would have to do it slowly, so that Eros and Athena could heal as they went. If they went too fast, Nyx would lose too much blood.

The angels, Sofreya included, stood on either side of the boulder, their arms outstretched.

"On my command. Prepare to push." Ash paused. "Push!" he commanded.

They combined their powers to nudge the boulder.

Nyx screamed as the boulder inched off them. The sound was horrifying. Ash could hear the wetness of their blood, the crunching of bones.

Ash could see the glowing healing mana that left Eros's and Athena's hands. "Push!" he shouted again.

They repeated the motions until at last, Nyx was free. Morpheus was beside them immediately, placing his calming, sleeping power into their mind.

"Nyxy will be alright," Eros stated.

"Ash!" Achlys shouted, pointing to the dark sky above.

A meteor shower of rocks was headed straight for them, glowing hot against the grey sky.

For Fates' sake.

Sofreya moved suddenly, manifesting a stretcher from grass, vines and dirt. She packed it together wordlessly as Eros and Athena moved Nyx onto it.

"Deymos, Sofreya, move ahead. Clear the path for us. Get us to the others," Ash commanded.

They moved.

The rest stayed behind to carry Nyx upon the stretcher.

They were running across the grassy clearing. Dodging. Ducking. Barrel rolling as piping-hot red rocks catapulted for them. Deymos and Sofreya worked together seamlessly to create a barrier around the group. Sofreya used a combination of her air mana and her demigoddess powers of creation to whip away rocks. Deymos used his shadows to deflect them.

They neared the base of Mount Gehenna.

Pallas came running to them. "Is Nyx alright?" he asked Ash.

Ash nodded. "They won't be able to climb though."

"No med evac?"

Ash shook his head.

"Shit."

They pushed the stretcher up against a tree.

"Morpheus, stay behind with Nyx until they wake up. Athena, you'll be their security." Ash commanded. He turned to the rest of his crew. "We need to keep moving. Climb the mountain and—"

A monstrous scream, one that Ash had hoped he would never hear again, echoed through the entirety of Tartarus. The ground shook. The trees bent from the force of it.

It felt like thousands of tiny poisonous spiders had run down his spine.

Typhon.

Ash would remember that scream for the rest of his life. Typhon had come out on Ash's very first Hrabrost Trial. The King of Mount Gehenna. A minotaur made of shadows and nightmares who stood thirty feet tall. At his beck and call, under his command, were the beasts of Mount Gehenna.

"Listen in!" Ash called out. Everyone rushed in closer, creating a half-moon shape around him. Ash grabbed a stick and crouched down on the ground, flattening the dirt in front of him with a swipe of his hand. "Situation. If you haven't fucking figured it out, that was Typhon. It means we're in for a shit fight." He drew a circle in the dirt before him. "Mount Gehenna is a steep climb." He drew three rings around the circle. "It is unknown what creatures have been released along with Typhon. All that is known, is that they will return to Mount Gehenna when Typhon does."

Ash kept is voice calm and steady. "Mission." He drew an X in the centre of the first big circle. "Return Typhon to the confines of Mount Gehenna, so we can all get out of this hellhole."

Ash looked at all his comrades. His Starlight. Her face was screwed into focus and determination. Which made him want to get this trial over with, so he could take her home and hold her.

"Execution. There will be two phases. Phase one will begin when we step away from this admin area." Ash pointed to the small pocket of forest they were currently standing in. "And it will end when we reach the opening of Mount Gehenna. Erebus, Pallas, Nemysis, Chronos." He pointed at the four angels. "You are Team Alpha." They nodded. "Deymos, Sofreya, Achlys, Eros, you're Team Bravo." Ash looked to Sofreya. To her credit, she didn't look the least bit scared. She was raging. Ready.

"Team Alpha, you will head up the mountain first and secure a safe position before the opening of Mount Gehenna." Ash drew a straight line running toward the X on the floor, stopping just a few centimetres before it. "You are to follow the commands of your team leader, Nemysis." The angels of Team Alpha nodded.

"Team Bravo, you will follow Team Alpha at a distance and occupy the safe position once it is secured and provide security from the rear." Ash drew another line, running parallel. "You are to follow the commands of your team leader, Deymos." Angels of Team Bravo nodded. "I'll be a few paces behind you all." As the words left his mouth, he couldn't help but look at Sofreya. Her eyes turned to worry. Ash didn't want to be separated from Sofreya. Not in the slightest but he also had the Aerial Legion to command and manoeuvre through this last trial. Just for this trial, she was one of his soldiers.

"Morpheus, Athena, when Nyx wakes, you are to climb Mount Gehenna and find me. You will be under my command as Team Charlie," Ash said. The two angels nodded. Morpheus looked less distraught as Athena pumped more healing magic into Nyx's body.

"Phase two begins when we leave our secure position on top of Mount Gehenna. As a team, we will fight to secure and detain Typhon." He highlighted the circle around the X again. "You will *still* be under the command of your team leaders. So keep your damned ears open. From there, we will combine our powers to reseal Mount Gehenna's entrance. Phase two will be complete once we return to our secured position for a debrief." Ash pointed at their secure position, just a few paces back from the entrance of the mountain.

"If you get lost, keep climbing that fucking mountain. If you get injured, keep climbing that fucking mountain. Whatever you do, do not stop. The mountain is mysterious and you *will* suffer a painful death if you stop for too long. Do you have any questions?" Ash scanned the group of angels. A day of rest had done them well. They would get through this trial as a team, hopefully with no casualties.

Everyone shook their heads. "Good. We leave in five minutes. Get some water in you. Who knows when we'll be able to stop." They all disbanded. Some turning around to their team leaders to discuss tactics, but not Sofreya.

Ash didn't care about water or preparation. He all but ran to Sofreya and pulled her close. He kissed her deeply, needing to feel their two souls intertwine for a fleeting moment. After a whole minute of breathing her in, Ash let go.

"What was that for?" she asked breathlessly.

"Just in case."

"Are you getting soppy on me?" She smiled mischievously.

"Only for you."

She peered up at him. So small and precious he just wanted to squeeze her at all hours of the day, but her voice was filled with worry. "You won't be far behind, will you?"

"I won't be far. You might not see me, but I'll be behind your team. Try not to cry, alright?" Ash teased, earning himself a hefty punch to the chest. Before she could pull away, he gripped her wrist and pulled her in closer. "I lov—"

Sofreya shut him up with a quick kiss. Her sweet breath dancing across his lips had that ability. "Why did that sound like the start of a goodbye?" She kissed him again. "We don't do that anymore, you big idiot. It's you and me until the sands of time claim us."

And she was fucking right.

60

SOPHIE

Sophie followed Deymos's command.

It was hard to not turn around and check on Ash, but she knew he was more than capable of handling his own. He was the freaking weapons master and leader of the Godlands Aerial Legion. He would be fine.

Her team, Team Bravo, ran at a gruelling pace. Deymos, Eros and Achlys, their legs much longer and powerful, were battling ahead. Sophie had to use a bit of her air mana to keep up. She *had* to keep up. Her chest burned with heavy breaths as they scaled the mountain together. Quiet. Focused. They were so close to the end.

Parts of Mount Gehenna were dark, black and jagged. Clouds obscured the very top. The other parts spat lava, adding another layer of difficulty to the task at hand. With every level they climbed, it grew harder and harder to breathe.

"Fuck!" Achlys shouted ahead of Sophie.

They all whipped their heads to the god of eternal night with his black wings and dark skin. A bright red snake flew into the air. "Snakes!" Achlys shouted again.

They didn't have enough time to register what he'd said when a sea of snakes covered the ground, striking at them in anger. Some were as thick as Sophie's legs, others were small but looked equally as poisonous.

Snakes? Why did it have to be snakes?

"Keep fucking moving!" Deymos commanded from the very front. He was using his shadows to stop the strikes of several snakes as he ran ahead.

Sophie followed suit, pulling out her blades to slice and dice as she dodged snake after snake. Her breathing grew ragged, and her legs ached.

Eros let out a yelp beside her. A snake had managed to lodge its fangs into his arm. Sophie threw her knife in a wide arc. It cut the snake clean in half before she caught it again. Eros pulled out the snake's fangs and shot healing power into his arm.

Sophie ran up to him. "You alright?"

"Thanks, Sophie," he breathed, planting a kiss on her forehead. "Let's keep moving."

Together they ran, slicing, dicing, kicking and punching their way through the sea of snakes.

Ahead was a hard ridge, two metres tall.

"Sophie!" Deymos shouted, touching his forehead with the palm of his hand. She learnt that it was a signal to go to him. She ran to Deymos, he hunched over a little so that he was on her level. "When you get up this ridge, you won't see us. It's an illusion, but we'll be right beside you. Do not look anywhere but ahead and up, until you reach a second ridge. Once you climb on top of that, we'll reach the position Team Alpha has hopefully secured. Got that?"

"Roger." Sophie nodded.

They were close. So fucking close.

"Alright! Let's move!" Deymos's voiced boomed, sending a tendril of terror through Sophie.

Sophie climbed up onto the ridge. Her hands burning from the heat of the rocks. The air was thick with smoke, coiling into her lungs and making her cough. As she clasped the rock edge with her hand, the sound of Typhon's screaming roared through the entirety of Tartarus. The mountain beneath her shook as if it were a monster coming to life.

Keep climbing. Keep moving.

Her fingernails cracked as she scaled the rocky ridge. Her legs strained as she pushed herself up. She could hear the grunts of the other angels. As she pulled herself over the rocky ledge a wall of thick smoke ambushed her.

Silence.

Gone was the soft hum of insects. The chaotic rustling of trees. The trembling of rocks, skittering across the ground. In its place was silence.

An illusion. Keep moving.

The dark smoke rolled and rolled, and the temperature plummeted, striking painful shivers through Sophie's body.

Sophie resumed her running pace. She could barely see ahead but she'd been warned times aplenty to not stop for too long. The others were nowhere in sight. Their absence left her feeling empty, unprotected and alone.

Find the second ridge.

The rolling smoke grew darker and darker. Thicker and thicker.

That's when she felt it. A presence. Something otherworldly, hovering a hair's breadth away from her.

She couldn't look back. She didn't want to. She ran faster and faster.

She couldn't see a thing.

Until a cold brittle hand laced its fingers through her hair and pulled her down to the ground with neck-breaking force. Dirt flung into the air with chaos as Sophie let out a horrendous scream that lanced through her throat. The back of her skull felt like it had been cracked open and whatever creature it was, had its rotten fingers in there, trying to cleave her head clean apart.

Death was a breath away. She could feel it. Her body felt entirely not hers. Her mana was panicking, rolling in dizzying circles. The ground was up, the sky was down. Blindly, with her own mana slipping through her fingers, Sophie pushed her air mana around her, letting out a sob. The sound of the creature scurrying back was haunting. It was all heavy thuds, wet movements, clicks and cracks.

Sophie clawed her way to her knees, each micromovement earning a warm trickle of thick blood down the back of her neck. Crying, she fumbled across the ground, a whimper leaving her as she desperately tried to right herself.

There.

The smoke was growing thinner.

Sophie crawled and scrambled to the light smoke.

She needed to go. She couldn't stop for too long.

The cold brittle hands wrapped through her hair again.

"Fuck off!" Sophie cried, the pain bringing a new wave of hot tears to her eyes. She managed to flip herself over and her entire body stilled. Cold sweat pooled all over her.

Above her was a banshee. A soulless creature and an omen of death. She knew it. Deep in her bones. A fear so debilitating shot through her chest and sank its yellowed teeth into her heart.

The banshee's long white hair was caked in dark crimson blood. Its eyes, hollowed. The sockets laden with rotten skin as it cried blood-red tears. A nasty scream etched into its face, and its hands were now firmly locked onto Sophie's neck.

No.

The air in Sophie's lungs dwindled down to paper thin. But as Sophie clung onto her last breath, she dug deep, pulling at her mana.

Please.

She wasn't going to go like this. Not in the last stage of the fucking Hrabrost Trials. Sophie screamed, expelling the last taste of life from her lungs as she manifested a giant ball of fire. The heat and force of it was deadly enough to knock back the banshee. It wailed as its skin boiled and shrivelled. Air had found its way back into Sophie's lungs. She crawled onto all fours, a mess of heavy limbs and let out another pained cry, dousing everything around her in *fire*. And when the sounds of Mount Gehenna returned, and the rolling smoke cleared, she knew she'd made it through the illusion.

Burning death was all around. The trees had been burned to cinders. Nothing but blank stumps and trunks remained.

Sophie wiped her running nose with the back of her hand. She was bleeding. Everywhere. Her eyes. Her nose. The back of her throbbing skull.

Too much power. Too much.

Sophie turned, fumbling to her feet. The second ridge was just a few paces ahead, but Sophie couldn't keep upright. She was a newborn fawn and the second ridge the salvation that she couldn't quite reach. She fell, more times than she could count. And as she hooked her fingers, broken fingernails and all, into the walls of the ridge, she began what was the most excruciating, godsforsaken climb. She didn't care if she scraped her knees, or broke her damned fingers again, or if her brain matter was spilling out the back of her damned head. She scaled the second ridge because there needed to be a tomorrow for her.

At last, Sophie rolled over the edge.

"Eros!" Deymos shouted. "Shit, Sophie, stay still. Stay with me." Sophie couldn't keep her eyes open. She was dizzy. So, so dizzy.

The sound of Eros sliding in the dirt toward her echoed in her ears. Too loud.

She felt warmth behind her head. Debilitating pain, as if her skull was being shifted around, echoed through her body. Sophie let out a cry. It was too much.

"You're okay, Sophie. I'm almost done, okay?" It was Eros's comforting voice.

Rough hands seized hers and Sophie looked up to find Deymos. His wholly black and yellow eyes looked down on her with worry. "Almost done, Soph. Almost done." He squeezed her hand tighter, and it only made her cry harder. She was all scared whimpers and panicked breathing, but suddenly her dread was gone. In its place was calm.

It was Deymos. He was taking away her dread and terror.

A sharp pain lanced across the back of her head again and the warmth of Eros's healing power pulled back. "It's going to scar, but she should be fine," Eros said.

"Sophie, do you know where you are?" Deymos asked, his hand holding her chin firm. He was assessing her.

"Tartarus."

"Do you know what you're doing here?"

"The Hrabrost Trials." How could she forget?

"Do you remember what we're to do next?"

"We need to get to Team Alpha so we can start—" The sound of Typhon's monstrous scream split through the air again. "—dealing with that motherfucker." Sophie spat out the blood that had pooled in her mouth.

"She's alright," Deymos stated, before squeezing her shoulder and helping her stand.

"Alright, I'll go help Achlys." The sounds of Eros's footfalls disappeared into the distance.

"What happened, Soph?"

"A fucking banshee. White hair. White face. Blood all over." Sophie shuddered at the thought, wiping the blood clear from her face. She'd be having nightmares for all eternity about it.

"I think she got Achlys too."

"She didn't hold back, did she?" Sophie scoffed, though tears were pooling in her eyes.

It was fucking terrifying.

Deymos rested a reassuring hand on her shoulder and surveyed the burned forest below the ridge they'd just climbed. "Looks like you didn't, either."

I didn't have a choice. It was life or death and Sophie sure as hell wasn't going to let a banshee take her life. A life that had only just begun.

"Let's keep moving." Achlys and Eros came running up to them. Achlys massaged his wrist, perhaps he'd broken it and Eros had healed it. There was no mistaking the haunted look in his eyes.

They needed to keep moving. The end of the Hrabrost Trial was a test away.

So together they ran. Across the incline of rocks only to hear the screams and grunts of the other angels. It made Sophie's blood run cold.

They were meant to wait for us.

As they rounded the mountain, Sophie's stomach dropped.

The mighty mouth of Mount Gehenna lay open. Hot fire scored every jagged edge. Sophie could feel its heat brush her cheeks from where she stood. The sounds of strange cries and shouts from creatures she knew were made of nightmares, echoed up into the air. Upon the dark edges was Typhon.

Sophie gulped.

His bull-like head and furry body was covered in shadows. He roared and dodged the angels of the Tienthan who sought to strike him with all their power. The dark sky above rumbled with thunder, and lightning flashed.

"Bravo, we need to close Mount Gehenna's opening. Alpha will push Typhon back in!" Deymos commanded. His hair was sopping wet as rain poured and his black eyes and yellow irises glowed with fervour. "Go!"

Achlys, Eros, Deymos and Sophie spread out, dodging the other angels and the throws of Typhon. His minotaur scream rocked the earth again, sending a few angels scrambling.

When they surrounded the opening of Mount Gehenna, they extended their arms, concentrating their power to close the giant opening. Sweat beaded across Sophie's brow, seeping into flaked and caked blood on her face. The heat billowing out of the mountain was almost as thick as a wall, making it increasingly difficult to concentrate. It seeped through her boots, melting the bottoms.

All four members of Team Bravo combined their powers, pushing into the mountain. Sparks of power flew in a rainbow of colours. Sophie could see it then. The edges of Mount Gehenna's opening, growing bits of rock. Smaller and smaller.

"Get down!" Nemysis's voice boomed across the mountain top.

Sophie hit the deck, her knees and elbows turning red and raw. She rolled onto her back in time to see Typhon shoot laser-like beams from his eyes. Not a laser, that was fire.

Are you fucking kidding me?

Typhon let out another roar and dived for one of the angels. It was Chronos. Her alabaster skin and white hair was stark against Typhon's dark pelt. He wrenched her into one of his hands and crushed her wings with the other. Her pained cry echoed through the air, slicing into everyone's attention.

A plume of darkness surrounded Typhon's hand, and in a blink, Erebus with his red hair and white wings appeared, slicing down hard with a sword he created from darkness. Black, foul-smelling blood spilled down Typhon's arm as the two angels fell unceremoniously to the ground. Without a thought, Sophie shot out her mana in time to soften their landing with vines.

"Chronos is down!" Erebus shouted through the fray.

Sophie turned to Deymos.

"Change of plans, Bravo, move in with Alpha and let's take this son of a bitch down!" he commanded.

Achlys roared a battle cry as they all turned to face Typhon together. Sophie pulled together her mana, using all the elements to strike the king of Mount Gehenna down. The Tienthan worked seamlessly, a well-oiled machine. While one half attacked, the other half pulled the beast down. But this motherfucker was strong.

As Typhon clawed through the next round of attacks, the air grew thin and cold. It sizzled.

BOOM.

Rock went flying everywhere. Bright white light scorched her eyes and Sophie fumbled back from the force of the power.

Lightning cracked as Ash crashed into Typhon with his powers.

Sophie moved quickly, pushing all her power into the ground. Vines shot out from the earth. She pushed and pulled, wrapping Typhon's limbs into the ground, pushing and pushing until his body crushed into the dirt. A mixture of darkness, night, shadows – pure, unfettered power – joined in, helping her push Typhon into the ground.

The king of Mount Gehenna roared, and a slight smile ticked upon his bull face.

Shit.

Pallas jumped up into the air, ready to strike Typhon's chest with a burning spear but the haunting sound of flapping wings burst through the burning maw of Mount Gehenna. The angels were plucked from the ground by a flock of harpies. One by one they were thrown into the air.

With no functional wings to aid their fall.

Sophie scrambled back. She wasn't going to let the vines go. They were so close to putting Typhon back in his damned jail cell. She pushed more power into the ground. Pushing him farther and farther, covering the entire mountainside with her vines, hoping that somehow she'd soften the Tienthan's fall too.

Ash moved to strike down the harpies as they attacked him from above.

We're outnumbered.

Sophie dodged, rolled to one side, and pulled out her makeshift rope dart. She spun and kicked as much as she could. Wedging the rocky blades into wings and pulling them down with all her might. Where she struck, the harpies came crashing to the floor.

One. Two. Three. Four.

Sophie kept moving even though her body was ready to give out.

Lightning flitted through the air, burning a few of the harpies to a crisp.

But they kept coming.

When the Tienthan downed two, ten more would appear.

Sophie couldn't see Typhon through the fray. And a panic so debilitating, like a hot knife held to her heart, worked through her when she couldn't see Ash.

It made her fight harder.

And when she thought things were teetering out of their favour . . . the darkness of night fell upon the harpies, they grew tired. Sleepy.

It was Morpheus, Nyx and Athena.

Relief manifested in a desperate cry.

They came charging into the melee with their weapons and powers, hacking through the harpies.

Together the Tienthan shouted. They screamed. They struck. They worked together as a team to nullify Typhon.

Ash's lightning struck again, and Sophie ran toward it. She pushed out her mana, immobilising Typhon with her vines while the others pushed him into the opening. With one last cry, the beast fell into the opening of Mount Gehenna.

As Typhon fell, he grabbed a hold of one of the angels.

Sophie's heart had never lodged itself so high in her throat.

It was Ash.

The Tienthan shouted, but Sophie was faster than all of them. Propelled on a wind of pure adrenalin. She spared no morsel of power as she dived for him. He was struggling against Typhon's grip and couldn't quite get free.

The heat of Mount Gehenna almost burned Sophie's skin off.

Ash roared, channelling all his lightning, striking Typhon in the chest. As he landed his powerful blow, Typhon let go but Ash was still falling, a flightless angel unable to use his wings.

"Grab my hand!" Sophie shouted.

As soon as their hands touched, it was like their powers melded together. Reunited at last.

Sophie shot out her vines holding onto the ledge of Mount Gehenna. The full weight of Ash bounced, tearing something in her shoulder. Sophie let out a cry, but she dared not let go. Below them was certain death. The guttural sound and cries, echoing up from below, chilled Sophie's bones.

Sophie propelled them up with the mana she had left, letting her vines take the full brunt of their combined weight. "CLOSE THE FUCKING OPENING!" Sophie shouted as they climbed and climbed.

And as Sophie and Ash spilled out onto the edge of Mount Gehenna's opening, she felt the full force of the Tienthan's powers wash over her body. The Tienthan were working together to close the opening and the sheer force of it pushed her back onto the ground.

Ash came crashing on top of her. "I fucking love you," he grunted before kissing her roughly.

"Don't say I didn't do anything nice for you." Sophie breathed heavily and let out a laugh. Ash scoffed as he pulled her up with him and joined in with the other angels.

Together, as a unit, they pushed all the power they had left into the earth, binding the opening of Mount Gehenna shut. Together they hummed something in an old language that Sophie did not understand. And as the words stopped, the mountain rumbled. Then quietened. The air grew less heavy.

Sophie could faintly hear the cries of Typhon from within the mountain.

They'd done it. They'd done it!

Sophie looked around. They were bruised and battered. Their breaths heavy and their eyes were wild, but they'd done it. They'd completed the trials.

A loud horn sounded in the air in the distance and a beacon of light sliced through the dark sky, starting at the base of the mountain.

They all looked toward it. It looked like the light was gradually dimming.

"Shit," Deymos gritted beside her.

Sophie looked to Deymos, then to Ash.

"Everybody, fucking move! Get to the damn beacon before the light gutters out!" Ash bellowed.

All the angels of the Tienthan sprang to action, beginning the final descent of Mount Gehenna. Sophie had no choice but to follow blindly.

"Ash?!" Her voice was all panic.

"That's our only way off Tartarus. If we don't get to it before the light dims out, we'll be stuck here until the next Hrabrost Trials."

Well, fuck that.

So they ran and ran.

They jumped, dived and rolled.

This was their out.

Sophie could see it now. The brightness of the beacon threatened to burn her retinas and her lungs were giving out. She pushed harder but with her height, she could barely keep up. From beside her, Ash laced his fingers through hers and shot her forward with him. Together they jumped into the light.

A burning sensation washed over her skin.

Not once did she let go of Ash's hand.

61

SOPHIE

"This year was a test of mettle unlike any other. Some of you suffered grave injuries." Ares nodded to Nyx who still had a paleness to their skin. Morpheus had his arms around them as the angels of the Tienthan sat on the ground of the training ring back on the Isle of Deos. As they stumbled through the beacon, they landed in the training ring and were brought straight to the attention of medics. "Others made decisions that weren't according to plan." He nodded to Nemysis. "While others proved themselves worthy, to be a part of the team." He nodded to Sophie. Her cheeks burned at the sudden attention and nods of agreement from the other angels.

Ash nudged his elbow into her arm, flashing her a proud grin.

Sophie turned even more red.

"Being a guardian angel in the Tienthan is in most parts challenging. It comes with responsibilities, but what makes every drop of blood spilled worth it, is knowing that the realms are safe, and that you have each other's backs in a team that will never own defeat. Congratulations, you made it another year," Ares said proudly.

The angels of the Tienthan burst into conversation. Patting each other on the back. Hugging each other. Laughing.

"BUT, before we take leave," Ares's deep voice shot through the group. "Sophie, will you please join me up the front."

Suddenly, Sophie felt tiny. Her stomach lurched in nervousness.

Shit.

Ash kissed her quickly on the cheek before pushing her up.

Sophie shot him an annoyed look.

He winked.

Asshole.

Slowly, Sophie walked to the front of the group and stood beside Ares. All eyes were on her. Her and her undeniably sweaty palms.

As she looked over the group of angels she'd just spent the gruelling week with, her heart warmed. Ash was on his knees, smiling brightly. His hair was all a mess. Eros was blubbering into Deymos's shoulder and Nemy gave her a firm nod of approval.

Ares fished a small white crystal from the pocket of space he often kept things in and held it up in the air between his fingers – the light of day making it sparkle. "For your reckless valour, your resourcefulness, fidelity and comradeship throughout the Hrabrost Trials, welcome to the Tienthan." Ares smiled as he struck the crystal into Sophie's back.

Sophie coughed at the sudden force. Her back instantly fell cool, her skin and bones moved in place as if something was crawling inside her. Pain lanced through her back bringing her to her knees but as soon as the pain appeared, it quickly rushed away.

Then she felt them.

Their heaviness and how they twitched and moved with the muscles of her back. Their feathers and how they tickled parts of her skin.

"Team, please join me in welcoming the newest guardian angel in the Tienthan. Sofreya Brighid Taliesin." Ares clapped loud and proud.

Sophie looked up to find the entire Tienthan standing up and cheering her on.

Sophie stood, a laugh bubbling in her throat and a smile so bright. She'd done it. She'd completed the Hrabrost Trials and now . . . now she had *wings*.

Her heart was bursting with pride.

She peered up at the large wings. Her feathers were a soft lilac and fluttered in the slight breeze. They felt powerful, strong. They were proof, not that she ever needed it, that she was capable.

The angels of the Tienthan surrounded her. Kissing her silly. Chronos even gave her a small nod and smile.

"Welcome to the family!" Eros squealed as he hugged Sophie.

He was immediately wrenched back by Ash and his little storm clouds. He said nothing as he prowled closer and claimed her lips. Sophie gave in fully, drinking in his woodsy sent. They were blood-soaked and worse for wear, but she didn't care because. Well. She was in fucking love.

"It's about time!" Morpheus whooped.

Ash smiled against her mouth. "You made it, Starlight."

Sophie pushed back in his arms. "And I saved your ass while doing it." She poked her tongue out, earning herself a tsk and another breathtaking kiss.

"Come on." Ash laced his fingers between hers. "Let's head home so we can finish what we started. Something about a whole week and doing whatever I wanted. Does that ring a bell?"

Sophie pulled back, the weight of her new wings throwing her a touch off centre. "Can we stop by somewhere?" Sophie's eyes turned murderous.

"Oh?" Ash raised his brows.

There was one shrivelled up god she needed to pay a visit to. She didn't have to say a word for Ash to realise what she was talking about.

"Oh." Ash's eyes turned positively murderous too.

Sophie enlisted the help of Ash, Deymos, Eros and Nemy for this one act of retribution.

They stood in front of the council building, its white marble glistening in the evening sun. The scales of justice had seemed to tip at a different angle than when she last saw it, perhaps in her favour.

"What about something like *the jig's up, bitch!*" Eros was rattling off one liners for Sophie to use.

"Shut it, Eros," Deymos grumbled.

Sophie looked to her new family.

"Are we sure he's in there?" Sophie asked.

"Yep, just got confirmation from Ares," Nemy said.

"Then let's get the show on the road." Sophie stalked up the steps of the council building, her wings tight against her strained back. They would get some taking used to. When she reached the large door, she took a deep breath and blasted the doors apart with her air mana. The sound of the splintering door echoed down the hall.

Whoops. Overkill.

Deymos added shadows all around her, making her aura dark. While Eros created billowing smoke. Ash carefully struck his lightning around her and Nemy pumped adrenalin into the air.

Sophie prowled to the centre of the council building foyer with the angels of the Tienthan in tow. "VESTES!" Her voice boomed and echoed through the entire building, almost waking the marble statues.

It was his slimy presence that she felt first. There he was. Entering the hall, dressed in a long flowing green robe. He looked down on Sophie, his chin held high. "What is a trai—"

Sophie cut him off, wrapping a lasso of fire around his neck. His face turned red as she took the air from his lungs and his lips cracked as she drew the water from his mouth. She forced him down on to his knees and a tiny struggling sound escaped his lips. She stalked closer and closer. She could see him assessing her wings, his eyes widening the slightest. "That's right, you bastard. Quake in fear. You really thought you could get rid of me," Sophie snarled.

She squeezed her magic tighter before dropping it all together. Vestes fell to the ground with a smack, groaning as his nose broke against the cold marble floor. At first it sounded like he was crying, his voice wheezing. But the wheezes quickly turned into a maniacal laugh.

"Oh Sofreya, Sofreya. It was a test, you see." His voice slithered into the air like an unwanted smell. "I knew you would make it. So strong. Just like your mother."

Sophie rolled her eyes. *Fates save me.*

"I loved your mother once, you know. She would have been my *wife* if she hadn't lost her mind and dignity to that *Fae* imbecile. I would have been your father, Sofreya. Don't you see? I could still be that if you want." Vestes was desperate. So desperate. She didn't need a father figure. She'd gone throughout her life with one that barely fit the bill.

Sophie looked down to her hands, pretending that she was totally buying into this last-minute save of his. She softened her eyes and even gulped for good measure. Slowly, she walked over to Vestes. His eyes were bright with false victory. She placed a soft hand on his wrinkly face, fighting hard not to gag as his musky odour violated her nostrils. She leaned in closer, her wings spreading high and mighty above her. "Get fucked."

His eyes widened.

Sophie smiled devilishly before awarding Vestes with the most brutal slap to the face. The sound echoed through the halls of the council chambers, all the way up to the sky where her ancestors would be smiling proud.

Vestes sputtered, his eyes somehow even wider than before.

Sophie could hear the angels behind her, holding back their laughter.

She pushed him down onto the ground again, his hands braced on the ground before her feet. She stepped closer, making sure to stand on his hand. "You do not know me, Vestes. I do not need a father. I am an angel of the Tienthan. A demigod. A Fae. A human. I am Sofreya Brighid Taliesin, and I am everything you are not. Cross me again, and I will fucking skin you alive. Do you understand?" Sophie intertwined all her elements including her vines and wrapped it around Vestes's neck. When he didn't answer, she tightened the noose again. "Do. You. Understand?"

His eyes grew bloodshot and his face red. He nodded once. Twice.

It was only then that Sophie let him go.

Smoke appeared in the middle of the room, just behind Vestes. Sophie had an inkling as to who it was. The air fell still and silently on a bed of rolling smoke, Ares stepped out, dressed in his golden armour, his spear in hand.

Vestes scrambled to his knees. "Ares! This *traitor* deigned to strike me in the face with her half-breed power. You must smite her!"

"Strike?" Ares scoffed. "I'd call it a redirection strike for the shit you dealt her." Ares struck his spear onto the ground, washing the white marble floor with glittering gold. He pulled out a golden note and read. "Vestes, God of Nothing, for endangering innocent lives and putting the safety and fate of the realms behind matters of your own personal gain, you are stripped of your powers." Ares struck the spear on the ground again. "You are stripped of your position upon Zeus's council." The spear struck the ground once more. "You are *banished* from the Godlands." Ares's golden spear struck the ground for the final time.

"No! N-n-n-o you can't do this to me! I'm a god!" Vestes tried to get up, but Ares's power held him down. His head was on a swivel, because one moment he was begging the god of war and in the next second, he was spitting venom at Sophie. "You! You half-breed! You spilled poison into the ears of all the gods. Wait until Zeus hears of this injustice! Wait until he—"

Thunder and lightning, more devastating that Ash's, split through the room.

"Wait until he what?" A soft yet deep masculine voice echoed through the room. From a puff of smoke, a middle-aged male with blond hair and fair skin, stepped out. He was wearing a black-as-night tuxedo and had tattoos across his hands, all the way up to his neck. He adjusted the cufflinks of his pristine suit and winked at Sophie.

Hmm . . . totally not what I was expecting Zeus to look like.

Sophie whipped her head to the other angels who were already down on one knee, their hands to their chest.

Oh shit. Shit. Shit.

Sophie scrambled to her knees and swore at herself. The god of all gods was here, and she was too busy comparing him.

"Sire! This *snake*"—he pointed at Sophie with a spindly finger—"has infiltrated the minds of your Aerial Legion. They have been compromised. You must smite her." His nostrils were flaring in all sorts of directions and his voice wobbled with anger.

"Oh hush, Vestes." Zeus snapped his finger and Vestes mouth literally disappeared from his face. All anyone could hear were panicked mumbles.

Impressive.

"Ares, make sure he's disposed of, will you?" Zeus said airily.

Ares's bright smile was all Sophie needed to see to know that he was going to enjoy every minute of *disposing* of Vestes. He stepped forward, picking Vestes up by the scruff of his neck and gave a mocking salute to his angels before disappearing on a puff of smoke.

Sophie bit down a smile.

Zeus, tall and fair, slowly walked to Sophie. His dress shoes clicked against the marble floor to a steady beat. "Let's have a look at my newest angel."

Sophie looked up. He had his hand out for her. She gingerly placed her hand in his, and he helped her up.

"Sofreya Brighid Taliesin, is it?" Zeus asked as he walked a slow circle around her, examining her wings closely, her tattoos. She felt like she was under a microscope. The microscope being the judging eye of the freaking god of all gods!

Panic. Sophie was panicking. "That's correct, sir." Sophie bit out. *Sir? Is that even what you would call Zeus?*

"Noble Lady of the Stars and Goddess of Fire. The name suits you," Zeus observed.

Umm . . . thanks, I guess? Sophie landed on saying nothing.

"You did well for your first time in the trials." He stopped right in front of her. "I was watching from Olympus. Well done." He smiled brightly and held his hand out for her to shake.

She took it and shook it firmly. "Thank you for accepting me into your Aerial Legion . . ."

"Zeus. We're all on first name basis here."

"Thank you, Zeus. For having me." She meant it.

"Taranis, is she yours?" Zeus pointed to Sophie's tattooed arm.

Ash stood up from his crouched position and nodded firmly, a gummy smile across his face.

"Thought I recognised the pattern somewhere." Zeus scoffed. "Love, hey?" He punched her on the arm.

Did Zeus, just punch me in the arm? Like he was a friend? Am I blushing?

Sophie laughed nervously. Her ears were positively red. "Yeah, totally." *Yeah totally???*

"Well." Zeus clapped his hands together, his power suffocating the room again. "I must take my leave. As always, it's great seeing you all. I'll be sure to visit over the coming weeks to see how everyone is going. Until then." He disappeared into a ray of light.

Sophie just stared and stared at the place he disappeared into.

Slowly, she turned on her heel to face the other angels. "Was that weird? Or was that weird?"

"He's a strange cat that guy . . ." Deymos admitted.

"He was kinda nice? But in the same breath could fuck up your entire life if he really wanted to. Psychotic. That's the vibe I got," Sophie explained.

"*I can hear youuu,*" Zeus's voice echoed into the room.

"Okay! We're going!" Ash wrangled them all up and pushed them out of the council chamber doors.

The sun had finally set, and the coolness of the evening had begun to fill the air.

Sophie sighed. "Well, what now?"

Before she could even think, or before anyone could reply, Ash threw her over his shoulder and shot them both into the air. "See you in a week, assholes!"

Sophie let out a squeal as they rushed through the air. Light laughter bubbled in her throat.

"Remember to wash thoroughly and pee after sex to avoid any urinary tract infections!" Eros shouted after them.

"And put a silencing bubble around your fucking villa!" Nemysis laughed.

Idiots. They were all idiots. And she loved every single one of them.

62

SOPHIE

Ash opened the door to his villa.

Calypso came bounding through the door, slobbering them both in kisses. "Oh buddy, we missed you too!" Sophie was on her knees, running her hands through his fur. She was the one who'd found him in Faery all those years ago and it was Ash who kept his promise. Sophie's heart squeezed. He kept his promise.

Ash crouched down on the other side of Cal, giving him a well-earned scratch behind the ears. "I bet Ares gave you more snacks than he was meant to."

Cal yipped and barked, confirmation enough.

Ash stood up quickly. "Did you want a coffee or tea or anything?" he asked.

Sophie looked up to him. "I'll have some tea. I'm not risking the whole coffee ordeal with you."

"On it!" Ash moved away into the kitchen. She could hear the sounds of a kettle boiling and the light clinking of cups.

Sophie moved to the couch with Cal in tow. She struggled to find a position that accommodated her new wings and after a few moments of troubleshooting, she landed on hanging over the edge. It would do for now. The hellhound immediately snuggled onto Sophie's lap.

"Did you want any sugar in yours?" Ash asked. Sophie turned to answer but the words were thoroughly lodged in her throat. Her mouth went dry and her jaw, imperceptibly dropped.

Ash was leaning against the door of the kitchen. His muscled, tattooed arms rested above him on the doorframe and the lines of his lower abs peaked through the bottom of his white shirt. A trail of dark hair disappeared into the band of his pants.

Oh my.

Sophie swallowed.

Clearing her throat, Sophie blinked away the desire from her gaze. "Just one sugar. Thanks." Her voice was impossibly weak. Heck, her freaking knees were weak.

Ash caught her eyes, returning a look that dropped to her lips then back up. He blinked before disappearing into the kitchen, returning to the tea.

Fuck the tea.

Sophie whispered into Cal's ear. "Can you head to Ares's house?"

Cal tilted his head.

"Your dad and I need some time alone," Sophie explained.

Cal let out a long puff of smoke from his nostrils and huffed.

Did this dog just give me attitude?

He trotted off the couch and slipped through the backyard, obeying Sophie's request.

Sophie moved from the couch. She needed Ash now. No distractions or disruptions. No veiled truth to stand in their way.

She walked into the small kitchen.

"I was just about to—" Ash started to turn when Sophie pressed a soft kiss onto his back and ran her hands underneath his shirt. He fell into silence. Her fingers danced lightly over his abs, the skin soft, warm. Is this what Heaven felt like? Her hands bound by want, found their way to his hips. She turned him so he could face her. His muscles hard, but his movements pliable. Willing. *Hers.*

She looked up at him. Those turquoise smoking eyes. The tufts of white hair sticking out among the inky strands from his nape. The lightning strike scar that danced upon his brow and high cheekbones. She would never get sick of him, or the way her stomach fluttered, among other things.

"I need you." Her voice was calm, a whisper.

Ash pulled her hand, splayed her palm and placed it upon his heart. She could feel it. The hard thumps. The racing beat that matched her own.

"I've always been yours."

He meant it. Every single word. Every single syllable. It had been twenty years since they'd been ripped apart upon the grassy hills of Soxis. Nine years since they reunited in the Summeiran forest. Less than a year since he saved her from the Wrenntian temple. Time, realms and veiled pasts had stood between them, stretching them apart. Now? It was just his cotton shirt.

So Sophie pushed him. Her hands upon his broad chest, she backed him up against the counter and commanded, "Take off your shirt."

He obeyed.

The way his muscles flexed and moved was unfairly hypnotising. His body was a devasting poem whose lines she wanted singed into her subconscious. Every line. Every curve. Every dip.

Ash's burning gaze did not leave her face as she hungrily traced the contours of his upper body. Slowly, she moved down his torso, running her fingers through his dark happy trail. Before she dipped past his waistband, she stopped. She looked into those turquoise smoking eyes again. "Take off your pants."

He obeyed.

Sophie swallowed hard.

Ash wasn't wearing anything underneath. He was fully erect. Just for her.

Sophie dared to look up at him. His eyes were dark, hungry, like he was daring her to make the next move.

So she took a step back to pull off her own shirt and pants.

They stood there, completely naked for just a moment.

Then another.

The air between them sizzled and cracked. The air filled with chaos, want and need.

Now nothing stood between them.

The guiding starlight had finally found her thundering storm. At long last.

Sophie moved in closer, brushing her hand through the curls of his happy trail again, all the way down so she could cup him fully. He hissed in pleasure.

The sinful sound shot a spike of adrenalin through her veins, and she desperately needed more of it.

Stroke.

Another hiss from his sweet lips.

The sound was fucking magnificent.

Sophie stroked him again. Slow, deliberate movements. Savouring every shiver. Every hiss. From the base, achingly across the velvet shaft and all the way to the tip. The way she collected his purrs was an addiction she had no intention of quitting.

Ash tried to claim her lips with his, but she pushed him back against the counter. She wanted this moment to pleasure him. She waited for him for so long. What was another moment?

Slowly, she sank down on her knees. Taking him into her hands, she kissed his swollen head softly, licking away the precum that had already appeared. She looked up at him, her gaze never tearing away from his as she licked her tongue from the base of his cock all the way to the tip.

"Starlight . . ." he breathed, pushing the hair out of her face and tucking it behind her ear.

She did it again. Her tongue slid along his entire length but this time, when she reached his head, she took him entirely into her mouth.

"*Fuck,*" Ash fluttered his eyes closed as his hand gripped her head. She sucked, in and out until she could feel his thighs tense, his abdomen flex. She couldn't help but smile, knowing that she was the cause for all this tension. What a fucking superpower.

His growl was the only warning she got.

He pulled her up from the ground, crashing his lips into hers and by the Fates she never wanted anyone more than him. They hungrily kissed, pushing each other from wall to wall. Through the living room and all the way to his bed where he gently lay her down onto her back, nudging her wings out wide. His frenzied kisses turned patient. Slow. Deep. Savouring. Sophie returned every languid stroke. Their tongues pushing. Tasting. Feeling.

They'd waited so long. They weren't going to rush a thing.

Wordlessly, Ash pulled her to the edge of the bed, gripping her thighs as he kissed her neck. Then her chest. Where his kisses went, followed his broad, calloused hands, touching every part of her skin and setting it ablaze.

Sophie grew breathless with every kiss and caress.

He trailed his lips against her stomach, breathing her in like she was the air he needed to survive. He moved his hands to her thighs and sank to his knees by the end of the bed. The image of a pious angel, bowing before his goddess. Slowly, he kissed burning trails from her knee, closer and closer to where she needed him most. Sophie propped herself on to her elbows and watched him worship her.

He spread her legs apart, his thumb just brushing against the edges of her core. Tiny little electric shocks ran up and down her legs. Her wings rustled involuntarily, another sensation that only added to the heady concoction she was already drowning in.

"You have no idea how much I want to taste you, Starlight," he growled. He looked at her hungrily as his hand pushed her firmly onto the bed.

"Show me how much," Sophie breathed.

Ash smiled a wicked grin.

He hooked his hands over her thighs and pulled her legs over his shoulders. She could feel his warm breath tickling her skin as he firmly pressed a hand onto her stomach and the other onto her thigh.

He kissed her left inner thigh.

Then he kissed her right inner thigh.

Then he kissed her fully.

Oh gods.

His tongue was firm. Slow. Patient. He licked all the way from the bottom to top, flicking at the last moment. Her eyes hit the back of her head as she moaned.

He growled against her as he did it again, this time slower, more excruciating.

"Ash, please," Sophie begged.

And he obeyed.

He was relentless. Unabashed. Un-fucking-hinged as he licked and kissed her to a steady rhythm. Her hips rolled uncontrollably as she gripped her hands into his hair, pulling him closer and closer. All the time, he kept his arms locked around her, his hand firmly on her stomach as he watched her writhe in the pleasure that he served her.

Already. She was so close.

Her eyes rolled and her moans were getting louder and louder. When her head fell back, Ash gripped her chin, forcing her to look at him as he tortured her. He growled hungrily as her legs shook, and her hips rolled. She was dancing on the edge now. And Ash knew it. She could tell by the way his eyes glinted, the way he growled, praising her for every one of her moans.

Sophie watched him. The way he devoured her. The sounds of his lips on her. It was too much. The distance between her breaths grew non-existent. His scent invaded her senses. His arms locked her in place. His eyes never wandered as she tipped over the edge and came hard, all over him. His cheeks were glistening with her as she bucked and plummeted from the edges of a world-shattering climax.

And when she thought she was coming back down to earth, Ash pushed his fingers straight into her, filling her up. He moved with precision, matching his pace to the pulses of her core. Suddenly, she was climbing again.

Fuck.

Ash pushed her farther onto the bed, resting her legs on top of his powerful thighs as he knelt between her. He continued his rhythmic, two-finger strokes as the thumb of his other hand circled her clitoris.

"Holy shit." Sophie couldn't stop shaking.

"I need you to come again, baby," Ash breathed.

Her hands gripped the bed as her back arched off the bed. His hands. His fingers. They didn't stop.

"I can't," Sophie breathed. It was too much. Her thighs were slicked in sweat. The bed, soaked.

"You can." Ash pushed his fingers deeper, curving them slightly until they hit that delicious spot. He worked her clitoris in excruciating circles. Sophie ground deliriously against his hands. Her eyes rolled back uncontrollably. She found herself standing on the edge again.

"Ash," Sophie moaned. Her breathing ragged as all hell.

"Yes?" He worked her harder.

"*Yes. Yes. Yes.*" She met every single one of her his strokes with her hips. All she could feel was the heat of his soaked hands. She was a fucking mess.

"That's it, baby." Ash increased his speed.

"ASH—" She was begging him now.

He rewarded her with one final, devastating stroke and Sophie swore she could see through the fabric of time itself. Her entire body shook as she came with a cry of ecstasy. Ash's name was the blessing on her lips.

"That's my girl," he groaned, slowing his pace, letting her ride out the last of her orgasm. He held his hands still as the last spasm left her body.

Ash leaned down, showering her entire body with sweet kisses before he claimed her lips. She could taste herself on his mouth and it satisfied every possessive atom in her body.

"You are a masterpiece, Starlight. A fucking masterpiece," Ash said as he kissed her lips again. He brushed the sweaty strands of hair out of her face.

She could feel the full length of him between her thighs. His tip just teasing at her entrance. He reached down to line himself up.

She needed him now. Every fucking inch of his body and soul.

Ash looked up to her, his turquoise eyes searching hers of purple.

Sophie nodded. Her words, lost to the wind. Her breath, lost to the space between them.

Slowly, he pushed himself in.

Sophie had waited so long to feel this. To feel him fill her. His soft, warm skin upon hers. He was overwhelming. Thick. Powerful. And when he fully seated himself inside her . . .

"Fuck," they both moaned.

She wanted to burn this feeling into her skin. Soak it into her damned bones until there was nothing left but their souls.

Ash pushed himself onto his hands, placing one hand just by her neck so she had nowhere to go. The other hand gripped her chin, his thumb tracing her lips.

Sophie kissed his thumb as he brushed past them. His firm grip forced her to look at him. "I see you, Starlight. And I love every single part of you. Dark, broken, bright and whole. Every single part," he declared.

"And I see you, Ash. And I will you love you until the sands of time claim us, until my soul is nothing but dust in the Elysian Fields. My *storm*," she answered.

As the words left her mouth, he began to move.

His strokes were deep. Intense. Filled with longing. Making up for lost time. They met each other, stroke for stroke. Their lips intertwined in a passion-filled dance. His hips rolled against her, pushing her to the edge again. Into a frenzy. Into another dimension. Their breaths mingled. Their moans interlaced with one another's in a symphony of sighs. Their kisses, hot and heavy. Cracks started to form through Ash's control. His strokes grew hurried. Sophie was eager to lose control with him. She needed to get closer. As if reading her mind, Ash moved his hand down to grip her hip, kneading her skin.

And that alone sent her over the edge. Sophie came hard and fast. A mess. Shock wave after shock wave. She screamed his name like it was the only prayer she knew, and he held her tight all the while.

With ease, he flipped them over so that he was sitting on the edge of the bed and she was sitting on his lap – her legs wrapped around his waist. They were still joined.

Sophie bent down to kiss him. Savouring the taste of his lips. The taste of him and the taste of this moment. She ran her hands through his long dark hair, gripped the soft white strands and leaned her forehead against his.

He started moving again. Pushing her up and down his length. Her thighs were soaked and so was his stomach. But they didn't care. They had found each other finally. And they were going to savour every dirty, sweat-soaked moment.

Sophie gripped him tight, a hand on each shoulder, gaining control. She undulated her hips, moving to the steady beat of their hearts. He watched where they were joined, where she moved on top of him.

"By the fucking Fates, Starlight. I'll never get enough of you." He squeezed her hips, letting out breathy moans as she moved faster and faster on his lap.

And as the intensity of another climax faded into her vision and claimed her muscles useless, Ash took control. He lay down on his back so that she straddled him. He moved her relentlessly, up and down until his entire body tensed. His strokes grew desperate. His moans the only song she wanted to hear for the rest of eternity. Their eyes never left each other's. They wouldn't miss this for the world. Not a chance.

"*Fuck. Fuck. Fuck.*" Sophie cried, each of her syllables matching the beat of his thrusts. She could die here. She really could.

"*Yes. Yes. Yes.*" It was his turn to pray.

It was the sound of his pleasure, the hisses of his S's and the roughness of his voice that sent her off the edge again, the shock waves, so violent she was screaming with pleasure and pain. He drew out her climax, placing his thumb onto her clitoris as he moved faster. Deeper.

"*Fuck!*" Ash groaned as he joined her climax with one, final stroke, her name now the prayer on his lips. She could feel him pulse inside her. Spilling into her. And she loved every moment of it.

As they both came down from the throes of ecstasy, she fell on top of him in a sweaty, breathless slump. He kissed her sweetly on the forehead, running his hands up and down her spine and along the ridges of her lilac wings.

They *were* sensitive. The feeling akin to someone running along their fingers along your sides.

They lay there for a moment. She could hear his rapid heartbeat as she lay on his chest.

"That was . . . I don't even . . . you are incredible," Ash breathed, a small laugh escaping his lips.

"Why did we wait so long?" Sophie laughed, looking up to him. He had an arm behind his head.

"Because someone wanted a clean slate."

"Hmm, I wonder who that was? What a naughty girl. Maybe you could teach her a lesson?" Sophie laughed as she drew circles on his chest.

"Hmmm . . . I could," Ash whispered into her ear. She felt his cock twitch against her thigh.

Sophie bit her lip.

Ash's rough hand found her jaw and pulled her close. Their foreheads now rested upon each other's, locked in a lover's embrace. Two souls once realms apart, now here. Together. Where they were meant to be.

Like the mirrors they were, hand in hand, wings outstretched, they said, "I love you."

Sophie knew it then, that she had finally made it home.

They spent the entire night wrapped in each other's embrace. Wading through the throes of pure, unadulterated bliss until they could no longer breathe. There was no telling where Sophie started and Ash finished. She could die in his arms tonight and she'd be happy.

It was well into the early morning before dawn when they both agreed to call it quits. Ash pulled her up from the bed and carried her to the bathroom. Of course, she kicked and squealed all the way. Her wings getting caught against things. She'd get used to them one day. For now, they were a flight risk.

Ash plopped her onto the toilet before standing guard just outside. When she was done heeding Eros's words of warning he came in with warm cloths.

"What is that for?" Sophie laughed.

"Well, I've got to help clean up the mess I made, don't I?"

Sophie rolled her eyes. "Who knew a mother hen was hiding under all those feathers?"

Ash scooped her up, earning a few more squeals. He placed her gently onto the bathroom countertop, the cold marble of it biting into her thighs.

"Ah, you forget." Ash placed himself between her thighs, before reaching down, pressing the cloth between her legs, soothing her raw skin. Sophie bit her lower lip. "I am a purely selfish angel." He bent down onto his knees, his face between her thighs. He looked up at her. Sophie couldn't help it. Her fingers combed through his inky strands, a little rougher in texture than his white hairs. She placed a kiss on his forehead. "The faster you heal, the more I can—"

Sophie punched him in the shoulder instead. "You dirty, smut-loving angel."

"Only for you, Starlight," he teased.

She went to pinch his shoulder.

He dodged her advances, before kissing her on her thighs and standing up. With her hand in his, he led her back to the bed, and pulled her close.

"How about a bedtime story? You can choose a book?" Ash said as he held her hands between them.

They were weary eyed, neither wanting to fall asleep. Fearful that if they closed their eyes, they would wake up to a reality where this wasn't real. Time, prophecies, and power tore them apart long ago, and they'd never let it happen again.

"I like the idea of that. Don't move, okay?" Sophie smiled, slipping out of the black silk sheets of his bed.

Sophie quickly pulled Ash's shirt over her shoulders and tiptoed out into the living room, across to the fireplace. The cold bite of the early morning pebbled her skin, but it didn't stop her from reaching up to pull the right horn of the draekin mantelpiece. Like the first time, the fireplace spun and groaned to life. She ran down the spiralling staircase in a hurry, eager to get back to her love. Though the library was dark, the soft flickering of the candelabras helped her see. Sophie quickly scanned the oak shelves and settled on Achilles.

When she turned to leave, something snagged against her mana. Like a soft poke, a nudge. It pulled her focus to a set of leather-bound journals, upon a lower shelf, hidden out of view. She crouched down, brushing her fingers along the well-worn spines. She knew exactly what these were. Ash's drawing journals. She remembered them from his nightmares. How could she forget? Little Ash. Nothing but the clothes on his back and the journals he loved.

She moved to the oldest, dated as far back as eighteen years ago. She pulled it out of the shelf, setting down the copy of Achilles on the ground. His drawings were vivid, real. No dreamy filter existed to dull their beauty. She knew the faces. King Gydeon. Riviera. Young Ash. As she flicked through the pages, the drawings got better and better. Gone were the harsh lines. In its place were soft ones that spoke to the time he spent on the renderings.

Her heart stopped when she spotted the drawing of herself. A draekin hatchling sitting on top of her head. More detail came through with each piece, the further she looked.

Sophie placed the sketchbook back, pulling out another from nine years ago. There she was a young girl at eighteen, hidden in the shadows of a tree. There were sketches of his own arms covered with the fated tattoo they shared, next to a feminine arm, much like hers with the same tattoos. There were sketches of his hands with a pair of feminine ones, their fingers intertwined.

Tears welled up in Sophie's eyes as she flipped through each page. There was a small note scribbled along the margin.

I don't know if I'll find you again, but these dreams and drawings will do for now. If they're all I ever have, then at least I was able to feel and see something . . . even if it's just on this stupid piece of paper.

A choking sound left her throat. Sophie snapped closed the sketchbook and ran up the stairs in tears. So long. He'd been waiting for so long.

She busted through Ash's bedroom doors to find him suggestively draped across the bed, a rose between his teeth. His eyes widened when he registered that she was crying. He quickly made the rose disappear in a puff of smoke and ran to her. "What happened? Are you okay? Was it the rose? I knew it was too much." He pulled her close as she laughed through her tears.

"No, no. I found these." She held up the sketchbook.

Ash took a step back and looked at the sketchbook as if it were a bomb. He gulped and straightened himself. He held his hands up defensively. "In hindsight, I can admit, it's a little obsessive."

"They're *beautiful*, Ash."

"They come from a dark place, Sofreya." Ash's head dropped a touch. He was ashamed of them. She hadn't forgotten the nightmares he succumbed to. The sad place he spent most of his years growing up, pining for his true family and friends.

Sophie rushed to him, pulling his face into her hands and kissed him deeply. "I see you. And I will always see you. No matter what."

Ash pulled her into a hug, burying his face into her shoulder, breathing her in deeply. "I know. I know." Ash pulled back, to kiss her again. "You know, I used to think . . . what could possibly exist that equals to the dawn"—he brushed her hair back behind her ear—"Is as beautiful as the moon"—he nuzzled his nose against hers—"and more radiant than the sun itself." He kissed her lightly. "Now I know for sure. It's you, Starlight. Always and forever."

He pulled her up into his arms. Sophie wrapped her legs around his waist and kissed him like her soul was on fire, and his lips were the only salvation.

63

KAINE

Kaine hissed at the atarangi demon as it continuously poked the needle into his skin. Poke. Poke. Poke. He'd been sitting here for hours. His arm draped across a table, numb. His skin rubbed raw, fresh with shadow ink. An ink made from the darkness of souls. That's what the demon was infusing into his skin. A special kind of ink only found in the Shadow Realm, known for the way it moved underneath the skin.

He thought about inking this pattern onto his flesh for a long time now. It would be a physical reminder. A reminder that his and Sophie's bond was real. That through Cam's betrayal, through the distance of realms and the spaces between, their fates were sealed. And the thought of seeing Sophie's face once she spied it . . . mother of Faery. There would be no denying their fate together, that was certain.

"It's done," the atarangi demon hissed.

Kaine sat up, admiring the shadowy ink that moved along his skin. From the crook of his left elbow, all the way to his hand, swirls and patterns lined his skin. It was Sophie's design, all the way down to the key on her index finger. Remarkably exact. But up close, the shadow infused ink moved and glittered in a preternatural way, making it entirely his own. A symbol, this was, that Sophie would never leave him. His first *true* love.

Castle Terrin's throne room hadn't been this crowded since the initial years of Queen Calliea's reign. Wall to wall stood the noble Fae of Summeira and Seaspun Bay while the castle grounds were littered with the lesser Fae from each court. A soft murmur washed over the crowd. Today was a momentous day as any. Today, Terr would be crowned king of Faery, alongside Queen Calliea. Together, they would see the full might of Faery returned.

Kaine stood a few steps from the dais, feeling numb. Bored even. Beside him was Lord Gulliver of Summeira and on his other side stood Lord Zavis of Seaspun Bay with his daughters. Queen Calliea stood upon the blood-red dais that had been decorated with black banners bearing the Shadow Realm sigil, a crow with ram horns.

Queen Calliea was dressed in a blood-red gown, a thorny crown with black diamonds sat upon her head as she held her chin high, looking intently at the doors of the throne room.

The ceremonial trumpets sounded and the royal guard at the door announced, "All rise for the coronation of His Majesty . . . Terr, the almighty ruler of two realms. King of the Shadow Realm and King of Faery." The door groaned open and dark smoke billowed in from outside.

As the trumpets heralded, Terr's massive eight-foot form slowly floated down the aisle. People gasped and bowed hurriedly as he passed them. Toward the dais, twenty royal guards stood on either side of the aisle, crossing their spears in the air to form a tunnel of sorts. Terr walked through the salute and slowly up the dais. His muscled back clenched and moved as he turned around to face the people of Faery who were on their knees. His people.

He took Queen Calliea's hand in his and together, they sat upon their thrones. A high priestess dressed in white appeared with a masculine crown, matching the queen's, in her hand. She rose on her toes to hover the crown above Terr's head.

Kaine could never have imagined that this was now Faery's fate. He never could have guessed it.

The entire congregation fell silent as they watched the crown, formerly King Gydeon's, placed upon the flaming head of Terr.

Kaine swallowed. There was a bit of sadness in him that he couldn't quite comprehend. Perhaps it represented the death of all that he knew.

The ceremonial trumpets ceased.

The high priestess spoke clearly and loudly. "Do you, Terr, swear that you will be faithful and bear true allegiance to Faery, its people and its interests, so may the gods help you?"

A beat past.

"I do," Terr hissed with a devilish smile.

Queen Calliea placed a pale hand upon his muscled blue forearm and smiled.

"Then today is a new day. Faery is blessed with a new saviour and king," the high priestess announced to the congregation.

"All rise," the royal guard at the door announced. He struck his spear on the ground twice. "Long live the king!"

The crowd burst into a cheer. "Long live the king!" they repeated.

"Long live the king . . ." Kaine said under his breath. He clapped slowly as he watched Terr and Queen Calliea share a kiss upon the dais.

Kaine couldn't help but feel like this was the start of something incredible.

Remember who this is all for.

64

SOPHIE

A whole week in each other's arms meant Ash and Sophie left no surface untainted. By the end of it all, Sophie still wanted more. She was a flower and Ash was the sun she so desperately needed. Today was the first day since the Hrabrost Trials that they would step out of his villa and back into reality.

Sophie sat by Ash's desk, scrawling a letter to Elowan and Zala. The last time she'd seen them, Sophie had promised that she would be seeing them shortly, but alas, the Hrabrost Trials had gotten in the way. The letter explained what had happened and when she would be returning to Faery. Sophie sliced the air around her with her mana, as Ash taught her, and sent the letter off.

"Hey sweet cheeks, ready to go?" Ash leaned against the bedroom door with his arms crossed. He was wearing his Tienthan uniform loincloth, showing off his tanned glory.

"Call me that one more time, and I'll be refusing you access to them moving forward," Sophie said seriously. It was anything but serious.

Ash rushed to her, pulling her up from the chair and pushing her onto the desk with enviable ease. He pushed her knees apart and showed her exactly how he felt. Sophie let out a yelp at the sudden movement.

"These cheeks"—he squeezed said cheeks firmly, earning a small growl from Sophie's throat—"are *mine.*"

The way he claimed her and called her his. *Ugh. My heart.*

He laughed softly, catching the desire in her eyes. Ash bent down and placed a kiss on her forehead. "Come on, let's go. We'll be late."

Distant clopping and neighing sounded from the stable. Ash walked before her, unlocked the latch and held the gate open for her. The smell of hay filled her nostrils immediately, making her nose wrinkle. Sophie pulled her wings closer to her on instinct.

She was a guardian angel now, funny that. A member of the Aerial Legion, the Tienthan. And as a guardian angel, she needed a mount. An arion.

Before her was the marble-made, open-air stable she had stumbled into many moons ago. Along the endless grassy hills, groups of arions roamed freely while others lazed upon beds of clouds eating hay.

"All you have to do is stand here." Ash pointed to the floor where golden wings had been hewn into the marble. "An arion will choose you."

"Oh, okay. That simple huh?"

Ash nodded.

Sophie stepped onto the golden wings and waited.

Nothing happened.

Sophie looked to Ash.

Ash shook his head and scoffed. "So impatient."

"Asshat," Sophie muttered before turning back to the rolling hills before her.

A herd of arions came galloping over a hill, headed straight to Sophie. Leading it was a pure white mare, its wings large and extravagant. Sophie remembered it from when she first visited the stable. Her name was Aika.

"You've got to be kidding me." Sophie smiled brightly.

Aika was headed straight for Sophie.

Sophie held her hand out as Aika slowed down and approached her. It was natural. Sophie ran her hand across Aika's white muzzle, earning herself an excited whinny. "It's good to see you again, beautiful."

"It seems like she was waiting for you," Ash came to stand just behind Sophie, brushing his hand through the mare's mane.

"What do you mean?" Sophie looked up at Ash.

"She has never claimed anyone to be her handler. Many Tienthan have tried, mainly for her pure white coat and genetics. She'll serve you well, Starlight."

"I bet she will." Sophie placed a kiss on Aika's muzzle.

Ash moved around Aika with grace, placing reins upon her. He then turned to the rolling hills and clicked his tongue twice. Lumen quickly came galloping over the hill straight to Ash's outstretched hand.

Together with their arions, Sophie and Ash strode outside the stables.

The sun was shining down on them Heat was thick in the air.

"Take it easy alright? A new arion will take getting used to," Ash warned.

Sophie ran her hands through Aika's mane, pushing her mana into the arion. She then looked back up to Ash with a cheeky grin.

"Ah shit."

"Last one there's a rotten egg!" Sophie cawed, squeezing her legs. She sounded two sharp clicks with her tongue. Aika thrusted them both into the air and together they flew to the top of the Isle's waterfall.

Ash was swearing under his breath in the distance but soon laughter found him. The sweet sound chased Sophie in the air as she careened for the other angels who were waiting on their arions.

They were all there. Eros, Deymos, Nemysis, Morpheus, Nyx, Athena, Chronos, Pallas, Achlys and Erebus.

"What? You assholes are too busy for us now?" Morpheus called to them.

"Sorry, not sorry!" Sophie teased as she flew over them with Aika.

"Now that they're here, LET'S GO!" Erebus cheered.

The angels whooped and shouted as they all jumped into the air with their arions. Ash had mentioned they did this first ride together as a team every year after the Hrabrost Trials. The only angel missing was Artemis. There were no updates to her whereabouts, as if she'd disappeared from all the realms. Ares had officially changed her active-duty status to AWOL.

When the last of the angels shot up to where they were all floating, Ash shouted, "To us!" He pounded his chest.

"TO US!" the Tienthan shouted together, pounding their own chests twice.

Together, they plummeted down the side of the waterfall.

Sophie roared with laughter and adrenalin as they all spiralled, dodging each other. She threw her hands out, running them through the clouds and along the spray of the water. The air around her was clear, crisp. Her heart felt steady and sure. The sun kissed her skin. In the chaos, Ash found her, circling her with Lumen. He reached out to touch her hand and together they pierced the sky.

This is living. Pure and true.

The other angels cawed their excitement. The sounds bouncing across the clouds in happiness.

When the waterfall dissipated and the edges of the Isle disappeared, they all steadied their flying and headed straight through the clouds. Sophie pushed her hands into Aika's mane and slowly, stood up on the arion's back. She wanted to feel the wind through her wings. She wanted to *fly*. As Aika whinnied in excitement, Sophie stood tall and tipped her head back, letting the sun soak her skin. And slowly, she let herself fall backward into the sky.

Sophie let out a cry of joy as she felt her wings against the wind. She turned and turned in the sky, following Aika closely.

"Starlight! What are you doing?" Ash laughed.

He flew underneath her, reaching out a hand. She stretched out her fingers, touching his.

"Flying," Sophie said matter-of-factly.

"I can see that."

"Come join me."

Ash scoffed and shook his head. "I fucking love you." In one swift movement, he jumped off Lumen and crashed into Sophie, his lips immediately finding hers. They were wrapped in a lover's embrace as they flew through the blue skies of the Godlands.

Sophie leaned into his ear and whispered something she'd long been thinking about.

Ash snapped his head back from their embrace. His eyes were wide with awe. With excitement. "When?" he breathed.

"Tonight?"

"Yes. A million times over, yes!" Ash shouted, laughter and happiness bubbling in his throat.

Sophie couldn't help it. She pulled him into another fate-sealing kiss as they flew through the sky. Nothing was holding them back. They had found each other again. And now what lay before them was a world unknown. A world that they'd tackle together.

Sophie smoothed the white sundress she'd found in the market earlier that afternoon and fixed the loose tendrils of her hair. With the help of Nemysis, purple flowers decorated her long braid. The thick heat had cooled, and the giant moon hung high in the sky. It cast a beautiful glow over the golden grass upon the Meadows of Mainn.

Sophie was nervous.

A small, warm hand found her shoulder. "Honey, you look absolutely breathtaking." Her mother's strawberry scent filled her nose. Sophie pulled her mother into a tight hug. She'd barely seen her mother since the trial but as soon as she made the decision to be here this evening, Sophie ran to her mother to tell her the news.

Danna couldn't be happier.

Ares popped his head into Sophie's vision. He was wearing his ceremonial garb, a bright golden armoured suit, with his blond hair neatly tied back. "Nervous, kid?" He laughed, pulling her into a hug.

"A little." Sophie chuckled.

"You're in good hands, Sophie. That kid will love you until the end of time. I know it. And if he hurts you, you know who to call." Ares winked.

"Thanks, Ares." Sophie placed a quick kiss onto his cheek.

Sophie could hear Nemy and Eros bickering behind her. They were placing fairy lights into the trees.

"No, you've got to droop it properly! The brief was *Twilight* not cheap Christmas light display!" Eros fussed and ended up snatching the lights of out Nemy's hands.

"Well don't ask for help next time!" Nemy shouted before she noticed Sophie walking toward them. Unlike Ares, they were dressed down. Nemy wore a silver chiton while Eros donned a sparkly loincloth. In his strawberry-blond hair, he wore a floral headband.

"Sophie! How are you feeling? Do you like the decorations? Everyone should be here soon. How exciting!" Eros sounded like he'd just ingested crack. His words were flowing a mile a minute.

"I'm nervous, but I'm ready and you've done exceptionally well, Eros. I love it."

"OH BY THE LOVE OF LOVE, I'M SO GRATEFUL!" Eros cried dramatically as he neared Sophie and pulled her into a hug.

Nemy chimed in and gave Sophie a quick squeeze of the arm before joining Danna and Ares.

"Do you want me to run you through the process again?" Eros asked a little more quietly.

"You'll slice our hands, bind them in a thread of Fate and we'll say our vows?"

"And don't forget you have to kiss him, okay? You can't be holding out on us hopeless romantics." Eros smiled suggestively at her.

Sophie punched him in the arm.

From the sky, the other angels of the Tienthan dropped in. They all shook hands and greeted one another before walking up the golden hill.

Sophie looked at the cove of trees Eros had kindly decorated in fairy lights for her. It was warm and welcoming. It was perfection for a night like this.

As the angels of the Tienthan crested the hill, Sophie went to greet them all, pulling them into hug after hug. Behind them all she spotted a mop of red hair and tanned skin awash with a blue glow. Cam had made it. She hugged him tightly until he complained that he would somehow die again if she squeezed any tighter.

Shortly after, Amina and the orphans of the Lost Home for Children appeared. Amina had her hands full but managed to wrap an arm around Sophie, congratulating her. The children ran up to Sophie, filled to the brim with excitement that they finally were attending a *real* royal wedding.

Sophie laughed as Tenerife came up to her and hugged her tight. She mentioned that she was no longer sad because she was no longer in love with her Acki. Apparently, there was another boy in her class she had a crush on. Sophie squeezed Tenerife's cheeks before pushing her to join the rest of the children.

When the moon had almost reached its peak in the dark sky, Sophie moved to the top of the hill. She sat on her knees in front of Eros while the guests sat all around them in a circle.

The sounds of Joe Hisashi's *Merry Go Round of Life*, the Godlands's orchestral version, played softly in the background as the fairy lights glowed all around them.

"He should be here soon." Eros grabbed Sophie's hand.

Ash was meant to be here five minutes ago.

Nervousness started in Sophie's stomach.

She looked to her mum, who raised her eyebrows in question, wondering where Ash could be.

Another five minutes passed.

Then another.

And then another.

Sophie's stomach had already been eaten away by worry. Now what lay there was dread. She knotted her hands into her white dress as she tried to ease the chaos in her chest. She didn't know whether it was worry for Ash or for herself, but the rotting feeling was growing more and more painful. Sophie knew now, what Ash had meant by love being a sharpened blade. She could feel its steel bite into her skin as she waited. Had her heart betrayed her again?

Where are you?

ACHERON

Ash thought the best day of his life was the day he found Sofreya again. Ever since that day, his life, his soul, his entire Fate-forsaken being grew brighter and brighter. But today had to top them all. For today was the day Ash was going to meld his lifeforce with Sofreya's. They were going to seal their fates, their souls, their bond and their *power*.

He'd never been surer about anything in his life. To think he was going to spend the rest of his immortal life riding the highs and lows of life with her. *Her*. He'd been counting his lucky stars since he'd found her again. There were far too many to count.

Ash looked at himself in his closet mirror and smiled. Tall. Strong. *Free*. His younger self would be proud right now.

Your dream came true.

Cal jumped up, tail wagging furiously, pushing into Ash's thighs. Dirty paw prints dusted on his loose white pants and blouse. "Ready to go, buddy?" Ash leaned down and fixed the white bow tie he'd made for Cal. "Looking sharp." Ash scratched Cal's forehead.

The hellhound spun in circles and his tongue rolled out the side of his mouth.

Suddenly, Cal fell eerily still. His head tilted toward the bedroom door.

Cal sniffed the air. His flaming tail was rim-rod straight and his hackles were up. Ash stilled. "Hey Deymy! You alright?"

No response.

Cal moved backward, barking violently at the door.

"Cal! Stop! Sit!" Ash commanded.

But the hellhound did not stop.

Ash pushed past Cal. "Ssh. On me," he whispered.

Immediately, Cal ceased his violent barks and glued himself to Ash's side. They were partners in crime. Ash pulled out a knife he'd hidden in his draw as he slowly advanced to the living room. The cool evening breeze flew through the house. The front door was left wide open. The faintest smell of sea and sunshine lingered in the air.

Shit. Where's Deymos?

Ash moved quietly to the front door, checking corners as far as his eyes could see. Cal prowled right next to him, ready to pounce once given the command.

Light footfalls sounded and grew closer.

Ash raised his knife, ready to strike.

"Acki!" Tenerife's tiny voice shrilled into the air.

Ash quickly tucked the knife away and bent down on one knee. Tenerife crashed into Ash, wrapping her little arms around his neck. "Hey Tene." Ash laughed. "What are you doing here? Where's Amina?"

Cal took a step back and growled at Tenerife.

She booped him on the nose, which sent Cal absolutely feral. His barks grew more violent.

"Cal. Go to your bed. *Now.*" Ash bellowed, confused by the way the hellhound was acting.

Cal whimpered before obeying. It didn't stop him from growling at Tenerife as he trotted into the bedroom, Ash closed the door and locked it at a distance with his powers.

Tenerife peered up to Ash with her dark onyx eyes. Her blonde curls were pulled into tiny pigtails. She pulled at his arm. "Acki?"

"Yes, Tene?"

Before he could stop it, hot pain sliced through Ash's chest.

Ash looked down to where his blood began to seep into his white blouse, stunned. A blade with a handle carved of the blackest stone laced in shadows and dark magic protruded from his chest.

No.

Tenerife's small hand was no longer small.

A larger hand was there now.

Blood gurgled up in Ash's throat as he stumbled back.

No.

Through the pain that threatened to pull him into a deep, sleepy darkness, Ash looked up. Where Tenerife stood a moment ago, stood a female. Her light-blue hair, sea-green eyes and iridescent skin was nothing like he'd seen before.

Her face was pulled into a scowl as she kicked him onto the floor.

He felt his chest almost cave as the force of his fall knocked the wind out of him. His wound wasn't repairing itself. Blood trickled all over his shirt and onto his hands as he clutched his chest desperately.

The female was upon him instantly, gripping her hand into his black hair. She yanked his head back as he sputtered more blood.

"What spell did you use on her? TELL ME!" She wrenched his hair tighter. "WHAT SPELL DID YOU USE ON HER!?" she screamed and spat in his face.

Ash had no idea who she was talking about. He gritted his teeth and shook his head as much as he could. He could feel the dirty clutches of death knocking on his door. He couldn't even reach his lightning. Something dark was stopping him.

The female, with her slimy skin, pushed her fingers onto his forehead, sending through a tendril of sea-scented mana.

Memories of Sofreya and the time they shared together flashed before his eyes. Her laugh. The way the sun reflected on her skin. The way her nose scrunched when she was angry. The way her lips felt on his.

"Ohhhh . . ." the female cooed. "He's not going to like that." She laughed fully. Her chest shook with joy, before she stood up, kicking him in the guts.

Ash let out a pained groan.

The sounds of her booted footsteps grew distant.

And as she left, a high-pitched ringing started in his ears. His vision grew hazy. All Ash could feel was the cold bite of the evening air. He could barely move. The hot burn of the shadowy blade was excruciating but was the only reminder that a small part of his soul was still hanging on.

The sound of a door crashing reverberated in the air.

Cal came clambering to Ash, whining and whimpering. He nuzzled his nose into Ash's arm as if to say *Quick, get up! What are you doing?*

But Ash couldn't move. He no longer had the strength. Whatever power the shadowy blade held was stopping him.

Tears spilled from Ash's eyes as he lay there helpless. The sounds of Cal's cries filled his ears as he let out pained cries of his own. Sofreya was waiting for him. She was counting on him to not break her heart. Yet here he was, on the floor, breaking the one promise he had made to her. The pain of that alone outweighed the physical gaping wound at his chest.

The Fates were cruel to exact this on him. Now of all times.

It turned out that love was not just the name in which people started wars. Love was the final embers of Ash's very existence. It was the cliff edge he clung onto by the skin of his teeth. If this were to be his final resting place, Ash found that he didn't mind. At least he had the privilege of holding Sofreya in his heart. At least he'd found her again.

She was all that mattered in his universe.

The starlight in his storm.

ENJOY THIS BOOK?

OR BETTER YET, WANT TO MAKE CRY?

Leave a review.
I'll cry happy tears knowing that someone's taken their time to read my work.
Every review helps.

Amazon

Goodreads

Acknowledgements

Wow. We've all just been through the ringer haven't we? Let's just take a couple of deep breaths and sit with what just happened. From Sophie *finally* unravelling her complicated past, to the *La La Land* inspired Ephemeral Ball **gush**, to the nightmare-fueled Hrabrost Trials and of course (how could we forget) finishing off strong with an almost wedding – we've definitely been through it all. Thank you for coming along on the ride with me.

Beyond Two Realms was a story that I dreamed of *long* before I wrote the first book, *Between Two Realms*. There's nothing I love more than destined lovers, mixed with childhood sweethearts. It's clear that Sophie and Ash are meant for each other . . . let's hope they get through book three in one piece.

This brings me to the acknowledgements. Thank you so much to you, the reader, for your dedication and support. These characters have lived in my brain for years and I'm glad they've found a safe place in yours. To Kat, my editor who somehow knows everything (I mean how much information can someone have in their brain??) and DOES everything too? It is truly amazing to see the work you do. You've been so supportive, insightful and just a dream to work with. There's no one I would trust more than you with this story. To Bec, my wonderful graphic designer. You always outdo yourself and I can't wait to see what you'll dream up for book three. To the Spicy Book Club, my biggest fan club since the beginning – where would I be without you and your tolerance for random, cryptic sneak peeks? Your patience and support astounds me.

Lastly, to my husband who inspired the dreamy Acheron and my fur-son Calcifer who inspired Calypso – this book wouldn't exist without you two.

ABOUT THE AUTHOR

Mazrine L Amaris is the Vietnamese–Australian author of the *Two Realms* series.

Based in Melbourne, Australia, she's only here to have fun. She's a creative at heart who enjoys writing stories she wants to read and making music she wants to escape to.

The pandemic catapulted her desire to dream up a story worth reading. Woven with her lived experiences, a bit of magic and a pinch of spice, the *Two Realms* series is a world she hopes is worth escaping to.

Keep in touch:

Instagram: @mazrinelamaris

Facebook: @mazrinelamaris

TikTok: @mazrinelamaris

Website: www.mazrinelamaris.com